Scarlet Wilson wrote her fi... and has never stopped. She'... service for more than thirty years, having trained as a nurse and a health visitor. Scarlet now works in public health and lives on the West Coast of Scotland with her fiancé and their two sons. Writing medical romances and contemporary romances is a dream come true for her.

Alison Roberts has been lucky enough to live in the South of France for several years recently, but is now back in her home country of New Zealand. She is also lucky enough to write for the Mills & Boon Medical line. A primary school teacher in a former life, she later became a qualified paramedic. She loves to travel and dance, drink champagne and spend time with her daughter and her friends. Alison is the author of over one hundred books!

Also by Scarlet Wilson

A Daddy for Her Twins
Cinderella's Kiss with the ER Doc
Her Summer with the Brooding Vet

Christmas North and South miniseries

Melting Dr Grumpy's Frozen Heart

Also by Alison Roberts

City Vet, Country Temptation
Paramedic's Reunion in Paradise

A Tale of Two Midwives miniseries

Falling for Her Forbidden Flatmate
Miracle Twins to Heal Them

Discover more at millsandboon.co.uk.

NURSE'S DUBAI TEMPTATION

SCARLET WILSON

MIDWIFE'S THREE-DATE RULE

ALISON ROBERTS

MILLS & BOON

All rights reserved including the right of reproduction in whole or in part in any form. This edition is published by arrangement with Harlequin Enterprises ULC.

This is a work of fiction. Names, characters, places, locations and incidents are purely fictional and bear no relationship to any real life individuals, living or dead, or to any actual places, business establishments, locations, events or incidents. Any resemblance is entirely coincidental.

This book is sold subject to the condition that it shall not, by way of trade or otherwise, be lent, resold, hired out or otherwise circulated without the prior consent of the publisher in any form of binding or cover other than that in which it is published and without a similar condition including this condition being imposed on the subsequent purchaser.

® and TM are trademarks owned and used by the trademark owner and/or its licensee. Trademarks marked with ® are registered with the United Kingdom Patent Office and/or the Office for Harmonisation in the Internal Market and in other countries.

First published in Great Britain 2025
by Mills & Boon, an imprint of HarperCollins*Publishers* Ltd,
1 London Bridge Street, London, SE1 9GF

www.harpercollins.co.uk

HarperCollins*Publishers* Macken House, 39/40 Mayor Street Upper,
Dublin 1, D01 C9W8, Ireland

Nurse's Dubai Temptation © 2025 Scarlet Wilson

Midwife's Three-Date Rule © 2025 Alison Roberts

ISBN: 978-0-263-32502-7

04/25

This book contains FSC™ certified paper
and other controlled sources to ensure responsible forest management.

For more information visit www.harpercollins.co.uk/green.

Printed and Bound in the UK using 100% Renewable Electricity
at CPI Group (UK) Ltd, Croydon, CR0 4YY

NURSE'S DUBAI TEMPTATION

SCARLET WILSON

MILLS & BOON

To any family that finds itself missing a key part.

I see you and I hear you.

Love is everything.

Treasure your memories.

PROLOGUE

Lyon, France

THE HOSPITAL ADMINISTRATOR looked at him again. 'Dr Dubois, do you understand what I'm telling you?'

Theo was never normally lost for words. But suddenly the leather chair he was sitting in felt alien to him, the bumps on his skin like some tropical disease, and the muddled thoughts in his head were surely some kind of pre-seizure thing.

Thing. That was where his medical brain had gone. Because absolutely none of this was normal. It wasn't real. It was a dream. Or a nightmare.

He felt something touch his hand. Colette, the hospital administrator, had moved closer and nodded to the gendarme in the room. Colette was formidable. A woman in her early sixties, she was always dressed impeccably and ruled this hospital with her iron will alone. No one crossed her path and lived to tell the tale. But today she was being nice to him. He recognised the look of empathy on her face, and it broke him just a little. She repeated her previous move and nodded to the gendarme.

But Theo wasn't ready for the gendarme to speak again.

'I spoke to her on Wednesday,' Theo said. 'I'd seen them a few weeks ago and offered to help again. I asked if she wanted me to go and get Max. She didn't sound great, but she told me she was fine. She told me she didn't want my help.' His voice drifted off.

The gendarme cleared his throat. 'Fleur—Ms Bernard was found on Friday after neighbours alerted us to the sound of a crying child. It seems as though it was an accidental overdose. We found some papers in her home that indicated you were her next of kin, and she wanted you to look after Max.' He paused for a moment. 'I'm assuming you're Max's father.'

The words jolted Theo back into this new reality. 'What? No. Fleur was my girlfriend at school. We haven't been together for more than ten years. But she asked me to be Max's godfather, and I agreed. She'd had a falling out with her family…' he took a deep breath '…because of the drugs.'

He raised his head as the enormity of the situation started to take hold. 'What does this mean?'

The gendarme looked a little awkward. 'Social services will be in touch with you about custody of Max. Do you happen to know if Ms Bernard has a will?'

Theo gave a wry laugh as he ran his hands through his hair in pure frustration. 'Yes, I know,' he said. 'I got her in touch with a free will service when her habit got worse. Told her she had to be responsible for Max. She wasn't listening to anyone, wouldn't accept any help. Social services had put support in place for her, but,' he sat back in the chair, his voice getting smaller, 'Fleur didn't want help. Her addiction had well and truly taken hold.'

A chill settled on his skin. He'd never admitted those words about his friend to anyone. She'd been on a path to destruction. The last time he'd seen her in person, she'd slammed the door on him. He'd been relieved when she'd answered the phone on Wednesday. He thought things might be getting better.

A hand rested on his shoulder. 'I'll take some more details from you, and social services will be in touch—probably tomorrow,' said the gendarme.

Theo nodded automatically. He spent the next ten minutes handing over Fleur's parents' details, the company who'd done Fleur's will, and asked everything he could about how he could arrange the funeral, and collect Max's things.

By the time the gendarme left, he felt as if he'd run a marathon.

He took a few moments, just breathing, and finally held up his hands to Colette. 'What am I going to do?'

Colette sat down in the chair next to him. 'Let me help you, Theo. Won't Fleur's parents organise the funeral?'

He shook his head. 'Fleur was a late baby. They're both in a care home now. Her father has dementia.'

Colette nodded. 'What about you? How equipped are you to look after a baby? Do you have family that can help? A partner?'

He shook his head again. 'My *papa* has multiple sclerosis, and my *maman* is his full-time carer.' He gave a smile. 'And no partner. Currently single.'

A furrow creased his brow, as the first wave of panic hit. 'I hardly know anything about kids. I've looked after Max lots of times, but I just winged it. I don't actually know how to do this for real. And what about my shifts? How on earth will I get childcare to cover my shifts?'

Colette lifted a piece of paper from her desk. 'First thing,' she said, 'don't panic. Take a breath.' She was watching him carefully. 'And, even though your friend may have put it in her will, if you don't think taking care of Max is the right thing to do, you need to have that conversation with social services. They won't ask you to take him unless you're fully prepared for all that entails.'

His stomach clenched. Was this what he would have chosen? No. Was this how he thought his life might go? Not really. But when he'd agreed to be Max's godfather, he'd known this could happen. When he'd lost his temper and told Fleur she had a responsibility to her child—to think about his welfare and make a will—he'd known who she would name. He had no idea who Max's father was. Fleur had never told him. Whoever the guy was, he hadn't been in their lives.

Theo took a deep breath. 'I'll take him. I want to take him. I'll make things work. I have to.'

She turned the piece of paper around and showed it to him. 'I wouldn't normally do this. You're a great cardiologist. We're delighted to have you here. But I understand how difficult things can be. I just got this. They're looking for specialist doctors. A cardiologist like yourself would be in high demand. They're offering very attractive packages for the right candidates. If you tell them you have a child and need childcare arrangements, I'm sure they'll be able to help.'

'Dubai?' Theo was speechless. He'd never considered working anywhere but France, his home. Sure, a lot of his friends were working in places all over the world, but his brain had just never gone there.

Colette gave a nod. 'Tax free too. Think how much you could save. Work there for a few years, come back with plenty in the bank, and it'll help your future with Max.'

All of a sudden, his brain started to go places. He currently had a small flat, and a mortgage. Long-term he'd need something bigger for him and Max. If he could save enough for a big deposit, he might even be able to drop his hours further down the line, to make sure he could meet all Max's needs.

Colette smiled. 'Just so you know—even those of us who carried a baby for months, and pushed him out—we all winged it. None of us know what we're doing. Even the ones that read the manual.'

He sighed, his shoulders finally relaxing for the first time since he'd been called into this office. Colette continued. 'I won't pretend that being a one-parent family isn't tough. It is. I know. But you can do this, Theo. I have faith in you. So, let me just say, I'll help you out over the next few weeks. And if you get this job, I'll still be here at the end of the phone for you. Day or night. Things can get on top of you. Sometimes it's overwhelming. But I can't tell you the joy you'll also feel watching a little person grow and thrive. Being a parent is a privilege. You're about to embark on the greatest adventure of your life.'

Her tone of voice was warm. He was seeing a whole new side to the hospital administrator—who was rumoured to know her own nickname of Attila, and not object to it. He reached into his pocket and pulled out his phone, scrolling until he found the last picture he had of Max and him together. Max was three, with rumpled blond hair. His T-shirt was stained with raspberry sauce from the ice cream he'd just eaten, and he was throwing his head back and laughing as Theo held him. The joy that Colette had spoken about was evident.

He took a deep breath and felt something settle over him. This was real. His future had just changed. He could do this. He turned his phone around to share the picture and smiled at Colette. 'Meet Max. He's just about to take over my life.'

CHAPTER ONE

Three months later

ADDISON BATES WAS NUMB. She'd been numb for the last four months. Ever since her fiancé had cleared out their joint bank account and disappeared into thin air.

Since then, it had been like peeling back the layers of an onion to find just how much debt he'd accrued in her name, and just how illegal some of his activities had been. The last straw had been the extra mortgage, in her name, on her property.

She'd considered herself a good judge of character. Sensible with money, and with her heart. But Stuart King had ruined all that. She'd left her engagement ring behind when she'd packed up the house, since she knew now it couldn't possibly be real.

The heat hit her as soon as she stepped off the plane in Dubai. It was a dry, searing heat. Not one she was used to. But she would have to get used it. It was her only possible chance of getting out of the escalating debt she now had against her name.

Of course she'd involved the police. But they'd politely told her the fraud investigation could take more than a year, and in the meantime her credit rating was lower than the belly of a snake and would likely remain that way, even if it was proved that Stuart had taken out the debts in her name.

So, Dubai it was. She'd known a few people that worked here. Her role as a sister in the coronary care unit back home, with previous experience in Cardiac ITU, made her a good candidate at the many specialist hospitals throughout the area. Her salary was more than she was used to, and came with an apartment in an apparently nice area.

She also wanted to get away from the mutual friends she'd shared with Stuart. She'd been aware of the judgemental looks and the apparent distrust from people. Did they really think she was in on it?

She shuddered. Dubai was a new start for her. At least she hoped it was.

The apartment was in a closed complex—the building was an actual skyscraper. There was a concierge. It was reassuring. She had to show proof of identity before she was allowed in and given her passkey. She was also given a list of rules and told that her belongings had already been delivered.

The floor-to-ceiling glass windows in her main living area gave a view over the wonderful landscape of Dubai, with all its majestic sights. She pressed one hand to the glass. It was like a city of clouds up here.

As she pulled her hand back, she could see her hand print and she shuddered. This whole place was pristine. She was already making a mess.

She'd asked for furnished accommodation and this looked like a show home. Sure, the apartment only had one bedroom, but the white walls and pale furniture gave the place a sense of space. That, and the views. The only room that didn't have a view was her bathroom, and she was thankful for that. Her bedroom looked out over the city too, and she wondered how it would feel to sleep here at night, practically up among the stars. The kitchen was small but practical. There were laundry facilities, and the whole complex had a swimming pool and gym area too.

As Addy looked around, she couldn't help but shiver. This place was lovely—perfectly respectable for her needs. But the rooms seemed to echo around her. The canvas was blank, and she'd thought that she wanted this, but now that she was here?

She took a breath and sank down into the comfortable cream sofa. It was overwhelming. Her interviews online, her resignation at her previous post, the way she'd stored up her few possessions before her flat was taken from her. The flight to Dubai almost seemed as if it had passed in the blink of an eye.

Now she was actually here, to do a job. In a country where she couldn't speak the official language. Though English was widely spoken here too. The hospital who'd employed her had reassured that she would likely work mainly with European patients.

But the thought of reporting there tomorrow suddenly seemed too real.

Addison sighed and looked around. She was lucky. Of course she was. She had a chance to earn good money, recover financially, then decide what she wanted to do with her life. It was nobody's fault but her own that she'd ended up in this position. She was too trusting. Too amenable. Or, at least, she had been.

That Addison Bates was gone.

The Addison Bates who was going to be the new sister in the cardiac ward, in the world-renowned Spira Hospital in Dubai, would be none of those things.

She wasn't here to be everyone's friend. She wasn't here to accommodate all the other staff.

She was here to give the best possible care to her patients, to make sure their cardiac care or surgeries were successful, their recoveries uneventful, and the staff worked diligently under her.

It was time to adopt a whole new mindset.

And she was ready.

CHAPTER TWO

'Dr Dubois? Mr Koch needs his pain meds reviewed.'

Theo took the chart from nurse and had a quick check of the notes. 'No problem, I'll go and review him, then prescribe something more effective.'

He was settling in. The hospital was vast. and while he'd thought his former workplace in Lyon had state-of-the-art equipment, it was nothing compared to what Spira Hospital had underneath its roof.

Nothing was too expensive, equipment was replaced frequently, and the staffing levels were above any he'd experienced before. Each nurse only had two or three patients to look after. He was supervising only one ward area, and another few beds in coronary care ICU. He had Theatre time every day in the specialist cardiac theatre, and didn't need to fight amongst other surgeons for time.

The on-call rota was less than he was used to, and he and Max were gradually finding their feet.

It had been like jumping into a freezing cold pool of water. Unprepared, and out of his depth. Max knew him, but had only stayed on a few occasions, and Theo's place hadn't been child friendly to begin with. Moving from France to Dubai had only been delayed by waiting for Max's passport to arrive. There had been no problem with Theo becoming responsible for Max, and that had him both a little sad and angry. Max was initially shy, but fun and intelligent. The world should be fighting for this kid—but Theo was the only one standing.

As for Spira Hospital? It was every bit as good as the frequent TV adverts showed it to be. His apartment was lovely and comfortable. The childcare arrangements better than he could have even imagined. And the area they lived in had lots of facilities.

Except it was lonely. There hadn't been a chance to make friends yet. His colleagues were courteous and kind, but it wasn't the same as having a wide circle of friends that you could phone at a moment's notice, or knock on their door to have a beer and a bit of company.

Theo gave a final glance at his computer, mentally listing the other things he needed to do this morning, and stood up to go and assess Mr Koch. He'd barely taken two steps when the unmistakable noise of an emergency buzzer sounded. It was dull, not directly in their area, but everyone went into autopilot. They'd been warned earlier that the arrest paging system was being reconfigured today. Although he wasn't on call, there'd been no confirmation the system was working correctly again. He turned to the room down the corridor where the buzzer was sounding and started to run. It was through the double doors. He could see an unfamiliar colleague up ahead grab the emergency trolley and tug it towards the room.

He knew this wasn't one of his own patients. He had four other cardiology colleagues who had patients in this hospital. But his body was designed to always respond to the sound of an emergency buzzer—no matter where he was.

As he crashed through the doors, he grabbed the back end of the trolley, giving it a helpful push into the room.

The woman pulling it let out a yelp. 'Careful!' She scowled, her eyes flashing. He'd never seen her before, but she was wearing burgundy scrubs, the sign of a charge nurse.

'Who's the patient?' he asked, ducking around the trolley and moving to the head of the bed to assess the situation.

'No idea,' was her short response. She glanced up at the monitor. 'Ventricular tachy,' she said, before pressing a button to inflate a blood pressure cuff already on the patient's arm.

There was a nursing assistant opposite, dressed in grey. He was tugging the pillows out from under the patient's head, and pulling them so they were flat on the bed.

'Someone tell me something,' said Theo, trying to keep his tone light, even though the situation was clearly serious.

'I called the code,' said the nursing assistant. 'One minute she was talking to me, the next her eyes just rolled and everything started alarming.'

Another nurse ran in, glancing in surprise at the people in the room. 'This is Isabel Aurelis,' she said quickly. 'Twenty-one. Multiple episodes of fainting and fast heart rate. We're investigating for Wolff-Parkinson White but she literally just got here. She's just had her bloods done. Hasn't even had an ECG yet.'

'Surely she had one pre-admission?' snapped the charge nurse. She had an unusual accent. Her dark hair was caught up in some kind of clasp, her expression was serious.

'And who are you?' asked the nurse. Theo could hear the hostility in the air. There was no time for this.

The other woman had stepped to the bed and was currently feeling for a carotid pulse at the side of the neck. 'I'll be your new charge nurse,' she answered. He placed her accent—Scottish, and strong. It would be easy to lose track of what she was saying. Her gaze flicked to Theo. 'No pulse.'

Theo moved fast, taking in the information displayed on the monitor and lifting the paddles from the defibrillator. 'Pulseless VT,' he said out loud. 'I'm going to shock at two hundred joules.'

He waited while the nurse placed the thick gel pads on the patient's chest area. 'Where is Isabel's doctor?'

'Dr Gemmill is due in sometime in the next hour. He knows Isabel is arriving.'

'Page him.' Theo glanced around. 'All clear.' He wondered how Dr Gemmill would feel about him taking over the care of his patient. It didn't matter—this was an emergency situation. Some doctors could be odd about another consultant stepping in. Once he was sure no one was touching the patient, or the bed, he delivered a shock, watching Isabel's back give a short arch as it was delivered.

His eyes went to the screen and he noticed the charge nurse's fingers went to Isabel's carotid pulse again. 'A flicker,' she said in a low voice.

Inexperience and anxiousness could sometimes make individuals too impatient with cardiac events. But Theo knew better. 'Let's wait,' he said calmly. He saw the smallest nod from the charge nurse, who kept her fingers lightly at the side of Isabel's throat.

His eyes went back to the monitor. There was the tiniest blip. After a few seconds, another. And then, finally, the comfort of seeing a QRS complex alongside a normal rate.

He stepped back, and breathed. Just like everyone else in the room.

Isabel Aurelis was a fortunate young woman. If this situation had happened anywhere else—somewhere that a defibrillator wasn't immediately available—it was unlikely she would have survived.

Theo reached for the electronic chart and automatically started adding tests. 'I want a twelve-lead ECG, twenty-four-hour monitoring to make sure we don't miss any future runs, a cardiac echo and I'll prescribe some amiodarone meantime to try and stop any abnormal rhythms.'

'Do you have authority to do that?' the charge nurse asked, a line across her brow.

Theo looked at her again. There was a weird vibe. An off vibe. But he didn't even know this person, and couldn't remember seeing her around here before. He opened his mouth to answer, but she'd turned to the nurse who'd run into the room once the code had been called, peering at the woman's badge for a few moments.

'Layla, you don't ever bring a patient onto this ward without consulting me first. And you certainly don't bring a cardiac patient up here without the most basic tests. No ECG? Has she had any pre-admission tests done? A full history?'

Layla's dark eyes widened. She opened her mouth to object, but the charge nurse raised her hand. 'This is my ward now. This incident will not be repeated.'

It was only a few words, but an icy chill flooded through the room. In any other circumstance, Theo might have raised his eyebrows in amusement. This wasn't how he conducted himself with other members of staff. Looked like this charge nurse was on a mission.

It was almost like she read his mind as her eyes suddenly met his. What an unusual colour. And he felt himself inwardly cringe that had been his first thought. What was that colour? Violet—or a funny shade of blue? Whatever it was, those eyes had a laser focus.

'Addison Bates,' she said in a clipped voice. 'I'm the new charge nurse for this ward. And you are?'

It was the tone of her words. Slightly confrontational, with an edge of challenge. Or maybe it was just the accent and he was misreading things. Whatever it was, it instantly set all the cells in his body on full alert.

'Theo Dubois.' He nodded towards the door, giving her a clear sign to take this outside. He started walking, quickly checking on Isabel's readings and giving a nod to the nursing assistant to remain in place.

Annoyance flooded Addison's face as she followed him out. Once they were clear of the door, he turned to face her. 'I'm one of the cardiologists from the ward next door. I was warned the arrest system was being reconfigured this morning, which was why I responded. So, yes and no. I do have authority to request those tests, though I'm not Isabel's doctor.' He glanced down at the chart. 'Dr Gemmill might overrule me once he gets here, but, until he arrives, I have a responsibility for Isabel's care. And—' he took a breath, aware that he didn't normally act like this, but the new girl had kind of annoyed him '—we don't have those kinds of conversations in front of patients here.' He looked at her badge. 'Charge Nurse Bates.'

He could see instantly she was aggrieved. Her dark pupils flashed and tiny pink spots appeared on her cheeks. He was trying to remember who she reminded him of. It was someone old-school. Someone either his *maman* or *papa* had liked, but the name escaped him right now. He was also trying not to notice how entirely attractive she was. Theo couldn't remember the last time he'd been attracted to someone in his workplace. Considering he'd only been here three months, and now had Max to look after, it wasn't as if a relationship could even be on the cards.

'You're new here. You should take some time to get used to the system and processes in place.'

Sparks practically flew from her. 'It might be my first day, but this is my ward, and there's no way I'm going to have a repeat of what just happened. An unknown patient...' she put her hand to her chest '...coming to *my* ward, with no proper notes, history or tests?'

Theo cringed. He knew what she was saying. He would never work like that, but he didn't want to speak for the consultants on Nurse Bates's ward. Was it wrong that he also liked how feisty she was, and that it totally matched her Scottish accent?

He pushed the thought from his head. 'We have a mixture of patients coming up here, both private and local.'

'I'm well aware of that,' she shot back. 'But the local patients present at Accident and Emergency. They're seen and assessed before they come to us.'

He gave the barest shrug of his shoulders. 'Then you'll have to speak to your own consultants about their arrangements for admission. They might not agree with having to run all their private admissions through you first.'

She held her hand out towards Isabel's room. 'Well, if this is anything to go by, the current process isn't safe, and I won't stand for it. Patients deserve better.'

The edges of his lips almost tilted upwards. He had to absolutely tell them not to. Because he was quite sure she wouldn't like it. A few strands of dark hair had worked themselves free of her clasp. With the flush currently in her cheeks, and her unusually coloured eyes, the new charge nurse was actually quite beautiful, and clearly passionate about her role.

He handed over the electronic tablet where he'd signed off all his instructions. 'Nice to meet you, Charge Nurse Bates,' he said. 'I've left everything for Isabel recorded. If you need me, I'll be just next door.'

He started down the corridor, then heard her clear her throat behind him. He glanced back as his hand reached the door.

'Addy,' she said. 'My name's Addy.'

He gave her a little nod of his head. 'Theo,' he replied, before disappearing through the door.

How to have a disaster on her first day—Addison Bates was clearly winning at this one.

Maybe she should actually be happy that Theo wasn't a doctor on her ward. This whole situation wasn't something she would want to repeat, for both professional and personal reasons.

She cringed at Theo's retreating back and turned back to deal with Isabel. Trust her to fall out with the first consultant that she met here, and it certainly didn't help matters that he was probably the most handsome man she'd seen in her life.

Not that she would ever trust a man again. That part of her life was well and truly over. She was here to get a new life, do a good job and work her way out of a financial black hole.

It also wasn't the first impression she'd wanted to make on her fellow nursing staff members. She'd need to resolve that issue too.

Isabel was propped up comfortably in bed now, with

the nursing assistant fussing around her, chatting easily, getting her a drink of water, offering to find out when she'd be allowed something to eat. Addy tried her best to paint a smile on her face.

'Isabel, how are you feeling?'

The girl blinked and looked at her, putting a hand to her chest. 'Like I've been hit by a truck.'

Addy smiled at the nursing assistant. 'I'm sorry. I'm Addison Bates, the new charge nurse. I didn't catch your name?'

'Omar.' He smiled. He was around twenty years older than Addy, and looked like he might have done this job for a while.

'Omar, would you mind finding Layla again, and asking her to chase up the tests that Dr Dubois ordered? And let us know when they might be arranged? Could you also ask her to page Dr Gemmill again, please?'

Omar nodded and disappeared out of the room.

Addy sat down next to Isabel. 'You've had a quite a day,' she said quietly. 'Would you like me to talk you through it and explain what happens next?'

Isabel gave an anxious nod. 'Can I have a bubble tea while you explain?' she asked.

Addy shook her head. 'Not right now, but maybe later. I'll ask you to stick to water right now, until your tests are complete and Dr Gemmill has reviewed them. He might want to take you for some treatment today.'

Isabel gave a sigh and rested back against the pillows as Addy talked her through the event. She explained how her heart rate had increased so much that it was no longer pumping her blood around her body the way it should. She took her time to talk about electrical impulses, and how an electric shock brought everything back to normal—that it was a known type of treatment for this kind of event.

Isabel still had one hand on her chest. 'I don't want that again. How can you stop this happening to me?'

There was a noise behind her, and Layla escorted in some staff who were wheeling equipment into the room. Layla introduced them. 'Paulo is going to do the cardiac echo and ECG, and Mariam here will take some further blood samples that were requested.'

Addy gave Isabel's hand a squeeze. 'Don't worry, I'll be back soon to explain the rest.'

She followed Layla outside and back to the nursing station. 'Sorry, for the abrupt arrival,' she said. 'We haven't had a chance to be properly introduced.'

Layla gave her a cautious glance. 'I'm Layla, I trained here and I've worked in cardiology for five years.' She gave a nod towards the double doors behind them. 'I go between both wards, depending on the staffing.'

Addy was still feeling on edge, knowing things had got off to a bad start. She hated that, particularly when she was working in a new place and really wanted people to like her. But she had to be true to herself.

She took a breath and gestured for Layla to sit down next to her at the nurses' station. 'I'm sorry about our initial introduction. I can promise you I'm not normally like that. I'm sorry if I upset or offended you by being so direct. I'm obviously new here, and saw some things that caused me concern.' She took another breath. 'Do you mind if I ask you a few questions about the ward?'

Layla gave a cautious nod.

'What happened today with Isabel's admission—is that normal practice here?'

Layla pulled a face and looked a bit uncomfortable. 'Yes. And no.'

Addy frowned. 'So, what does that mean?'

'It means that some consultants do it, and others don't.' She bit her bottom lip. 'Some of the consultants are very casual. They'll either see a patient privately, or take a phone referral and just arrange for them to come in. Although the doctor has assessed them, the patient notes don't normally get sent to us until the patient is actually in the bed. And, if they've seen one of those consultants privately, although they need a string of tests, they don't get ordered until the patient arrives.'

Addy wondered how best to deal with this. She knew for sure there was no way to let it continue. She decided to take a soft approach. 'Layla, you don't know me. I'm Addison Bates, I've been a general nurse for twelve years. I've worked in Accident and Emergency, Cardiology, Cardiac Intensive Care, and assisted in Theatre for cardiac procedures. I've been a ward sister for four years, and like to think I have a problem-solving approach.' She looked into Layla's dark eyes. 'Can you see any issues with the current arrangements we have?'

Layla gave a nod and a sigh. 'I hate not knowing the patient's history before they get here. Sometimes we have to wait a few hours for the electronic notes to arrive, along with the patient instructions. Often we just get a call from one of the consultants, or their secretaries, to say that a male or female patient is arriving, and they'll be along later. Sometimes they give us a diagnosis, sometimes they don't.'

Addison drew in a breath. 'Has anything like what happened today ever happened before?'

Layla wrinkled her nose. 'Not exactly. Some minor issues maybe. But nothing as bad as today.'

'And is it all the consultants that do this, or only some?'

Layla shook her head. 'Just a few.' She pointed to some names on the board next to them. 'None of the consultants in the ward next door do it. Theo—Dr Dubois—who was just here, he's new too, but he's very specific about any of his private admissions coming in, has a whole plan specified, tests prearranged and a time agreed with the ward staff for admission.'

'Theo is new?'

'Yes, he and his little one just got here from France.'

'He has a kid?'

'Yes, a little boy I think.'

She shouldn't be asking these questions. She knew she shouldn't be asking these questions. But they'd just erupted without any thought. Why was that?

Was it the sexy accent that had come out of his mouth when he'd talked? Or was it his tall build, brown hair and soulful-looking eyes?

Addy gave herself a shake. She had poor taste in men. She had history. Last time she'd got herself in a relationship she'd ended up with a repossessed house and a multitude of debts. Theo Dubois was likely a charmer. And that was the last thing she needed to be around. Hopefully he had an equally beautiful wife who took up all his time.

This job was important to her. This job was a chance to build some resilience, restock her life, and her goals, and try and reset things for herself. There would barely be any time for friendships, let alone anything else.

The only person she needed to concentrate on in Dubai was herself.

Layla was still sitting next to her. 'Let's have a chat

about this later,' said Addy. 'I think I can do something to try and put processes in place to help get things better organised.'

Layla gave a shrug of her shoulders. 'Good luck,' she said. 'Some of the staff here can be a little old-fashioned.' She straightened her uniform as she stood up. 'I'll go back and deal with Isabel until Dr Gemmill arrives.'

Addy nodded as she picked up a nearby notebook and started writing a few things down. She needed to focus. She would spend the next few days on the ward learning as much as she could.

And then…she would make some suggestions.

CHAPTER THREE

HE WAS TIRED, and definitely a little bit crotchety, as he juggled the shopping, his backpack and a very sleepy Max in his arms.

It was barely six pm. The hours at Spira were everything they'd promised to be, with better staffing levels, good childcare arrangements and less on-call than he'd had back in France. But as he looked at the little head resting on his shoulder, he wondered if he'd made the right decision.

Max had been in the nursery-cum-daycare centre for the last nine hours. The staff there were great. They played alongside the kids, taught them some basic language skills and helped keep them entertained, fed and rested. But Max was always exhausted when they got home.

And as a new dad, Theo didn't even know if that was normal or not. He might text Colette later. She'd been true to her word, and been happy to answer any queries he had. She'd even spoken to him late at night, when he'd been worried about Max crying in his sleep and the nightmares he'd been having. Having a soothing, rational voice at the end of the phone—from someone who'd done this before—was a relief. He could, of course, have called his *maman*, but she had enough stresses of her own without Theo adding to them.

As he reached for the keys in his pocket, his shopping slipped from his hand. The contents spilled on the floor just as the elevator doors pinged along the corridor. He couldn't even look up, his eyes fixated on the tub of chocolate ice cream—Max's favourite—that had tipped open and seemed to be melting on the floor like a mini volcanic eruption.

'Whoops,' came the voice with a hint of amusement. 'Let me help you.'

It was that exact moment when Max chose to open his eyes, see his destroyed ice cream and let out a howl.

Things really couldn't have gone worse. Or maybe he shouldn't have had that thought.

Because in the next second he was staring into a familiar pair of violet-blue eyes. Addison Bates gave a jolt as she recognised him, gathering his undestroyed shopping items from the floor. She had a bag of her own, and after a second's pause, she put all the items in together.

Her dark hair was down today, landing on her shoulders in soft waves. She was dressed casually in jeans, a white T-shirt and a lightweight navy blazer. It was kind of impossible not to notice how good she looked.

Max buried his face into Theo's chest while squirming, leaving him with no hands free to help.

'Thank you,' he said quickly, then gestured to his door. 'I'll get inside in a moment and clean up that floor.'

The ice cream trail had almost reached Addison's shoes. She didn't seem too worried. 'Are your keys in your backpack?' she asked.

He shook his head and tried not to squirm himself. 'In my pocket,' he admitted, still keeping hold of the sobbing Max.

She tucked the shopping bag under one arm, held up both hands and raised her eyebrows. 'Shall I?'

He hesitated for only a second. This was clearly going to be the worst new neighbour meeting in the world. He tipped his right hip towards her. 'Be my guest.'

She didn't fumble or mess around. Addison slipped her slim hand into his pocket. He felt a short wave of heat from her palm through his thin trouser pocket as she scooped out the electronic keys and scanned his door.

Certain cells in his body started a Mexican wave that he was absolutely intent on ignoring.

The door clicked open and he breathed a sigh of relief. 'Thank you,' he said, hoping for an easy retreat.

'I'll stick these in the kitchen,' she said, gesturing to the shopping she'd crammed under one arm and then heading into his apartment.

'Sure,' he murmured, taking the briefest of seconds to wonder how she knew where to go, then realising their apartments were probably very similar.

He walked in, paying attention to Max, stroking his hair and muttering soothing words as they both flopped down on the comfortable sofa.

Max wasn't a child who did big dramas. He was clearly overtired, and Theo hoped it would settle soon. 'My scream,' the little guy sobbed into Theo's neck.

'Don't worry about the ice cream,' he said quietly, 'I'll get some more tomorrow.'

As he kept talking in a low voice to Max, it took him a few moments to realise that Addison had clearly looked around his kitchen, found some supplies and was outside, on her hands and knees, cleaning up the mess from the pristine tiles that lined the hallway.

'You don't have to do that,' he said, feeling embarrassed, but she waved one hand and gave a small shout in return.

'No worries.'

He smiled at the broad accent. Addison Bates had been quite sharp the first time he'd met her, but he sensed there was something more beneath the surface. Everyone had a reason for working in Dubai, everyone had a story. He'd learned that quickly since he got here.

For many it was money. The rate of pay over here was much better, along with the tax benefits. For some, it was the country and the experience. For others it was escaping a past life for whatever reason, and finding a new place to call home. Or it was the work-life balance. Better pay, a possible reduction in hours and the added benefit of childcare.

Even though it had only been three months, Theo knew that, back home in Lyon, he would have struggled to manage. There was still the occasional hiccup here, but nothing that, so far, had been insurmountable.

As Max started to settle in his arms, he continued to watch Addison, cringing as he saw just how gloopy the ice cream was to clean.

Max was paying attention now too. 'No ice cream,' he said in his saddest voice.

Addison's head lifted and she shot Max the biggest smile. 'Actually, I might be able to help.'

Her gaze shifted to Theo, and even from this distance those violet blue eyes were mesmerising—more so when they held his gaze. Was he imagining this? It had been a while since Theo had dated. Maybe he'd just forgotten all the rules. How could a few seconds feel like the longest stretch in the world?

And then she blinked, and returned her attention to the floor she was cleaning.

Theo stood up and set Max down on the floor. 'Here, let me get that,' he said, still embarrassed at their second meeting, walking out to the corridor to join her. Maybe it wasn't only Max that was overtired and he was just overthinking things.

'It's fine,' she said again, moving into his kitchen area to deposit the used cloths in the refuse bin. She picked up the shopping bag she'd left on his countertop. 'And I might be able to save the day.' She tipped out the contents of the bag that had a mixture of his and her groceries.

There, in amongst the fresh fruit and vegetables, cold meat and cereals, was an identical tub of chocolate ice cream. She bent down to Max. 'It seems that you and I have the same favourite ice cream. How about I give you this one, and you can still have some tonight?'

Max's eyes widened. He reached out for the large tub. 'Can I, Theo? Can I?'

He should say no, but he could see the potential joy in Max's face and he didn't want it to be removed. 'That's really kind,' he said to Addison. 'But…' he knelt down next to Max '…we really should share. Would you like to join us?'

There was a moment's awkward silence. His stomach gave a little flip and he realised he might have made her uncomfortable. 'I'm sorry,' he said quickly. 'You likely have a family of your own to get home to.'

He saw her swallow as she met his gaze. 'Nope, it's just me.' She took a breath, 'And I'd love to share some ice cream.' She smiled down at Max. 'And you're really doing me a favour. I was likely going to eat the whole thing myself in front of the TV, so sharing is definitely a better option.'

His brain immediately flooded with a million possible scenarios. She could be waiting for family to join her. She might be the first to get a job here, and other members would come along later. His eyes looked to her left ring finger and he saw it was bare. The one thing that stood out in her words was 'just me'. Then something prickled in his brain. Just how lonely the night ahead she'd planned was.

But how dare he? A night with ice cream in front of the TV was likely what half the population might dream of. He had no business passing judgement.

A small voice broke into his thoughts. 'Do you have spwinkles? We have spwinkles. I can give you some. I have mashmallows too.'

Theo couldn't help but grin broadly.

Addison gave him a curious stare. 'His English is great, but you're French, aren't you?'

Theo nodded. 'His mum was bilingual, and because he was introduced at an early age he seems to have picked it up no problem. The nursery workers at Spira mainly speak English to him and he appears to manage well.' He took a breath. 'Let's get this ice cream out. Why don't you have a seat?'

He gestured towards the table in the main room. Addison and Max sat down together while Theo gathered some crockery and cutlery. He gave the ice cream scoop to Addison as he set out the bowls.

'One or two for Max?' she asked.

'One,' he said, at the same time as Max said, 'Two!'

They all laughed as he gathered the ice cream decorations and brought them to the table. 'Chocolate sprinkles, multi-coloured sprinkles, marshmallows and chocolate sauce.'

He sat down in the chair next to her and gestured to the table. 'And this is why I said one scoop. The sugar explosion after this will be massive.'

Addison smiled in agreement as she scooped out ice cream into the bowls. Max held up both kinds of sprinkles. 'What kind do you want?'

Theo held up his hand for a second. 'Oh, I'm so sorry, I forgot my manners. Max, this is Addison Bates. She works at the hospital with me.'

'Addy,' she corrected quickly. Her eyes met his for the briefest of seconds. 'My friends call me Addy.'

'Addy,' Max repeated as he looked at her. 'What kind?'

She pointed. 'Definitely chocolate.' She pushed her bowl towards him as he shook the tub, giving her a generous sprinkle.

It was clear he liked to be in charge of the sweet treats as he decorated everyone's bowl. 'I'll have to prise them out his hands later,' said Theo under his breath to Addy.

She seemed perfectly at ease sitting at their table, chatting away to Max about nursery and what he liked doing. For a second, Theo felt a sudden chill—what if she asked something about Theo's mum? But maybe she'd heard from elsewhere about his circumstances, because she didn't bring it up at all.

It struck him that he'd never done this before with Max—sat down with another female joining them. He'd spent a few days with his *maman* and *papa* when he'd first taken custody of Max—one for a bit of support, and two because he knew his next stop would be Dubai, and he wasn't sure when they'd all get the chance to be together again. Being with Max on his own had become his new normal, and this right now? It was nice.

'How are you settling in?' he asked.

She pressed her lips together for a second. 'It's certainly different.'

'What do you mean?' That sounded as if she wasn't too sure about her new place of work.

'I mean...' She gestured to the view from his living room. 'The apartments and facilities are nice.' She looked around. 'Mine is a little smaller, but it's better than a million other places I've stayed.' She bit her bottom lip. 'Spira is taking a bit of getting used to.' She reached up and twisted a lock of her dark hair around one finger. At first he wondered if she was nervous, but she looked more thoughtful than anything else.

He gave a contemplative nod. 'For me too. The technology is state of the art compared to what I'm used to at the hospital in Lyon. I thought the equipment we had there was good. But this stuff? Everything has been brand new to me.'

She pulled a little face. 'The equipment has been fine. It's some of the systems and processes that make me flinch.'

He knew immediately what she was referring to. 'You think they're unsafe?'

He watched her as she clearly considered what to say. 'Not deliberately so. But sometimes casual isn't good. I've written some new standard operating procedures for the wards, for all staff, and handed them into the staff governance group for approval.'

'You have?' He gave a half-smile. 'Well, you don't waste any time.'

'I don't,' she agreed, and shifted in her chair.

'So, what brought you to Dubai?' he asked. It didn't seem like too intrusive a question, and he imagined she'd be asked it a number of times over the next few weeks.

'I needed a change,' she said without hesitation. 'I was already a charge nurse in a cardiac unit in Glasgow, and had worked in cardiac ICU and assisted in Theatre for cardiac procedures. My experience meant I had a few jobs to choose from over here.'

'So, you didn't come for the sun, the money and the accommodation?'

She sent him a half-smile. 'Let's just say they weren't my main reasons, but were definitely added extras.'

She gave a little sigh, and he knew better than to pursue that comment. Instead he asked the question that was playing around in his mind. 'Do you have friends over here already—or some that might join you later?'

She shook her head. 'I don't know a single person. And no, no one will be joining me.' She looked down at her nearly empty chocolate bowl as she said those words. There was an edge of melancholy, and he realised he'd accidentally pushed more than he should.

'Well, I'm sure you'll make plenty of friends now you're here. The hospital has good social clubs, its own gym and I think around half of this building is filled with hospital staff.'

'Do you go to any of the clubs?' she asked.

He nodded towards Max, who now had his head leaning on one hand and was stirring his nearly empty bowl. 'It's a bit hard to go to clubs when it's just me and Max. I work enough hours already. I don't want to look for a babysitter to take more time away.'

'It's just you two?'

He gave a nod and hoped she wouldn't ask for any more details in front of Max.

She gave him a thoughtful look. 'Well, if you ever have an emergency, and I'm not working, I'll be happy to help.' She held up her hands. 'Not pretending to be a kid expert, but I've babysat for lots of friends in the past.'

He couldn't help the almost sigh of relief he let out as he gave her a genuine smile. 'That's great, thank you. The hospital nursery and daycare have been my only help for Max, so it would be nice to have an emergency back-up plan. Thank you.'

She shrugged. 'No worries, I'm only two doors down. So just give me a chap if you need to.'

He frowned for a second.

She let out a laugh. 'A chap? It means a knock at the door. One of my many Scottish sayings.'

He smiled. 'Okay, I get it.' He looked over at Max. 'I think it's time for a bath and bed for someone here.' He nodded towards the empty carton of ice cream. 'And thanks for that. I'll replace it, I promise.'

She stood up, clearly taking his words as a cue to leave. 'Don't worry about it. Your boy needed it far more than I did.'

She didn't stand on ceremony. Just gave a wave and saw herself out, gathering up the rest of her shopping and closing the door behind her.

Theo listened to the silence echo around the apartment. Max now had his head on the table and was virtually sleeping.

He hadn't had a female friend in this place since they'd got here. Was Addy even a friend? It was literally only the second conversation that they'd had. But she'd been helpful, good with Max and he'd sensed a certain vulnerability around her.

Maybe that should send red flags to him. Max's mum had been vulnerable. He needed stability for Max. That had to be his priority right now. So, no matter how much he thought she was attractive, and how easy she was to be around, he couldn't let himself get distracted. His relationship with Max had to be paramount right now. Nothing else could interfere.

He inhaled. A hint of her perfume was still in the air around him. His skin prickled. He liked it. And he liked the fact it was still there.

He reached down and picked up Max to take him through to the bathroom. 'Nice lady... I like Addy,' he murmured sleepily as Theo rubbed his head.

'I do too,' Theo responded, feeling a little sad. 'But you're my most important person,' he whispered into Max's ear. 'And we're going to do just fine.'

CHAPTER FOUR

SLEEP HAD EVADED Addy the last few nights. She wasn't sure if it was because of the shift in time zones, or that her thoughts had been invaded by a handsome doctor she was trying not to think about.

But the fact the HR director was waiting to meet her this morning couldn't be good. 'Miss Bates, can we chat please?'

Her stomach did a complete somersault as she nodded and followed her into a nearby office.

The woman gave her a smile. 'Just a small change in some details,' she said hastily.

'What do you mean?' Addy was doing her best not to let panic overwhelm her.

'I've been asked to move you to the ward next door.'

'What? Why?' Addy felt stunned—she hadn't had any time to settle in yet.

The director sent her a sympathetic look. 'We think you might be better suited to the other cardiac ward environment.'

'Excuse me?' What was happening here? Addy shook her head. 'I don't think I understand.'

'It's felt you need some time to settle in.'

'I agree,' said Addy, feeling automatically defensive. 'Which is why I don't understand why you would move me within a few days.' The woman just kept looking at her. Did she think Addy knew more about this? 'Isn't there already a charge nurse in that ward?'

'Yes, there is, we're just going to swap you both.'

'And have they been asked what they think of this?'

The HR director gave a smile. 'You're not contracted for a particular ward—just a particular speciality. And you will both be remaining within that speciality.'

Addy sat back in her chair. 'You're going to have to give me more details. What is this really about? Have I upset someone? Has there been a complaint?'

She couldn't imagine that there had been. All interactions with patients and their families had been good.

Something sparked in her brain. 'Is this because I asked for some processes to be reviewed?'

The look on the director's face told her all she needed to know. It was clear she hadn't wanted to tell Addison herself.

Addy leaned forward. 'What happened on the ward on my first day was unsafe, and could have had a different outcome. Patient safety has to be our first concern.' She used the word 'our' on purpose.

'And it is,' said the director quickly.

'Are you clinical?' asked Addy.

'Excuse me?'

'Do you have a clinical background?'

The director shook her head. 'No.'

'Then how can you really know about patient safety, or how the current processes—or lack of them—put patients at risk?'

Addy put her hand to her chest. 'That's my job. It's my job to make sure our ward is as safe as we can make it. That's why I put those suggestions to the clinical governance group. I'm sorry if some of your consultants didn't like it, but they should at least have the courtesy to tell me.'

'It's been decided you would be better suited to the other ward area. The change will be in place from today onwards.'

Addy straightened in her chair. 'I didn't come here to cause trouble. I came here for a new start. But if I see something that puts my patients at risk, as Charge Nurse, I have a duty of care, and I have to act as their advocate. This won't go away on its own. We *all* have a duty of care to our patients.'

She let the words hang for a few moments before standing up. 'The processes,' she licked her lips, 'I didn't put them forward for one particular ward, I put them forward for the whole speciality.'

The director swallowed and met her gaze. 'I know.'

'And the clinical governance process—it won't be halted once papers have been submitted?' This was really important. One person's ego shouldn't be allowed to compromise patient safety. If it was, she would walk, no matter how much debt she was in.

The director gave her a hint of a smile. 'Once the papers are submitted, they can't be discounted. They'll have to be considered by the whole committee.'

Addy let out a breath. There was still a chance she could make some changes around here.

The director stood up and spoke in a low voice. 'Just move next door, continue to do your job, and keep your head down. The committee processes generally take around six weeks. By that time, you might find that some have warmed to your ideas a little more.'

Addy gave a nod of her head. 'Okay then.'

Her head was spinning. Part of her wanted to have a tantrum. Clearly, at least one of the consultants had thrown a tantrum of their own. Maybe they hadn't realised they were being so lackadaisical. She wondered if Spira was like every other hospital she'd ever worked at—with a gossip grapevine that spared no one. Could it be they'd realised their own practices were now being discussed by others?

Addy almost groaned out loud. She hadn't thought through all the idiosyncrasies and egos of simply trying to improve practice. With hindsight, it was probably because she didn't know everyone yet. If she'd taken some time to get to know people, she might have realised who to tread carefully with in order to get what she wanted.

But, in the meantime, that would have left patients at risk. And that just wasn't on her game card.

She turned back to the HR director, wondering if this poor woman had had to listen to some consultant ranting and raving about her. 'Thank you,' she said with a nod before walking down the corridor, through the double doors and onto the other ward.

If the other staff knew she was coming they were very easy about it. The ward clerkess immediately gave her a smile. 'Charge Nurse Bates, come and I'll show you where to store your bag, and then I'll show you the office.'

This ward was practically a mirror image of the other, but Addy smiled sweetly and let herself be shown around. She then spent an hour asking the various nurses on duty to give her a rundown of their patients and any immediate issues.

She took some time to talk to the two physiotherapists allocated to the ward, then arranged to meet the ward pharmacist. If she'd still been at home, in an NHS hospital, all of these people would have been the same from ward to ward.

But Spira mainly had people allocated to one ward only. Which then made her wonder about Layla. She'd told her she worked between both wards. Had she managed to upset one of the consultants on the other ward too?

Once she'd finished talking to the staff, she went back into her office. It was clean and tidy, and it appeared that the other charge nurse had moved out their things—or perhaps someone had done that for them.

The desk opposite hers had a computer set up, an odd-looking mug and a half-eaten packet of biscuits. But the rest of the place was pristine.

'Maysa,' she called to the ward clerkess. 'Do I share this office space with someone?'

Maysa smiled at her. 'All of our consultants have their own offices, but some like to work on the ward while they're here.' She raised her eyebrows at the desk. 'The biscuits belong to Theo. He always says he likes to do things right away, in case he forgets.'

Addy wrinkled her nose. 'Why would he forget anything?'

Maysa kept smiling. 'He just has so much on his mind all the time, being on his own with Max and having to learn about being a parent.'

Addy blinked. 'What do you mean…learn about being a parent?'

Maysa's head tilted to the side. 'Oh, he hasn't said anything? Of course you've not really been working with Theo yet. Max isn't his biological child. He's his friend's child, and she died a number of months ago. Theo is Max's godfather, and he took on the role of parent after Max's mother died. They are such an adorable pair.'

Something clicked in her brain from the other night. Max had called Theo by his name. Not Papa or Dad. Theo. She hadn't thought much of it at the time, but it had obviously lingered in her head.

'I live right next to them.' It came out before she had time to think about it.

'You do? That's nice.' Maysa gave her a curious look. 'Do you have any experience with kids? Theo is always looking for advice. He was kind of thrown in at the deep end.'

'He didn't spend much time with Max before?'

Maysa gave a small shrug. 'He showed me a picture of him holding Max when he was younger. I don't think he lived close by his friend, but he definitely visited. Max seems comfortable with him. I'm not really sure what the circumstances were.'

Even though her brain instantly wanted to know everything, she was trying not to ask too many questions. She'd assumed that Max was Theo's son. She'd also assumed there was a mother somewhere in the mix.

Maysa shook her head. 'Anyway, Theo comes in here often. Omar Iqbal comes in too. He's very nice. Lovely family.'

Addy pressed her lips together in a smile. 'Thanks, Maysa.' It was clear if she wanted to know anything, she just had to ask Maysa. She also realised that the whole ward would know she lived near Theo and Max by the end of the shift.

It was odd. That whole short episode in Theo's house had been replaying in her brain for the last few days. At times she wondered if she was misremembering things. But she was sure there had been a few moments when their eyes had caught—when something had buzzed in the air between them.

It was stupid. She had just got here. And the last thing she needed was any kind of flirtation or hint of a relationship. But she couldn't pretend Theo wasn't attractive. She couldn't pretend that French accent didn't wake up parts of her body she'd vowed would remain dead for a while. And no one could ignore Max. He was definitely a cute kid.

What kind of single guy took on their friend's kid on their own?

She contemplated if she'd have the guts to do the same, but, thankfully, she'd never been in that position.

She carried on with her work, completing off-duty for the coming month and looking over some of her staff's previous appraisals. She'd taken a few notes with ideas for staff development, but she wasn't quite sure who to run them past. Maybe the HR director could point her in the right direction now they were on more familiar terms?

The events of this morning started to edge away at her. She'd kept a handle on things, but secretly she was annoyed. While most of the staff she'd worked with in her life were good human beings, she'd come across the occasional misogynistic, chauvinistic person who thought they were better than everyone else. Who talked down to those around them and expected the world to jump at the snap of their fingers.

Thankfully this breed of person was slowly but surely disappearing in hospitals, but it seemed that Spira might still have a few hidden among their ranks.

She would have liked to think that the HR director would have told the potential person to wind their neck in when they'd approached her about Addy. But it seemed not so. This was likely someone who could cause a fuss, and staff around them had spent most of their time placating them. Didn't people realise that this only encouraged their behaviour?

The more she thought about it, the angrier and more indignant she became. She knew she had to temper her annoyance. She was brand new in this role, and it might even be that the person who'd complained about her had wanted her dismissed. The last thing she should do was to behave in any manner that might give them an excuse to be rid of her.

Addy had always conducted herself in a professional manner at work, and she had no intention of changing that.

The door opened and Theo walked in, talking on the phone to someone. 'Can I get that chest X-ray done urgently, please? I need to know for sure if this patient is in a degree of heart failure, or if there's anything else marring the clinical picture.'

His presence in the room made her catch her breath. She tried not to notice how handsome he was, or the way her body seemed to react to the smell of his aftershave.

He looked up in surprise at Addy. 'What are you doing here?' he asked as he finished the call.

She raised her eyebrows. 'You mean you haven't been part of the plot to destroy me?'

He sagged down into the seat across from her with a look of bewilderment on his face. At least that was a good thing.

'I've not been here long enough to plot anything,' he said easily. 'I'm not important enough, and I don't have enough hours in the day. But...' He took a breath and looked amused. 'I might be up to plotting some kind of coup at a later date.'

She leaned forward. 'And why would that be?'

He leaned back and folded his arms. 'Let's just say I'm watching and waiting. Biding my time.'

'Are you planning on becoming leader of the world?'

He shook his head and grinned at her. 'You forget I have a three-year-old. Leader of the world is tame. He'd expect me to be leader of the universe.'

She was struck by the words he'd just said, and what Maysa had just told her. He didn't sound like a new parent. He sounded like an old hand. Maybe he'd just taken to his life change a whole lot better than she had.

'Okay.' She nodded in agreement. 'If that's what Max wants, it's your job to get it.'

He gave a small smile and looked at her again. 'Seriously, what are you doing here?'

She sighed and held up her hands. 'I've been moved. It's apparently to help me settle in.'

She saw something flash across his face. 'Oh,' was all he said.

'That's it? Oh?' Her tone was more annoyed than she meant it to be.

He pulled a face. 'I did wonder how you and Dr Gemmill might get on.'

'So, it was Dr Gemmill who complained about me?'

He held up one hand. 'Hey, hold on. I don't know if *anyone* complained about you.'

'Well, someone has. That's why I've been moved.' She took another breath and tried to be more reasonable, definitely not wanting him to notice the tears that were threatening to prick at her eyes. 'Well, that and the fact I put some papers into the clinical governance committee, suggesting new processes for the cardiac speciality.'

He let out a small laugh. She could tell he was shocked.

'You mentioned that the other day. I take it you ran it past the rest of the staff first?'

She gulped. 'Is that how you normally do things around here?'

This time he raised his eyebrows at her. 'You know that old saying about bringing others along with you on the journey?'

She shook her head. 'Nope. Exactly how old is that saying?'

He laughed while shaking his head. 'If you wanted to change a protocol, a process or write a new standard operating procedure at your last place, how did you do it?'

She frowned. 'It was easy. I revised the protocol or process, asked a colleague to check what they thought, and then I just sent it in to the clinical governance committee.'

'You didn't need to have a whole load of meetings first, to get everyone's opinion?'

She shook her head. 'The clinical governance committee was very inclusive. They would discuss the papers, then send them out to everyone who'd potentially be affected for comment. People would send back some thoughts, or make tracked changes to the document, and it would come back to the group for further discussion and approval.'

She could tell from the look on his face that things didn't happen like that here. Addy put her head in her hands and groaned. 'I take it it's not so straightforward here?'

He let out a sigh and ran his fingers through his dark hair. 'Well, it should be. But some people don't like change.'

She flung up her hands. 'All I'm asking for is safe planning for known patient admissions.'

'I get it, and I agree, but...'

'But?' She could feel herself becoming defensive, but she knew she had to speak up.

'But try and build those relationships first. I'm sure you could be persuasive if you want to be. There's more than one way to do things.'

Addy was definitely annoyed. She was always passionate about work and doing the right things for her patients. 'So, I should pussyfoot around someone who should be better about planning?'

A deep frown creased Theo's brow. 'Pussyfoot?'

She stood up in frustration. 'Tiptoe around them instead of getting straight to the point.'

He nodded. 'I get what you mean, but not everything needs to be a battle.'

She shook her head. 'You tell me you agree with me, but then backtrack with just about everything else you say. Do you want patients to be safe or not?'

The words came out, and she realised how they sounded. Theo shifted his position in the chair and she cringed. She'd likely just annoyed him. 'Of course I do. And I don't follow the same practices as he does. You've brought attention to it now. I bet most of the other consultants had no idea he was being so casual about things. It will go through the clinical governance process and it will likely be approved.'

She was beginning to regret her move. 'I can't sit on things that I think should be improved. I'm always on the side of the patients.'

'As you should be, but I still think you need to try and get to know some of the staff around here.'

She narrowed her gaze, but he dropped his voice. 'If you took some time, you might see that the key person here is Dr Gemmill's secretary. She's a really nice person. If you told her that him casually phoning to say a patient is coming in with no real details is unsafe, she could probably fill in most of the gaps.'

'It doesn't stop his bad practice. What does he learn if I do that?'

Theo stood up and her heart sank. She was being too pedantic. Did she really need to make this point to a brand-new colleague that she was hoping to get on with professionally?

'You're right,' he said. 'What does he learn? But the likelihood is he won't be here much longer. He's been making noises about retiring. Going to his secretary would be the quickest fix.'

'There's other things.' The words were out before she could stop herself.

She could tell he was trying to be careful. 'Other improvements?'

'Yes and no. Staff development. There doesn't seem to be any kind of rota system for professional development.'

'What do you mean?

'Within cardiology, we have the two wards, the cardiac ICU and the cardiac theatre.'

He frowned. 'But they're all specialisms.'

'And you work in all three. Why don't our other staff have that opportunity?'

She could see the recognition in his eyes. 'You think they should?'

'I think it might be good if that opportunity was there for staff.'

'You'd have to clear it with the theatre charge nurse, and the charge nurses in ICU.'

'Would you be opposed to it?'

He paused. Then, 'No.'

'But? I sense there is a "but".'

'But some consultants might be wary about having staff in Cardiac Theatre who aren't familiar with procedure.'

'I get that. But what happens when they get a new member of staff? Aren't they allowed a period of time to become familiar with the processes?'

'I guess so. I've only been here three months, and all the staff I've met so far are extremely competent.'

'I hear what you're saying. Let me think about it a bit longer, and then I'll meet the other charge nurses and try to come up with a plan. Just think…in a year's time we might have staff who've worked in all three areas and could help anywhere if required.'

She could feel the enthusiasm building inside her—even if Theo wasn't entirely convinced.

He looked at her carefully. 'I've only been here three months and I'm still learning things. Give yourself a chance to get familiar with the place and the people. Then, if you see something you want to change, talk to me. Maybe we could do it together?'

She knew he was trying to be helpful. And while his French accent was soothing, things still felt a little hierarchical. 'You mean a doctor can change things, but a nurse can't?'

He sighed. For the first time she noticed how tired his brown eyes looked. Maybe he'd had a bad night with Max?

He walked to the door, turning before he left. 'No, what I mean is it would be better if we worked together, that's all.'

He disappeared and she sat back down with a thud. Was this what her work life was going to be like now?

She realised how defensive she'd been. She was annoyed about the move and was taking things out on him.

It was unfair, and she knew that. That was part of being new—she didn't have a friend she could vent to yet. To moan with about the day-to-day things in the workplace that meant very little, but could irk a lot. Theo was the only person she'd even made friendly overtures to. Why was she now trying to push him away?

Her stomach gave an uncomfortable roll. Maybe this was for the best?

The underlying feeling of attraction towards Theo was making her question herself. She didn't want or need someone to flirt with. She really just had to focus on doing her job.

And if doing her job made Theo fall out with her? So be it.

CHAPTER FIVE

It had been an uneasy few weeks. Theo was doing his best to spend his hours at work concentrating on the job, and his hours at home concentrating on Max.

But it seemed like Addison Bates was drifting through both parts of his life like some kind of cartoon ghost. It felt like every time he blinked, she was there.

On the ward, talking to the charge nurses in ICU, with patients and in the office at work. Then, there was the long corridor at home, the elevator, the nearby shops, the gym and the running track at the park.

They were being civil to one another. And things were fine. Except for the undercurrent that was still there between them.

Occasionally he'd catch her eye. Both would look away quickly, but it always seemed like a zap from above. Something he was purposely trying to avoid.

Theo sighed as he packed up things for him and Max. Today they were going out together. Dubai had a multitude of places to visit for leisure, entertainment and learning. Spira frequently offered discounted tickets to many popular attractions. Theo had already taken Max to two of the adventure theme parks, and a water park. Today he was trying something educational—the Museum of the Future.

They took the Dubai Metro to the unusual oval torus-shaped building set upon a green hill. 'What's that?' asked Max as soon as he spied the glass and metal building.

'That's where we're going today,' said Theo.

He glanced at his ticket. Every ticket allocated a time, but it looked like they would still have to queue. He made sure Max's baseball hat had the flap out at the back to cover his neck as they walked over.

They'd only been waiting a few minutes when they heard a slightly awkward voice behind them.

'Hey, guys, fancy seeing you here.'

'Chocolate lady!' said Max, before Theo even managed to turn around.

Addy was wearing a beige shirt dress, and was already kneeling down to talk to Max by the time he shrugged off his backpack. 'Hey.'

She looked up at him through her dark lashes and he remembered which old-school actress his mother had admired: Elizabeth Taylor. It was Addy's flawless skin, and definitely the colour of her eyes, that sent a jolt of recognition. Of course Addy had a much more modern hairstyle, but it brought a smile to his face.

'What are you doing here?'

She kept talking to Max. 'It's Addy, but I'll answer to chocolate lady if you want.' She stood up and gave a slightly embarrassed shrug. 'I guess the same as you. Spira gave me discounted tickets, and I don't want to spend any time in the mall in case I spend all my earnings.'

She looked up at the unusual and impressive building. 'Have you been here before?'

He shook his head. 'I think it might all be a bit too old for Max, but we'll give it a go. Something to pass the day and keep us out of the heat.'

She glanced up to the sun as the queue shuffled forward a little. 'I wasn't really expecting to queue, I thought with the timed ticket you would just walk right in.' She looked down at Max and Theo could almost read her mind.

'Complete sunblock,' he said quickly. 'And the rest of the queue is in the shade so we should be fine.'

Thankfully, this wasn't quite as awkward as work. 'Well,' said Addy, 'you've got a three-month head start on me, so after the museum what else can I do on my days off?'

'I'm not sure my recommendations will work for you.'

The queue shifted forward. 'Why's that?' she asked lightly.

She was different out of work—more relaxed. Not hampered by worry about standards, staff and patients. Was it wrong to think that he liked this version of her best?

'Because my recommendations consist of theme parks for kids. We've gone to two so far. Plus a waterpark.'

She half-pulled a face. 'I don't mind theme parks, but I'm not a waterpark fan. I'm too pale and burn too easily. It's just not worth it for me.' She glanced over at Max. 'What did you do with the wee man?'

She said it so casually she obviously didn't give it a second thought. But when he burst out laughing she looked around, as if looking for the source of his amusement.

'The wee man?' he said. 'You sounded so Scottish there.'

Her hand gently tapped his arm. 'I hate to remind you, but I am Scottish, and that is just one of my many turns of phrase.'

'I like it,' he said approvingly. 'Makes you sound like the guy in the ancient Scottish police TV series that my *maman* and *papa* used to watch. They dubbed it with a French translator who still had a Scottish accent.'

'Oh, no.' She shook her head. 'That just sounds so wrong. And, anyhow, the original series was the best. You should listen to it in its pure form. Even some of our English counterparts weren't quite sure what was being said.'

'Oh, I've looked online. I loved the way the main guy said *mhurrr-der...*' He mimicked the Scottish accent, but it was still infused with his own French one and Addy couldn't stop laughing.

'*Mhurrr-der*,' she said helpfully, her Scottish accent identical to the TV show.

'You win,' he said, shrugging in defeat and shooting her a wide smile, then pointed back at Max. 'The "wee man", as you call him, had one of those swimsuits that covers him from neck to toe, and a hat. So, there was no burning. We only stayed for a few hours.'

They'd reached the entrance to the museum now and were hit with a welcome blast of air conditioning. 'Finally,' he breathed as they scanned their tickets and made their way inside the very modern building.

'Mind if I hang around with you both?' Addy asked.

The words had just been forming on his lips to invite her to do the same. 'No problem,' he said quickly and gave Max's hand a squeeze. 'We'd like that, wouldn't we?'

'Will there be ice cream?' asked Max.

Addy laughed. 'Oh, I think I can stretch to buying us all an ice cream.' She smiled as Max held out his other hand to her.

What on earth had she got herself into? Things all seemed so simple in her head. She'd met her colleague and neighbour by accident, and since they were both at the same place, and didn't have any other company, it made sense for them to stick together.

The building was big, consisting of seven floors. Three of those focused on ecosystems, bioengineering, outer space, resource development and health and wellbeing, while other parts were dedicated to young ones. Most of it was over Max's head.

There were other exhibits on health, water, energy and future technologies, but the best floor for Max was the one dedicated for children.

They'd followed other people and started on floor six, working their way down, but it seemed like it hadn't been the best idea.

Theo looked relieved when they reached the kid's floor. 'I did suspect this place might be a bit too old for Max,' he said. 'But I guess I didn't realise quite how much wouldn't be interesting to him.'

He looked disappointed and she got a weird feeling in the pit of her stomach. What must this be like for him? The ward clerkess had told her that he'd taken responsibility for Max unexpectedly, and that he sometimes looked for advice. Plus, he was on his own with the little guy. Being a single parent was tough enough without being thrown in at the deep end.

'Come on, Theo,' she said encouragingly. 'There has been something at every exhibit that he could play or interact with. And it's not like we've spent a long time at those. Once Max has played with what's there for him, we've moved along.'

He groaned and waved his hand to the floor in front of him. 'But I probably should have brought him straight here.'

Addy put one hand on her hip. 'Has Max looked bored

to you at any point? Has he complained? Or asked to move along?' She shook her head. 'No, he hasn't. As for this,' she smiled, 'now it's time to let him run loose, and for us to follow his lead.'

She was feeling little twinges that she really didn't want to feel. It was clear how passionate he was about doing a good job parenting Max—and she wondered how that might impact on any other relationships he could have.

This floor was designed around future heroes letting kids play a part in a game. It might have been a little bit advanced for a three-year-old, but Theo and Addy played alongside him to keep him entertained.

Finally, they were all exhausted. 'How about something to eat?' asked Theo, pointing at the elevator to the restaurants on the seventh floor.

Max was starting to tire, so he carried him in his arms until they picked a restaurant set in the rooftop garden with a nice breeze. He applied more sunscreen to Max, even though they were in a shaded area.

They sat back and perused the menu. 'Spaghetti bolognaise or cheese and tomato pizza?' Theo asked Max.

Max put his finger to his mouth and looked thoughtful. Addy honestly thought she'd never seen a kid look so cute.

Kids have never been on her radar. She didn't mind them. She'd babysat on occasion for friends and she quite liked playing 'auntie'. It meant she got to do all the fun stuff without the hard commitment of rules and parenting. There had been an occasion when one of her friends had been broken from lack of sleep with her new baby and Addy had offered to take the colicky baby overnight to let her friend get some undisturbed rest.

She'd spent most of the night pacing, listening to the

heartbreaking high-pitched cry, and realised exactly why her friend looked exhausted. To be honest, it had put her off for a bit. But she'd never taken the time to really consider having a family. She guessed it had always been in the back of her head that she might like to have one at some point. But with all the drama about her fiancé and the debts, there had just been no time to consider anything.

But now, sitting here with Max, for the first time, she thought about it.

She was thirty-two now. She'd never considered her biological clock ticking. But how long would it be before she could trust someone again? Right now, that seemed like never. What if she didn't meet someone that she could form a relationship with? Would she be brave enough to be a single parent like Theo?

She blinked. Imagining the costs of requiring a sperm donor and IVF. She would likely never be in a position to afford any of those costs—at least not while she still might be fertile enough to produce viable eggs.

She felt a nudge at her elbow and realised the waiter was next to them. 'A glass of pinot grigio, some sparkling water, and the pepperoni and honey pizza, please,' she said quickly, pushing away the thoughts that had filled her head in the blink of an eye. Sometimes she scared herself.

Theo ordered for himself and Max, then relaxed back into his chair. 'Good view,' he said, looking around them.

She nodded in agreement. 'Not quite as good as the apartments though. I sometimes feel as if we sleep amongst the stars.'

He gave her a smile. 'Been brave enough to sleep without blinds?'

She grinned. 'The first night. Do you try to look around to see if anyone can see in?'

He nodded. 'There's nothing quite so creepy as thinking someone might actually watch you sleep, is there?'

She shuddered and laughed. 'And then you realise that no one in the world is interested. What could they possibly have to gain? So you lie there, looking at the black sky and twinkling stars, and it feels a bit like camping as a kid.'

'You camped?' He seemed surprised.

'Didn't everyone?' She wrinkled her nose. 'Or was that just in Scotland?'

He smiled again. 'Not, that was France too. We definitely camped.'

She opened her hands. 'Don't get me wrong. I'm an appliance girl. I like electrical sockets. And home comforts. But I have, on occasion, lain on a blown-up mattress, in a field somewhere, and looked up at the stars.' She raised her eyebrows. 'Until it rained of course.'

He gave her a good-humoured smile. 'You don't like the sound of the rain on your tent?'

Her eyebrows raised mockingly. 'And then you put your hand up to touch the inside of the tent and it's wet? Shortly followed by the deluge?'

He laughed out loud. 'Should have bought a better tent.'

'Should have stayed at home,' she said quickly, raising her wine glass to him.

There was something so nice about this. Max was drawing with some crayons that the waiter had brought them. Theo was slowly sipping a cool beer, and Addy's wine was refreshing and light. They were shaded from the bright sun, and the breeze around them helped keep them cool.

Addy looked around at their surroundings and let out a small laugh. 'If you'd told me six months ago I'd be working in Dubai, looking at this view, and having lunch at the top of a museum, I'd have thought you were writing a work of fiction.' She gave him a soft smile. She didn't need to say the words for him. She knew his life had changed in unimaginable ways too.

His brown eyes went automatically to Max's blond head—he was still colouring. Green apparently was his favourite colour. Theo let out a long sigh. 'Me too,' he agreed, but the look in his gaze was affectionate. 'We all wish we could go back and change things sometimes. But what's done is done. And I'm not sorry that I'm here.'

His gaze met hers. Even though she'd just had a drink, her mouth felt dry. Was he being philosophical, or direct?

There was a zing in the air. And she wasn't imagining it. The breeze wasn't making her skin prickle. His gaze was.

It would be so easy to think he was looking back over his life and just saying he was glad he had Max. But the words seemed a bit different. When he'd said, 'I'm not sorry that I'm here,' it had been as if the 'with you' might have been unspoken, but seemed to be hanging in the air between them.

And it didn't matter how much she told her skin not to tingle. Or how her brain kept telling her any kind of relationship was the last thing she needed—those dark brown eyes of his seemed to pull like an invisible string across the table.

She gave a little cough and picked up her glass again, raising it towards them. 'Me either,' she added quickly, hoping she wouldn't be asked to qualify what that actually meant.

Thankfully the waiter arrived, setting down pizzas for them all. Max happily started eating, then chatting with his mouth partly full about his favourite movie with little yellow creatures in it.

'Slow down,' said Theo, leaning over him and putting a hand on his shoulder. 'Don't talk with your mouth full. You'll have plenty of time to tell Addy the story.' He looked over. 'At least, I think you will. Are you in a rush?'

Something washed over her. It was the oddest thing and seemed to come out of nowhere. Was she in a rush? No. Last time she'd been in a rush it would have been sorting out one of the many disasters she'd been left with back home. But here?

It was a sweeping sensation of loneliness that almost took her breath away. She was here today through pure chance and good luck. If she hadn't met Theo and Max she would have spent the whole day on her own. She'd been here just over three weeks now, and she still hadn't really had a chance to make any friends.

Dubai was a wonderful place, but everywhere she looked people were busy—laughing, chatting, exercising—and it made her feel even more lonely.

But lonely was safe, she reminded herself. If she was lonely, she wasn't being taken advantage of, or manipulated. She had to keep reminding herself of that.

'I'm not in a rush,' she finally answered, looking down and concentrating on her pizza. The last thing she wanted to do was let him know she was embarrassed by the answer. But Max's little hand brushed against hers.

He beamed at her, and she realised he'd finished his pizza, and wanted to tell her the whole movie story. So, she finished her pepperoni and honey pizza and sipped her wine while she listened to his tale. It was clear the yellow creatures were favourites.

'How many movies are there?' she asked Theo.

His brow furrowed. 'I don't know. Six? Seven? Feels like about one hundred.'

'There's another one soon!' Max beamed. 'You should come with us.'

Theo made a strange sort of sound. 'Now, Max, we can't assume that Addy will be free to come to the movies with us. She might be working, or have plans with friends.'

The little slightly sticky hand slid into hers. 'But we're your friends, aren't we, Addy?'

'Of course,' she agreed quickly, acknowledging the little ache in her heart.

She had to try harder. She had to put herself out there in the world. Sealing herself off because of how Stuart had treated her wasn't a long-term solution.

Theo's words made her realise she might not be welcome to join them. Maybe she hadn't even been welcome today and had just been too unaware to pick up on the signals.

He'd been trying to give her an easy get-out clause. She should take it. And take the hint in general.

'I've had a great time today, Max. And I've loved seeing the museum with you. But Theo is right. When your next favourite movie comes out, I could be working or have other plans. And I'd hate for you to miss out. So, you go ahead with Theo, and maybe you can tell me all about it some other time?'

Kids weren't subtle. And she could see the hint of confusion and hurt in his face. 'Okay,' he said unsteadily, his gaze flicking between her and Theo.

Theo's face was steady. He waved his hand to get the check and paid before she even had a chance to offer.

Five minutes later they were outside the museum. She knew that Theo and Max would head towards the metro and, although that had been her plan too, she didn't want it to seem like she was trying to stay around them.

'I have a little shopping to do,' she said.

Theo gave her a nod.

'I want to add some colour to the apartment. Put my own mark on it.'

He hadn't asked her for an explanation, so she wasn't quite sure why it seemed important to justify her shopping arrangements.

She bent down in front of Max. 'I've had a lovely time. Thank you for letting me hang around with you today.'

Before she straightened up, Max reached over and touched her face. The unexpected move instantly made her recoil, but Max still smiled at her. 'Thank you, Addy,' he said.

Theo bent down and swooped Max up into his arms. 'Sorry,' he muttered hurriedly.

But it was her that felt embarrassed. Max had just been doing what three-year-olds do. Why had things suddenly got so awkward?

She stood up, conscious of the heat rushing into her cheeks. 'No problem,' she said, trying to keep her voice light. 'I'll see you guys later.'

And with a wave of her hand, and no idea where she was going, she rushed off.

CHAPTER SIX

Theo groaned as his pager buzzed, knowing what it would be without even looking.

He sighed as he picked it up. Yep. Another colleague off sick.

It seemed that half the hospital had picked up some sort of bug. Public and environmental health were currently investigating. No one knew yet if it were some kind of norovirus or gastroenteritis, or where the origins lay. Their Accident and Emergency department was also full of patients from surrounding areas.

'Another one?' asked Maysa as she walked in.

He nodded. Maysa picked up her phone. 'I'll let Addy know. She's trying to keep both wards staffed, and Cardiac Theatre. One of the charge nurses from Cardiac ITU just phoned in too.'

Theo groaned. He'd been keeping his fingers crossed all week that Max wouldn't pick anything up. Some of the children in the daycare had been affected, and these things spread like wildfire around children. He couldn't be at the hospital, and taking care of a sick child, and he wasn't quite sure what he would do.

Well, actually he did know. He would phone in sick too.

The ward phone rang and Maysa answered, looking into the office where Theo was sitting, just as Addy came through the double doors, pager in one hand, notepad and pen in the other.

Theo looked up as Addy came into the room. 'Everything covered for you?'

'Almost,' she said, pulling a face. 'What about you?'

He groaned. 'Another two doctors off sick, but I have cover for the next few days at least.'

There was a slightly awkward pause between them. It had been this way since their day together at the science centre. Theo couldn't quite work out if he or Max had upset or offended Addy in some way, but the friendly, relaxed manner between them had been stilted these last few days, and neither one of them appeared to understand it.

Theo wondered if she didn't want to appear too friendly at work. People did talk. And that was the last thing they both needed. Particularly when any chat would be unwarranted.

But Addy had stuck in his brain. Max had asked after her a few times, even checking if Theo had replaced her chocolate ice cream—which, embarrassingly, he hadn't.

She'd seemed happy during lunch. He'd caught the affection in her eyes for Max, and it had filled him with relief. He'd had friends before who were never relaxed around children, and that made things awkward for everyone. In the past, he'd been on the sidelines, either trying to placate a worried parent, or a nervous and short-tempered friend. Now he was the main event. Max would always be by his side, and he was conscious that he never wanted to put anyone in a position where they might be uncomfortable.

He didn't even know Addy's past. She might have been married. She could have had fertility issues of her own. Or she might consciously have decided she never wanted a family. They weren't close enough to have those kinds of conversations, which left him with a world of questions that circled around and around—especially late at night.

He tried to reexamine everything he'd said, wondering if he'd made her feel unwelcome in any way. If he had it hadn't been intentional. But the truth was he couldn't remember every word he'd said. He just knew that something seemed to be a little off between them right now.

It shouldn't matter. It shouldn't bother him. They were neighbours and work colleagues. That was it.

But it did. It made his stomach squirm in an uncomfortable way he hadn't experienced in years. Because he couldn't remember being interested in someone like this in a while.

Maysa knocked on the open door. 'I think you're both going to be needed,' she said, with a grave look on her face.

'What?' asked Theo promptly.

'A VIP downstairs in Accident and Emergency. Chest pain, dehydrated, and suffering from diarrhoea and vomiting the last few days.'

Theo frowned. Usually one of their junior doctors covered the floor in Emergency. But it wasn't unheard of for a VIP to ask for a consultant. He'd only met an extremely rich oil man and an international rugby player so far, both of whom had been regarded as VIPs when they'd attended with cardiac symptoms.

'They're certain it's cardiac and not just dehydration?' he asked as he stood.

Maysa pressed her lips together. 'It's not them that's certain. It's the patient.'

Both Theo and Addy looked up.

Maysa shrugged her shoulders. 'It's Dr Gemmill.'

Theo looked directly at Addy. 'Come down with me.'

She put her hand to her chest. 'What? Me? No way. He hates me. I'll only make whatever symptoms he has worse.'

Theo shook his head. 'Who's covering the cardiac theatre?'

She closed her eyes for a second, realising where this was going. 'Me,' she admitted. 'Everyone else has phoned in sick or has sick family members they can't leave.'

Theo's gaze met hers. 'Then if I need to take him straight to Theatre, it's best if you're with me.'

Addy didn't pretend to hide her groan, but she nodded and followed him down the corridor.

Theo knew he was being logical about this. If his colleague was unwell, he didn't want to waste time.

They reached Accident and Emergency in record time. One of the staff gave them a nod of acknowledgement and pointed towards a room at the side.

Theo could hear Dr Gemmill's voice before they even reached the doorway. He wasn't renowned for his good manners.

'Dr Gemmill,' said Theo as he walked into the room, smiling at the nurse who'd clearly drawn the short straw. He watched the monitor's electronic picture of Dr Gemmill's heart for a few seconds. Then he picked up the twelve-lead ECG that had already been performed.

Dr Gemmill took this as his cue to talk. 'You? There's no one else on duty?' The creases on his brow deepened. 'And what's she doing here?'

'Addy is likely to be assisting me in Cardiac Theatre this evening, since all other staff are sick,' said Theo, keeping his temper in check and his voice steady.

Addy looked over his shoulder. 'Non-stemi,' she murmured, recognising the type of heart attack Dr Gemmill had suffered at a moment's glance.

Theo tried not to smile. He'd known she was good, and he suspected he was about to find out just how good.

'Can you see if the lab results are available?' he asked.

'They're not,' snapped Dr Gemmill.

Theo stepped closer to him. For the nearly four months he'd known this colleague, he'd always been quite lean. But today his skin was papery, waxy and almost looked as if it had collapsed in on itself.

Theo glanced at the IV running on the other side of the bed. 'Can you turn that up?' he asked Addy, as she searched on one of the nearby tablets for the blood results.

Her hand reached out and she upped the rate in a few seconds.

'Do you want to give me some history?' Theo asked Dr Gemmill. He could see on the chart his first name was Alan, but he knew better than to use it. 'You're clearly very dehydrated. How many days have you been unwell?'

'Just treat my MI,' growled Dr Gemmill. 'That's what you're here for.'

'If I don't like your blood results, I won't be taking you to Theatre,' Theo said succinctly. 'I won't take a dehydrated patient who's at risk of further clots or stroke without ensuring you're stable first.'

'We both know what I need,' Dr Gemmill snapped.

Theo nodded. 'After fluids, yes. But not before.'

Addy handed over the tablet. 'Blood results just in.' He wondered if she would try to remain clear of Dr Gemmill, but no. She bent over him. 'Dr Gemmill, let me check your IV site.'

He scowled as she bent over to look at his diminished veins, clearly checking to make sure the fluids were still running in correctly. The veins in patients with dehydration could often collapse.

'Might need another site,' she said softly.

Theo sighed. 'Okay, your cardiac enzymes are consistent with what the ECG shows us. But your urea and electrolytes mean we have to delay Theatre. I'll run them again in half an hour, after we get another IV into you.'

'You'll overload me, you fool!' Dr Gemmill exclaimed.

Theo merely turned the tablet around to show Dr Gemmill his own results. 'I won't overload you,' he said quietly. 'But you clearly have a limited volume circulating right now. If we want your angioplasty and stent insertion to be a success, we have to delay.'

There was silence in the room. Addy moved around and inserted another IV while the doctors looked at each other. She'd run the other IV through, and connected it, before they finally spoke again.

'Would you take a patient with these blood results for stent and angio?'

They both knew the answer was no. And they both knew the older man wouldn't admit it.

'I suspect,' said Theo, 'that you might be unique. You might actually be a patient whose heart attack has been caused by dehydration, rather than atherosclerosis.' He raised his eyebrows slightly at his colleague. 'Although your age goes against you, you have no other real risk factors I can see in your chart—we both know that means little. Any family history?'

'No.'

'Your cholesterol levels have always been good. Ever a smoker?'

'No.'

Theo sighed inwardly. 'Anything else I should know before considering you for Theatre this afternoon? Allergies?'

'None.'

Addy had finished what she was doing and was talking in a low voice to the nurse.

'What are you whispering about over there?' snapped Dr Gemmill.

Theo felt himself bristle. He knew that, right now, Dr Gemmill was likely terrified. He was about to put his life into Theo's hands, and Theo had no doubt that the mere thought was crippling him with anxiety.

The man was arrogant, over-confident and downright rude as a human being. But he was also a patient. Theo's patient. But no matter who he was in this hospital, Theo wouldn't allow him to talk to staff like that.

It turned out Addy could more than handle him. 'You,' she said succinctly. 'We're talking about you, Dr Gemmill. I'm talking with Faizah here about getting a portable chest X-ray arranged, and what time to get your next set of bloods taken. All being well, I'm also giving her some pre-op instructions for you, since I'll have to go and prepare the cath lab.'

She gave Dr Gemmill the sincerest smile.

'Apologies, I would normally stay with a patient to talk them through everything and make sure they were fully prepared for Theatre, but unfortunately, as you know, there's a shortage of staff, and I'm very *particular* about things.' She laid some emphasis on the word 'particular', and then continued. 'I like to ensure everything in my theatre is laid out exactly as I like. I want to ensure everything is perfect.'

Theo could see all the words that Alan Gemmill actually wanted to say bubble beneath his skin. There was nothing wrong with anything Addy had said, or how she delivered it. But Alan Gemmill was no fool.

Addison Bates had just let him know in the nicest possible way that she was no slouch, and he was lucky to be in her hands.

She shot Theo a beaming smile. 'Dr Dubois, I take it I can leave all the consent procedures with yourself while I go and prepare Theatre?' She glanced from Dr Gemmill to Theo. 'Providing of course the future blood results are sufficient.'

He gave her a nod and didn't let himself smile as she left the room in a few strides. Theo glanced at the clock. He turned to Faizah. 'Optimal reperfusion time is ninety minutes for best effect.' He gave her a time. 'Can the bloods be taken then? I'll phone the lab and let them know I need the results fifteen minutes later.'

Faizah nodded.

'Great, then these are the rest of the instructions for Dr Gemmill.' He wrote up some medications and timed observations. Finally, he finished the consent procedures with Alan Gemmill, and asked the most important question.

'Can I call someone for you? A family member or a friend?'

His colleague still had a disgruntled expression on his face. Theo actually wondered if he had anyone. 'I called my wife and left her a message. She hasn't replied yet.'

Theo stopped the million questions that immediately sprang into his head. 'Do you have any idea where she currently is?'

'At her club.' His words were staccato.

'And where's that?'

He murmured an address and Faizah raised her head.

'Oh, I know that place. I know someone who works there. Let me call and see if I can get a hold of her.'

If Theo had blinked he would have missed the tiny movement in Alan Gemmill's shoulders, which might have indicated a little sigh of relief.

Maybe the guy did have some feelings after all. 'Do you have any questions for me, Dr Gemmill?' Theo asked.

The older man shook his head.

'Then I'll go and get scrubbed for Theatre. I'm hoping your blood results will be a bit better and we can get started as soon as possible. If there's a problem, I'll come back and let you know. Otherwise, I'll see you in the cath lab.'

Addy was thanking her lucky stars she'd made a few visits to the cardiac theatre, to meet the charge nurse and get shown around. She'd sown the seeds of her idea of rotating staff, and it had gone better than she'd initially hoped. Luca, the charge nurse down here, had wanted to chat further, and explore how best they could manage things.

However, Luca was currently on a two-week holiday to the US. She suspected if he knew about the sickness levels at Spira right now, he would jump back on a plane, but that didn't help her or Theo today.

She talked to the anaesthetist on call, and to the theatre technician on duty. The theatre was prepared in record time. It wasn't difficult—this was a permanent cardiac theatre, so the main pieces of equipment remained in place.

She looked out the theatre packs, angio lines and stents, before briefing the imaging technician and finally going to change into scrubs.

By the time she was at the theatre sink, Theo was next to her. 'Bloods okay?' she asked.

He nodded. 'Not normal as yet, but improved. Enough that I'm confident to do the procedure.'

'The anaesthetist, Hal, is on standby if you need them.'

Theo gave a nod. 'He said he would have a chat with Dr Gemmill in pre-op to let him know he was available if sedation was required.'

'Does everyone jump to Dr Gemmill's word?'

Theo gave her a sideways glance as he scrubbed. 'No. To be honest, I think Hal would take great pleasure in anaesthetising the guy. Probably wanted to do it for years just to keep him quiet. But that's hardly a thing you can say out loud.'

Addy grinned at his frankness. 'Well, I know the charge nurse down here thinks very highly of Hal. Says if he's ever sick and needs an op, he's calling Hal on his way in.'

'Now, that's praise indeed from a colleague,' said Theo as he dried off his hands. Then they finished gowning and gloving.

Addy stood at his side as Dr Gemmill was wheeled into Theatre and positioned on the table. Theo hadn't been joking when he'd said everything was state-of-the-art here. They had a bi-plane system, which captured 3D images faster because they used detectors on two axes instead of one. It looked like two giant arms shaped like Cs, which could be moved and manipulated around the table where the patient lay.

Dr Gemmill was still scowling, but Addy kept smiling and talking in a reassuring manner as the technician ensured electrodes were placed where they should be and the BP cuff was in place. They were ready to start.

Theo started to talk. His accent was rich and thick.

She'd never been in the cath lab with him before, so didn't know if this was his normal manner, or if he might actually be a little nervous.

Treating patients that you knew was always different and sometimes difficult. Addy had been part of the resuscitation of a previous colleague and it had stuck with her—no matter that she knew everything had been done perfectly.

Addy draped the groin area, where Theo would start the procedure. She cleaned it with the orange-coloured antiseptic that was used all over the world, then he injected local anaesthetic to numb the area.

Dr Gemmill was quieter than she'd expected, and she suspected the anaesthetist might have given him something to relax him. It was probably better for everyone.

But whether Dr Gemmill was listening or not, Theo talked him through what he was doing. He made the small incision, inserted the sheath then passed the catheter, watching its ascent as he guided it along the coronary artery.

A thin flexible wire was then inserted down the inside of the catheter once they found the narrowed area in the artery. Theo had been right. There was little evidence of plaque inside the arteries—which was usually common in patients with cardiac conditions. However, when they reached the left coronary artery, there was clear sign of blockage—a thick clot.

Theo inserted some medicine specially designed to dissolve the clot in a harmless way. Then he inflated the balloon to relieve the blockage and allow the blood to flow through the heart. The tiny stent was already in position. As Theo deflated the balloon, the stent stayed in place as it was designed to.

Dr Gemmill's heart rate remained steady throughout, with only the occasional ectopic beat. Theo finished by inserting some contrast dye to monitor the blood flow through the heart and ensure there were no other blockages.

The whole procedure took just under thirty minutes. The balloon, wire, catheter and sheath were all removed, and Theo applied pressure to the wound, talking comfortably to Dr Gemmill until he was happy the wound was sealed.

They had a short talk about pain relief, future plans and the need for possible antithrombotic medicine in the future. Dr Gemmill was scornful—so he was obviously feeling a bit better—and was confident that dehydration had caused his blockage and he wouldn't require anything else. However, he did accept that Theo would ask him to be reviewed by one of their specialist colleagues to discuss this further before he was discharged from hospital.

When Dr Gemmill was wheeled out through the door, Theo and Addy let out big sighs of relief as they tugged off their theatre caps.

Addy bent down and shook her hair out, tossing it back over her head when she was finished. Her dark, normally smooth hair had some kinks and curls.

'Phew,' she said. 'I've too much hair for these theatre caps. They kill me.'

He laughed at her. 'It does seem to have doubled in size.'

She glanced about, looking for a mirror, but there was none. 'Is it that bad?' She stalked around, patting her inflated hair. 'Humidity. It plays havoc with me. My hair is just too thick. I'll need to find a good hairdresser to help me thin it out.'

Theo had folded his arms and was leaning against a wall. 'Thinning out your hair. That's actually a thing?'

'Of course,' she said, pulling her scrub top free of her trousers and letting it hang. The theatre changing rooms were surprisingly warm.

Theo stuck up his hand to feel the air. 'Think the air conditioning's broken in here?'

She laughed. 'Either that or they spent so much money on all the equipment they can't afford to turn it on. Maybe they're just trying to stop us all hanging around by making it a sweat-fest in here.'

This was the first time they'd been alone since their day at the science centre. It felt nice again. It felt right. And as soon as that tiny thought entered her head, she could feel the wave of panic circling her again.

'I really need to shower,' she said, heading to her locker to grab her things.

Theo gave a nod at her sudden move. He was watching her carefully, she could tell. 'I'll need to finish up my notes. Are you working on the ward tomorrow?'

She nodded and then her feet stopped. She turned around. 'Is that going to be a problem?'

Theo looked puzzled. 'No. Why? I was only asking for continuity of care.'

But Addy froze. 'You know he doesn't like me. He moved me off his ward.'

Theo moved next to her. 'But I'm his consultant.' He patted his hand against his chest. 'So, he'll have to stay on *my* ward, not his.'

She shook her head. 'He won't want me anywhere near him. And I bet he's a complainer.'

Theo looked at her quizzically. 'You are more than fit for him. That's how you say it, isn't it?'

A smile hinted at her lips. 'Maybe,' she agreed reluctantly. Then she gave a big sigh. 'But he's a cardiac patient who's just undergone a procedure. The last thing I want to do is add any stress. It's probably best I'm nowhere near him.'

'Then try not to be.'

'You know what the staffing is like.'

'I do,' Theo agreed. 'And so does he. I expect you to treat him like every other patient.'

She instantly felt her hackles rise and opened her mouth to answer, but Theo's soft hand rested on her shoulder. 'Like the excellent nurse that you are. You're experienced, have lots of knowledge, and likely know as much as any of us. Don't be intimidated by him. Think of him as one of those patients who are nasty, rude and tetchy because, deep down, they're scared. He's just had a life-threatening event. Right up until his chest pain today, Dr Gemmill probably thought he was going to live for ever.'

She was conscious of the warm feeling of his palm through her thin scrub top. They were inches apart, and the only two in the changing room. The heat wasn't just coming from the air around them. It was coming from inside.

She tilted her head upwards. He was close enough for her to see the tiny scratchy stubble around the edge of his jawline. His brown eyes were a little bloodshot—probably from the pressure of today. But, this close, she could also see just how long his dark eyelashes were. Women would go to war over eyelashes like those.

She could smell him. That cologne that he wore. She'd noticed it a few times. Hints of it were still there—amber, woody, but still fresh. She tried not to suck in her breath. That would just be too weird.

His fingers moved a little, one coming into contact with her skin. There it was—the reaction that she'd known would happen. All of the cells in her body coming alive in instantaneous response. Instead of sucking a breath in, she let a breath out, in an odd kind of sighing way.

In that instant, she saw his pupils dilate, and he leaned towards her.

Neither of them had spoken. They didn't need any dialogue. Their bodies were doing all the talking.

The door swung open behind them and both of them jumped.

The theatre orderly's gaze narrowed for a second, as if he realised what he'd almost seen. Then he said, 'There's a woman outside to see you. Somebody Gemmill. She won't go to the waiting room. Believe me, I've tried.'

A smile broke across Addy's face and she stepped back. It was odd. Her body was on fire, but she now felt strangely relieved.

What would have happened if they'd kissed? It could be a disaster. They barely knew each other. Addy was here to get her life in order, and she certainly hadn't achieved that yet.

But as Theo stepped back his hand brushed against her bare arm. Only in the slightest way, his fingers making a lightning soft trail down her forearm to her wrist.

The zap was like being hit by a magic wand. The pads of her fingers tingled—as if they were crying out to grab his hand as it drifted away from her skin.

It was the smallest move, and looked almost unintentional, but as Theo walked to the door, she saw his sideways glance at her. 'I'll speak to Mrs Gemmill,' he said, his voice huskier than usual. 'See you back outside.'

And then he was gone. Leaving her more in need of a shower than she had been before.

CHAPTER SEVEN

It turned out that Mrs Gemmill was probably the most interesting patient's relative that he'd met in all his years as a doctor.

She was big. She was flamboyant. She was loud. And she was the biggest sweetheart he'd ever met.

Mrs Gemmill wore hats, and they usually matched her lipstick and her shoes. She went to a variety of 'clubs'—most of which Theo was sure he'd never see the inside of.

Addy stood next to him with her arms folded, watching the spectacle at the end of the corridor as Mrs Gemmill said hello to every person, in every room, before reaching her husband.

'She's got to be old money.'

Theo looked at her. 'What do you mean?'

'I mean, I think Alan Gemmill married up. She's a lady. I bet she actually has a title. Have you heard the number of charities she's involved with? She goes to Ascot every year. Wimbledon. She's gone to the Grand Prix in Monaco. And she never boasts. She talks about these things as if they were every-day normal.'

Theo leaned over and whispered in her ear. 'Do you think he ever gets a word in?'

That made Addy grin, her smile spreading across her

face. Her violet eyes turned to him. 'You know, I doubt it, and funnily enough, that makes me happy.'

Alan Gemmill had stayed a day longer than usual because it seemed the dehydration was taking a few days to recover. He was a little unsteady on his feet, and his blood pressure was generally low. All in keeping with an older patient who'd had a bug for a few days and become severely dehydrated—and that was all without taking into consideration his MI, angioplasty and stent insertion.

Theo was quite sure the man would have dragged himself out of the ward any way he could, if possible. But it seemed that Mrs Gemmill had some kind of background knowledge herself in medicine, and was happy to go along with Theo's recommendation that Dr Gemmill stay until all his levels were entirely normal and he was fully fit again.

And it seemed that her husband was not getting a chance to overrule her.

'I'm going to bask in these few days,' said Addy as she took a cookie from a huge basket on the desk—also supplied by Mrs Gemmill. 'He snapped at me as I changed his IV, and she put him back in his place in a heartbeat. She was literally mortified by him, and I don't imagine she has any idea how he normally is at work.'

'Did you get a chance to meet Dr Gemmill's secretary when she came down?'

Addy nodded again. 'It seems that she and Mrs Gemmill are in cahoots.'

'Cahoots? What's that?'

She gave a quiet laugh. 'It means they're in an alliance together, a partnership, and it generally means up to no good.'

Theo took a couple of seconds to get his mind around

that one, then nodded in approval. 'Maybe that's the only way they manage him.'

Addy turned to face him. They had managed to stay at arm's length for the last two days. Memories of the changing room had flooded his mind at all possible instances, along with the eternal what-if question.

The main focus of the question was central to him and Max. He'd never been a single parent before, he'd never tried to date anyone while he was a single parent. So many things were new to him. Should he have rules? Should he have actually tried to date someone before allowing them to meet Max?

Maybe Max should never meet someone he dated—unless... He couldn't even think about the unless. It was a million miles away.

Addy knew about Max. She'd met him. She seemed good with him. But he was conscious he didn't know so much about her. He didn't want to take a chance on something that could be fleeting and then damage any future working relationship.

But, as the floral scent of her perfume drifted under his nose, he wondered if fleeting and casual might be the way to go. It had never really been his style. But maybe he could keep any relationship fully at arm's length, and keep Max cocooned from that part of his life. Would that work better? Would that keep Max from making friendships with women that might actually do him more harm than good?

He just wasn't ready for this. For the myriad of what-ifs that had been circling his brain. And this wasn't the kind of thing he could pick up the phone to Colette about. Any Max-related question was fine. But how to have a love life as a single parent? Colette would put him firmly back in his place if he tried to ask for advice on that issue. The thought brought a smile to his face.

'Any chance he might retire now?' asked Addy, her voice hopeful.

Max shrugged. 'I'm his doctor right now, but I don't think he'll want to have the conversation with me about reducing his workload. He's fixating on the fact his MI was likely caused by dehydration. I think if he could get away with it, he'd write up his own case for some journal.'

'Why don't you?'

Theo spoke quietly and couldn't keep the smile out of his voice. 'It's unusual but not *so* unusual that I want to tell the world about it. Last time I saw a case like this the guy was in his late twenties, fit as a fiddle, and worked in a printing factory where the temperatures were through the roof—and it was in the middle of summer. Now, that case was interesting, and the consultant I worked with at the time wrote it up. This one? Not so much.'

'You don't think Dr Gemmill needs the fame?' Amusement was in those eyes.

'I think that's the last thing he needs.'

She gave a sigh and continued to nibble her cookie. 'His wife's nice. I wonder how he managed to catch her.'

'Catch her? Somehow I think if I said that you might give me trouble.'

'Maybe.' She shrugged good-naturedly. 'I just find it fascinating that a person who's a tyrant and a grump at work managed to find such a charming wife.'

'She is charming, isn't she?'

Addy tapped him on the arm. 'But you know what that means now, don't you?'

He was focusing on the tiny spot on his arm that her fingertip had just touched. It was ridiculous how his eyes went there. Or how, when she'd been right in front of him two days ago, close enough to kiss, he could see both shades of blue and violet in her eyes, merging to make that heart-stopping colour. How her skin had been so perfect, even though she'd just taken off her surgical mask. And her hair…oh, her hair brought a wide smile to his face.

'Hey,' she said, nudging him with her elbow. 'Pay attention.'

'Sorry.' He gave himself a shake, trying to pretend his mind hadn't gone to other places.

'You know what this means, right?'

He was bewildered, and still wondering if, even though they were on the ward, they might be standing a little too closely.

'I haven't got a clue.' He sighed, hoping this didn't mean she would move.

She threw up her hands. 'His patients. They're yours right now. Including…' She waited, as if he would throw out the name. But she gave up in exasperation. 'Isabel Aurelis.'

The young girl who had arrested on their first meeting.

'But that was almost a month ago. She was discharged after a few days.'

Addy tapped the side of her nose. 'But her investigations haven't been completed. She still has episodes and symptoms.'

He frowned and looked at her. 'And how would you know that?'

'Layla,' she said promptly. 'She's doing some learning right now, and she's based her patient case on Isabel and her potential condition of Wolff-Parkinson-White Syndrome.'

'I can get away with looking after the patients that Dr

Gemmill currently has admitted—or who are scheduled for procedures that shouldn't wait. I don't think I'll get away with calling in one of his private patients.'

'I have contacts.' Addy beamed.

Her hair was back under control, smooth and gleaming under the hospital lights, caught in a burgundy scrunchie that matched her uniform. Theo wasn't sure what way he liked it best.

He groaned. 'Dr Gemmill's secretary.'

'Finally,' she said, throwing up her hands again. 'She'll bring Isabel in if you ask.' Her tone changed, as she clearly tried to make herself sound innocent, as if she hadn't planned this to get Isabel's care reviewed.

He took a breath. 'You are going to get me in all sorts of trouble.'

She winked. 'Hope so.'

It was so easy and natural between them. And he liked it. He liked being around her. Even when he tried to find reasons not to.

The thought of Addison Bates getting him into trouble did all sorts of things to him that it shouldn't.

He picked up a cookie. 'I will see her *if*, and I mean if, she still has symptoms that need investigating, or *if* she still needs test results explained to her.' He waved the cookie as he walked down the corridor.

'I understand,' Addison said brightly, with a big smile on her face.

And he knew she was indeed going to get him into trouble.

Seven hours later she was sitting on her sofa with the weirdest feeling sizzling in her belly. It was like an itch that she wanted to scratch but didn't exactly know where it was. There were a million things she could watch on TV or streaming services, but it wasn't what she wanted to do.

She started to pace, looking out at the dark sky, the outline of the skyscrapers and the twinkling stars above. Her phone pinged and she sighed as she picked it up. But the sigh was quickly extinguished when she realised who the sender was.

Are you free to come over? I have a debt to repay.

She looked down at her 'lounging' outfit. Soft beige joggers and a matching giant off-the-shoulder sweatshirt. She should change. She should find something more alluring to put on. But as she hurried through to the bedroom and caught a glance of herself in the mirror, she stopped. Some of today's make-up was left in place and her hair was in a half-up, half-down style, because of how she'd been lying on the sofa a while ago. If she changed, how long would that take? And should she really dress up to go practically next door?

She looked down again. Her clothes were fine. Not what she would wear to go shopping, but they were clean, no stains—certainly good enough to go two doors down. She gave herself one panicked spray of light perfume, then grabbed her key and her phone.

He opened the door with a big smile on his face. She was glad she hadn't changed—he was wearing an old shirt, some shorts and a pair of worn-in designer flip flops that he'd probably got in his youth.

'Wine or beer?' he asked.

She looked around. 'Where's Max?'

'Sleeping.' He looked relieved as he said the words. 'It's just us.'

That sent a little tingle to her stomach. 'Wine,' she said. 'White if you have it.'

Two minutes later they were perched on his sofa, looking out at the dark night.

'I was doing this next door,' she said as she sank into the cushions. 'Don't you like to do this?'

He laughed. 'Sometimes it's all I can do.'

'What do you mean?' She turned slightly to face him, letting one of her arms rest on the back of the sofa, her knee pulling up too.

He gave a sigh, but kept smiling. 'By the time I get back from work, collect Max, feed him, bath him, play with him, I just don't have the energy for chat shows or action movies.' He waved his arm at the dark sky through the glass. 'This is as good as it gets.'

'You've turned your sofa to face it,' she said, looking around. 'I like it.'

'Don't get fooled.' He laughed. 'The rest of the time it's definitely facing the TV. Max is a special expert on certain kids' shows.'

She let her head fall back. She felt surprisingly comfortable in here. 'I'll bet he is. What's his favourite?'

'Some guy walking around an empty nursery, playing with the toys and singing.'

She shot him a sideways glance. 'That sounds a little bit creepy.'

Theo laughed too. 'It does, doesn't it? Honestly, it's fine, and he sings along and does all the actions. Nothing dubious. I promise.'

She took a breath and then asked, 'So, how is Max?'

'What do you mean?'

'I mean, he had a big change some months ago. He's with you, you've moved. How's he doing?'

Theo closed his eyes for a few seconds and she wondered if she'd got too personal. But she couldn't deny the attraction between them, and they were becoming friends. It felt right to ask.

His dark brown eyes met hers. He bit his lip before replying. 'He's doing fine. At least I think he is. He has the occasional nightmare, and that freaks me out, because I don't know everything he was exposed to, and all the research now tells us that the first two years of a kid's life are formative.'

Addy nodded. She'd heard that too—particularly when she'd had to work with traumatised adult patients. She reached out her hand. 'But that doesn't mean you can't shape what comes next.'

He let out a breath and she could sense his body relax a bit more. His hand closed over hers. She shifted a little so she could still drink her wine with her other hand, and it brought their shoulders side by side.

'I worry I don't spend enough time with him. I worry that I don't have an extended family here. It feels disloyal to France to bring Fleur's child here and bring him up in Dubai instead of back home.'

'Isn't seeing the world a good way to shape a kid's life experience? You already told me he's bilingual. His English is great.'

Theo shook his head a little but smiled. 'Oh, he keeps his French for when he's having a temper tantrum.' He raised one eyebrow. 'He might know a few phrases that he shouldn't.'

'Does he have many temper tantrums?'

'Not really. I mean, I don't think he has more than any normal three-year-old.'

'Then surely that means you're doing a good job?'

He took a sip of his wine.

She could tell he was still stressed, still worrying. 'And isn't it the job of every parent to always secretly worry?'

She leaned a little bit forward, so she could get a good look at those eyes. Should she actually be worried about Theo?

'I guess so,' he said, but the tone of his words sounded defeated.

'So, how are *you* doing?'

The edges of his lips turned upwards. 'Aren't you supposed to say that like Joey from *Friends*?'

She laughed and made an attempt to mimic the character, then shook her head. 'No, I just can't do it. The Scottish accent is too strong.'

He nodded in agreement, then tilted his head as he looked at her. 'No one has really asked me that since I took on Max.'

'Then you're hanging around with the wrong folks.' Addy had never been one to beat around the bush.

He gave a sad kind of smile. 'That's not strictly true. My *maman* asks, but she has enough to worry about.'

'What's wrong with your mum?'

He shook his head. 'Not my mum, my dad. He has multiple sclerosis and my mum is his full-time carer. It's partly why I moved to Dubai. When they knew I was going to take care of Max, my parents asked if I wanted to move back home with them. But I knew that was unfair. My mother would have wanted to help out, and she really isn't able. She has enough to deal with, and I didn't want to put any more strain on her, or on them.'

'How's your dad doing?'

'Okay,' said Theo carefully. 'His deterioration has

slowed. He can still manage things with assistance. I'm hoping that he'll stay like that for a while.'

She could see from his face that she didn't need to ask the next question. Should his father get worse, Theo would want to be there, he would want to go home to France. She didn't blame him at all.

'So, you didn't answer,' she persisted. 'How are you doing?'

He met her gaze, and she could feel the invisible barrier between them. There were a million things he didn't know about her. She wasn't sure she would ever be ready to share—not when her past made her look like a fool. It made her feel so vulnerable, and she didn't want to share that with anyone.

'I hope I'm doing okay,' he said, this time with a bit more confidence. 'Mind you, having to do surgery on a colleague was a bit nerve wracking.'

'You don't say?' she mocked.

'But I'm glad it was you that was there.'

She gestured with her wine glass towards her chest. 'You mean, so I could deflect his bad mood, and keep you safe.'

He smiled but shook his head. 'No, because I know that you know what you're doing. I was confident in the person standing next to me, so it meant I didn't need to worry.'

'Thank you,' she said simply, then leaned forward and whispered in his ear. 'But let's not have a repeat, okay?'

She was so close to his ear that when he turned his face towards her his nose brushed against her cheek. They both froze for a second.

She blinked, conscious that he'd silently set his wine glass down. He reached over and took hers from her hand.

Their faces were only inches apart, and she could feel his warm breath next to her cheek.

'Hey, did you get me here under false pretences?' she whispered.

His voice was low. 'What do you mean?'

'You said you had a debt to repay?'

One of his hands moved to her cheek, his fingertips running down the side of her face. He gave her a lazy kind of smile. 'There's a problem with that now.'

'Really?' Her breath was catching in her throat at his touch. 'And what might that be?'

'Well...' it was almost a drawl '...if I repay my debt, we'll both have to move. I kind of don't want to do that right now.' His warm hand moved to her waist, slipping under her loose top and resting on her bare skin.

She smiled and closed her eyes for a second, enjoying the buzz. 'I kind of don't want you to move either, but I still want to know what this debt is.'

His head bent a little, his lips connecting with the soft skin at her neck. She tipped her head back as his mouth explored the area at the bottom of her throat, then moved up to her ear.

His lips touched her ear. 'Chocolate,' he whispered with a laugh. 'We owe you chocolate, and Max reminded me to pay our debt.'

'You bought me ice cream?' Her eyes connected with his. They widened as she challenged him, shifting her hips to move astride him, as his fingers danced up her bare back.

'Yep,' was all he could muster from her change of position. 'Sure you want to do that?'

She arched her back a little towards him. 'Oh, I'm sure.

Now,' her fingers drew down one side of his face, 'I hope you got me all the trimmings.'

His dark eyes flashed in confusion, but he couldn't remove the smile from his face.

'What trimmings?'

'You know…' Her fingers moved down the front of his T-shirt, sliding underneath as he caught his breath. 'All the things that Max likes. The chocolate sauce, the sprinkles, the marshmallows.'

Her eyes were sparkling as she said the words, taking delight in teasing him as they spoke. All her previous precautions were dancing out through the window. It was funny how his touch could do that to her.

Scotland was a distant memory. She was miles away from thoughts of debt and betrayal. All she wanted to think about was the here and now. They were both grown-ups. This could be whatever they wanted it to be. She was capable of having some fun with her friend. Everything else could just wait.

'So, you like all the trimmings?' he said again, at the base of her throat.

Her hands moved, tugging his T-shirt over his head, then mimicking the act with her own soft top. She glanced over her shoulder into the dark night. 'Think anyone can see us?' she asked.

'Couldn't really care,' was his muffled reply as he pulled down one strap of her bra, then released the back clasp with the other hand.

She could stop this. She could stop this now if she wanted to.

But she absolutely didn't. Because the only thing on her mind right now was Theo Dubois, and just how good this could be. The anticipation was currently killing her.

She asked one final question as she glanced at the door in the corner. 'Any chance Max might wake up?'

Theo shook his head. 'Even if he has a nightmare, he stays in bed. I go to him. He never comes to me.' His eyes met hers. 'We're safe.'

'Good,' she replied with a grin as she pulled him down sideways, then on top of her. His lips touching hers was like heaven.

She could tell that her breathing was shallow. They had both been waiting for this moment. It meant their first kiss was breathless, in a mad teenage kind of way, which made her instantly smile and think of a million movies. Breathless in a way that made her legs liquid, even though she was lying down.

His teeth were on her lips, his tongue was in her mouth, and a million blood cells were currently racing around her body.

His chest was against hers and she could swear she could feel both their racing hearts through their skin. The groan that came from the back of his throat almost undid her.

He stopped for a second, as if he were trying to catch his breath. 'Addy.' His voice was a low growl. 'Are you sure about this? We've only known each other a few weeks.'

'Five,' she responded without hesitating, because it was front and foremost in her mind. She didn't care that she'd told herself she wasn't looking for a relationship. She didn't care that they hadn't had the chance to talk about all their past issues. All she cared about was the right here and now. The feel of his warm body against hers. The touch of his hand on the skin at her back.

'What if people ask about us? Notice a change between us?'

She was smiling and in real danger of clashing teeth with him as their kiss deepened. 'Let them wonder,' she breathed, moving her kisses around to his ear. 'Let's keep this here. Between us. We can tell them when we're ready.'

She was sliding her hands to his front, across his chest, then winding her hands around his neck so she could pull him even closer.

'I can live with that,' he said, then lowered his head to make her forget about anything else.

CHAPTER EIGHT

THE REDIRECTED LETTER came like a bolt out of the blue. Her solicitor knew where she'd relocated to, but this letter was from the police, saying a new inspector was in charge of her case, and criminal charges might be brought. She should attend for interview immediately.

It had been sent more than a month ago, and it had finally made its way to her in Dubai. Addy thought she was going to be sick.

She'd spent the last week floating around in a pink bubble, spending as much time as she could with Theo and Max. No one knew that they were dating or in any kind of relationship. Even Addy wasn't quite sure how to define it.

What she did know was the feel of his skin against hers, the touch of his fingers and lips, had cast some kind of spell over her. All she wanted was more. She hadn't stayed overnight at his place yet. But walking the few steps between their apartments in the early hours of the morning was rapidly becoming the norm.

She couldn't remember being this excited or happy at the start of any of her previous relationships. Being around Theo was hypnotic. But her giant pink bubble had just been burst with a letter-shaped pin.

She spent more than an hour trying to get hold of her

solicitor. Finally, Laura let out a huge sigh when she heard the news. 'Leave it with me. Let me deal with this.'

'But what does it mean? It was me that spoke to the police about Stuart. It was me that wanted to bring charges against him.'

She heard Laura draw in a deep breath. 'He's reappeared. He's causing trouble. He likely outstayed his welcome wherever he went and thought that things would have blown over back home. He's denying he took out the new mortgage or some of the debts. He's telling the police it was all you, and it doesn't help that his return coincided with the original inspector retiring.'

'But what does that mean for me?'

'Nothing. It means nothing. We know some of the debt was taken online. They have no signatures to prove it was you or an electronic footprint. You gave two previous interviews, which more than covered anything they need to know. Leave me to deal with this. Send me a photo of the original letter.'

Addy could feel the wave of panic coming over her. The timing could not be worse. She'd just started to settle into life in Dubai, she'd met someone, she'd just taken some tentative steps towards a new relationship—and now this.

'He's a parasite.' Laura's voice cut into her thoughts. 'He doesn't want to be held accountable for his actions. I'm pretty sure he'll just be setting up his next target, and then he'll disappear again.'

'He doesn't know where I am, does he?' Sudden fear had struck into her heart. Stuart had never been physically abusive towards her, but she didn't know what he might do if he was pushed.

There was a brief pause. 'Not as far as I know. Addy, let me deal with this. I promise I'll be back in touch, okay?'

Addy hung up the phone, her heart racing. She dug into the fridge and pulled out a big bowl of fruit salad, sitting at her table and eating her way through it. A sugar rush always helped when she felt like this. And now wasn't the time for the chocolate ice cream Theo had given her the other night.

She leaned her head in her hands. Just when things had started to look good.

With Dr Gemmill still recovering and not at work, some of the tension in the workplace had disappeared. Word on the street was that his wife was in the process of persuading him to take retirement.

Addy was due to hear back from the clinical governance committee next week around her submission, and she was hopeful it might have some feedback she could work with.

As for Theo? Well…

He filled every part of her thoughts, both day and night. Or at least he had, until now. He still had no idea of her past or history. She still had no real desire to tell him. When he'd told her the other night that he had confidence in her when she was by his side at work, her heart had almost swollen to fill her chest.

Addy always managed to put on an outwardly positive appearance of confidence. But the real truth was all the dealings and deceptions with Stuart had stripped much of her confidence away. Things had all seemed as if they were slotting back into place—and now this.

She put down her fork, before she sent her body into overload. Her phone rang before she had a chance to think.

'Laura?' she asked.

The voice at the end of the phone was confused. 'No, it's Theo. Is everything okay?'

Heat flushed her cheeks. 'Yes, yes, everything's fine. What's wrong?'

She heard his deep breath. 'I hate to ask you this, but the daycare have asked if I can go and pick up Max. He's running a temperature, but I have a patient requiring surgery for an implantable defibrillator in the next hour. I really don't want to cancel or delay.'

'It's fine,' she heard herself say without really thinking about it. 'I can collect Max.'

She heard a huge sigh of relief. 'Thanks. I wouldn't normally ask, but—'

'Where's the card for your apartment?' she asked. 'And do you have medicine I can give Max?'

'In my locker—the code is one, nine, six, seven—and, yes, I have kids' paracetamol and kids' ibuprofen. He's had them before with no problem and can take them alternately if running a temperature. I promise I'll be back in a few hours.'

'You'll be back when your patient is stable,' she cut in. 'Don't worry about Max. I can manage him for a few hours. If there's any problem I'll get a message to you.'

'I know,' he said, and there was a warmth in her skin.

He meant it. He trusted her. He trusted her with the most precious thing to him. She grabbed her light jacket and made her way to the hospital. It was literally only five minutes from the apartments. When she reached daycare, Theo had already phoned to say she was on her way.

The staff gave her a note with his temperature readings. He was flushed and sleepy when she picked him up. She'd never actually carried Max before, and three-year-olds were heavier than expected. But she heaved him up on one hip, and he tucked his arms around her neck as he sagged into her.

If he objected to her picking him up, he didn't say.

By the time she reached the apartment, he was like a leaden weight in her arms. She scanned open the door, carrying Max straight through to his bedroom.

She laid him on of the bright bed covers and took off his shoes. It only took her a moment to find the ear thermometer Theo had said he kept in his kitchen cupboard. Thirty-eight point five. High, but not enough to panic. She found the medicine, measured it out and propped him up a little, getting him take it along with a few sips of water.

All he wanted to do was sleep. And Addy knew the feeling well. On the few occasions she was sick, she just wanted to sleep too. The air conditioning in the apartment was on, and she made sure it was set at a level to keep him comfortable. She contemplated stripping off his T-shirt and shorts, but then settled on checking there was no obvious rash on his torso or back.

Children were always a worry. Infections, viruses, meningitis. She hadn't asked Theo if Max had been given his childhood vaccinations, but she was sure he wouldn't have left him at risk. She seemed to remember having to provide her own vaccination history for entry into Dubai as part of her visa requirements to stay and work here.

She wrote down Max's current temperature along with the time she'd given the medicine, and the amount, then settled in the chair in his room. It seemed wrong to sit in the other room. It didn't matter he was sleeping. She'd been asked to care for him, and she would.

She kept an eye on the clock and took his temperature half an hour later. It remained the same and she swithered about giving the other medicine. But another half an hour on it was at thirty-eight degrees. She gave Max a little shake and persuaded him to drink some more sips of water, before letting him sleep again.

She'd just walked through to the kitchen to look for something to drink herself when Theo came through the door.

It was clear he was worried, as he hurriedly said thanks and went straight through to Max's room. She wanted to walk after him, but decided to give him some time on his own. He came back, just as she was pouring some juice from a bottle in the fridge. He had the little note in his hand. Addy gave a shrug. 'The daycare had started it so I just kept it going. He'll be due his temp again in another five minutes.'

Theo ran his fingers through his hair.

'How's your patient?' she asked.

'Good,' he said as she handed the juice over to him and poured another glass for herself. 'Everything was straightforward, and they'll page me if there are problems overnight.'

She paused. 'Want me to stay?'

The words hung between them for a few seconds, as if they were both contemplating what that might mean. If, for some emergency, Theo did get called back to his patient, what would he do? If Max had already been sent home from daycare, they wouldn't accept him into the emergency overnight childcare at the hospital.

'That would be great,' he said. His eyes met hers, and she swallowed, trying to work out if it was just nerves, or something else.

It seemed like saying something without saying something. This would be the first time in a week she hadn't crept back to her own apartment in the early hours.

He went back through to check on Max again, took his

temperature, wrote it down, then gave him the alternate medicine after getting him to drink a little more.

'Any idea what it is?' she asked.

He shook his head. 'Paediatrics was never my speciality. I've bought a Dr Spock book, another called *What's that Rash?* and joined an online group where people run symptoms past fellow parents.'

She folded her arms and looked at him in amusement. 'The kind of group that all healthcare professionals cringe about?'

'Exactly that kind of group. And I like it,' he said, smiling as he waited for her barrage of abuse.

He opened his fridge and cringed. 'Not much here. We were planning on scrambled eggs on toast tonight, or pancakes and bacon.'

He looked at her expression and pulled out a plastic tub from the freezer. 'I'm better at this, honestly. I have pasta with five types of veg in it, bolognaise with hidden veg and lots of bases for homemade pizzas.'

She laughed. 'Dessert. What I really want is dessert.'

He went into the bottom tray of the freezer. 'Chocolate fudge cake, two minutes in the microwave and it's a dream.'

'Done,' she said rapidly.

A few minutes later they sat down at his dining table, spoons in hand. But Theo didn't start eating. He just sat for a few moments, fixing his gaze on the table.

She reached over and brushed her fingers against his. 'What?'

He blinked. 'What would I have done if you weren't here?'

He looked panicked. It had obviously played on his

mind at points throughout the last few hours. 'You would have worked something out,' she said steadily.

'But what?' he persisted.

She held up her hand. 'They knew your circumstances when they took you on. Everyone gets sick kids. Your only option for childcare is the care they provide. They also know that. If Max is too sick for daycare, or the night option if you're on call, they have to provide cover.'

He ran his hands through his hair. She was starting to realise this was a sign of his nerves. 'For him, or for me?'

She stopped for a minute. It would make sense for them to provide a sitter if Max was sick. Because that would have to be less expensive than paying another doctor to cover Theo's shifts.

'Because I have no intention of leaving Max when he's sick, with someone that he and I don't know.'

It was reasonable. She knew it was reasonable. And it was clear this was on his mind because he'd never been in this position before.

'Well, I guess you need to chat to someone about that.' She looked him in the eye. 'If I'm not working, and there's an issue with Max, then I'm happy to help, just like today. But if I'm working too, I'm not sure what the answer is.'

She was careful with her words. She didn't want to presume he would want her. She also needed to protect herself and her new role here. She couldn't pull a sickie because someone else's child was sick. And she hoped Theo would never ask her to. Was her job less important than his? It was a road she didn't want to go down.

The reason she was here, in this role in Dubai, was to support herself and get her head back above water. Lots of staff she knew had issues when their children were sick. It was a common problem—it was a fact of life that children tended to catch a myriad of minor ailments when they were young. While she was happy to assist when she could, she didn't want to become a crutch that Theo would expect was always available. Things were brand-new between them. It wasn't fair on either of them.

But, as she'd watched Max sleeping, his pale blond hair against the dark blue pillow, something in her heart had definitely pinged. Was this her biological clock finally telling her at thirty-two it was time to consider if children would be part of her future?

She'd watched other friends meet partners and have families, and it had never really featured in her head. It had always been in the place of *someday*, but it struck her today that the word *never* had not been one of the options she'd considered.

Of course, she didn't know if she could have children. Most people didn't until they started trying. There was nothing significant in her medical history. No past cancers along with invasive treatment…no gynaecological issues. But what if, with no opportunity of choice, she was already a no?

She hated these thoughts.

Theo looked worried, and tired again. Was he getting enough sleep?

'How about I sleep on the sofa?' she asked.

He blinked as if he hadn't had time to give her sleeping place much thought. She didn't want to suggest they sleep in the same room, particularly when Max was sick. Although Theo had said he always stayed in his own bed, Addy didn't want to bank on that.

'You can have my bed,' he said. 'I'll likely just sleep in the chair in Max's room. I want to keep checking his temp to make sure I keep on top of things.'

She wouldn't have expected any less. His fingers brushed against hers. 'Thanks, Addy. I really appreciate this.'

'No problem,' she said.

'And if I get called back to the hospital for any reason, I'll come and let you know before I go.'

She gave him a smile and a nod of her head. After another quick check on Max, she headed through to Theo's room. It wasn't a typical guy room. There were no dark colours. All his bedding was cream, but as soon she rested her head on the pillow she could smell him. The aftershave he wore, the scent of his skin, which was quickly becoming addictive.

I'm in trouble was the first thought in her head, rapidly followed with, *How truthful should I be?*

The letter and call to the solicitor had her worried. She knew she hadn't done anything wrong. She knew she'd been deceived by someone who'd likely done it before. It would be embarrassing enough to admit that to Theo, but what about the potential complications? The police might now suspect she wasn't innocent. They might want to charge her with something. That would put her job and work permit at risk. She hadn't declared any convictions because she didn't have any.

The last thing Theo would want is a potential criminal around his child. What if he didn't believe her?

Her stomach clenched and she wrapped her arms around herself as she lay in bed.

She was unsure about everything. Should this relationship continue? What if she got closer to Theo and Max, and then something happened that would make her have to return to Scotland? Max had already had a change in his life. How would Theo feel if the next woman he introduced Max to then disappeared from his life?

Her night was unsettled. Addy got up a few times, to check on both Theo and Max. Although Max was sometimes restless, his temperature didn't go any higher, and he slept for most of the night. He wasn't even surprised when Addy went in and spoke to him in the morning before she left for work.

Theo walked her to the door, giving her a hug and a kiss on the cheek. He gave a half-hearted smile. 'Sorry, we likely spoiled all your plans for last night.'

'I had no plans,' she said without hesitation, 'And I was happy to help.' She nodded over his shoulder. 'Will you be okay today?'

He nodded. 'I'm not scheduled to work today. I'll just have a lazy day watching Max and hopefully getting him on the road to recovery. Hopefully see you at work tomorrow.'

She gave a smile and headed out of the apartment and into her own. She blinked as she opened the front door and the brilliant sun met her, since none of her blinds were closed. What struck her most of all was the emptiness of the place, and the starkness of the décor.

She'd meant to get a few things to brighten the place up, but just hadn't got around to it yet. As she walked around, she realised she'd been here six weeks now, and the place didn't even look like her own.

Why was that? Her last flat had been full of her things—some of which she'd had to get rid of when she knew the place was being repossessed. Was that why she was reluctant to decorate? In case things got taken away from her again?

Addy sagged down on her own sofa. She was here for

a fresh start. She'd met someone new. Things were looking good. She had to start focusing on the future—her future, and not the one that her toxic ex was trying to drag her into.

She looked around. It was time to put down some roots. Give herself something to fight for. Theo and Max were worth fighting for.

She was worth fighting for. She had to believe that.

CHAPTER NINE

THEO WAS GLAD that Max's temperature had settled and things appeared to be back to normal. He was a doctor, he should be able to handle a sick child, but the truth was it had caught him unawares.

It wasn't even the practical stuff—like having to find alternative childcare. It was the gut punch to the stomach that Max was sick. He couldn't really control it, and the fear of what if something actually happened to him?

He'd never been a parent. He'd never had a kid. This whole range of emotions had swept the feet out from under him. Theo had never had this responsibility before. It was all on him.

And he wasn't a fool. He'd known this when he'd taken on the future care of Max. But the emotional part had been overwhelming.

He doubted Addy even realised how much it meant to have another human around him at those moments. He was treading so carefully. They were only just together. The spark and passion between them was electrical. He was finding it hard to strike the right balance here—even though they'd spent every evening together for the last week. Tonight was the first time she'd stayed overnight—and Max hadn't even noticed. Theo was still finding his feet around being a parent. He couldn't expect her to take on his responsibilities alongside him. It wasn't fair to her, or to Max.

But a tiny part of him hoped for the future. Addison Bates was in his mind most days, and definitely every evening. A glimpse of her eyes, a flick of her hair, the sound of her laugh. Parts of him were being touched that he hadn't exposed in a long time.

If he could have sat down and planned a future, he wouldn't have met Addy yet. He would have settled in Dubai for a few years, cementing the relationship between him and Max. Then he would have got to know someone slowly, gradually introducing him to Max over months, before finally deciding to date.

But life had made its own plan for Theo. Maybe they'd already moved things too fast? But it was too late now, and he didn't have any regrets about her. She was a good person. He liked her straight-talking on the ward. She was kind to Max. She'd helped out without hesitation when he really needed it. She'd made something burn deep inside him that he hadn't even realised he needed. It was almost like he craved her, and that brought a smile to his face.

At work, they caught each other's eyes throughout the day like secret messages. There were definite secret smiles. But had anyone noticed yet? He didn't think so. They were still professional. But it was amazing what you could say to each other in an office on a ward that looked out on all the staff when the door was closed and they were at either end of the table. He just hoped no one could read lips.

She knew him, and she knew his life. But what did he really know about her? Not too much. Although she'd filled him in on the basics, he wanted to dig a little deeper.

He wanted to know more, because he sensed there was still a barrier between them.

It was up to him to push a little further.

The staffing numbers on the ward had slowly got back up to normal. His workload had slightly increased because he and the other consultants were spreading Dr Gemmill's workload and patients between them.

It was fine. He still wasn't anywhere near as busy as he'd been in the general hospital back home in France.

The phone in the office rang and he answered it, talking to one of the Emergency physicians. He listened to the case. 'Fifteen-year-old, plays rugby, collapsed today on the pitch, was slightly cyanotic on the field. His ECG shows some unusual changes, his cardiac echo shows signs of apparent strain, and his chest X-ray also shows a slightly enlarged heart—but not significantly so. I know he's under eighteen, but this is a large kid, adult height and weight, and I wondered if you'd consider admitting him for cardiac review?'

Theo's decision was made in an instant. 'Have you taken bloods? Good, then add these tests to his panel and send him up. I'm happy to review his cardiac issues.'

He walked along the corridor until he found Addy. He gave her a smile. 'Charge Nurse Bates, as per our newly agreed admission protocol, I'd like to let you know about a fifteen-year-old we're admitting from Accident and Emergency after a collapse on a rugby field, and a number of unusual cardiac findings. Here's his details and the tests that have been run.' He handed her a slip of paper he'd taken notes on.

'Does he have a parent with him?'

Theo cringed. 'Oops. Forgot to ask.'

She shook her head. 'And that's why I'm the boss. If

he took unwell at school, he might have come directly via the rugby pitch. I'll make enquiries to ensure his relatives are notified and are on their way.'

He leaned over and whispered in her ear. 'I'm making dinner tonight. Singapore noodles. Do you prefer chicken or prawn?'

She took a quick glance sideways to see if anyone was listening. When she was assured their conversation was private she beamed at him. 'Both.'

He smiled. 'Both it is.'

By the time the patient came up from Emergency, his bloods were already available. Theo went directly into the room, wheeling a machine behind him so he could show the results to his patient.

'Khalid, I'm Dr Dubois. I'll be looking after you.'

Addy walked in behind him. 'Mum and Dad have just arrived downstairs and are on their way up.'

Theo sat down at the side of the bed. 'Tell me what happened today.'

Khalid was a fit-looking fifteen-year-old. He was as tall as Theo, had defined muscles and had obviously been playing rugby for a while.

Khalid put his hand to his chest. 'I don't really know. I was playing rugby, my legs started to feel heavy, my breathing hurt and then everything went black.'

'Any episodes like this before?'

Khalid frowned. 'I've been trying to get fitter. But instead of getting easier, I feel like things are getting worse. I don't have the same stamina. My running sprint times are going down, and I get out of breath easier.'

'Is this recent?'

'Fairly recent.' The boy gave a sigh. 'I go to the gym too, usually every day. I've been taking protein shakes.'

He prodded at one bicep. 'My muscles are building okay, but I'm still overtired.' He looked annoyed. 'Other guys in my team can last much longer than I can.'

There was a noise behind Theo, and he turned to see the anxious faces of Khalid's parents, who'd obviously heard some of what had been said.

His mum rushed over and put her hand on her son's head. 'Are you okay? They told me you'd collapsed.'

'What's wrong with him?' Khalid's dad directed the question to Theo.

Theo held out his hand. 'Dr Dubois. I'm a cardiologist and I'm looking after your son.'

'A cardiologist? Something's wrong with his heart?' Worry creased their faces, as well as Khalid's.

Theo held up one hand. 'Accident and Emergency have asked me to review Khalid. They ran a number of standard tests when he came in that I'm just about to check over. One of the things that was reported was that Khalid's lips were blue—we call it cyanotic—when he took unwell. Since he has no history of asthma or lung problems, and his temperature was entirely normal, because his lips are blue, the next thing we check is the heart.'

He wasn't sure he'd relieved any of their stress, but at least they all looked as if they understood. He faced both parents. 'I was asking Khalid about his fitness and he's telling me he's been feeling more tired than he thinks he should. Have you noticed anything that worries you?'

His dad held his hand towards the bed. 'Well, he's a teenager. They're meant to sleep a lot, aren't they?'

Khalid's mum wrinkled her nose. 'I guess he does seem more tired than usual. He started rugby in the last two years and he's been doing really well. But he's lost his spark in the last while.' She grimaced as she said the words, knowing that her son was overhearing her.

But Theo just nodded, taking in all the information. He'd already had a look at the test results, and Khalid was currently attached to a heart monitor and blood pressure cuff.

'Has your son been unwell at all in the last year?'

There were some exchanged glances. Finally, the mum shrugged. 'He had a bit of a fever more than a month ago, a rash, and his tongue was red and swollen. We were told he'd had a possible allergic reaction to something. But we never understood what. It's probably been since then that he hasn't really got back to normal.'

Theo swallowed, his mind instantly going to a place that could explain what the tests showed, and the boy's current symptoms. It wasn't good.

'Okay. Exactly how long ago was this?'

The mum pulled out her phone. 'It was when we were invited to a family dinner. Khalid didn't come as he couldn't eat much. Here,' she turned her phone around, 'just over six weeks ago.'

Addy moved across the room and put a hand on his shoulder. She knew where this conversation would go.

Theo spun the monitor around so Khalid and his parents could see it. 'Okay, this is a scan of Khalid's heart. See these parts?' He pointed to particular sections. 'This is part of the heart muscle, and it looks as if it's under strain. You can see it here, and here. It's thicker than normal, meaning the heart is having to work harder to circulate the blood.'

He pulled up Khalid's ECG. 'I know this just looks like squiggles, but it tells me quite a lot. It also says that Khalid's heart is showing signs of strain.'

'He's never had heart problems,' said the dad quickly.

Theo gave a nod to indicate that he'd heard. 'I also looked at the blood tests. They show signs of inflammation in Khalid's body.'

Theo took a breath. 'From the previous symptoms you've told me about, and how Khalid is now, I think the event six weeks ago wasn't an allergic reaction. I think Khalid had Kawasaki disease.'

'What's that?' asked the mum.

'The diagnosis is unusual,' said Theo steadily, 'it usually shows in children under six, but can be diagnosed in young adults. It sounds as if it was missed.'

'So, you can fix it?' asked the dad. 'Give him something?'

Theo kept his voice calm. 'Kawasaki disease is an inflammatory disease that affects the blood vessels and heart. If it's picked up early, there are treatment options, and we will look at some medicines for Khalid. But if it's missed—Khalid's was—there can be long-term effects.' He turned to face Khalid. 'Some of the symptoms you have today make me think there could be damage to your heart and surrounding blood vessels. This can also happen to children who are diagnosed quickly and given treatment.'

'Where does this come from? Did he catch it from someone?'

Theo shook his head. 'No one really knows the cause as yet. Some researchers think it's the body's own response to an infection, some think that certain genetic factors predispose people to the condition. There's also been research into environmental factors, but nothing definitive has been found.'

Khalid put his hands to his chest. 'Am I going to die?'

It was the hardest question to answer. Because the real truth was, he just didn't know. Depending on the damage the disease had caused, Khalid could be at risk.

'We need to find out how your systems have been affected, and then we look at how we can monitor or minimise any damage that's been done. I'm going to start you on a really simple drug called aspirin straightaway, because it's good at preventing any clots forming.'

'What about my rugby, and the gym?'

This time Addy stepped in as she moved to the side of Khalid's bed. 'The doctors need to get as much information as possible right now. Once they have it all, they'll be able to let you know about future plans.'

Theo turned to the parents. 'We'll run some more tests, but I'd like to refer Khalid to a specialist I know. He's actually a paediatric cardiologist in another city. Although Khalid is almost an adult, this disease usually presents in children younger than Khalid, and this paediatrician is an expert in people with this disease and their ongoing care. Are you happy for me to do that?'

Both parents nodded and Addy handed over some literature she'd printed off for them on the disease and its treatments.

They excused themselves and went to decide on more tests.

Once they hit the office, Addy turned to face him. 'Do you think he could have an aneurysm?' It was a known consequence of the disease.

'I'm praying he doesn't, but we'll run the tests anyway. From his symptoms I'm guessing he already has some narrowing of the arteries and could be at risk of an MI.'

Addy shuddered. 'A possible MI at fifteen? Please, no.'

She turned to her computer and pulled up the records. 'Did anyone see Khalid when he was unwell? This shouldn't have been missed.'

'I'll need to dig deeper,' he said. 'Someone must have seen him to suggest an allergic reaction. Or they may just have searched for "swollen tongue" online? In any case, if we find out Khalid was seen somewhere, we might need to suggest some training.'

'It's unusual at this age,' said Addy in a more conciliatory tone. 'I remember seeing a research article on the diagnosis of a twenty-one-year-old. That seemed old.'

'It is.' Theo nodded in agreement. 'But the long-term issues are just too great to ignore. If we find out this was missed, we need to take steps to make sure it doesn't happen again.' He'd finished writing up the rest of the tests that needed to be done, one of which was an angiogram to see if the coronary arteries were damaged.

'This poor kid,' said Addy. He could tell from her expression that she was worried about him. 'What if we have to tell him that rugby and the gym won't be on the cards for a while?'

'I'm hoping my colleague Brin Edson will be able to help with this one. He really is an expert, and even with risk factors involved he wants to keep these kids as healthy as possible and living their lives the best possible way.'

'Will he be able to see Khalid? You said he lives in another city?'

Theo nodded. 'Berlin. But we have the internet now—tests can be ordered, results sent and online consultations arranged. He's the best, and that's what Khalid should have. These are unique circumstances.'

'They are,' she agreed, then gave him a soft smile. 'Thank goodness you were working today.'

He shrugged. 'I'm sure one of the other cardiologists would have caught this.'

'But would they have known where to refer?'

'Maybe not, but we're a team. If someone had told me about this case, I would advise them to consult Brin. I know about him because I attended a number of international conferences he's spoken at. This could just as easily have been another lesser-known condition, and maybe one of them would have pointed me in the right direction. We're all here to help each other and find the best thing for our patients.'

'Did anyone tell Dr Gemmill?' she joked.

He leaned back and then raised his eyebrows. 'You earned a clean sweep at the governance committee. You must be pleased. Everyone agreed with the suggestions and accepted the paper with no concerns.'

'That's only because Dr Gemmill is still off,' she replied, still smiling.

'Well, it doesn't matter what he thinks if he comes back,' said Theo. 'Because it's been agreed through all the processes. He'll need to follow them like everyone else.'

'It won't get me moved back to his ward though,' said Addy, her expression sad.

'Why would you want to go back there…' he held up his hands '…when you can work here with me?'

Her eyes gleamed and she gave him a wicked smile. 'Well, of course, I wouldn't. But…' She paused for a second. 'It still feels like I got hounded out of there, because I dared to question some of the practices.'

'Would you do anything different?'

She pressed her lips together. 'Probably not. It's unlikely he would have listened even if I'd spoken to him.' She held up one hand. 'I may have decided to speak to his secretary, but that wouldn't have solved the root of the problem.' Her gaze met Theo's. 'So, no. I wouldn't do anything different.'

'And that's why I like you,' he said.

She raised her eyebrows across the table at him.

He continued. 'Because you're stubborn, determined, and at the bottom of it all is good patient care, so who can argue with that?'

She leaned across the table towards him. 'Is that the only reason you like me? Or...' she smiled at him suggestively '...is it also because we share a love of desserts?' She winked. 'And a few other things?'

He laughed. He'd held his breath for a second, wondering what she might say.

'Come to think of it, you haven't mentioned dessert for tonight. You better remember to put that in the plans too.'

He rolled his eyes. 'Don't worry, I won't forget about dessert.' Then he stopped and looked at her again. 'What are your plans for the weekend?'

She shrugged. 'Not much. Shopping. The cream walls and furnishings are closing in around me. I need some colour in the place. I meant to get some things the other week, but time just got away from me.'

'What kind of shopper are you?'

'What do you mean?'

'Are you a mall girl? Or would you be willing to look in some of the markets and souks?'

She didn't hesitate for a second. 'Millionaire malls? No thanks. But I'm not sure where any of the markets are yet. I've not had a real chance to look around.'

'If you don't mind a few tag-alongs, Max and I will be happy to show you the markets and the souks at the weekend. I think you might find things that you like.'

She smiled. 'A weekend with my two favourite guys. Sounds like a plan.'

He leaned forward and sighed, putting his head in his hand. 'Honestly. You're too easy to charm. I haven't even told you my ulterior motive yet.'

Something fleeting passed her eyes and he saw her tense for a second, but then it disappeared. 'Dr Dubois, what is your ulterior motive?'

He gave a broad smile. 'It involves someone aged three. A very dark room. And the millionth movie about little yellow characters.' He raised his eyebrows. 'I might even try to touch your leg in the dark.'

She laughed. 'You want to go to the pictures?'

'The what?'

She grinned. 'The pictures. That's what we call the cinema in Scotland.'

He frowned and shook his head. 'So, you call going to see a film or a movie "the pictures"?'

'Of course, and so should everybody else—it would save a whole lot of hassle.'

He loved that, when her Scottish accent came through thicker than before and he had to concentrate on her words.

'So, will you come?'

'Is there popcorn?'

'There is.'

She leaned forward. 'Then I'll come.' Then she whispered, 'And just between you and me, I kind of like those yellow creatures.'

A warm feeling spread through him. He was almost sure other staff in the department had started to talk about them. But honestly? He didn't care. As long as this relationship didn't affect their work, it was no one else's business.

Relationship? Had he thought about it in those terms before? No, because he wasn't quite sure what to call it. Using the word relationship might be presumptuous.

But it didn't feel like that to him. In fact, as the word settled in his brain, it felt quite comfortable. He was happy around Addy. After their prickly start, he'd liked her almost immediately. She was easy to like.

And she was making an impact at work. Staff had started to realise just how scarily organised she was. She had spreadsheets for costs, rotas and some baseline information on average stays on the ward.

She'd set some staff the task of reviewing the wards' standard operating procedures, and preparing some new ones for tasks that hadn't quite made it to that stage yet. This was a teaching hospital, and it was good to have a start-to-finish plan for some procedures to show students before they accompanied staff on their rounds. It helped their learning and gave them a good minimum baseline.

The idea around staff rotating was also taking wings. Apparently, some staff had asked in the past and been turned down, but with Addison's backing, the planning processes were now in place, and it looked like it would be starting soon.

Her organisation and leadership were being noticed in the space of a few short months. Now Dr Gemmill wasn't around, he heard more of the consultants saying how good she was. She'd assisted in Theatre more than once during the sickness period, and had also taken charge of a night shift in the cardiac ICU after a member of staff had a sudden family bereavement.

People were seeing Addison for who she truly was.

And it wasn't just staff and management. Feedback from patients was good too. Her bedside manner was straightforward but fun. She encouraged questions and had the patience to take her time explaining things at a level patients understood.

He'd heard on the grapevine that she'd been invited on a few staff night outs and turned them down. But she had joined the local hospital book group and was apparently a vociferous reader.

But the most important thing to Theo was how things were between them. She was good to Max. She didn't mind teasing or flirting with Theo as long as no one else was around, and the buzz he got when she looked at him with those violet eyes…

It was the first time in a long time that he was considering something more serious. He couldn't deny the attraction, or the feelings he had for Addison. They'd naturally fallen into a pattern of spending every evening together. Maybe it was time to have a conversation about being official? Letting others know they were actually in a relationship? Maybe this weekend would be the right time?

He could swear he almost felt a fizzing in his belly. But he wanted to do this. He wanted to have the grown-up conversation. They had a connection that neither of them could ignore, and which they continued to act on, most nights when Max was in bed. He knew how she took her coffee. What biscuits were her favourite. What she preferred to watch on TV. Which old-school nineties band was her secret favourite. And knowing all of these things sent a warm glow around him. One that he wanted to continue, to grow and develop. He smiled to himself. Could little yellow characters assist him? He'd have to wait and find out.

* * *

'I would never have found this place,' said Addy as she looked from side to side underneath her wide-brimmed hat.

The market was buzzing, stalls and small stores everywhere. There was a huge array of wonderful smells. The constant background noise of voices and shouts of laughter was pleasant and welcoming. But the thing that captured her attention most was the bursts of colour.

Furniture, clothing on people, clothing for sale. Items for houses in a wide range of hues. She was trying to pretend she couldn't see all the gold that was available for barter, as she wasn't there to spend vast amounts of money. She wasn't sure she would ever be in a position to do that again. But rugs, vases, cushions and prints… they were all on her mind to bring some colour into her apartment and make it feel more like home.

They threaded themselves through the bustling crowd. Max was fascinated, stopping to stare at things, asking multiple questions and being taken in by all the street vendors around the sides.

They moved into a bigger area and Addy's eyes were caught by a giant sofa. It was in the window of one of the stores and was covered like patchwork in a bright array of fabrics. She'd seen similar designs in some magazines in the past—all with spectacular price tags.

'Wow,' was all she could say.

Theo followed her over and grinned. 'Now, that's perfect.'

'You think?' she asked, eyes full of excitement.

'It's my dream. If I spilled something on that, you'd never know.'

She nudged him in the side and groaned but he grabbed her hand and pulled her inside.

'Let's try it,' he said, pulling Max up onto his knee as he sat and Addy down beside him. The giant sofa gave a *hmph* noise as they all sat down, making them burst out with laughter.

Addy ran her hand over the array of fabric. Some velvet, some heavy stitching, some linen, some felt more like a rug. But the colours were like an explosion—reds, yellows, oranges, browns, the odd patch of purple or green. It was like a whole story being told beneath her eyes. And the padding was just luxurious.

She looked out through the store window and realised people were looking in on them. It made her laugh out loud. She ran her hand across the fabrics again, then moved it down to the wooden claw foot. It might not be to everyone's taste, but she loved it.

'Well, this would certainly give you a burst of colour in the apartment. You wouldn't need anything else.'

She rested her head backward. 'If only.'

'I like it,' said Max.

'So do I,' said Theo. 'But Addy spotted it first.'

She gave a sigh and stood up. 'This will be well outside my price range. Come on, guys, I need to find a vase and some cushions.'

Her hand trailed across the back where the price tag was. Feeling just a little curious she flicked it over. Her gulp was a kind of semi-gulp. It wasn't as pricey as she feared, but the little savings she had in the bank she needed to keep. If the solicitor phoned to say the police were demanding she return at short notice, she'd need money for flights, and somewhere to stay for a few days.

Theo was by her side, looking at the tag. 'Well, that's

okay,' he said, his brown eyes connecting with hers. 'Are you going to get it?'

Spoken like a man who'd never had his house repossessed or had to account for everything he spent.

She couldn't help it. It made her ultra-defensive. 'Not in my price range,' she said quickly. 'Let's just get the things that are.'

As soon as the words were out of her mouth, she wanted to kick herself. This was definitely a conversation she didn't want to have.

'Okay,' Theo said quietly behind her, but she could hear the question in his voice and it made all her senses go on alert. Theo had never mentioned money. As far as she knew, he didn't have any money concerns. His biggest issue had been childcare, and he'd solved that by taking the job in Dubai.

Hoping he was following her, she moved quickly to a stall with brightly coloured vases, picking a medium-sized one decorated in merged swirls of pink and red. Then she chose two cushions with red backgrounds, and a bright tablecloth for the table just outside her kitchen.

By the time she'd finished, Max was back by her side eating some small sweets. Theo held out a bag. 'Want some?'

She shook her head, feeling awkward and a bit foolish. 'I'm done, I've got everything I need. These should brighten my apartment up a bit.'

'Shall we head back?' he asked. 'We'll need to drop those things off before we go...' He hesitated, and then added, 'To the pictures.'

He said the words in the worst Scottish accent ever and she couldn't help but laugh. 'Okay then, give me a hand.'

She handed the vase over to him and they travelled back to the apartment to drop off her purchases.

Even as she glanced around the space, there was a little knot in her stomach. The patchwork sofa would have been more than perfect for this place. It would have drawn the eye straight away and sent a message of warmth, happiness and welcome. It stung her so bad, her breath caught somewhere in her throat.

She blinked back the tears that threatened to fall and walked her vase over to her side table. It was lovely. The cushions on her sofa were good too, and the tablecloth on the dining table just outside the kitchen tied everything together.

Her apartment was coming together—just like her relationship with Max and Theo. There was a constant flutter around her heart and buzz around her stomach. Everything felt too good and too soon. And, the trouble was, Theo had no idea that the tower they were magically building together was actually teetering. Another letter from the police or phone call from her solicitor could bring this perfect world she'd accidentally created crashing down around her.

And what she knew above all else was that she really, really didn't want that to happen. She took a deep breath and fixed a smile on her face.

'Better than I could have hoped for,' she said quickly to Theo and Max, who were patiently waiting for her, and she ignored that knot again. 'Let's go and meet my favourite little yellow people.' She grabbed her bag and held her hand out to Max. He threaded his hand into hers with an innocence that made her catch her breath, and then she headed back out into the Dubai sunshine with them.

* * *

Theo wasn't entirely sure what he'd done wrong. But from the look on her face, and the snap of her words, he'd suddenly realised that money must be an issue for Addison.

It was easy to forget these things when their accommodation came as part of the employment deal—lots of staff stayed in these luxury apartments. Maybe she had family issues and had to send a large part of her salary home. One of the doctors that he worked with had told him freely that he sent more than half his salary home to support his mum, dad and disabled sister. Not all countries had free health care available or government assistance for those unable to work.

That was the trouble. He still didn't know her well enough. But that wasn't stopping the flood of feelings he was getting caught up in.

He had to try and get her to trust him. To talk to him more. Because he wanted this to work. He was more invested than ever.

Every time she walked into his apartment his heart seemed to lift a little. Each time he watched her effortlessly interact with Max it sent a warm sensation through his veins. He might not have been ready. But it looked like the world had other plans for him.

He'd bought the tickets for the cinema online. As soon as Max saw the posters with his favourite yellow characters he started bouncing up and down on his toes. It only took Theo a few moments to buy them popcorn before they were filing their way into the dimmed cinema.

Max sat between them to begin with. Then changed seats partway through the film because he had to go to the bathroom. By the time Theo sat down next to Addy, he could tell she'd started to relax again.

When they finally left the cinema, he reached out as they exited the row, and she took his hand.

They travelled back on the Dubai Metro and, when he suggested picking up takeout on the way back, she was happy to agree.

Max was wilting—the fun of the market, then concentrating in the cinema had all got too much for him. Theo carried him the last few yards to the apartment block, and laid him down on his bed when they got home.

Instead of sitting at the table, they kept their takeout in the boxes and sat on the sofa together, with cans of soda on the floor next to them.

Once they'd started eating, Theo decided to dig a little deeper.

'So, what about Scotland? Are you planning on going back, or will you stay here now?'

She gave a half-shrug. 'I haven't made any decisions yet. I wasn't sure how things would go here, or if I'd like it.'

'And do you like it?' he asked, with a gleam in his eye.

He watched her for a second, and as he waited he had a flash of fear that her answer might actually be no. But she let out a little sigh, her shoulders relaxed. As her gaze met his she said, 'Better than I thought I would.'

He smiled and then gave her a slow nod. 'It's tough going somewhere new where you don't know anyone. Because of the circumstances I'm in, it's not like I can meet new people and go out for a beer together.'

'Your fellow consultants would go out for a beer?' She raised her eyebrows, clearly in disbelief.

He laughed. 'The rest of the cardiologists are a bit older than me. But there's some surgeons my age, a couple of anaesthetists, and a group of physios that have started a football team. If I was here on my own, that's the kind of thing I might do.'

She looked at him for a moment. 'But, if you were on your own, you wouldn't have come here, would you?'

He shook his head. 'No, you're right, I wouldn't have.' He took a slow breath. 'Things are exactly the way they should be.'

Her nose wrinkled just a little. 'So, you never get angry at Fleur? You never wonder why she couldn't beat her addiction for Max, or maybe have let you know who his father was, so he could have played a part in their life?'

The question troubled him, but only because the answer wasn't too nice. 'I did get angry at Fleur—lots of times. That's part of why I pushed her into making a will. But Fleur was an adult. And she'd been my friend, but I wasn't responsible for her. I'm not an expert on addiction, but I, and the rest of her friends and family, tried to support her. But addicts frequently push people away. I'm pretty sure Max's father was an addict too, and I know that, although she'd reduced her use during her pregnancy, Max still had to go through a withdrawal regime after he was born.' He put his hand to his chest. 'And honestly, that made me furious, that she'd done that to her baby. But I didn't doubt she loved him. When I watched them together, there was genuine love and affection between them. She just loved her addiction more.'

Addison shuddered. 'That's terrifying.'

He looked at her expression. 'It is, but it's not unique. My biggest worry for Max is the stuff I don't know about.'

'What do you mean?'

It struck him for a moment that this was not where he wanted this conversation to go. He wanted to learn more about *her*. But things had kind of got turned around, and the truth was, Addy was so easy to talk to.

He sighed. 'The research about kids says their first few years are the most formative. I have no idea what Max's day-to-day experience was. I hope it was good. But I know that sometimes Fleur would have been using drugs, and I wonder if he remembers being ignored or neglected.'

Her hand reached over and slid into his. 'You have no way of knowing that. And I get what you say, but you're assuming the worst. You know that she loved Max. Didn't she?'

He nodded. 'But her addiction was real. It took over parts of her life.'

'Did you meet many of her friends then?'

He wrinkled his brow. 'Sometimes. Most were fleeting, in and out of her life, dealing with their own issues.'

'But…' She was clearly taking her time with this answer. 'They may also have helped her when she needed it. Maybe if she was having a bad spell, one or other of those folks would have looked out for Max. He's a sweet kid. Pretty adorable.'

She was trying to be reassuring, and he admired her for it, recognising this was a line of conversation that could never come to a definitive conclusion.

'I hope so,' he said. 'I hope that's what happened.'

There was silence for a moment before he met her violet gaze again.

'You didn't really mention what made you leave Scotland.' He knew he was pushing. But it felt like it was time.

She started with the normal words. 'Opportunity, better money, a new start.' But as her words tailed off, they both realised this was the expected answer, not the actual truth.

He kept his voice steady. 'You know that this is building to something, don't you?'

She gave the briefest nod of her head.

'And Max has become my world.'

She nodded again.

He ran his fingers through his hair. 'So, I've met someone, unexpectedly, that I really like.' He locked gazes with her. '*More* than like.'

She held that gaze and he continued. 'And I hope…' His heart gave a little flutter. This could be the moment he made the biggest fool of himself on the planet. 'That she likes me too. Likes *us* too.'

Addy seemed as though she were frozen in place.

He kept going, hoping he wasn't about to wreck things between them. 'So, I realised that I don't know that much about her—that much about you. And I wondered if there was anything you needed to tell me?'

Her head had lowered but now whipped fiercely up. 'What, you think I'm some kind of criminal?'

He jerked back as if stung, wondering why that had been the first place she'd gone. He held up one hand. 'No, not at all. You just haven't said much about your family, or your friends, or anything about past relationships, and I just thought I should ask.'

Her eyes looked fierce now. 'Did it ever occur to you that if people don't talk about something there's a reason for that?'

His stomach was cringing. 'Of course, I know that. But the more time I spend with you, the more I want to know about you. Is that wrong?'

But the words didn't seem to placate her. It was clear that all her red flags had gone up around him. 'So, you think I'm a risk?'

He shook his head again. 'No, no, it's just that—'

He didn't get to finish as she cut him off. 'So, you *do* think I'm a risk.' It wasn't a question, it was a statement. Since when did trying to get to know someone a bit better set off this kind of response?

He could keep trying to placate her, or he could just cut right to the chase. 'I'm trusting you, Addy. I'm trusting you with being around Max, and sometimes being alone with him. And I do trust you. But you've also heard me tell you how much I worry about him. If I'd thought about this more, I maybe wouldn't have introduced you both so quickly. Five months ago he lost the central female in his life. Now I've let someone else in. And I've done it because I wanted to. It felt right. It felt good. But I have some questions. Are you telling me I shouldn't ask?'

She stood up. 'Frame it however suits you. But some parts of people's lives are private. We are all entitled to privacy, Theo. I don't need to tell you all my personal friendships or relationship disasters. That's for me to know. Not you.' She took a few steps. 'You know that Spira will have done a whole host of checks on me—like they did with you—before I started here. If there was anything significant, they wouldn't have offered me the job. What more do you need? My medical history? My family genetics?'

He stood up too. 'Whoa. This is getting way off track.'

'Is it?' He could see the anguish on her face, and immediately wondered why he'd let this reach this point. It never should have. But that deeply protective instinct in him was going wild. At the heart of this was a little boy. He'd just revealed his own vulnerabilities around his fears for Max. He couldn't say for sure, but he didn't think he was being unreasonable. He'd clearly hit a nerve with Addy—and he absolutely hadn't meant to. But his father-bear instincts were roaring loud and strong. He couldn't just think about himself any more. He and Max were a partnership, and he always had to take Max into consideration.

He lowered his voice. 'Addy, I'm just asking you if there's anything I need to know. If you're in trouble in any way, I'd like to help you.'

'I've never asked for your help,' she spat back.

Theo's shoulders sagged. While they were both on edge, this would never get anywhere helpful. He knew that, and he sensed she did too.

She walked over to the door. 'Thanks for the nice day,' she said, 'but I'm going to go home now.'

And before he had a chance to say anything else, she was gone.

Addy was furious. A fury that she couldn't contain, or really explain. In the few steps she'd taken down the corridor, hot, angry tears had spilled down her cheeks.

By the time she'd fumbled with her key card and got inside, her shoulders had started to go too.

The bright cushions, vase and tablecloth were like a gut punch now. She'd bought them to bring hope, joy and welcome vibes to her bare apartment. But they practically screamed Theo's and Max's names at her. This wasn't how this was supposed to go.

The phone in her apartment was blinking. She couldn't remember it ever doing that before, and she pressed the button to listen to the message.

And then the day just got worse.

'Hi, Addy, it's Laura Palmer here. I've spoken at length to the new inspector in charge of the case. It seems Stuart King has been laying on his charm quite heavily and appears to have almost convinced this man that some of the responsibility lies at your door. I've asked him to investigate digitally around IP addresses, for the loan agreements and signatures. I already know that one of the loans that was digitally signed was agreed on a date you were working a twelve-hour shift in Glasgow. However, he wants to reinterview you regarding the whole fraud episode. He initially insisted on an in-person interview, but I've persuaded him that would be unreasonable due to costs. He's agreed to a video interview, but we have to arrange a day and time. Can you get back to me when you get this message, please?'

Addy felt her legs go from under her. Her head was spinning. She'd already given an array of statements around Stuart's fraudulent activities. What else could they want?

Something flicked in her brain and it was like her blood had suddenly run cold. It had been a throwaway comment. Theo had likely meant nothing by it. But when he'd arranged this day together, he'd remarked she was too easy to charm.

What did that actually mean? Was she a fool? She thought she knew everything about him—but what if he'd been untruthful? What if, right now, Addison was being played, just like she'd been with Stuart? Hadn't she learned anything from that whole experience?

Her whole body was trembling now as she slid to the floor.

Was she misjudging everything?

She tried to calm herself and take some deep breaths. Things were just overwhelming her. The pressure of the mess she'd been left in back in Glasgow had been too much to cope with. She'd always been methodical and organised. To know that someone she'd loved had played her, had outsmarted her—it had made her question everything she thought she knew. The way that he'd also created doubts about her amongst their friend group had been the most hurtful aspect of all. For the first time in her life, all the fight had gone out of her. Once she'd finished with the police—when she knew the full extent of the accumulated debt and her flat repossession—she just wanted to get away.

The contact from her lawyer had taken her back to square one.

Her heart rate started to slow, and her breathing eased.

Theo Dubois wasn't Stuart King. He was a good guy. An honest one. But she still didn't want to share all this with him. Shopping today had freaked her out. The sofa had been gorgeous, and she would have loved it. But if she'd tried to purchase it, he might have thought it odd that she didn't have a credit card, and that wasn't a conversation she wanted to have.

A relationship had been the furthest thing from her mind when she'd come here. But it was almost like someone had landed Theo and Max on her lap. It felt fated—meant to be—and right now there was a chance she was going to blow everything.

What must he think of her?

Her experience with Stuart was clouding her emotions and making her overthink things. Not every guy she met would be some kind of con man. She'd been unlucky. She knew that. But she had to try and move on.

She looked up at her phone on the table. If she really wanted to move on, she had to put everything behind her. And right now that would include talking to the police again. It didn't matter that she didn't want to relive any of this. Stuart was clearly up to something again, and was likely trying to clear his path to the next con.

She put her hand to her heart. He'd ruined her faith in herself, and her ability to trust. But that wasn't Theo's or Max's fault. She had to judge them on their own merits, no matter how hard she was finding things.

As she held her hand at her heart, she realised something. She loved them. She loved them both as a package deal—because that's what they would always be. It had sneaked up on her. But she had to acknowledge her true feelings. She was far too afraid to say those words out loud, but she couldn't help the wealth of emotions that were buried deep. Maybe that's why she was reacting so badly to things? Admitting that she loved them could change everything, and the world was spinning too quickly as it was.

She bent forward and let her head rest on her knees. Theo had already told her he 'more than liked her'. What would he think of her reaction today?

It must have shocked and surprised him. She could feel embarrassment sweep over her and more tears came to her eyes. She was so unsure about herself right now.

But the one thing she was absolutely sure about was that she wouldn't let Stuart King impact on her life any more. He'd destroyed the life she had back in Glasgow, and he wouldn't destroy the one she had here.

She did have to speak to Theo. She did need to tell him the truth about her past. But she wanted to do it on her own terms. She wanted to do it when she'd sorted things, so she could look him in the eye, be truthful and let him know she was out through the other side.

Then she would be ready to dive into this relationship with her eyes and arms wide open.

CHAPTER TEN

THEO WASN'T QUITE sure what had happened. One minute they were having a nice day together and the next... It still baffled him.

Had he misjudged everything? Maybe he'd misinterpreted her level of interest in him. Had he pushed her too far, too fast? He couldn't help the feelings of shock and disappointment he'd had around her reaction. There was nothing like telling someone he cared deeply about that he more than liked them, only to witness them pick a fight and almost sprint for the horizon.

Everything felt so terribly wrong. Maybe this was all his fault? Maybe he should have kept things going in their own easy way, without hinting at more, or a deeper connection. It was clear that Addy wasn't ready. Or at least wasn't ready for any more with him.

That made him sadder than he'd ever expected. He didn't just 'more than like' Addy. He loved her. But there was no chance to say that, and it seemed like the last thing she might want to hear.

For the next week they tiptoed around each other at work and in the apartment block. No real conversations. No real connection again.

Max kept asking if they could visit, or if Addy would visit them. Then he stayed mysteriously quiet about her.

And that set off a whole lot of other worries that he'd let his little boy form an attachment with someone who might not really care about him.

But then there were a couple of texts out of the blue. The first was from Addy.

Was planning to drop into daycare to see Max. Is that okay with you?

He didn't answer straight away because he was momentarily stunned. Part of him wanted to jump in the elevator and go down there too. Maybe they could actually talk?

But something told him not to. This was about Max, not him. What was best for Max? His brain spun round and round.

One of the nurses came and asked him to prescribe something, so he texted back quickly.

Fine.

But when he went to pick up Max later, he never mentioned a word about Addy coming to see him. It was strange—and not like Max at all.

He waited a few moments before talking quietly to one of the staff members. 'I know Addy came down to see Max earlier but he hasn't mentioned her. Do you know if she told Max not to say anything?' he'd asked.

Doria, one of the staff, shook her head straightaway. 'I was playing alongside Addy and Max with another little boy. She never said anything like that at all to him.' Doria then pressed her lips together in sympathy. 'Maybe Max is picking up on something. Can you think of a reason he wouldn't tell you? He's kind of young to make that decision.'

But Theo knew exactly why Max wouldn't say anything, because he'd been in the room when Theo and Addy had exchanged words. It made his heart ache to think of the impact he was having on his son—because that was how he thought of Max now.

Max had likely suffered enough trauma in his life. The last thing he needed was any more. Theo's job was to make him feel safe and secure, and if his son wasn't telling him something, he needed to ask himself why.

The next day on the ward he walked into the office where Addy was sitting and closed the door behind him. She looked up in surprise.

'Is something wrong?' Although they'd worked together this last week, she'd barely met his eyes. She'd just kept everything professional, with no real discussion.

'Yes,' he said bluntly, sitting down.

'What?'

'Max hasn't told me that you've been to see him at daycare.'

There was an awkward pause between them and Addy's brow furrowed. 'Okay,' she said slowly.

'That seems...strange.'

'I agree.'

'Why did you go to see him?' The question came out blunter than he meant.

She licked her lips slowly. 'I missed him, and I wanted to make sure he was doing okay.'

'You could have asked me how he was doing.'

She let out a long, slow breath. 'I could have, but it wouldn't be the same.'

He could swear a hand squeezed around his heart. Asking if someone was okay and seeing for yourself was entirely different. He appreciated that.

What also struck him was the fact that, when he'd challenged her on it, she was straight. She wasn't sorry at all that she'd seen Max.

And he knew. He knew how she felt.

'I don't want my son keeping secrets from me.'

She took a deep breath. 'I didn't ask him to.'

'I know.'

Tears pricked her eyes. 'So, where does that leave us?'

There was silence for a few moments before he added, 'I miss you, Addy. *We* miss you.'

'I miss you both too.' She put her head in her hands. 'I know this is my fault. I know it is.' She bit her lip. 'I have no right to ask, but could you just be a little patient with me please? I have a few things I need to sort out.'

Silence hung in the air between them while he turned things over in his mind. He knew better than to push again. So he didn't ask for details.

He spoke in a low voice. 'I don't want my little boy to get hurt. He's fond of you, Addy, you know he is.'

The tears spilled down her cheeks. 'And I'm fond of him too. I want to be around him. I want to be around you both.'

Theo let it hang a little longer, and then finally said, 'So, how do we fix this?'

She gave a huge sigh of relief. 'How about we all just take breath, and spend some time together again?' She put a hand on her heart. 'I promise, from my end, I will fix this.'

He smiled and moved around the table towards her. He wasn't going to push her again. He had to make the decision to take her on trust. Because he did want to spend time with her again, and he knew Max did too. 'What do you have in mind?'

'We could do a movie night at mine, or we could take Max swimming. I saw some lessons advertised and thought it might be good for him to start.'

Theo sat back and looked at her. He was impressed. 'I kept meaning to look for some.'

'Well, I've found them. Want me to set it up? We could go in after his lesson and get him practising and have some fun.'

He held up his hands. 'Absolutely.' He leaned forward and caught a whiff of her light perfume. 'How did we get so lucky to meet you?'

She turned her violet gaze towards him and gave him a wink. 'Well, I'm from Scotland, so I guess I must be your lucky white heather.'

His heart gave a swell. It was like the awkwardness had temporarily evacuated the building, and he was here for that. He much preferred it when things were like this.

He still wondered what had caused her reaction before. But since he didn't want to go back there, he wasn't going to ask any questions. If Addy wanted to tell him then she would.

The ward phone rang just as Addy was walking past the nurses' station. 'Cardiology. Charge Nurse Bates.'

'Addy? It's Adhil from Accident and Emergency. We are absolutely slammed. We don't even have a cubicle free. I've triaged a young man in the waiting room who I'm sure has cardiac symptoms. No tests yet. Do you have a consultant free that can see him, if I send him up escorted?'

Addy leaned forward to double check Theo was still on the ward. He was just finishing with a patient in one of the side rooms. 'Yep. Dr Dubois is here. I'll let him know. Give me some details.' She lifted a pen and took some notes. 'Yep, yep...got it. Let the staff know I'll meet them at the elevator.'

She hung up the phone and hurried down the corridor, meeting Theo and Layla as they exited the room. 'We've got an emergency admission coming up, triaged by Adhil in Accident and Emergency, but they don't even have a cubicle to assess him in. Severe chest pain, breathlessness. Twenty-four-year-old male. On his way now. No tests completed as yet.'

She turned to Layla. 'We'll use room three-two-three. Can you bring along the ECG machine and the ultrasound please?'

Theo looked at her. 'Why is Accident and Emergency slammed?'

'RTA, multi-vehicle. Adhil didn't want this young man to get lost in the noise down there when they're already assessing multiple patients.'

Theo nodded. 'Which elevator?'

'South side.'

They both moved quickly and, as soon as the elevator doors opened, they grabbed either side of the trolley.

There was a nurse and porter from Accident and Emergency, and the young man was already on oxygen, with a heart monitor and pulse oximeter in place.

They moved along to the room and transferred him quickly to the bed. The nurse handed over the notes in her hand. 'I'm so sorry, you know we would never usually do this.'

Theo scanned the notes and nodded. 'It's fine, I get it.'

He moved the patient's side. 'Hi, Rio, I'm Dr Dubois, and we're going to take care of you.'

Addy made some quick notes on a chart at the end of the bed. 'BP low, tachycardic and pulse ox ninety.'

From first glance, this was a young, fit-looking man, but it was clear to see he was having trouble breathing and was using all his accessory muscles around the chest to assist.

Theo didn't hesitate—he lifted the transducer from the ultrasound machine that Layla had just wheeled in.

'Rio, I'm going to use this to get a better look at what's going on in your chest. It won't hurt, I'll just slide it across your skin.'

He put some gel on Rio's chest and flicked the machine on.

'How long have you had this chest pain?'

'S-since yesterday,' wheezed Rio.

'What happened yesterday?' asked Theo succinctly.

He was rapidly scanning the structure of the heart and the blood flow through it.

'R-rugby,' wheezed Rio.

Theo's head whipped from the monitor to Rio. 'Did you get hit in the chest?'

Rio nodded.

'Did it hurt straightaway?'

'Took my breath away. But not like this.'

Theo nodded and pointed to the screen. 'Rio, I think you've got something that's called a cardiac tamponade. It can happen for a variety of reasons, but it's likely because you've had a direct injury to the chest. Have you got shorter of breath since the incident?'

Rio nodded again. He looked half-panicked, and half-exhausted.

Theo pointed to another part of the screen. 'There's a sac around your heart called the pericardium. It has two layers and there's normally a little fluid between them. Because you've had an injury to your chest, extra fluid has built up in those layers, meaning that your heart can't pump effectively right now. This is called a pericardial effusion. And what we need to do right now is take the fluid out to reduce the friction on your heart and let it beat properly again.'

Addy had recognised the condition as soon as Theo had put the transducer on Rio's chest. She'd already pulled the emergency trolley into the room, as one of the drawers held the equipment for reducing the pericardial effusion. Cardiac tamponade was often a cardiac emergency and she was sure Theo wouldn't want to delay.

He gave her a nod, and within a few minutes she had the pericardial needle and catheter ready to go as Theo washed his hands and put on some gloves.

Layla kept her eyes on the observations. 'Blood pressure is dropping,' she noted.

Addy drew up the lidocaine, and handed the smaller syringe to Theo, as Layla wiped the area with some antiseptic. 'Just a small prick to numb the area for you,' he said to Rio. 'This might feel a bit tingly on your skin.'

Rio made a face as the lidocaine was injected. Theo waited a few moments until he was sure it had started to take effect.

Addy adjusted some of the cardiac leads to ensure they would have a clear signal while Theo was draining the fluid. Sometimes draining the fluid could lead to a number of extra heartbeats, or a change in the heart rhythm. It was important the leads were in the correct position to give them that information during the procedure.

'Will this hurt?' breathed Rio.

She could see the anxiety on his face and reached out to hold his hand. 'It might be a little uncomfortable, but it shouldn't cause you pain.' She nodded to Theo.

He gave her a hint of a smile. It wasn't obvious. It was just for her. But it made her heart swell. Because she knew what it meant. He trusted her. He trusted her as his colleague for this procedure—to monitor the patient, to keep the situation calm and to assist in any way she could.

A sense of pride swept over her. And a little piece of herself slotted into place.

She used to feel like this at her work every single day. Confident, happy and sure of what she was doing.

It suddenly struck her how, for a time, that had been taken from her. When everything had gone belly up, when Stuart's fraud had made her walls crumble, and when colleagues had looked at her with a hint of distrust in their eyes, the one clear thing that had always been steady in her life had disintegrated around her.

Coming to Dubai had been part of putting her life together again. She'd known that. It was why she'd stepped on the plane.

But she hadn't realised how much his actions—which had absolutely nothing to do with her work—had affected her confidence in her own abilities.

And once she'd got here, it didn't matter what her qualifications were, or what her professional history was. As soon as Dr Gemmill had been annoyed by her challenges, and had her move ward, what little confidence had been left had been stripped from her too.

It was like a lightbulb going off in her head.

She could do this. She had recognised what was wrong with this patient. She knew the procedure well. She knew exactly what would be required, and that the patient needed to be distracted right now, and to hold still during the procedure.

But that one little look from Theo had just made all the pieces fall into place for her.

She sat down next to Rio and started talking to him, taking one of his hands in both of hers, and encouraging him to try and slow his breathing—all while keeping an eye on the monitors.

Theo had a steady pair of hands. Pericardiocentesis needed the steadiest.

Using the ultrasound as a guide, he inserted the needle into the observed gap between the two layers of the pericardial sac. Threading the catheter into place, and then using a three-way tap, he slowly and steadily allowed some of the fluid to drain. It was a delicate process, and everyone in the room knew it.

Addy kept her eyes flicking to the monitor while talking steadily to Rio. His breathing was slowing all the time. It was clear that the gradual reduction in fluid was releasing the pressure on his chest in a positive way.

Layla was keeping her eye on the fluid amount from the other side of the bed. By the time she said the words, 'Three hundred mils...' it was clear Rio was benefiting from the procedure.

He wriggled his shoulders a little and Addy gave his hand a squeeze. 'Try and stay still. This will only take another few minutes, and you'll continue to feel the pressure easing.'

He grimaced but nodded, taking in a long slow breath. The level on his pulse oximeter was gradually rising as the blood started to pump more efficiently around his body and his oxygen levels increased.

Addy took a breath herself. This was one of those procedures where everyone in the room could see the difference the process made. Improvements were rapid for patients.

'A few ectopics,' she said quietly as she kept her eye on the monitor. It was clear Rio had no indication of this. Every person in the world could have ectopic heart beats every day with no ill effects, but in these circumstances it could mean something different.

'Slowing slightly,' said Theo with a nod of his head.

Everyone was watching the monitor. The space between the two layers had reduced, but it was clear there was still some fluid to collect. 'That's been some blow to the chest,' said Theo gently, trying to help distract. 'I'm actually surprised you aren't black and blue.'

Rio pulled a face. 'I never bruise much. I broke a bone once, and apart from the swelling there was no bruising at all. I think, at first, the doctor thought I'd come in with some kind of sprain.' He gave a wide smile. 'He'd been quite dismissive with me, until he saw the X-ray and realised I'd need plates and pins to put my bones back together.'

Theo shot him a smile as he continued with the procedure. 'You must have a good diet, excellent platelets and a good collagen level. All reasons why some people don't bruise as much as others. Genetics can play a part too.'

'So, I should be grateful?'

'Absolutely,' said Theo. 'But, I have to warn you, sometimes if the bruising is deep it takes a few days to develop and show on the surface of the skin.'

Rio took a few more breaths. 'It's definitely starting to feel a bit more comfortable.'

Four hundred and fifty mils, mouthed Layla silently. The amount of fluid was significant.

All eyes went to the monitor where the space between the layers had now reduced. There was always a minimal amount of fluid. It was necessary to remove friction between the two layers as they moved when the heart beat.

Theo watched carefully then turned off the three-way tap. 'Okay Rio. That's us. I'm going to order an X-ray to ensure there's no obvious damage to any of your ribs or lungs after the hit from the rugby ball, and we'll need to monitor you quite closely overnight today and into tomorrow.'

'Why? What can happen?'

'Occasionally fluid can build back up. We might give you some IV fluids to maintain your blood pressure. I'll order some more ECGs throughout the day to ensure everything is going back to normal. I'm also going to order some medicines to keep you comfortable and hopefully stop any inflammation of the heart.'

'But I can play rugby again, can't I?'

Theo caught Addy's smile as she shook her head and gave a short laugh.

'Can I do this one?' she asked.

Theo nodded as he snapped off his gloves and moved to the sink to wash his hands.

Addy looked at Rio. 'You can absolutely play rugby again, but only when Dr Dubois says it's safe. We need to make sure your heart has completely recovered before you start vigorous exercise again. Given your age and fitness level it will likely only be a few weeks.'

'So, I'm benched for the next two weeks?' He'd jumped on the word 'few'.

She wagged her finger at him. 'Remember, we still have to check you have no other injuries to your ribs, or your lungs. That could also affect your recovery time.' She raised her eyebrows at him. 'It could be up to a month.'

He groaned and leaned his head back on his pillow, as if this were the worst thing in the world. It was clear Rio didn't realise just how serious a cardiac tamponade could be.

'Your heart is the most important muscle in your body. It's just been under a lot of stress. You need to let it recover. You only get one,' she added with a wink. 'Remember how sick you felt less than half an hour ago.'

'Okay,' he groaned, but it was good-natured. He looked back at Addy. 'You seem like you'll be fit enough to tell my coach that.' He gave an approving nod. 'The Scottish accent will probably keep him in his place.'

Addy held out her hand. 'Give me his number. He'll be putty in my hands.'

She felt good as she phoned the coach and told him about Rio's injury and recovery time. She understood exactly why Rio had wanted her to phone, because of the coach's initial reaction and the fact he thought he could 'negotiate' Rio's recovery. But Addy had dealt with people like this before. She made sure that he knew he would have to be patient and wait for Rio to get the all-clear. She only had to mention the words 'insurance' and 'liability' for him to pay attention.

After that, she spoke to some other relatives whose family matriarch had suffered from a severe MI and required coronary artery bypass. They were so grateful for the care and attention their family member had received, and Addy was touched by their sincerity and admiration.

By the time Rio's chest X-ray was reported on, and his first set of ECGs had been repeated, both of them were over their shift time. Rio's blood pressure had stabilised now he was on some IV fluids, and his immediate pain had eased. He was eating some toast by the time they were ready to leave.

Max chatted easily when collected from daycare, and Theo invited Addy to join them for dinner. They debated the contents of his fridge, before she returned to her own apartment and brought back some chicken to make some pasta for them all.

He came and stood behind her, sliding his arms around her waist as she was stirring the pasta and sauce in a pot. She leaned back against him. 'I feel as if I need to make a disclaimer about my cooking skills not always being the best.'

'And you think mine are?'

The warmth of his body permeated her thin T-shirt. She liked it. It felt natural. It felt right. 'I can promise faithfully that the chicken is properly cooked. But after that? It's just a chance we all have to take.'

'Maybe long-term we should try and teach Max to cook. It could save us all.'

A little tremor went through her skin. Long-term. He'd said the words 'long-term', and that was clearly how he was starting to think now.

It delighted her. It excited her. And it also terrified her.

Was this too soon? Because part of her head said yes, but her heart had a mind of its own.

She liked the routine they were falling into. She liked being able to look across the ward and communicate with Theo without actually saying anything.

She waited until the pasta had been served and eaten, and Max was in bed, before she finally took a breath to speak.

She was lying against him on the sofa, drinking a glass

of wine, and staring out at the beautiful night sky. 'Today's the best day I've had in a long time,' she admitted. It was time to open up—even just a little.

She sensed his body reacting a little. 'What do you mean?'

His arm was around her neck, and his hand draped down towards her chest. She started tracing her fingers along the back of his hand. 'I mean today, on the ward, at work, was the happiest I've been in a long time.'

'You mean since you got here? Do you think you've settled in?'

She paused and licked her lips, wondering how much to say. 'Yes and no. I've never done anything wrong at work. But my confidence was knocked at the last place. I'd always been super proud of my job, and what I did, but then some things happened, and I started to hate going to work. To hate the place I'd always loved.'

He shifted as he tried to get a better position to look at her. 'Did something happen at work?'

She shook her head. 'No, that's the sad thing. Some stuff happened outside of work. It wasn't anything to do with work at all. But I felt as if people looked at me differently, treated me differently. And the place I'd loved working at, and been confident in, made me feel as if I were under a microscope. I second-guessed myself when I'd always been happy with my decisions and clinical care.'

'Couldn't you speak to someone? Didn't you have a boss you could go to?'

She sighed. 'It just didn't work like that. The old consultant I worked with—he never listened to anything outside work. So I know he had no issues with me. But you know what a hospital is like. Rumours come from outside, and then everyone's looking at you. People stop talking when you come near and you know you've been the topic of conversation.'

'But...' she could tell he was speaking carefully '...if this is all external, and nothing to do with work, people had no business making you feel uncomfortable. You should have spoken to HR, asked them to stop the rumours.'

She'd only given him a tiny hint of what she'd been through. But he was taking it so well, being supportive and not judgemental at all. A tiny voice in her head urged her to say more—to tell him all about the debt, the fraud and the current issues with the police.

But it was too much to tell him all that. After a tense week, they were just back to where they wanted to be. She'd asked him to be patient, and he'd agreed. The last thing she wanted to do now was spoil the moment they were in.

So she gave a soft laugh and laid her head back against his shoulder. 'You know it doesn't work like that. It's all "he said, she said" and you can't really prove anything. There's just tension—an atmosphere—and the place that always felt like home feels different.'

He ran a finger down her cheek. 'So, how do you feel about being here?'

She bit her bottom lip and looked into his brown eyes. 'Better. Now I feel better.' She pulled a face. 'For a while, it was touch and go.'

'You mean with Dr Gemmill?'

She gave a nod. 'It was like jumping out of the frying pan and into the fire. I'm too passionate about patient care not to say anything. When they moved my ward, I thought they were actually going to sack me.'

Now he did sit up straight. 'Honestly?'

She nodded. 'And I didn't really know anyone. I didn't know who to speak to. I'd just got here. I didn't have any friends.'

'You could have spoken to me.'

She gave him a sad smile. 'But I thought you were on his side. I thought you agreed with him.'

He sighed and pulled her closer. 'I'm sorry you thought that. I was trying to offer advice. I didn't appreciate that you might be feeling like that.'

He stroked the side of her face. 'They gave you the job because they know you're capable and competent. Your references must have been good—so it's clear they thought you could do the job. Do you know they interviewed twenty candidates for your role?'

'What?' Now it was her turn to sit up. She was totally shocked.

He smiled. 'Spira is a competitive place. People want to work here. But they want the best.'

She sat back again. 'Wow, I didn't know that.'

He pulled her closer to him. 'And it's not just Spira that wants you. Max and I want you too.'

She shivered. A good shiver. One of excitement and anticipation.

'You do?'

He nodded. 'I know things have been a bit tense between us up until now. I guess I didn't know how you were feeling, and I guess you also realise how I'm hanging in here by the seat of my pants when it comes to Max.'

'He's a great kid, Theo,' she said. She couldn't hide the affection in her voice. 'I love being around him.'

'And he loves being around you. He talks about you all the time.'

'He does?' She pressed her lips together. 'This last

week I missed being around him. It's why I went to see him at daycare.'

'I figured,' he said gently. 'So, where does that leave us?'

She smiled. 'Where do you want it to leave us?'

His deep brown eyes looked at her carefully. 'I want us to be around each other. I want you in both of our lives, but I don't want to rush you into anything if you're not ready.'

She reached over and put her hand on his chest. 'I didn't expect this. I didn't come here expecting to find someone. Or two someones. But this is what I want,' she said, her stomach slightly knotted. 'I want us to be together too.'

He bent forward and kissed her lips lightly. 'What about Max? You know how I feel about things.'

She closed her eyes and smiled as his lips danced across her cheek. 'I love him,' she said easily. 'In an ideal world we would have dated longer before I met Max. But I get that you come together.' She gave a shrug. 'I never had a plan around children. I never thought no. I just figured children would happen at the right time in my life.' Her eyes opened and fixed on his. 'I guess the world just knows better than we do.'

He ran his fingers through her hair. 'So, you're happy. We can take some time and figure out things together. We'll have to be up front and tell HR that we're dating before someone else does.'

'I'm happy to do that.' She laughed. 'What's the worst that can happen—they'll move me again?'

His brow furrowed. 'You don't honestly think they'd do that?'

'I don't know what the rules are. Some hospitals don't

like staff dating and working together. Just in case something goes wrong and they cover for each other.'

'But that's not going to happen. I'd prefer to be up front with people. If they want to give us a set of rules for the workplace, then that's fine.'

She licked her lips. 'So, what about Max? What do we tell Max?'

He paused for a moment. She could imagine the number of conflicting thoughts that were going through his brain.

She put her hand on Theo's chest. 'How about we don't do anything at all? We see each other. We spend time in each other's apartments.' She raised her eyebrows. 'You might even let me have a sleepover. But we don't sit him down and make a big thing of it. We let it develop naturally. He's used to us being around each other. We let *him* get used to us.'

Theo gave a few small nods, and Addy continued. 'And if you notice anything—if he's having nightmares again, or his behaviour changes—we can take a few steps back.'

His shoulders relaxed a little and she knew that he must have been worried.

'Let's take this easy,' he said. 'Easy on us, easy on Max. If I'm too intense, if I'm not intense enough—just tell me. If I don't sleep, I know that I get short-tempered.'

'Is this our cue to tell each other all our faults?'

He grinned. 'Go on then.'

'I sometimes snore. So, I might be responsible for you not getting enough sleep.'

He leaned over and whispered in her ear. 'That better not be the only way you keep me up all night.'

She snaked her arms around his neck. 'That's something we could discuss together.'

There was a gleam in his eyes. 'When would you like to start?'

She pulled him on top of her as she slid down the sofa. 'How about now?'

CHAPTER ELEVEN

THE WARD WAS almost full. Only two beds were free, and both were assigned to patients coming in for investigations or procedures.

The last few weeks had been perfect. They'd seen each other every day and night. Max appeared entirely comfortable. He loved snuggling up on the sofa with Addy and telling her his daycare stories. They'd visited an aquarium, a water park and a mall with a special area for kids.

Things were so easy between them. Theo had learned her favourite foods and movies, and she'd learned his. They laughed together, supported each other and encouraged Max's learning in any way they could.

For the first time since he'd got Max, Theo didn't feel on his own. It felt instead like he was building a relationship and a family, and that made him proud and happy at the same time.

Occasionally his head flipped back to what little that she'd told him about her old job and loss of confidence. She never mentioned past relationships, or what had caused those tensions at the hospital. But she'd asked him to be patient with her. So he had to believe, if there was anything important, she would tell him when she was ready—even if he had to wait a bit longer.

His pager sounded, and he answered immediately. It

was his secretary. 'Dr Dubois,' she said, 'you asked me to update you on Isabel Aurelis. I spoke to her yesterday after all her assigned tests were completed. She was supposed to report today for admission, but she's over an hour late. I've tried her mobile with no response.'

Theo felt an uncomfortable prickle go up his spine. 'Where does she stay?'

His secretary read off the address.

'And do we have a next of kin for Isabel, a parent or friend?'

'Yes, I have contact details for both of her parents.'

'Can you try them please?'

He replaced the received and walked down the corridor to find Addy. She was chatting with one of the other cardiology consultants over preparing a patient for a procedure.

Theo rested his hands on his hips. 'One of Dr Gemmill's patients was supposed to come in today. She hasn't appeared.'

The other consultant gave a soft laugh. 'They've probably gone to the tennis club or the cricket club instead.'

Theo shook his head. 'Unlikely. She's only twenty-one. Previous admission for investigations of Wolff-Parkinson-White.'

The other consultant's eyebrows raised. 'The one who arrested and caused the ruckus?'

Theo nodded and Addy answered. 'Well, we all know it was me that caused the ruckus, because she was admitted with no real details. But that's a worry. Is there any chance she's taken unwell?'

He sighed. 'My secretary is trying to get hold of her next of kin. I'm hoping she's a young lady with a better offer who forgot about her admission today.'

'Has she had any other episodes?' the other consultant asked.

'That's the problem,' said Theo. 'She's had a number, but was still under Dr Gemmill. I had to contact her to try and get her tests all completed since her symptoms were worsening.'

His pager sounded—he walked to the wall and picked up the phone. 'Yes, okay, I see. Where are they? No one? Okay. How would they feel about us visiting?' He met Addy's violet gaze. She knew exactly how worried he was.

He hung up the phone. 'Her parents are in Gibraltar. They've tried her too, and one of her friends couldn't get hold of her this morning.'

'Are you going to send someone to her address?' asked the other consultant, his face grave.

'Actually...' said Theo, looking at him.

'Go.' He gave a wave of his hand. 'I can cover here. Who will you take with you?'

'Me,' said Addy. 'I'll give the keycards for the medicine trolley to Layla, and let the sister in the next ward know where we're going.'

She ran to the office and grabbed a few things, sticking them in a bag, before joining Theo at the elevator a few minutes later. They grabbed one of the porters to borrow a Spira staff car, and he drove them the short distance across the city.

Isabel stayed in a complex much more luxurious than the one the hospital hosted them in. A concierge was waiting at the door for them.

'You are the doctors from Spira?'

Theo nodded and the man strode swiftly towards another elevator. 'This takes us straight to the penthouse,' he said. 'I was just about to go up. Mr and Mrs Aurelis have phoned.'

The elevator was speedier than normal and Theo realised on the ascent that there were no other buttons. This must be exclusively for the penthouse.

There was an outer door that the concierge opened with his sensor. 'Ms Aurelis?' he shouted in a booming voice that took both Theo and Addy by surprise.

He started walking through the hall to the main living room, which was empty. It had vast views and exquisite furniture. 'There are four bedrooms, a study, three bathrooms, a dining room, kitchen, dressing room and laundry room,' he said briskly, waving his hand. Theo and Addy took that as their cue to help with the search.

They both ducked into other rooms. Theo was first into a bedroom, walking right round the whole room and checking inside the adjoining bathroom. Next was a study—he even checked under the desk.

Then he heard a shout. 'In here!'

It was Addy, and by the time he'd raced through she was on the floor of another bathroom. Isabel had clearly been about to either shower or bathe, as a number of glass bottles had broken and spilled liquid on the floor. Addy had covered her with a bathrobe and a towel while she checked her airway, breathing and circulation.

'She's breathing...it's shallow, but it's there. Her heart rate is very fast.' Addy reached into her bag and pulled out the portable monitor that she'd brought with her, fastening a few electrodes to Isabel's chest.

Theo was down on his knees next to her. He gave Isabel a little shake on the shoulder.

'Isabel, can you hear us? It's Dr Dubois and Charge

Nurse Bates from Spira Hospital. You've had a turn, and we've come to check on you.'

His eyes flicked to the monitor now the rhythm was showing on the screen. 'Rate two-twenty, SVT, we have no way of knowing how long she's been like this.'

He looked back across to Addy, since Isabel hadn't responded yet. 'Do you have a BP cuff?'

She nodded. 'It's manual,' she said apologetically, pulling a stethoscope and BP cuff from the bag.

He fastened it around Isabel's upper arm, inflated the cuff and listened with the stethoscope at her inner elbow. 'Eighty over fifty. Not great.' He pulled some adenosine from his pocket and looked over his shoulder at their porter, who was standing at the door. 'Get us an ambulance please. We're taking this patient in with us directly.'

He injected the adenosine, hoping to reduce Isabel's heart rate and stabilise things. As he looked up, he realised the concierge looked stricken. 'Can you call Isabel's parents back? Let them know we've got her and we're taking her back to Spira for a possible procedure this afternoon? They can call us later for more information.'

Addy had her head low, whispering in Isabel's ear as they continued to monitor her. 'Cardiac ablation?' she said.

'Unless we see a direct improvement,' he said. 'We can't leave her like this. And it has a good success rate.'

They waited patiently. Isabel became a little more aware of her surroundings but was still semi-conscious. Her heart rate slowed only a little, and it became clear they were going to have to continue her treatment.

By the time the ambulance arrived, they were ready to leave straightaway. Addy had grabbed some things from Isabel's cupboards and bathroom, equipping her stay for a few nights. The concierge locked up the penthouse and said he'd arrange a cleaning service.

Addy had phoned through to Spira to set up the cath lab for an emergency ablation procedure.

They went straight through Accident and Emergency to the cath lab. There were few staff available to prepare Isabel, so Addy completed the normal admission paperwork with all her details and medical history, and drew an emergency set of bloods.

By the time she'd finished, Theo was ready to start the procedure. Addy threw on a set of scrubs, standing in the background to observe.

It was clear Theo had done this many times. He inserted a sheath into a vessel near Isabel's groin before threading the catheter up towards her heart. The catheter electrodes—long thin wires moved up into the heart— were then delicately put into place as they all watched the whole process via a camera. It was a delicate procedure, because Theo had to find the abnormal tissue that was sending the rogue electrical impulses, then make sure the electrode catheter was in exactly the right spot before sending an energy pulse that destroyed the rogue tissue. As they watched the monitor, they could tell the procedure had been a success—Isabel's heart rate dropped and reverted to a normal rhythm.

Addy smiled as she heard the collective sigh of relief from everyone in the room. She moved over next to the trolley. 'I'll take her through to recovery,' she volunteered with a nod to the anaesthetist.

Isabel quickly started to come round. She was still monitored and on oxygen for a period of time, but her blood pressure improved and her heart rate stayed in a regular rhythm, at a normal rate.

An hour later, Addy took her up to the ward.

The consultant who'd been left on shift smiled but raised his eyebrows at her, handing her a pile of sticky notes. 'Mr and Mrs Aurelis are very anxious to speak to one of you. They're flying back from Gibraltar but wanted to speak to someone before their flight took off.'

Addy smiled and put the notes in her pocket. 'I'll phone them as soon as I have Isabel settled in her room.'

Layla joined her, and Addy gave her a handover, arranging for Isabel to get some food. 'She'll be staying for overnight monitoring and will be reviewed in the morning, with a view to potential discharge, all being well.'

Addy tapped her pocket. 'Isabel, I'm going to phone your mum and dad. Layla, warn the night shift that Isabel might have some late-night visitors.'

She shot them both a smile, then spent the next thirty minutes on the phone to some anxious but very grateful patients.

Theo appeared, to write up his notes, and heard the tail end of the conversation. He grinned when she finished. 'Well, this has been a bit of an unusual day.'

'It has been.' She nodded in agreement and then looked at the clock. 'Do you want me to pick up something for dinner, or collect Max from daycare?'

His eyes darted to the clock and he groaned. 'Pick up Max, please, and I'll sort out dinner. Do you want my key card?'

She shook her head. 'I'll take him to mine. You can give us a knock when you finish up.'

'Thank you.' He smiled at her, and her heart gave a little leap. The crinkles around his brown eyes and the expression on his face touched every part of her. It was the casualness. The sureness of each other. That fire still burning between them. And the trust.

No matter how they'd got here, she was absolutely sure about what she wanted for her future. It had two names. Theo and Max.

She still hadn't told him everything. The calls between her and her lawyer had increased as events continued to get worse back home. She definitely didn't want to leave Dubai, but it was now becoming a distinct possibility. Anxiety pricked at her that she hadn't told Theo everything, but she knew she would…as soon as she had a clear plan for what would happen next. The last thing she wanted to do was put any extra worry on him.

She was learning how to be a mum by default and was absolutely loving it. She'd asked some friends at the book group she was attending for a few hints on things, and they'd been more than delighted to help. From making food a bit more child friendly, to helping their attention span, to dealing with tantrums, and getting them to help around the house safely. Some of their suggestions were things she hadn't even considered, and she'd enjoyed feeding back to them too. Making new friends as an adult was always slightly awkward, particularly when she'd no starting point in Dubai, but the book group was an absolute godsend. Who'd known reading romance, crime and historical novels could teach so much?

Addy swung her bag over her shoulder, had a quick check to make sure no one was looking in the office, then gave Theo a kiss on the cheek. She gave him a wave as she headed to daycare.

Max was sitting scrunched up in a corner. Usually he was full of beans and waiting for one of them to appear.

'Okay, honey?' she asked.

He nodded but kept his head down.

She checked with a member of staff. 'Everything okay with Max?'

The staff member nodded. 'He's been a bit quiet this afternoon, but he says nothing is wrong.'

Addy thanked her and collected his backpack. 'Come on. We'll go home to mine until Dad finishes work.'

That was another thing that had changed in the last few weeks. Max had started to call Theo 'Dad' instead of Theo. Neither of them had tried to correct him, and she could see how secretly proud he was of the title.

They walked home, rather slowly, but the few times she offered to carry Max he refused.

When they reached her apartment, she dumped their stuff and settled him on the sofa. 'Let me check your temperature,' she said quickly, feeling his forehead. He didn't feel warm...

As she checked his temperature, she noticed her answering machine blinking red.

Max temperature was fine. But he was rubbing his eyes. 'I'm sleepy.'

'Okay, honey,' she said, picking up a nearby blanket. 'Did you do a lot in daycare today?'

He gave a scowl. 'Not really. Just fought with Rueben. I don't like him.'

Addy knelt down in front of him, watching as he lay his head on a cushion. If something significant happened, the daycare staff would always tell them. 'What did you fight about?' she asked carefully.

'A dinosaur.'

Addy waited for more information, but none came. 'Doesn't daycare teach you to share, or take turns?'

Max kept scowling. 'I'd only just got it. I told him he could have it later.'

'And what did he do?' asked Addy, hoping she got a good answer.

'He pushed me.'

'He did?'

Max nodded. 'So I bit him.'

Addy felt her stomach flip over. 'Oh, no, Max. We don't bite other people. That's naughty.'

If daycare had missed this altercation, there was a chance Rueben might go home with a bite mark somewhere, and that would likely create havoc. She should really phone them.

Max pulled his blanket up. 'I'm tired,' he said again, and closed his eyes.

Addy's mouth was half open, and she was ready to say something, but she took a deep breath and closed it, touching his little head once again.

She would have to tell Theo when he got back. Max had generally been well-behaved around her. She'd only seen him throw a temper tantrum once, and she knew he'd been overtired at that point.

But biting was serious, and her stomach churned as she thought how she would feel if Max had shown her a bite mark on his skin today.

She stood up and stretched. There was no point tackling this now. She'd talk it through with Theo once he got home. If Max had a sleep right now, he might be in a better mood once he woke up.

She moved over to the phone and remembered there was a message. She pressed the button to listen. It was Laura, her lawyer. 'Hi, Addy. Listen, I'm sorry, but things have taken a bit of a turn. Can you phone me urgently please?'

Addy's stomach lurched. She felt a wave of panic.

She pressed the buttons to dial Laura, her hands shaking so much that she put the phone on speaker mode rather than holding it.

'It's Addy.'

'We have a problem.'

'What do you mean?'

'The new inspector is threatening to put a warrant out for your arrest.'

'What?' Her legs wobbled and she started to shake. 'How on earth can he do that?'

'He claims you've been uncooperative about being interviewed.'

'I've sent him my shifts three times. He's never asked me to meet him.'

'I went through that with him, but he says you're being deliberately uncooperative.'

'Surely it's his job to arrange a time that suits? This job at Spira is different from other posts I've had. In theory I have to be available seven days a week, twenty-four hours a day. But the reality is I have to be there for the busy periods. And since most of Spira's cardiac admissions are arranged, that's usually Monday to Friday between eight and five. So that makes me unavailable for the inspector during those hours.'

'I know that,' said Laura. 'But it seems that he's talked to Stuart again and dreamed up some more charges.'

'Like what?' She could feel cold sweat breaking out on her skin.

'Fraud, extortion, cyber-crime, theft and corruption.'

'What?' Her throat was dry and her brain was going into panic mode.

'How can this be happening? I've offered to speak to

him. He's conjuring up charges without having a clear picture of what went on.'

'Addy?'

The voice cut through the noise in her brain. Theo was standing in the doorway with a look of confusion on his face.

For a moment, all words left her mind—it almost seemed as if she'd lost the ability to talk.

Laura kept talking. 'He's serious, Addy. He wants to put out a warrant for your arrest. He might even contact your employers. I'm thinking you'll have to come back to Scotland.'

Addy turned away from the phone to see Theo's face.

'I… I can explain,' she stuttered.

'Where's Max?' he asked, his face blank.

'He's sleeping,' she said, pointing to the sofa that she'd turned to face the window.

'Sleeping? Why is he sleeping?' Theo crossed the space in a few strides.

'He said he was tired. And daycare said he'd been quiet this afternoon. We talked when we got home and he told me he'd been fighting and bit another kid.'

She kept on glancing at the phone, conscious that Laura would hear her. This wasn't how she wanted to deal with things.

'What?' Theo's face whipped around to look at her again as he knelt at the sofa. 'You should have phoned me.'

'I would have, but…' Her voice tailed off.

Yes, she probably should have phoned him, but she hadn't wanted to make a big deal out of it in front of Max, and had hoped they would've had a chance to talk privately.

'Max?' Theo's voice was quiet as he tried to shake Max awake.

Addy started to speak. 'Laura, this isn't a good time right now. I'll need to call you—'

'Max!' Theo's voice was sharp now, and it stopped her mid-sentence. 'Max!'

She recognised the tone and ran over to his side. He was shaking Max sharply now, but Max was definitely not waking up.

'What's wrong with him? What have you done to him?'

'What? Nothing. He was talking to me earlier. I checked his temperature…it was fine.' She put her hand onto the little body and tried to rouse him too.

Theo started running his hands over Max's body. Touching his stomach, his limbs, then pulling up his eyelids to check his pupils.

Max gave the tiniest groan, but that was it.

There was no question. Max was unconscious.

Theo ran his hands around his son's head and stopped short, his head snapping around to her. 'What's this lump?'

'What lump?' She tried to get a look, but Theo was blocking her way.

His voice was like steel. 'My son has a lump on his head and he's unconscious. What have you done?'

Fear gripped her, along with a wave of anger. 'I told you! He was fighting with another kid at daycare. But he never said he hit his head. He didn't complain about his head at all. He just said he was tired. Daycare didn't say anything at all.'

Her brain was whirling. She reached over to touch Max's head, instantly terrified when she touched the lump. It was definite. But his skin was unbroken, there was no blood.

'What do we do?' she asked, all her nursing background flooding out the window, leaving her scared and panicked.

'*We* do nothing,' Theo spat out as he gathered his son in his arms. Then he clearly had second thoughts. 'Phone an ambulance. I'll meet them at the front door.'

Her trembling fingers cut the call to Laura without a word and dialled for an ambulance. She gave the details, telling them Max was unconscious and his father would meet them at the door.

All of a sudden she was furious that she hadn't taken Theo's key earlier. If they'd been in his apartment she could have gathered some things for them to take to the hospital. She grabbed Max's backpack from earlier, her own jacket and bag, and ran to the elevator. She had to know. She had to know that Max was going to be okay.

But by the time she reached the ground floor, the ambulance was already there, and Max and Theo were bundled inside, Theo talking to the paramedic. As she scrambled to get closer Theo saw her and his eyes cut her dead.

'Stay,' was the only word he said before the back doors of the ambulance were slammed.

The siren sounded. Her legs buckled and sent her onto the pavement as the two people she loved most in the world disappeared, leaving her with no idea of their future.

CHAPTER TWELVE

Theo did his absolute best not to vomit all over the back of the ambulance or get in the way of the paramedic who was tending to his son.

The overwhelming urge to panic and rant and rave was right on the tip of his tongue. He'd heard a colleague say once that when someone had crashed into her car, with her children in the back, she'd panicked, checked her children were okay and grabbed them and ran—not even talking to the person who had crashed into her. The calmest doctor he'd ever known had told him that, in that moment, she couldn't talk to anyone, and just ran to a friend's house that was nearby.

Theo had been bewildered by her words. Now he understood them entirely.

They arrived at Spira within minutes. A few of the staff recognised him and one of the Accident and Emergency doctors came over straight away.

'Theo? What's wrong?'

'This is my son, Max, he's three. He's unconscious and has a lump at the back of his head.' He struggled with the next words as a wash of guilt embraced him. 'My…friend picked him up from daycare. He was fine but quiet. Daycare didn't report anything, but my friend said that Max told her he'd been in a fight today. He was tired. She let him sleep.'

'How long has he been sleeping?'

Theo took in a deep breath, thinking what time Addy had picked him up. 'It will be about two hours, maybe longer.'

He should have picked Max up. Would he have noticed there was something wrong?

'Any vomiting? Irritability?'

'I don't think so…'

He said this just as Max, who was on his side, vomited everywhere.

'Let me do some neuro obs and take a good look at him,' said the doctor, wheeling the trolley into the resus room.

The staff moved quickly, almost without saying a word to each other. They knew exactly what they were doing. They took his observations, filling out a neuro chart and shining a light into Max's pupils. Then they took some time to examine the bump at the back of Max's head.

'I really need more information about what happened at daycare today,' said the doctor.

'So do I,' muttered Theo.

'And I'm sorry, but I have to ask the question. Is there any chance he could have been injured by your friend?'

Theo had put a hand on the wall behind him. After everything he'd just heard on that call, all the secrets Addy had been keeping from him, did he think she could have hurt Max? Why had she been keeping secrets? Why on earth were the police pursuing her, and why did they think she was guilty of fraud? He had so many questions tumbling around in his brain. He'd thought it was wrong to push her. He'd promised to be patient. Now it seemed there was so much he didn't know. But did any of that mean she would hurt Max?

'No,' he said. 'It's Addison Bates, the charge nurse from my ward. She would never hurt Max.'

The doctor disappeared for a few moments and came back. 'He's still unconscious. I'm taking him for an emergency scan.'

Theo knew he should try to get more information from the daycare, but there was no way he was leaving his son's side. He strode along next to the trolley as they wheeled it through for the scan, and sat outside as the detailed scan took place.

He knew, in these circumstances, they would report on it immediately.

Fifteen minutes later, the doctor joined him outside the waiting room. 'Dr Baz, the neurosurgeon, is on his way to Theatre. Max has an acute subdural haemorrhage. They need to release the pressure.'

Theo was thankful he was sitting down—his whole body crumpled and he put his head in his hands.

'Is there someone I can call for you?' asked the other doctor.

After a few minutes, Theo took a deep breath and sat up straight. 'No,' he said with conviction. 'No one at all.'

Addy was pacing. He'd told her to stay. He didn't want her there. He'd asked her what she'd done to Max—he'd actually said those words out loud, and now her heart was broken. She had no idea how much he'd heard of her call to Laura. She had to presume he'd heard everything. But there had been no chance to discuss it. No chance to tell him about her evil ex and his actions, that she'd done nothing wrong—at any point.

But she had. She had done something wrong. She hadn't taken the opportunity to tell Theo what had happened in her past. He'd told her his past, and how he'd got Max. He'd shared with her openly, and she hadn't paid him the same courtesy. All to save face? All because she was scared she'd look foolish?

She wanted to turn back the clock so badly right now. But not for her. For Max. Why hadn't she paid better attention? Why hadn't she at least phoned the daycare to ask what had happened?

Max was her favourite little person on the planet, and she'd failed him.

She had to know. She had to know how he was. She knew that by calling she might put fellow colleagues in a difficult position. Some knew that she and Theo were together.

She picked up the phone. 'It's Addy,' she said when someone she knew answered. 'How's Max?'

The person paused a little. 'He's just gone to Theatre. Are you coming in?'

She held back the retch in her throat. 'What kind of injury is it?'

'Subdural,' came the reply. 'Theo looks terrible. Where are you?'

Where was she? On the floor of her apartment, with her head between her knees.

'On my way,' she said.

No matter what the consequences, she had to be there. She had to be there for her boys.

CHAPTER THIRTEEN

Two days passed in a blur. Max's surgery was successful. He was fitted with a shunt for twenty-four hours, and it was removed when the surgeon was sure the swelling and bleeding had passed.

Theo never left his bedside. Someone from the daycare came down to see him, distraught after they'd viewed security tapes that had shown the two three-year-olds clearly fighting, and the other boy pushing Max over so the back of his head struck the corner of a table. He jumped up and bit the boy in retaliation, and then the two boys started playing together again. It had all been over in seconds, and none of the staff had noticed at the time.

At first Theo was confused. Of course, he would have gone to them at a later date and asked for an explanation, but the manager gently explained that Addy had gone to see them. She'd let them know about Max, and asked them to supply Theo with more details in case the surgeon asked.

He was stunned. She'd asked to get in a few times and he'd just said no. He couldn't think about her, or anything that he'd heard in that call, because his primary focus had to be Max.

When Max opened his eyes and smiled at him, it felt as if the elephant on his shoulders had finally left. For the first time in two days he could breathe. And then he cried. Max had rapidly become his whole world. He hadn't asked for this. He wasn't even sure he wanted it at first. But welcoming Max into his life had been the best thing he'd ever done. Now he understood why people who were parents would do anything for their kids. It didn't matter that he wasn't Max's biological dad. He felt it, inside, and he knew that would never change.

So when Max finally started speaking and asked, 'Where's Addy?' the pain in Theo's heart was so acute he felt he couldn't speak.

Max loved Addy. And so did Theo.

But he'd been so blindsided by things these last few days he hadn't been able to think straight.

He cringed as he remembered some of the things he'd said to her—what he might even have accused her of. It didn't matter that he'd done it without thinking, it was an unforgivable thing to do. He understood that now.

He stroked the top of Max's head. 'Don't worry, honey. I'll find her later and bring her here.'

When Max fell asleep again, he ducked out to head to the apartments. He tried her door but got no answer. He tried her phone too, but it went straight to message. He hesitated for a few moments, wondering what on earth to say, before finally hanging up and deciding to try again later.

As he went back downstairs, he approached the concierge, who immediately asked how Max was. Theo filled him in and then asked the question. 'Have you seen Addy?'

The concierge looked uncomfortable. 'She's gone—she didn't tell you?'

'What?' Theo felt as if the floor had just opened beneath him.

The concierge nodded. 'She went to the airport. Said she had to go back to the UK to sort some things out.'

'But she's coming back?' He could hear the edge in his tone.

'I'm sorry, Dr Dubois, I don't know. The apartment is still in her name, but she didn't tell me her intentions.'

Theo gave a nod and went back upstairs. He looked in despair at her closed door before opening his own. He walked over to the floor-to-ceiling windows.

A world of possibilities was out there, but he didn't want them without Addy. They were a family. They were meant to be together. He should never have snapped at her. He should have let her visit Max. Now he didn't know if he would get that chance.

His heart felt as if it had been ripped in two. How on earth could he explain to Max that she'd gone?

A tear slid down his face as he turned away from the window. He'd made the biggest mistake of his life, and he had no idea how to fix it.

CHAPTER FOURTEEN

By the time she landed at Glasgow the rage had built inside her for hours. Laura had strongly advised her to come home. She'd booked them an interview with the new inspector. Addy had left Dubai knowing that Max was out of danger, but she hadn't been able to see him. She longed to see his face again, and longed for a chance to talk to Theo.

But first she had to deal with the chaos that Stuart King had caused in her life again. And she was done with it. Laura kept trying to talk her down, but Addy had taken as much as she could. 'I've travelled nearly five thousand miles to sort this out. You can bet I'll answer the inspector's questions, and then let him know I have no intention of letting this man ruin my life again. My patience is done. I've left behind a three-year-old that I love who's recovering from brain surgery to be here. If this man is so gullible that he believes what a liar and fraudster says—just because he has the gift of the gab—then he's clearly a fool.'

'Please don't say that,' pleaded Laura.

'I might,' bit back Addy. 'You're just here to advise.'

She spent two days being questioned. Things were heated. But Addy could answer every question, explain every transaction. Give proof of shifts and of being in other places when, apparently, she'd applied for loans or remortgaged her house. She was angry. But she was also precise and consistent.

By the time she left, she had been guaranteed, in-person, that there would no investigation into her, no charges and no further need to remain in the country. But that wasn't enough for Addy. 'What about Stuart King? This man has tried to ruin my life twice. He can't be allowed to do this to anyone else—even though the likelihood is that he already has.'

The inspector assured her that they now had multiple pieces of evidence that would allow them to bring charges against Stuart King. He would be arrested in the next few days.

The relief was immense, but so was the sadness.

Theo might never speak to her again. She might never get to be in Max's life. She'd been hurt beyond belief when Theo had uttered the words *'What have you done?'* But she also understood he was panicking, and he'd walked into a situation that she'd had time and opportunity to tell him about, but she'd chosen not to.

He had a right to be angry, he had a right to be suspicious. But how could she continue at Spira if he was going to hate the ground she walked on?

It would be unbearable, because she loved him—she loved them both. They were her perfect family. And life would never be the same if she didn't have them alongside her.

So, she pulled out the last of her recent savings and bought a ticket back to Dubai. Worst-case scenario, she could pick up the rest of her things and give formal notice to HR.

Best-case scenario? She couldn't even dare to hope…

CHAPTER FIFTEEN

It had been five long days. He'd watched her apartment every day and asked the concierge if he'd heard anything. He'd also promised the concierge that the item he'd had delivered to her apartment was entirely expected. She'd just forgotten to let the concierge know.

His senses were on high alert, and his door had been ajar the whole time. So, when he finally heard some footsteps in the corridor, his heart missed a few beats.

Max was home now, and sleeping peacefully. He'd made a full recovery, but Theo was off sick for the rest of this week, to give Max some recuperation time and allow him to get fully back to normal. He'd swithered about leaving altogether and not using the Spira daycare again, but he was satisfied by the explanation from the staff, and their promises. Max had even asked when he could play with this Rueben again.

His breath caught in his throat as he heard the steps. They didn't slow at all as they passed his doorway. He only made it to the corridor in time to see her door open and hear the gasp of shock.

He moved swiftly. Her hands were still at her mouth as she took in the giant patchwork sofa in place of the previous standard cream one.

He spoke in the quietest voice possible. 'Thought it might hide the baked bean stains if Max and I come here.'

She spun around to look at him. He could see everything in her eyes. She looked weary—exhausted, even. Then she swayed a little and he caught her elbows.

'Addison?'

She shook her head and took a few deep breaths. When she lifted her head again there were tears in her eyes. 'How's Max?'

His heart swelled at her first words. How could he ever have doubted her?

'He's good. He's recovering and might go back to daycare next week. He's asking for you.'

'He is?'

Theo nodded, wondering where on earth he should start.

'I'm sorry,' he said simply. 'I'm sorry I doubted you, and I'm sorry I blamed you. I was wrong. I had no right to do that. And I could offer excuses—I could tell you I was panicking—I could tell you I couldn't think straight. But none of them are good enough, and I know that.'

She didn't answer. Just looked at him.

'I love you, Addy. Max loves you too. We want you in our lives. I don't care about what I heard on the phone, because I trust you. I do.'

She blinked and then licked her lips. Her voice was flat. 'I'm tired, Theo. I have an ex who has tried to ruin my life not once, but twice. Leaving me a pile of debts that weren't mine and having my house repossessed because of his actions. I came here for a fresh start. I didn't tell you any of that, because frankly I didn't think you needed to know. But he came back. With a new inspector on the case, who believed most of what came out of my ex's mouth. I was under suspicion. I went home to sort it out.'

Her violet eyes were steely.

'And all of a sudden I'm tired of not feeling in control of my own life. You walked into my apartment and treated me like crap because of a conversation you heard but didn't understand.' She put her hand on her chest. 'Can you imagine for one second how I must have felt, realising that Max had become unwell on my watch? That he needed brain surgery and I hadn't noticed or understood?'

Her voice was angry now.

'And you wouldn't let me see him! The little boy I had taken into my heart and loved as if he were my own. If things had gone wrong, I would never have got a chance to say goodbye. Can you imagine what that did to me?'

Theo raised his hands. He wanted to crawl into a hole in the ground. He was imagining if something had happened and he hadn't got a chance to say goodbye. It would have been imprinted on him for ever. He would never, ever get over something like that. And he could potentially have done that to Addy, the woman he loved. The shame was overwhelming.

'I am so, so sorry. I panicked. All I could think about was that Max was unconscious. I felt guilty because I hadn't picked him up myself. Would I have noticed anything? Probably not. Would I have done anything different from you? Probably not. But my son was sick, and I hadn't been there. Max has never been seriously ill with me before, and, the truth is, I couldn't handle it. I told you from the start I was winging it. I know nothing about being a parent, Addy. And maybe I shouldn't be. Maybe I'm not cut out for this, and Max deserves better.'

She paused, then took a breath, gesturing him over to

the patchwork sofa he'd bought her. They sat down together, looking out at the skyscraper view of Dubai.

Tears were falling down her cheeks. She spoke softly but steadily. 'You are a great dad, Theo. And you're just what Max needs. Don't doubt yourself.'

His hands were shaking. 'But look how much I messed up with you. I love you, Addy. From the bottom of my heart, I love you. *We* love you. I want us to be a family together, because I can't imagine doing this with anyone else. I wouldn't want to do this with anyone else.'

Her tears were still falling. 'But look at us, Theo. Look what happened between us. I should have told you earlier about my life back home. But I was partly ashamed. Ashamed that a man had manipulated me and committed fraud in my name. It makes me look stupid and gullible, and I didn't want that. I didn't want to tell you I'd been that person.'

'That's what affected your work?' he asked quietly.

She nodded. 'People talk. Stuart charmed people. They liked him. And when all the gossip started about fraud and money issues they looked at me differently. I could tell they were thinking I'd been involved. Can you imagine how that felt?' She shook her head, then met his gaze with her tear-stained eyes. 'It just felt like it was my own mess to clean up. I didn't want to drag you into anything. You had enough going on being a parent to Max.'

His words were gentle. 'But I could have supported you too.'

'I'm sorry,' she whispered. 'I should have trusted you. I should have told you. I'm so sorry that I didn't tell you.'

He reached over and threaded his fingers through hers. 'I'm sorry too. I'm sorry someone put you through all that. But wouldn't it be better, if something bad happens, to have someone supporting you? Someone having your back and fighting for you too?'

'Of course,' she whispered, her voice shaking.

'Then I will be,' he replied. 'From today, and for the future.' He closed his eyes for a second. She could sense he was nervous. 'We'll be there for each other.'

They interlinked their hands together and Addy leaned back into him, the warmth of her body against his. He kept talking in a low voice. 'And, if we're serious about each other, and want to be together, then should we consider Max too?' His brown eyes looked down and met hers. 'Right now, Max has only one adoptive parent. But he could have two. Then he'd be ours. Not mine.'

She let out a long, slow breath. 'My instinct is to say yes, right away. But we have a little boy's heart to consider. What if we try and we don't work?'

'We will work,' said Theo steadily. 'I'll move heaven and earth to make us work. I can't imagine life without you.'

'And where will our future be?' she asked, looking out at the skyline.

'Wherever you want it to be.'

'I'm from Scotland. You're from France. And I know you might want to go back eventually and support your mum.'

He gave a slow nod. 'If my father's condition goes downhill, you're right, I would want to support my *maman*.' He gave her a smile. 'You have no idea how much she is going to love you.' He took a moment. 'Would you object? Would you want to stay here?'

It was Addy's turn to take a moment. It was clear she was considering things. Then she gave him a smile. 'I want to be wherever you and Max are. I can be content anywhere if I have my boys by my side.'

'You mean it?'

She nodded. 'You and Max are family to me.'

He dropped a kiss on her forehead. 'Can we really make this work?'

She gave a slow nod. 'But for Max's sake we have to take things slow. We've had a rocky few weeks. Do I want to be Max's parent? Absolutely. But let's do things at a pace that fits in with him.'

He tilted her chin up towards his and brushed a kiss against her lips. 'I love you, Addison Bates, and I'm so glad that we found each other.'

She returned his kiss with a smile. 'I love you too, Theo Dubois. Now, let me see my boy.'

EPILOGUE

One year later

THE WEATHER IN Lyon was beautiful, and Addy couldn't wipe the smile from her face. The adoption had been finalised last month and she was now officially Max's parent.

They'd arranged their wedding in Lyon so both of Theo's parents could be there, and guests had come from Scotland and Dubai to join them.

Theo and Max were already in the hotel's gardens, standing beneath a giant arch of flowers as they waited for her. 'I have the ring,' said Max in a comic whisper to the crowd, which caused much laughter.

Her dress was a cream satin floor-length sheath, with a cowl neckline and thin diamond belt, and her bouquet was sunflowers, because yellow was now Max's favourite colour.

Her dad grinned, kissed her cheek and walked her down the garden aisle as the music started.

The last year had been so much easier than what had come before. Stuart King had finally been jailed, and Addy had been able to give her evidence in court via video.

People at Spira had accepted them easily as a couple, and their relationship had thrived. Addy had let herself trust again, and Theo had relaxed into his role as a parent, sharing the responsibilities with someone who loved Max just as much as he did.

By the time she reached the top of the aisle Max was bouncing on his toes. 'Look at the ring,' he said proudly, opening the box and letting the diamond-set wedding band sparkle in the French sun.

She let out a little gasp—because she hadn't seen it yet. They'd skipped the engagement part and decided to move straight to the wedding.

Theo's hand slid into hers, and Max stood between them, each holding his hand as they said their wedding vows.

'I love you, Mrs Dubois,' said Theo as he slipped the ring onto her finger.

'Love you too,' she replied as she slipped his thick plain band onto his.

The celebrant lifted her arms to the crowd. 'And I now take great pleasure in pronouncing Addy and Theo as Dr and Mrs Dubois. You may kiss the bride!' she exclaimed. Theo beamed and dipped his wife backwards for a kiss.

'Me too!' shouted Max as he was lifted into their arms.

They kissed his cheeks in unison.

'To family,' Addy declared to her friends.

'To family!' they replied, and they all celebrated well into the night.

* * * * *

*If you enjoyed this story,
check out these other great reads
from Scarlet Wilson*

Melting Dr Grumpy's Frozen Heart
Her Summer with the Brooding Vet
Cinderella's Kiss with the ER Doc
A Daddy for Her Twins

All available now!

MIDWIFE'S THREE-DATE RULE

ALISON ROBERTS

MILLS & BOON

CHAPTER ONE

'WHO *IS* THAT?'

Philippa Gordon could feel her gaze being drawn and then caught, despite the fact that her attention had been centred on the staff huddle gathering in front of the whiteboard at the back of the central nurses' station for the shift handover. The ward receptionist was talking to new arrivals at the desk—an anxious-looking, heavily pregnant woman in a wheelchair and her even more anxious-looking partner. Other incoming night shift midwives and support staff were busy chatting and finding notepads and pens.

Pippa didn't realise she'd spoken aloud until Sally, who was updating boxes on the whiteboard, glanced over her shoulder.

'New consultant,' she said. 'Lachlan Smythe. Starts tomorrow.'

'What's he doing here at this time of day, then? It's seven p.m.'

'Moving into his office, I believe.'

A second glance was irresistible—and it wasn't simply because this man was more than attractive enough to invite second glances. *This* was the famous Lachlan Smythe who, according to the hospital grapevine, had been headhunted from a top job in a major American hospital for the sought-after HoD position at The Queen Mary Hospital's Birthing Centre.

Pippa had a legitimate reason to be watching him now. She would be working with the man, after all.

'Younger looking than I expected,' she murmured.

'*Better* looking than *I* expected,' Sally whispered back. 'Lucky us. I met him earlier. He seems very nice.' She looked past Pippa. 'Everybody ready? I'd like to get started so that some of us can head home on time for once.'

There was a chorus of assent and a shuffle as some people took chairs and others crowded closer.

'Right… Room One, we have Mary McGovan. She's forty-one weeks gestation; G4 P3 so she knows what she's doing. No red flags. Came in at eighteen hundred hours and currently six centimetres dilated. Suzie, you've got a student midwife with you tonight, so this should be a perfect introduction.'

Pippa took one more glance as the new HoD passed the reception desk. Mr Smythe's CV was apparently notable for the number of prestigious hospitals he'd worked in, his cutting-edge research projects and an impressive list of peer-reviewed articles in leading medical journals. No wonder he had such a confident air about him—as though he already felt as if he belonged here.

She hoped he was as 'nice' as Sally believed. Their last HoD had, unfortunately, been one of those old school surgeons who was inclined to dismiss the opinions of staff members who were further down the pecking order, like nurses or midwives. She could feel the corners of her mouth curling upwards a little. It had to be a good sign that he was carrying that large cardboard box himself instead of finding a porter to shift his belongings. Especially when it looked like an awkward and rather heavy burden. It had to be an effort so it was a surprise to see him suddenly turning his head over the top of the box.

Oh, Lord...

Pippa knew the feeling that someone was watching you and how it could send a shiver down your spine. When it was strong enough to make you turn it was usually because it felt creepy enough to make the hairs on the back of your neck stand up, and here she was with a smile on her face, probably *looking* creepy. Hastily, she straightened her face and turned to focus on Sally and the whiteboard. She wasn't quite fast enough, however. For just a heartbeat there, they'd made eye contact that *she* could feel, even at this distance.

What was *that* about?

Pippa took note of the rooms assigned to her that included an older woman, Linda, having her first baby at the age of forty-two after IVF intervention, and Helen, who had been admitted at three centimetres dilated, with regular contractions, but was slow to progress. As one of the most experienced midwives on the shift, she was being assigned to any labour that could be potentially more complicated. She'd already lost any interest in the new boss she had yet to meet. These women were the reason she was here and each one of them would remind her of why she was so passionate about this job.

'Room Six, Stella Braithwaite. Thirty-six years old, twenty-one weeks gestation, G2, P+1. Came in at sixteen hundred hours and is having intermittent contractions. Ultrasound and monitoring suggest they're Braxton Hicks and the cervix is closed but she's understandably very anxious so we're keeping her in and doing thirty-minute obs. Pippa, I've put her on your list, too.'

Okay, maybe some women and their stories were more of a reminder than others. The '+1' designation meant that Stella had lost her first baby before the twenty-four-week mark and that put her at much higher risk of losing a second baby. It wasn't just Pippa's professional interest that was captured by this case.

This was personal.

Stella was the first person on her list that she went to introduce herself to as the handover finished. Her heart went out to the woman who was lying stiffly on the bed as if she was too afraid to move a muscle. As Pippa knocked and entered the room quietly, both Stella and her partner were staring at the screen of the CTG monitor beside the bed and Pippa knew that they were watching the lines forming and listening to every blip of their baby's heartbeat.

She'd been there. Too many times. She knew that fear.

'I'm Pippa,' she introduced herself. 'I'll be looking after you tonight, Stella.'

Stella nodded.

Her partner was holding her hand tightly. 'I'm Tony,' he said.

Pippa took in the information on the screen of the monitor. 'That's looking very reassuring,' she said.

'Is it?' Stella sounded doubtful. 'Are you sure?'

'I'm sure.' Pippa picked up the thin strip of graph paper that was pooling on the floor to run between her hands and see what had been recorded recently. 'Did someone explain what we're keeping an eye on?'

'The baby's heart rate,' Stella said. 'If it slows down or gets irregular, it's a concerning sign.'

'And that bottom line is the strength of the contractions,' Tony added. 'If they get stronger it means it's likely to be real labour starting and not those false contractions.'

'Braxton Hicks.' Pippa nodded. She was still rapidly scanning the graph paper. 'We measure contractions in millimetres of mercury—like a blood pressure. If it's real labour, they'll be between forty and sixty millimetres. The strongest one I can see here is no more than fifteen millimetres. And they're getting further apart.' She smiled at Stella—aiming for a mix of reassurance and encouragement. 'I know it's not easy, but try and relax. Stress—and fatigue—are both triggers for Braxton Hicks.'

She couldn't miss the look that Stella and Tony exchanged.

'What is it?' she asked.

Stella bit her lip.

'She thinks this is her fault,' Tony admitted.

'What?' Pippa was horrified. 'Of course it isn't.'

'That's what I keep telling her.'

'But Pippa said that stress can trigger it.' Stella's eyes filled with tears that spilled over. 'I tried not to get stressed. I really did but…but…'

It was Tony who filled the silence. 'We're at exactly the same day it was when we lost our first baby,' he said. His voice cracked. 'Twenty-one weeks and three days.'

Oh…

Pippa had to pull in a deep breath. To find that courage that she knew she had, despite—or perhaps because of—knowing exactly what that would have been like. It was termed a late miscarriage because the baby was too early to survive. It was referred to as a foetus and it would have fitted into the palms of their hands but it would have *looked* like a real baby. And it would have hurt beyond measure.

She sank onto the edge of the bed and reached for Stella's other hand. 'I totally understand how stressful this is,' she said. 'But there's absolutely no sign that it's about to happen again. The CTG is normal. Your ultrasound was normal. You're very close to being past the day you were dreading and we're going to be here to look after you until you feel more confident. Now…have you both had something to eat since you came in?'

They both shook their heads.

'I can recommend our cafeteria, which will be open for another couple of hours. They do a really good lasagne. Or you could get sandwiches and have a picnic. I'll be coming in to see you whenever I can but you can push your buzzer any time and, if I can, I'll come straight away.' She gave Stella's hand a squeeze and stood up. 'I'd better go and do some work now.'

The next person on her list was only two rooms away and she begged for an update on her dilation status as soon as Pippa introduced herself.

Within minutes, she was the second woman to burst into tears in front of Pippa.

'You've got to be kidding. I'm only *halfway*?' Her head flopped back onto the pillows. The hand holding the mouthpiece of the Entonox cylinder hit the mattress. 'I thought I could this,' she moaned. 'But now I don't think I can. Terry's fed up, too. He went to find some food ages ago and he hasn't even bothered coming back yet.'

'Six centimetres is good,' Pippa said. 'It's past halfway and it's progress. You were only three when you came in.'

'That was *hours* ago.'

There were tears streaming down Helen's face now.

'But I'd been having contractions for fifteen hours before I even came in. *Fifteen* hours! I'm so tired. And it hurts…'

'I know.'

'Do you?' Helen glared at her. 'How many kids have you got?'

'I haven't got any of my own.'

Oh, boy…this was clearly going to be one of those nights with too many poignant reminders of the past. She'd had plenty of practice keeping it hidden, however, and still managed to find a smile for Helen.

'I've lost count of how many babies I've helped into the world, though,' she added with a smile. 'So, I do know a lot about it.'

'It'll be worse when it's your turn,' Helen said. 'You'll see.'

Pippa stripped off her gloves and stood up from where she'd been perched on the side of the bed to do the internal examination. She was only in her mid-thirties so why wouldn't people make the assumption that she was just putting off motherhood? What would it be like in ten years' time when people might start thinking she was selfish because she'd never wanted to have kids, or worse—feeling sorry for her because she couldn't?

'You really are doing well, Helen,' she said. 'And baby's still coping with the contractions, but I'd like to leave the monitor on for a bit longer unless you want to get up.'

Helen's head shake was miserable and Pippa took hold of her hand. The slow progress of this labour was clearly beginning to take a significant emotional toll and that was something that had to be taken into consideration in the management of this baby's arrival. 'Maybe I should get one of our doctors to come and have a chat to you about what we could do to help?'

'Like what?'

'More pain relief might let you get a bit of rest. Some sleep, even. You might want to have another think about having stronger medication or an epidural. Or an infusion to help make the contractions stronger.'

'But I said I don't want drugs. Or an epidural. I wanted to have a natural birth.'

'I know.' Pippa was sympathetic. 'Maybe you'd like to try the pool again? Or the birth ball? Or walking around?'

Helen shook her head again. 'I'm too tired.'

'When did you last have a wee?' Pippa asked.

'I can't remember.'

'It's really important,' Pippa said. 'If your bladder's full it can make it harder for baby's head to descend and it can slow things down by making the contractions less effective and more painful.' She reached for the chart on the end of the bed to see if the midwife who'd been with Helen on the day shift had recorded the information.

'*Oww...*' Helen's loud groan, as a new contraction started, seemed like agreement with what Pippa was telling her. She pulled the mouthpiece close enough to suck in a deep breath of the mix of nitrous oxide and oxygen.

Helen spat out the mouthpiece as the contraction ended.

'I *have* changed my mind,' she groaned. 'I just want this baby out. *Please...*'

'I'll find someone to come and see you,' Pippa said.

She found Sandy, the consultant on duty tonight, at the nurses' station, hanging up on an internal phone call.

'We're down one anaesthetist,' she sighed. 'There's some horrible gastric bug going around and she's had to go home. The staff shortage might mean we can only have one theatre open tonight and we've already got a potential C-section waiting in the emergency department and keeping my registrar busy. Fingers crossed we don't get any more. Could be a long night.'

'At least we've got a new consultant on board from tomorrow.'

'A new Head of Department, even.' Sandy's raised eyebrows made her look hopeful. 'Maybe he'll look at improving our staffing issues.'

For some odd reason, Pippa found herself glancing away from the reception desk. In the direction she'd seen Lachlan Smythe going, carrying that box, a couple of hours ago.

It was highly unlikely he was still in the building.

Even less likely that he'd look at her again and give her that strange impression that he already knew who she was. Or that *she* was the person he'd been waiting to meet?

She shook off the ridiculous notion.

'Have you got a couple of minutes?' she asked Sandy. 'We've got a woman in Room Three. Primigravida, cephalic presentation, but slow progress of just on two centimetres in over four hours. Mother's getting tired and distressed enough to be ready to discuss modifying her birth plan.'

Helen chose to have IV pain relief and her response to the oxytocin infusion that Sandy had offered was rapid. Less than two hours later, she gave birth to a large baby boy who started crying loudly the moment Pippa lifted him up to put on his mother's chest.

'Sounds hungry already,' she said.

'Just like his father, then…' Helen reached to touch her baby but she was smiling up at Terry.

'He's beautiful,' Terry said, swiping tears off his face. 'Just like his mum.'

Pippa clamped the cord and showed Terry how to cut it. She did an Apgar score on the baby and recorded his weight and time of birth.

'He's looking very healthy,' she told the proud parents. 'Have you got a name for him yet?'

'Jack,' Terry said. 'After my dad.'

'One of my favourite names,' Pippa said.

'He's still crying,' Helen said, as she took the baby back into her arms. 'Can I try feeding him?'

'I was just about to suggest that. Look at the way he's turning his head...he's already trying to latch on himself. Put your hand behind his head and bring it up to your nipple and then wait until his mouth is really wide open—like a frog—and put in as much of the nipple as you can. Here... I'll help...'

Baby Jack was sucking within seconds, both parents mesmerised by his talent. It left Pippa free to monitor the third stage of labour, delivering the placenta and checking that it was intact. She had fifteen-minute observations to do on both mother and baby for the first hour after birth and, in that time, Pippa also stitched up the episiotomy that had prevented any serious tearing from the birth of a baby who weighed just over ten pounds.

'There you go, all done.' She smiled at the perfect picture of a brand-new family in front of her, the mother lying back in the circle of the father's arms, the baby asleep in *her* arms. 'I'll leave you in peace for a little while to get to know each other but I'll come back and check on you soon. Ring your bell if you need something before then.'

'Could I get this needle out of my hand before you go?' Helen asked. 'I don't need that infusion now, do I?'

'I'd like it to stay in a bit longer,' Pippa told her. 'But I'll unhook it from the tubing so it won't be such a nuisance.'

Lachlan Smythe leaned back in his chair and checked his watch.

Good grief...it was nearly midnight. It wasn't simply the time it had taken to fill the bookshelf with his textbooks and hang his framed degrees on the walls of his new office—there had been a glitch with getting access to the computer systems he needed and he didn't want to be waiting for someone from the IT department first thing tomorrow morning.

He wanted to hit the ground running. He'd learned, thanks to moving around so much, that it was the best way to get to know a new hospital and his new colleagues. It could make the first few days feel like navigating a professional minefield, for sure, but there was nothing like a good challenge to make you feel really alive, was there?

Lachlan loved his work as an obstetrician. He'd spent too many years letting his research work and teaching cut into the time he spent doing what he'd put so much passion into learning to do extremely well—helping people realise their dreams of creating their own families and keeping mothers and babies safe during the birthing process. Accepting this position at The Queen Mary Hospital was a step back to the work he loved the most and he couldn't wait to get started, but there was an unexpected tension to this particular appointment.

There was more to this than a purely professional

change in his life. He'd grown up here. Not just in London but *here*, in the heart of Richmond.

He glanced at the small photograph in a silver frame that had become a permanent desk ornament after so many years. An image of two adults and two small boys. His family. He'd been eight years old. His brother Liam had been five. They were grinning at each other, while their proud parents beamed at the camera above their heads. Lachlan loved this photo. Because this represented the happiest part of his life. Before any of them knew the horrors of what lay ahead for them all as a family.

Was the importance of this picture partly why he'd chosen to take this new position? Because the memories he knew he could only find in this tiny patch of the planet were the only links he had left to his family?

Maybe…

But professional considerations would, as always, take precedence over anything so personal and it was far too late to be here. If he didn't get a decent sleep he wouldn't be in top form for his first day on the job.

Lachlan left his office and walked towards the doors at the other end of the ward that led out to the elevators and stairwell. Unencumbered with boxes this time, he slowed as he passed the central hub of the ward with its reception desk, banks of computer screens, filing cabinets and the ubiquitous whiteboard.

The whiteboard that he'd seen that staff member standing in front of the last time he'd walked past. He had no idea who she was but she'd been wearing scrubs and a lanyard and was taking part in a shift handover so she had to be one of his new colleagues, but in that moment he'd turned his head she'd been looking directly at *him*.

Smiling at him.

As if she approved of what she was seeing?

It should have been somewhat disturbing but Lachlan decided that it had made him curious. Was she just a smiley sort of person? Maybe he'd get the chance to find out. He'd certainly recognise her easily again. Who wouldn't with that long braid of distinctively red hair?

There was a phone ringing on the desk. Lachlan slowed his pace as he realised there was no one here to answer it.

The area was deserted.

A quick scan of the whiteboard told him that there was an emergency Caesarean underway in Theatre One and that the rest of the staff were probably all occupied in the rooms of a very full ward. He saw the capital letters of the word BORN written across boxes in several different rooms, the most recent of which had been in Room Three.

The phone stopped and immediately began ringing again. He was about to answer it himself when he noticed a digital display beside the whiteboard light up, along with the sound of an alarm.

Room Three, it relayed. Code Red.

Code Red was an urgent call for medical assistance for a patient whose condition was rapidly deteriorating but wasn't yet in a cardiac or respiratory arrest, in which case a crash call would have been made. He wasn't familiar with the response to an alarm like this in The Queen Mary. Would available staff have been bleeped in other areas of the hospital? He couldn't see anyone emerging from rooms to get somewhere else in a hurry.

He was moving himself, however.

Where the hell was Room Three?

She'd been out of the room for less than fifteen minutes. Just long enough to do another set of reassuringly normal observations on Stella and point out that she hadn't had a contraction strong enough to show on the CTG in the last ninety minutes, have a quick bathroom break and scribble an update on the whiteboard to record the birth of a baby in Room Three.

Terry was holding his son as Pippa went back into their room. Helen was lying back on her pillows and she was looking…

…extremely unwell. She was very pale and was that a sheen of perspiration on her face?

'I'm so cold,' she said as soon as Pippa reached her bedside. 'And kind of dizzy. I think I'm going to be sick…'

Pippa grabbed a container and gave it to her. She put her fingers on Helen's wrist to find a pulse that was far too rapid. Her breathing was also rapid and yes…her skin was cool and clammy.

Pippa's own heart rate was increasing noticeably as she flicked back the bedcovers to see a bloodstain that was already large enough to be visible on either side of Helen's body and legs. The absorbent sheet beneath her hips was heavy enough to confirm a sudden, severe blood loss.

'Oh, my God,' Terry whispered. 'What's happening?'

A massive post-partum haemorrhage was what was happening but there was no time to try and explain in any detail right now.

'Helen's losing a bit of blood.'

A lot of blood. Quite possibly a life-threatening amount of blood.

Pippa reached to push the alarm button at the head of the bed to summon emergency assistance.

'I'm going to lie you flat, Helen, and put a mask on to

give you some oxygen. And then I'm going to take your blood pressure.'

'I'm scared,' Helen whispered.

'I know, sweetheart.' Pippa was careful to keep her tone calm and reassuring as she moved swiftly. She put a plastic mask over Helen's mouth and nose and turned on the wall supply of oxygen. She reattached the tubing to the IV line and rolled the small wheel to start fluids running again. Then she wrapped a blood pressure cuff around Helen's upper arm. 'Don't worry, we're going to get this sorted,' she said as she pushed a button to start an automatic blood pressure recording.

Pippa was thinking as fast as she was moving. She might have to push the cardiac arrest button to summon the kind of assistance she needed because she'd seen that both the consultant and registrar on duty in the ward tonight were in Theatre with an emergency C-section for a breech presentation baby that had decided to make an appearance earlier than expected.

'I'm going to start massaging your tummy again,' she warned Helen. 'It might be a bit uncomfortable but it looks like your uterus needs a bit more help to shrink properly.'

Helen cried out in pain as Pippa pressed down on the top of the uterus, which was still on the high side for someone who had just given birth. Terry made a distressed sound at the same time. He was pressed against the wall, almost as pale as Helen, clutching the bundle that was baby Jack, who let out his own whimper. The fresh absorbent sheet she had tucked under Helen's hips was already soaked with fresh blood.

Please, Pippa begged silently. *I need help...*

Even as the plea formed in her head, the door was opening…

She would have been happy to see anyone, but she was astonished to see the last person she could have imagined responding to this emergency call.

Lachlan Smythe?

CHAPTER TWO

LACHLAN BARELY REGISTERED that it was the staff member he'd been thinking about only minutes ago as he introduced himself to her—and the frightened-looking man holding a baby. His focus then shifted to the woman on the bed who looked as though her level of consciousness was dropping.

'What's happening?' he asked succinctly, as he rolled up the sleeves of his shirt, thrust his arms into a gown and pulled some gloves from the box on the wall.

The midwife—Pippa, according to her name badge—kept massaging the woman's uterus as she responded.

'PPH. Estimated blood loss at least six hundred mils. Last blood pressure was ninety-six over forty-eight. Heart rate one twenty-six. Pulse ox ninety-seven. Uterus was a bit slow to start contracting but there wasn't any sign of excessive bleeding in the first hour after birth.'

'Background?'

'Primigravida. Labour of more than twenty hours before she accepted any intervention. Large baby born just over an hour ago.'

Lachlan nodded at the information. A long labour and a large baby were both risk factors for a uterus that was simply unable to contract efficiently which was, by far, the most common cause for a post-partem haemorrhage. Trauma and retained tissue also had to be considered.

'Any tears?'

'No. She had an episiotomy that was straightforward to repair.'

'Was the placenta intact?'

'Yes. It's still here, if you want to check.'

He would, but not now. He moved to the wall phone and punched in a number. He needed to alert the blood bank that they might need to activate a massive transfusion protocol. In the meantime, he'd need units of whole blood, red blood cells and fresh, frozen plasma. He needed to get an operating theatre on standby in case they couldn't stop the bleeding with drug therapy and massage. He also needed more hands on deck. Pippa was clearly competent and managing an emergency situation impressively calmly but there was a lot that was about to happen. A physical examination of the patient. Drugs needed to be drawn up and administered. Blood samples taken. Constant monitoring of vital signs.

'When did the bleeding start?'

'Within the last twenty minutes. Sudden onset with pallor, diaphoresis and syncope.'

'Is that IV-line patent?'

'I think so.'

'Good. We'll need to get a type and crossmatch, stat. IV trolley?'

'Just there.' Pippa nodded towards the wall where the man was now holding a crying baby.

As Lachlan moved the trolley closer to the bed, he took a moment to reassure the man that they were doing what was needed to deal with this complication. As soon as more staff members arrived, he would designate someone to stay with him.

Right now, he had only the midwife Pippa to work with and he had to hope she was as good at her job as she appeared to be on first impressions.

She was taking another set of vital signs. 'Blood pressure's dropped to ninety over forty-five,' she told him quietly. 'And GCS is down to thirteen.'

A dropping level of consciousness took this to a new level of concern. Shock due to blood loss was the leading cause of maternal fatalities.

'We need another IV access,' he said, as he took a blood sample for a type and cross match and full blood count. 'This one's marginal.'

More staff arrived. Lachlan asked the midwife to take a set of vital signs every five minutes and to weigh the soaked absorbent sheets to get a more accurate estimate of blood loss. A support worker was dispatched to get the blood samples to the laboratory as quickly as possible and bring back the units of blood products and he asked Pippa to insert a Foley catheter to ensure that bladder distention wasn't contributing to the failure of the uterus to contract.

Lachlan tried, and failed, to get a cannula into a vein on Helen's hand. Worryingly, the IV line in her other hand looked as if it wasn't patent any longer.

Pippa saw that he was trying to find another palpable vein and handed him an alcohol wipe and then a cannula.

'Can't feel anything,' he said quietly. 'She's as flat as a pancake. I'll give it one more try, but then we'll look at an alternative.'

'A cut down?'

Lachlan shook his head. He was carefully changing direction and depth with the needle but there was no flashback to indicate he was anywhere near a blood vessel.

'Intra-osseus?' Pippa was opening a drawer on the IV trolley.

'No. I'll do an external jugular cannulation. More effective and we can use a larger gauge needle.' Lachlan gave up on the arm. 'Can someone give us a head down tilt for the bed, please, and, Pippa, let's take Helen's pillow away and could you turn her head to the side for me and help her keep as still as possible?'

Pippa was no stranger to high-intensity medical emergency situations although, fortunately, they didn't happen very often and very rarely with as dramatic a presentation as this massive blood loss.

There were more people arriving in the room now. She'd noticed when Terry and baby Jack had been ushered out to be cared for elsewhere and she'd seen the supplies of blood arriving. The on-duty consultant, Sandy, had come down from Theatre, having left her registrar to finish the final suturing after the C-section she had performed but she didn't take over Pippa's assistance for Lachlan. She stood to one side and double-checked that the placenta was intact and there was no retained tissue that could be causing the bleeding.

'You were right, Pippa,' she confirmed. 'I can't see anything missing.'

This wasn't the time but Pippa was aware that she would remember later that it felt good to have her skills recognised, even in a small way, in front of not only a new senior colleague but their incoming HoD. The only thing that mattered right now was doing everything they could to deal with the emergency and Pippa was completely focused on what she was being asked to do. She didn't want her part in this resuscitation to be found wanting in any way.

Sandy could have stepped in at that point and taken over Pippa's position but perhaps she wanted the opportunity to watch the way Lachlan Smythe was managing a life-or-death scenario.

It was quite likely, Pippa thought, that Sandy was just as impressed with his performance as she was herself.

He was so calm.

So in control.

And his clinical skills were faultless. He'd made the cannulation of the large neck vein, which wasn't exactly an everyday procedure, look very easy—even with Helen's low blood volume.

'Pop your finger on the vein for me, would you, Pippa?' The almost casual request had been the only indication that the task was challenging. 'Just above the clavicle. If you occlude it, I'll get a much better target.'

They had been working closely together with the cannulation of the external jugular vein and then the drawing up, checking and administration of more drugs. They were working fast and were close enough for their arms and hands to touch at times, but not because they were getting in each other's way. It felt seamless in fact, as if they'd worked together on many occasions over a long period and yet it had only been minutes since this emergency had unfolded.

It made Pippa remember, for just a heartbeat, that strange frisson when he'd first made eye contact with her. That notion that he'd recognised her. That maybe he knew more about her than she was comfortable with.

Lachlan just seemed quite comfortable as he gave

Helen a thorough physical examination to look for any hidden trauma that could be causing the bleeding. He nodded with satisfaction as he palpated her abdomen.

'Uterus is definitely firmer,' he said. 'We're going in the right direction.'

He looked up a short time later to catch Pippa's gaze as she was hanging another unit of blood onto the IV pole.

'Great suturing on that episiotomy,' he said. 'Very neatly done.'

The tension began to fade and Pippa focused on Helen, providing more reassurance as her blood pressure slowly came up enough for her to become more aware of what was happening around her.

'You're doing well,' she assured her, slipping a pillow beneath her head again. 'The bleeding's slowed right down and your blood pressure's coming up. You'll start feeling better very soon.'

'Where's my baby? Where's Jack?'

'Jack's been taken to the nursery so that he can be checked by a paediatrician and looked after until you feel better. Terry's with him. It's okay, Helen. It's all going to be fine.'

And it was. One by one, the extra staff in the room went back to other duties. The standby for Theatre was cancelled and the blood bank informed that the haemorrhage was under control and no further supplies were needed. The intensive care unit was contacted to arrange for Helen to be transferred to receive the intensive monitoring she would need for the next few hours until she could be admitted to a post-natal ward.

'I'll go with her,' Lachlan said. He stripped off his gloves and blood-spattered gown. 'I'd rather do the handover myself.'

Pippa found herself, for the second time tonight, watching this new staff member walk away. It was the middle of the night. Lachlan Smythe wasn't due to officially start work here yet until the morning. He could be going home to his own bed at this point but it felt as if that hadn't even occurred to him.

Yeah…his commitment to his work was definitely impressive.

Pippa was making a mental list of the immediate tasks she had ahead of her as she refocused on her own work. Room Three needed a thorough clean-up and Stella was overdue for her next set of observations. It was quite likely that there would be more deliveries that Pippa could assist with for the rest of this shift, but with a bit of luck she might soon be able to take the proper break she should have had a couple of hours ago.

Talk about jumping in at the deep end.

Lachlan had expected to meet his new colleagues in the controlled environment of a staff huddle and a quiet tour of all the wards that were part of his department. He needed to get familiar with the locations of the operating theatre suite and the outpatient department before his first lists started on his second day on the job and he was hoping for a bit of quiet time to get up to speed with any protocols that might well have been updated since he'd last worked in a UK hospital.

He'd found his way back to the labour ward easily enough after handing over Helen's care to the ICU staff and finding her husband, Terry, to tell him what had happened and reassure him that the emergency was over.

His head was spinning somewhat, in a combination of fatigue and the sense of displacement of being not only in a different work environment but in a different country than he had been only a matter of hours ago. The stress of unexpectedly being in control of a situation that could have ended very differently had been a curve ball, not to mention the number of new people he'd met, spoken to on the phone or worked with. He might have difficulty in remembering every name but he wasn't going to forget how impressed he'd been with the systems in place and such an efficient response from everybody involved, given the time of night and low staffing thresholds.

He certainly wasn't going to forget the person he'd worked most closely with, who'd been the first to start dealing with what was an alarming adverse event that could make even the most experienced medics feel more than a beat of panic.

That midwife.

Pippa.

He didn't know her last name yet, but he fully intended to compliment her on her skills and thank her for her assistance before he went home to try and snatch a few hours' sleep. She'd been brilliant to work with.

Outstanding, in fact.

She'd been doing all the right things before he'd arrived and then she'd simply slotted in to work with him as if she was totally in sync with the way he worked. As if she was familiar with the way he thought, even. She was calm under pressure and clearly experienced. If he had to guess—although he usually avoided guessing ages when it came to women—he'd put her in her mid-thirties. Was she one of those heroic women who were busy raising their children but still holding down what could be a challenging career? Did she have a supportive husband, perhaps? And a beloved family dog who would be overjoyed to see her arriving home after a long night shift?

Just why he was so curious was too difficult to fathom, probably due to the fuzzy edges that fatigue was giving his thoughts. Maybe that was why he was standing, staring blankly at the whiteboard in the central area of the labour ward. Pippa's name was beside the line for Room Six and the last update had put its occupant into the transitional stage so she was probably busy ushering another new life into the world.

He should go home.

But was it worth it? It wasn't just the travel time, including quite a long walk to the staff parking area. He hadn't unpacked anything in the apartment he'd taken on a short-term lease before he'd decided the priority should be to sort out his office. There was no linen on his bed or towels in the bathroom. He might be able to unearth a mug but he hadn't been to a supermarket yet either, so there was no coffee or milk in the fridge. This was, in fact, one of the very rare occasions when he had to wonder if work should always take priority over his personal life.

'It's Mr Smythe, isn't it?' The ward receptionist looked away from the computer screen in front of her. 'Can I help with anything?'

He read her name badge. 'Thanks, Rita,' he said. 'And please call me Lachlan. Tell me, what's the morning traffic like these days, coming here from Notting Hill? I've been away from London for a few years now.'

Rita looked to be in her fifties and had a welcoming,

motherly vibe that was no doubt much appreciated by stressed young couples arriving to face a major event in their lives. She wasn't looking very reassuring now, however.

'Awful,' she said. 'It would take you a good thirty minutes at this time of night with no real traffic and in rush hour…goodness me, I'd be leaving at least an hour before I wanted to be here. Ninety minutes, even.'

'I thought that might be the case. Maybe I'll just stay here and find some coffee or a comfortable chair for a snooze. I'd rather like an early start and to be here for the shift changeover. Great way to get the feel of a new hospital.'

'We do have some on-call bedrooms near the staffroom, if you want to be really comfortable—on the other side of the corridor where your office is. They get booked by the registrars on call but I could check to see if there are any available?'

'Thanks, but I have a splinter skill I learned as a junior doctor of being able to sleep just about anywhere for short periods of time. If I can find a hot shower later, I'll survive until day's end.' He smiled at Rita. 'It's my own fault. I should have been home many hours ago.'

'Just as well you weren't, from what I heard,' Rita said. She smiled back at him. 'Welcome to Queen Mary's, Lachlan. You know how to make an entrance, that's for sure. There are some nice squashy armchairs in the staffroom. I've fallen asleep in them myself at times. The coffee's not bad and there's always plenty of toast. The showers in the locker rooms are good. At least they are on the women's side. Can't say I've tested the men's showers.'

'I'll let you know, for future reference.' Lachlan turned

away, laughing. 'I'll go and find some of that coffee. And toast. I've just realised I forgot to have any dinner. Oh... if you see Pippa and she's got a free minute, can you tell her where I am? I'd like to talk to her.'

'He wants to talk to me?' Pippa had just written BORN across the status box on the whiteboard for Room Six. She turned to frown at Rita. 'Why?'

'He didn't say. But he did say that he was living in Notting Hill.' Rita raised her eyebrows. 'That's rather posh, isn't it?'

'People might say that about me, living in central Richmond, but I can assure you that my rented cottage that's about the same size as a postage stamp is very far from posh. What else did he say?'

'That he wasn't going home. He's going to stay here and eat toast and drink coffee and then have a shower and be here for the shift changeover at seven-thirty a.m.' Rita blew out a breath. 'Have you ever met a new consultant who's quite so...hands-on?'

'No...but at least he seems to know what he's doing.' Pippa had an image of those hands right now. Moving confidently and swiftly to perform the fine motor skills of using a single finger to occlude a vein at the same time as removing a needle from a cannula, screwing a plug into place and attaching the tubing of an IV giving set.

'I am overdue for a break,' she added. 'Guess I could go and have a coffee and see what he wants to talk to me about. You'll know where I am if anyone needs me.'

Pippa hoped her sudden nervousness wasn't showing. She could feel her heart racing and it felt like an effort to suck in a new breath. Had she done something wrong earlier? Maybe she had underestimated how boggy Helen's uterus had been post-delivery but she hadn't been bleeding unduly and it hadn't been painful to have her tummy massaged. It had definitely begun contracting before she'd left her alone in the room.

Her heart sank like a stone at the sudden thought that he might, instead, want to tell her that Helen's condition had deteriorated again and that baby Jack was in danger of losing his mother.

No…she might have only met this man a few hours ago but she was absolutely certain that if he had any involvement at all with a patient who was in trouble he wouldn't be in the staffroom drinking coffee and eating toast.

The thought of toast made a knot form in her stomach. Or was that due to her nerves? She didn't think she'd done anything wrong. She'd delivered two healthy babies. Helen's emergency had been successfully dealt with without her needing to go to Theatre. Stella was peacefully asleep now and it looked as if the scare she'd had for her pregnancy might be over.

Maybe she was nervous for a reason that had nothing to do with anything professional. There was something about this man that was…a little unsettling, that was what it was.

Or… Pippa stifled a yawn. Perhaps she was just tired. And hungry.

At three-thirty a.m. she would have expected to find a few weary-looking staff members taking a break, but the only person in the room was Lachlan. He had a newspaper open in front of him on the central table and he put down a half-empty cup of coffee with a grimace.

'Coffee's great when it's hot,' he said. 'And revolting when it's cold.' He smiled at Pippa. 'That'll teach me for getting stuck on a crossword puzzle.'

Oh, my...

That was a real smile. One that reached his eyes enough to crinkle the corners. Eyes that were almost as dark as her own, but they weren't brown. Even in this light, she could see that they were blue. His hair was brown, though. Brown and wavy and soft looking.

He wasn't just attractive, she realised. He was...absolutely gorgeous.

And that knot in her stomach had just sent off a volley of sparks that were travelling through her body at the speed of light. Oh, help...*she* was attracted to him.

Hastily, she looked away. She stepped away even, heading for the bench.

'Rita said you wanted to talk to me?'

He sounded as if he was still smiling. 'I did. I just wanted to tell you how well you managed that emergency with Helen. If the other staff members in this department are half as good at their jobs as you are, I'm going to enjoy working here very much.'

'Oh...' Pippa could feel her cheeks going pink, which was never the best look for a redhead. 'Thank you.' She felt too shy to tell him that she'd been just as impressed with him. 'I'm going to make myself a cup of coffee,' she said instead. 'I can top yours up for you if you like?'

'It's okay. I suspect I've had more than enough caffeine.'

Pippa opened the bag of sliced white bread on the bench and then went to the fridge to get out some butter and a block of cheese. She flicked on the sandwich maker.

'Can I interest you in a cheese toastie instead?'

'Now you're talking...'

Oh-h... The approval in his voice was a verbal caress. Pippa took extra care to butter the bread right to the edges and fill the sandwich with extra cheese so it would turn out to be crispy and brown and irresistibly delicious. She wanted to give him that pleasure. And she wanted to see the expression on his face when he took that first bite.

She closed the top of the sandwich maker and clipped it shut. It might be a good idea to shut off the direction her thoughts wanted to go in as well.

'Have you had an update on Helen?' she asked.

'She's doing well. No signs of any further excessive bleeding, but they'll keep her in ICU until they're sure she's not going to have any complications from the aggressive fluid replacement. Terry's with her. Jack's being looked after in the special care baby unit but he's fine.'

Pippa risked a sideways glance. She couldn't help it when she could hear the smile in his voice again. She wanted to see it as well.

'They've got you to thank for a happy outcome,' Lachlan said quietly. 'If she'd been left much longer with a bleed like that, it could have been a very different story, so thank you.'

'I think the fact that you were still in the building was what made the real difference,' Pippa said. 'I have to say I was very surprised to see you come through the door. And relieved, I have to confess. It was a scary situation.'

'Intense,' Lachlan agreed. 'Bit of a trial by fire in getting to know a new colleague, yes?'

'Yes…' Pippa lifted the fragrant toastie from the machine to a plate and opened a drawer to find a knife. 'Speaking of fire, we'll need to wait a few minutes to eat this. It'll be like molten lava in the middle.'

'Good. Maybe you can help me with the crossword clue I'm stuck on while we wait.'

'Sure.' Pippa sat down opposite him. 'Shoot.'

'Six letters, a U in the middle and a D at the end. Clue is "Succinct description of an old woman who lived in a form of footwear".'

'The one who lived in a shoe? Who had so many children she didn't know what to do?'

'That's the one.'

Pippa laughed. 'Stupid?' she suggested.

She was still laughing as she watched the smile on his face turning into a grin and then heard his own rumble of laughter. It was a rather delicious sound.

Even better, *she'd* made him laugh. How good was that?

Too good.

She could feel those sparks again. Not just in her body—it felt as if the air was thick with them. They were settling on her skin and getting caught in her hair. She was breathing them in. She could taste them on her tongue and they were just as delicious as the sound of his laughter.

The strident sound of her pager beeping had never been so welcome.

Lachlan Smythe was her new boss. He might not be wearing a ring but that was no guarantee he was single.

Two red flags.

He was also a *doctor*, for heaven's sake.

Pippa should know better.

She *did* know better.

'Gotta go,' she said, reading her pager. 'New human arriving.'

'But you haven't had any of your sandwich.'

'It's all yours.' Pippa was on her feet and turning towards the door. The sooner she put some distance between herself and Lachlan, the better. 'Consider it a welcome gift. Enjoy...'

She walked away without looking back.

CHAPTER THREE

Fecund.

The answer to that crossword clue should have been instantly obvious to an obstetrician.

But, deep down, he was delighted that he'd missed it. Because Philippa Gordon—he'd learnt her full name in a departmental meeting this afternoon—had made him laugh.

He liked her.

He really liked her.

But beneath that humour was something that felt even more of a connection. Wasn't there a proverb about many a true word being spoken in jest? Was Pippa, like him, working with babies because she loved them but she didn't want—or couldn't have—her own?

Whatever.

It was none of his business.

He hadn't seen her since the day shift had come on board after the night of that dramatic post-partum haemorrhage and she'd gone home for some well-deserved sleep, and he hadn't given her a second thought throughout the busyness of his first official day as the new head of obstetrics at The Queen Mary.

He found himself thinking about her again that evening, however, when he was finally in his apartment, making up his bed. Counting down the minutes until his head could hit the pillow because he was quite ready to sleep the clock around after such a full-on start to his new position.

A trial by fire, indeed, as he'd said to Pippa.

And that was kind of an appropriate turn of phrase, given the colour of her hair. Long hair. Tightly wound into a braid. What did it look like when it was unravelled? Was it straight or wavy? He was sure it would feel soft. Silky…

Lachlan shook his head as if it would be enough to shake off a disturbingly inappropriate direction for his thoughts to be going in. He went into his bathroom and turned the shower on. Briefly, he considered turning the temperature control to cold in the hope that this could be doused.

This…*attraction*.

It had been there from the first moment he'd laid eyes on her. It had been simmering in the background and easily ignored when he'd been working so closely with her but…oh, man…when she'd made him laugh, it had suddenly exploded into something that was new territory for Lachlan. He'd never been this attracted, this quickly, to anyone since he'd been a teenager and hadn't yet learned that it was better for everybody involved to keep a tight control of that kind of thing. Otherwise, you were playing with fire, and it was inevitable that someone would get burned.

Thoughts of flames seemed to be a recurring theme around this woman and Lachlan thought he knew why. It was because the heat they produced could be dangerous unless very well controlled and Lachlan's interactions with women were always very well controlled. It wasn't that he didn't enjoy female company or appreciate having a healthy sex life. Not at all! He loved women as much as he loved babies. He enjoyed the familiar sensations of a physical attraction and the building of a friendship that could include the pleasure of sex. Under controlled conditions, of course. There were boundaries that would never be crossed and if that wasn't understood and accepted right from the start then the attraction would never go any further.

But this felt different.

So different, it was like nothing Lachlan had ever experienced before.

This one was fierce enough to be a warning he couldn't ignore and he would be well advised to back away.

Fast.

Heads of departments didn't do Queen Mary's twelve-hour night shifts that ran from seven-thirty p.m. to seven-thirty a.m. so it was no surprise that Pippa's path did not cross with that of Lachlan Smythe for the rest of that week.

It should have made it so much easier to deal with that unusual level of attraction to a man she'd only just met and knew nothing about. Her boss, no less. She needed to parcel it up and put it where it belonged—well away from her professional life. Given that it was a strong enough feeling to make a shiny thing she would be better not to even consider playing with, she needed to keep it away from her personal life as well.

It was making it far less easy that she continued to be too aware of his appearance in her world and to be learning things about him despite not having sought the information. The hospital grapevine was humming with reports of the most recent senior appointment. Conclusions were being drawn and opinions whispered and Pippa had heard far too many of them for comfort. It was impossible not to hear them on a quieter night shift.

Have you seen the new HoD of Obstetrics? Phew... he's a bit of all right, isn't he?

Someone who's seen his CV says he's single, but he's forty years old so he must be divorced. Nobody's heard of an ex-wife, though. Or any kids.

Maybe he's gay.

He was born and bred in London but he's got seriously itchy feet. He's lived in the USA, Australia, Canada and Switzerland.

He got into ocean swimming in Australia to keep fit. He's been asking about good places to go wild swimming around London.

Wild? As in naked? Hahaha... I'm in...

He's very, very good at his job. He hadn't even officially started work here but he virtually single-handedly saved the life of a first-time mother who could have bled out.

That snippet had made Pippa shake her head. Not that she was about to add her two cents' worth and remind people that she had been there as well, along with a cast of many others, including some unseen but crucial staff members in places like the blood bank.

But others had made her curious.

Why was he single?

Why did he keep moving? Not just hospitals or cities but whole countries? Continents, even. Was he running away from something? Or some*one*?

And...*did* he ever swim naked?

By the time she'd finished the week on nights that, fortunately, she didn't need to do very often, the grapevine had the new topic of a juicy scandal involving a married cardiologist and a young technician from the catheter laboratory. Pippa made a considerable effort to ignore any details about that development and the unwelcome trips down memory lane they could push her into, but on day shifts there was far more distraction available and it was relatively easy to avoid company in the staffroom or cafeteria, where that kind of gossip was most likely to be shared.

Maybe she should have tried harder to avoid the information she seemed to have gathered about Lachlan Smythe, but that was partly human nature at work, wasn't it? Toying with attraction was more than pleasant. Her personal memory lane was rather too full of painful potholes. It was so much easier to swerve the prospect of pain than deny yourself a flash of pleasure.

While it would be relatively simple to avoid gossip during a day shift, Pippa knew it would be more likely that she would have to interact with their new HoD. There were complications in childbirth that demanded the attention of someone more highly qualified than she was as a midwife. An awkward presentation, perhaps, or a multiple birth or a baby in distress. An instrumental or surgical delivery was always in the hands of an obstetrician and, of course, there were ward rounds, outpatient clinics and just…being in the same workspace.

Pippa was, however, confident that the odds of Lachlan being the senior staff member she worked with more than any others were low and, even if she did find herself working in close proximity to him, she was just as confident that any personal attraction would not undermine her ability to do her job well. That the winds of fate were providing a test for her resolve on her first morning back on day shift was a little disconcerting but it was a good thing, Pippa decided, as she began to prepare a nervous woman for an elective C-section on the only day of the week that Mr Smythe had a full theatre list.

She would start as she intended to continue.

Completely focused.

Without revealing the slightest hint that there could be any less than professional thoughts in her head. Hopefully, those weird sparks would have burned themselves out by now.

It would be no different than it was to work with the anaesthetist, Peter, who came in to administer the spinal anaesthetic.

'So this is Kate Mulligan,' she told him, turning the wrist ID for Peter to check for himself. 'She's thirty-two and is thirty-eight weeks pregnant. She's in for an elective C-section this morning due to a Grade Two placenta previa that has a margin of less than two centimetres from the cervical os.'

'Hi, Kate, I'm Peter. I'll be giving you your spinal anaesthetic and looking after you in Theatre. How are you feeling this morning?'

'Terrified,' Kate admitted.

'I can give you something to help with that,' Peter said. He smiled at Pippa. 'Can you draw up a dose of midazolam for me, please? We'll let that take effect before we get started.'

Pippa had worked with Peter on many occasions over the years she'd been at Queen Mary's. He was a perfectly nice guy but there had never been any sparks between them. She would channel this feeling of professional ease when she got to Theatre.

She supported Kate as the cannula was inserted into her back and the medication delivered to provide complete anaesthesia from the waist down. She helped her into a theatre gown, took off her nail polish and put tape over the rings she was wearing. She took another set of vital signs on Kate and printed a strip of the CTG recording on her baby.

'You're going to meet your daughter very soon,' she said. 'How exciting is that?'

It was Pippa's job to take the CTG machine up to Theatre and go through the pre-operative checklist with the theatre staff. Both Kate's husband and Pippa needed to get dressed to be in the operating room during the surgery. Covered from the hat over her hair to the disposable booties on her feet, Pippa suddenly felt almost as relaxed as Kate was, thanks to her medication. She was completely disguised. The surgeon about to come in from the scrub room would probably not even recognise her, especially as she stood back then, with no further responsibilities until the baby was delivered and handed into her care.

That feeling of protection lasted as Lachlan came in with his registrar, chatted to Kate for a moment, on the other side of the drapes pinned up as a screen, and then positioned himself to begin the surgery.

'All set?' He actually had the scalpel in his hand and was poised to make the first incision as his glance raked the staff around him.

Pippa could hear the murmur of assent but didn't make a sound herself. Lachlan's gaze had only grazed hers for a microsecond but she knew he had not only recognised her, he was pleased to see her.

And dammit...she had to stand here, outside of the

sterile field, and feel the sparkle that was still there. Increased, if anything, by observing not only Lachlan's surgical skills but the way he interacted with both his team and his patient.

'Are you ready, Kate? We're going to take the drapes down so you can see your baby being born.'

'I…think so… I won't be able to see too much though, will I?'

'No. Your tummy is hiding all the gruesome bits, I promise. I'm going to lift her out and, if she doesn't need any extra help, we'll put her straight onto your chest and wait a minute or two to cut the cord. Okay?'

Kate's response was more like a sob. 'Okay…'

Pippa was standing close now, with a sterile towel across her hands. If the baby needed resuscitation, she would be put onto the towel rather than going straight to the skin-to-skin contact with her mother. Pippa would take her to the heated cocoon of the resuscitation unit to one side of the room, to do the first Apgar score and get her dry and warm. They had a paediatrician on standby if they were needed.

But this baby opened her mouth and gave her first cry the moment she was eased out of the womb. Lachlan handled the slippery little bundle with great care as the nurses lowered the drapes and he carried the baby to lay her gently onto Kate's chest. Pippa stepped in so that she could cover the baby with a towel to help keep her warm and do the first Apgar score and for just for a heartbeat, as he lowered the baby, her gaze caught Lachlan's. Being so much closer this time, she could see the crinkles at the corners of his eyes and the warmth that made them such an incredibly dark blue.

He was happy, she realised. Not because someone had

made him laugh this time, but because he was holding a new, precious baby in his hands that he'd helped arrive safely in the world. She knew that happiness. It filled her own heart every time. It was the best of moments and it was what had kept her in this job because it never failed to balance the worst of moments, even if it couldn't eliminate them.

This connection, on what was both a professional and personal level, was exactly what Pippa had needed. It made the nuisance of navigating unwanted sparks worthwhile. She could respect this man. Even better, she could appreciate working with him instead of hoping to avoid it and, on a purely instinctive level, she was quite sure that she could trust him.

It should have worn off by now.

Lachlan had been in his new job for nearly three weeks now. He could find his way around The Queen Mary with no difficulties at all. He was familiar with most of his new colleagues and quite comfortable running his departmental meetings and liaising with other Heads of Departments. He was enjoying the clinical work and loving being back in his hometown. So much so that he was stopping on his way home to have a look at a property on the market in Richmond because he was already sick of getting stuck in rush-hour traffic at both ends of his working days.

It was the only real fly in the ointment of this decision to come back to the UK.

Although he was also slightly disappointed that ignoring the unusual level of attraction he felt towards Pippa Gordon wasn't making it vanish as quickly as he'd anticipated.

It didn't help that he seemed to see her more often than any of the other midwives who worked in and around the birthing suite. And he didn't just see her. He worked with her. A lot. How was it that she seemed to be present almost every time he did a C-section—elective or emergent? And yes, as such an experienced midwife, she was going to be given the more high-risk mothers to care for, but she seemed to get more than her share of births that needed obstetrical assistance. He'd even spoken to her in the outpatient department this afternoon.

Okay…that had been his choice. But he'd known she was working in the antenatal clinic and that she'd want to know the results of the latest reassurance scan on Stella.

'Her Braxton Hicks contractions have settled to completely normal levels and everything else is looking good. She's still a bit anxious, but getting past the twenty-four-week mark and knowing that the baby is viable has been a real boost.'

'I know, I saw her in the waiting room. She's so much happier. Getting well past the stage that she had lost her first baby has been a big help. She's not going to stop being anxious, but she did say that she was going to go and buy a Moses basket when she gets to twenty-eight weeks and I know what a big deal that is for her.'

'She mentioned you in her appointment with me. Said that you were the best possible person who could have looked after her that night she got admitted. That you really seemed to understand what she was going through.'

Pippa seemed to appreciate the feedback. They'd shared a smile, nothing more.

It had been a purely professional interaction. So why was he thinking of her as he headed away from work? And when the attractive estate agent was giving him signals of being interested in more than selling him this property?

'It's a stunning property,' he told her.

It was. A detached Edwardian house that was almost spitting distance to Marble Hill Park, with an upstairs view across the Thames to the huge expanse of Richmond Park.

'I think four bedrooms might be a little too big for me, though,' he added.

Why was he even looking at a family home?

Especially one that had a view to Richmond Park. He'd learned to ride his bike on the green spaces and pathways of that park. He'd helped his beloved younger brother Liam to get good enough to ditch his training wheels before he even started school.

Before the first signs of possibly the most heartbreaking type of the hereditary disease of Huntington's—the rare juvenile form that would slowly but inexorably destroy and then finally take his life when he was only fifteen.

But the tragedy of the disease and how it had affected the whole family hadn't been the first thing he'd thought of when he'd noticed the view, had it? It had been a happy memory of racing each other on their bikes. Of the triumphant smile on Liam's face when Lachlan had let him win. Of the family picnic they'd been having that day. While still incredibly poignant, he could feel the notes of joy in that memory and that was…priceless.

He'd only been half-listening to what the estate agent was saying about getting a feel for the market and how this was the most exceptional property she'd seen in a long time.

'I'll contact you if anything smaller comes up for sale,' she said finally. 'Check out the area while you're here, though. It's got a lot going for it. There's a fabulous pub just a few blocks away. And a shopping precinct that's got a good supermarket.'

Lachlan did check it out. Not the pub, but he did need some groceries and the local supermarket was one he liked for its ready-made meals that only needed a few minutes in the microwave to taste like home cooking.

He was heading from the frozen food section to the checkout when he rounded a corner and came too close to crashing his trolley into someone else's.

'I'm so sorry,' he said. 'I wasn't paying attention.'

'That's not like you.'

His head jerked up at hearing a voice he recognised instantly.

'Pippa! What on earth are you doing here?'

She was smiling at him. 'Exactly what *you're* doing. Except…' She glanced into his trolley. 'I do tend to buy things that need cooking.'

Yes. Her trolley was full of fresh vegetables like tomatoes and garlic and spinach. She had fresh pasta as well. Olive oil and Parmesan cheese.

Lachlan was a big fan of Italian food.

She was wearing jeans. And a top that was a pretty shade of yellow. And her hair was loose, flowing down her back like a silky curtain. It was straight.

Lachlan was a big fan of straight, silky hair. Especially when it was hanging loose.

'And I live around here,' Pippa added. 'I thought you lived in Notting Hill?'

'How did you know that?'

'Ah…'

Lachlan saw the pink flush in her cheeks. Why was

she embarrassed? Because she'd obviously been talking about him?

Because...she was also feeling that static electricity sensation that happened to him whenever he was too close to her?

It was stronger than ever right now. Because they weren't at work. This wasn't, in any way, a professional encounter but he didn't want it to become awkward.

'I was looking at a house for sale,' he told her. 'I'm hoping to live a bit closer to work myself. The estate agent told me to check the area out on my way home. She said there's a great pub nearby.'

'The one on the other side of the supermarket car park? The White Swan?'

'That's the one. Is it as good as I'm told?'

'I've never been.' Pippa shrugged. 'I don't tend to go into pubs by myself.'

She was by herself? *Single?*

'Neither do I,' he said.

Lachlan could hear a voice in the back of his head.

No... Don't do it. Do. Not. Do. It.

He ignored the directive.

'You wouldn't have the time to pop in with me now, by any chance, would you? That would mean we could both find out whether it's any good without looking like dodgy characters who like to drink alone.'

His invitation hung in the air between them for a split second. Long enough for Lachlan to wish he'd kept his mouth shut. Oh, help...did Pippa think he was hitting on her?

Was he hitting on her?

He was just about to open his mouth again and give them both an easy way out by telling her he'd actually remembered a prior engagement, but she beat him to saying anything.

'Why not?' Her tone made it a perfectly reasonable suggestion. One with no strings attached. 'I've always wondered what it's like inside.'

Lachlan had lost the slightest inclination to withdraw his suggestion. He was, in fact, feeling delighted. He didn't care that his smile probably looked more like a grin.

'I'll meet you on the other side of the checkout.'

CHAPTER FOUR

It was everything you could want in a traditional English pub.

Hanging baskets full of bright flowers outside, the gleam of polished wood on the bar and tables inside. Old copper pots, kettles and vintage lanterns dangled from the beams and there were horse brasses and faded oil paintings on the walls.

It was cluttered and cosy and comfortable. Popular enough in this after work time slot for the available seating to look limited.

Lachlan let go of the heavy door he'd held open for Pippa. 'Why don't you see if you can find us a seat?' he suggested. 'What can I get you to drink?'

Pippa met his gaze. She wasn't sure she should be here at all, let alone having a drink with her new boss. This was starting to feel too much like a date. But that tingle in her gut was telling her that she would be an idiot to walk away, so she shrugged instead.

'Ah, why not?' she said. 'I'm walking home. A glass of prosecco would be lovely.'

'I might join you.' Lachlan grinned. 'Just for one. Although, with the traffic out there, I won't be driving any more than a walking pace, anyway.'

Pippa moved off as she spotted people getting up

to leave a table near the fireplace. Not that it was cold enough to warrant an open fire, but the flicker of flames certainly added to the welcoming ambience. It also made her think of that warning not to play with fire.

Was that what she was doing, spending time with Lachlan that had nothing to do with anything professional?

He didn't seem to be worried about it. 'This is nice,' he said as he came to the table with two flutes of fizzy wine. 'It's a long time since I've been in a pub. Or even out with a colleague. I have a bad habit of making friends and then changing jobs and countries and leaving them all behind.'

Was he thinking he might become friends with her?

Would she want to be friends with him?

It was worth consideration. Being friends, with the definite boundaries that automatically imposed, might defuse an attraction that could be a nuisance. Or would spending time with him like this make it worse? It didn't seem to be having that effect right now. Pippa was interested in learning more about him, not imagining what it might be like to be kissed by him.

Well…okay…maybe that *was* hovering in the back of her mind.

She hastily lifted her glass for a first sip of her wine.

'I did hear that you moved around a lot,' she said. 'Where were you before you came to Queen Mary's? Somewhere in the States?'

'Johns Hopkins. In Baltimore, Maryland. It's a general hospital that's got a great focus on teaching and research.'

'It's one of the world's most famous hospitals. I have heard of it.' Pippa laughed. 'I've heard of Washington DC as well. That's part of Maryland, isn't it?'

'Next door neighbour. DC stands for District of Columbia. It's not a state and doesn't belong to any state. Cool place to visit. Have you been there?'

'I haven't been out of the UK in years. Haven't changed my job, either. Maybe I'm not as adventurous as you are.'

'I love new challenges,' Lachlan admitted. 'And fresh starts. Arriving somewhere with no baggage, other than what I put my clothes and books in.'

'So you travel alone?' Pippa hastily reached for her glass to take another sip of her drink. That was a rather personal question, wasn't it? She risked a quick glance and found that he was watching her.

'Always.' He lifted an eyebrow. 'How 'bout you?'

'If I was going to travel it would definitely be alone,' she agreed.

Lachlan's other eyebrow rose as well. 'You sound very sure about that.'

'I'm sure about many things.'

Lachlan laughed. 'Good for you.'

It was the second time she'd made him laugh and it felt even better than the first time. This was like a compliment—as if he approved of her being so sure of her own mind.

'So you live around here?'

'How did you know that?' She was deliberately repeating the question he'd disarmed her with earlier, but the curl of his mouth told her he knew exactly what she was doing and he wasn't remotely embarrassed.

'Because you told me you were walking,' he reminded her. 'And in the supermarket I do believe you said "I live around here".' His eyebrows rose and his glance was suddenly noticeably more intense. 'How did you know where *I* lived?'

'The grapevine,' she muttered. 'Not that I normally pay any attention to gossip but...you did create a bit of a buzz when you arrived. Especially after riding in on your white horse and saving a life before you were even officially on duty.'

'*We* saved a life,' he said firmly. He took a longer sip of wine. 'So...what else were people saying about me?'

'Only good stuff. How well respected you are in your field. Some people wondered what made you come back here. Especially to Richmond, when you could have got a job at another world-famous hospital like Guy's or Great Ormond Street.'

'I grew up here,' Lachlan told her. 'Learned to ride a bike in Richmond Park. Were they saying anything else I should know about?'

Pippa had had just enough wine to make her feel ever so slightly mischievous. 'I did pick up on the rumour that you didn't seem to have a wife. Or kids.'

Lachlan's face stilled and Pippa would have decided that she'd overstepped a boundary but his gaze was steady.

'No,' he said. He held her gaze even longer. 'How 'bout you?'

'No,' she replied, using the same tone he had—as if it was no big deal or wasn't up for discussion. But then she felt guilty because she'd been the one to step onto such personal ground. 'Been there, done that,' she said. 'Wouldn't recommend it.'

'You've been married?'

'Just the once.' It was time to lighten the atmosphere, Pippa decided. 'He decided to upgrade.' She kept her tone and expression deadpan. 'To an obstetrician.'

Lachlan grimaced. 'I apologise on behalf of my specialty,' he said.

Pippa snorted. 'He was a cardiologist.'

Lachlan was just as deadpan as she had been. 'In that case, I apologise on behalf of my gender. Possibly all of mankind.'

It was genuine laughter this time and Pippa remembered just how sexy it was for a man to be able to make you laugh.

They both sat in a companionable silence then, finishing their drinks. It was Lachlan who broke it.

'This really has been nice,' he said.

'It has,' Pippa agreed. Too nice. Lachlan was intelligent, easy on the eye, easy to talk to and he'd made her laugh. What more could any girl ask for?

'Can we do it again some time?'

It was Pippa who caught and held *his* gaze this time and she knew it was a very direct look. She had felt the muscles around her eyes emphasising the focus. She might as well have had a speech bubble above her head like a cartoon character.

'I'm not hitting on you,' he said. 'I like your company and...' if she wasn't mistaken, there was a mischievous glint in his eyes now '...I'm the new boy at school, you know? It's good to make friends.'

Pippa shook her head but she was smiling. Lachlan dropped his gaze to the bags of groceries she had beside her chair.

'Are you sure you want to walk? I could give you a lift.'

'I'm sure,' Pippa said. She got to her feet and bent to pick up the bags. 'Thanks for the drink, Lachlan. Maybe I'll see you at work tomorrow?'

'You will. And you're welcome. You didn't answer my question, though.'

Pippa's expression was intended to suggest careful thought. 'I'll check the rule book,' she said. 'Just in case there's some fine print about drinking prosecco with your boss.'

'You have a rule book?'

'Of course. Don't you?'

'Are we talking professional or personal?'

'Both,' Pippa said. 'And in this instance the rules could be in two different sections.'

The way Lachlan lifted his eyebrows was a mix of surprise and genuine interest. 'Which are?'

'Professional relationships,' Pippa said. 'And…dating.'

'Ah…'

Oh, help…why had she got carried away enough with this idea of a rule book that she'd said that out loud? Now they were both thinking of being in each other's company when it could be more than simply two colleagues bumping into each other away from work.

And for her, at least, the prospect was a little too enticing for comfort. Pippa turned away with a shake of her head, as if she was dismissing an inappropriate suggestion.

But she could hear him speaking quietly behind her as she walked away.

'It's your book,' he said. 'And I get the feeling that it's you that makes the rules.'

The knowledge that Pippa Gordon's husband had left her for another woman was a snippet of gossip that Lachlan would have ignored if he'd heard it from anyone else. He might not have even believed it, in fact. For heaven's sake, the woman was gorgeous. Competent. Funny. And she could, presumably, cook Italian food. What had the guy been thinking?

He found himself wondering how long they had been married for. Long enough for her to be so devastated she had no intention of trying the state of matrimony ever again, anyway. She must have been very deeply in love, Lachlan decided.

Weirdly, even though he had no intention of ever getting married himself, he felt jealous of the guy.

He hadn't been averse to marriage.

And Pippa had chosen him.

He only saw her in passing the next day, but there was something different about the way she smiled after they exchanged greetings.

They had met each other outside of work hours and their shared workspace, which had opened a door into something different, and spending even a short time together had been...nice.

Very nice.

They had a great basis for friendship. A connection in a shared career that would never leave them short of something interesting to talk about but, more importantly, they had made each other laugh about things that had nothing to do with work. About that stupid crossword clue and him offering an apology on behalf of every person on earth that shared his gender.

He loved having made her laugh.

It wasn't that often that someone made him laugh with such genuine amusement.

Didn't that make them halfway to being friends already?

Lachlan hoped so. He thoroughly enjoyed the company of women and it was very hard to have a genuine friendship with someone of the opposite sex without courting expectations.

He liked Pippa. He liked that she was confident enough to make her own rules.

He had his own rules about relationships and dating that were clearly stricter than Pippa's, given that she had been married, but he'd like to hear more about hers and ask which ones she found worked especially well. Who wasn't up for a bit of self-improvement, after all?

He didn't ask, of course. But he did appreciate the occasions their paths crossed, even if it was simply in the corridor or an outpatient clinic. Working together in Theatre or on the ward was a bonus.

He liked the way she was with the women she was supporting in labour—encouraging and appreciative of their efforts, she knew how far to push them but also had a good instinct for a woman or baby who was getting into difficulties. He had only been working here for a short time but he knew that if it was Pippa calling for assistance it was very unlikely to be a false alarm.

Not that he immediately knew it was Pippa when he responded to an alarm in Room One, having gone past the reception area to check his pigeonhole for mail on the way back to his office from a meeting. He walked into the room to find a woman kneeling on the bed, the midwife hidden behind her. He recognised Pippa's voice the instant she continued with her instructions.

'Put your head right down on the bed, Ashley—that's it. Bum up in the air as high as you can. That's great...'

'What's happening?' The man standing near the window was looking confused. 'I don't understand. I thought it was a good thing when the waters broke.'

Lachlan knew exactly what was happening. He went to

pull gloves from the box on the wall. 'Cord prolapse?' he queried tersely. It was the obvious reason to put a woman into a position where gravity could help take the pressure off an umbilical cord that had come out in front of the presenting part of a baby.

'Yes.' Pippa's face appeared as she straightened to move to the end of the bed. She was also donning a fresh pair of gloves. 'The waters broke about two minutes ago when I put the CTG on to monitor the heart rate and contractions. Some meconium. It's been a long second stage. Cord prolapse was visible. And pulsatile.'

Pulsatile was good. It meant the baby was still alive. The priority was to keep pressure off the cord until they could deliver this baby, which needed to happen as quickly as possible.

Another midwife came through the door in response to the alarm. 'Get Theatre on standby, please,' Lachlan told her. 'And get a paeds team on standby too.'

The CTG straps were still around Ashley's belly and he could see that the baby's heart rate was slower than he would have liked.

So could Pippa. 'You're going to feel me putting my hand inside,' she told Ashley. 'I'm going to be pushing on baby's head, just gently.'

'Why? *Ow...* Why do you need to do that?'

'To stop baby's head pressing on the cord,' Lachlan explained, stepping closer. 'What was the last heart rate you recorded, Pippa—before the cord prolapse?'

'One forty.'

'It's back to one twenty now. Up from ninety-four.'

'Good. I'll switch to external supra-pubic pressure as soon as I'm sure the head is above the pelvic rim.'

'I want to push,' Ashley groaned.

'*No*. Don't push,' Pippa said urgently. 'Not yet.' She looked up at Lachlan. 'She's fully dilated,' she told him. 'And I can feel that the cord's still pulsatile.'

She held his gaze, knowing exactly what he was weighing up. It was possible that a vaginal delivery could be quicker than a Caesarean but it would require a team effort from the mother, the midwife and an experienced obstetrician. Lachlan might have been more reluctant to consider it if he didn't have this much faith in Pippa.

'Any contra-indications to an expedited delivery?'

'She's tired,' Pippa said. 'But she'll give it everything she's got.'

'Forceps kit?'

'On the trolley. There's a gown there, too.'

'Ashley? Do you still feel ready to push?'

'Yes.' The word was a sob.

'Okay. We're going to wait for your next contraction and then I'm going to let go of baby's head and help you turn onto your back. We're going to need your baby to be born as fast as possible so you are really going to have to push hard. I'm going to help as much as I can and Lachlan is going to help with forceps, but you've got an important job to do.'

'I can do it...' Ashley was breathing hard. 'I want to do it. Ooh... I can feel another contraction starting...'

Pippa looked up at Lachlan, who was shoving his arms into the gown a midwife was holding for him. He held her gaze and then gave a single nod before glancing up at the clock.

'Let's go,' he said.

Pippa's hand was aching and badly cramped by the time she could release the pressure she'd been putting on the baby's head. She also glanced up at the clock as she helped Ashley turn onto her back. They had a limited time frame to get this baby out because its oxygen supply was going to be compromised as soon as Ashley started pushing the baby's head down, which would press the cord against the pelvic bones and prevent the movement of life-sustaining oxygen. If they couldn't get the baby delivered in time, it would be fatal.

'Push...' Pippa encouraged Ashley. 'Push, push, *push*. Keep it going... That's it... Don't stop... Push again...'

She glanced up at Lachlan, now gowned, gloved and masked and looking every inch the surgeon he was. He had to be as aware of the tension in this room as Pippa was but he gave the impression of being completely calm and in control. More staff members were in the room now and a nurse was helping with the medical equipment on the trolley, unrolling a sterile kit that had the forceps Lachlan was going to use to help this delivery happen swiftly. He lubricated the first blade and kept his hand across the back of it to protect Ashely as he slid it into place. With the second blade in place, he locked them together and positioned his hands, ready to provide gentle traction to augment Ashley's next push. He gave Pippa a tiny nod.

'I need you to push again,' Pippa told her. 'Even if the contraction is wearing off. Take a big breath and push down...as hard as you can.'

Ashley was still gasping from her efforts. 'I *can't*...'

'Yes, you can, sweetheart.' Pippa's voice was calm. Confident. 'You're doing *so* well. One more push...as hard as you can. That's the way. *Push*...'

'I can see it.' Ashley's partner sounded awed. 'Our baby's coming, Ash...'

The baby slid out, looking completely limp. They needed to move fast. Pippa grabbed a warmed sterile towel as Lachlan clamped and cut the cord. He took the suction bulb from the midwife and cleared the airway of the infant. Pippa briskly but gently dried the baby but the stimulation wasn't enough to start it breathing. She put another towel across her hands and Lachlan lifted the tiny body and put it onto the towel. Pippa turned and took it to the resuscitation unit at one side of the room, where they could keep the baby warm. The paediatric team hadn't arrived yet so it was up to her and Lachlan to resuscitate this baby boy.

'Why isn't he crying?' Ashley was trying to sit up. 'What's happening? Is he going to be all right?'

Her partner was watching in horror. The other midwife was moving in to support them both.

Pippa knew where everything they needed was kept in the drawers of the unit. She handed a stethoscope to Lachlan and took out a tiny bag mask unit to put over the baby's mouth and nose and provide the first breaths.

The disc of the stethoscope looked huge against the baby's chest but it was moving as air filled the small lungs and when Lachlan's gaze caught Pippa's she found she could breathe again as well.

'Heart rate's over a hundred,' he said. 'And look… he's pinking up.'

The baby took a breath for himself as Pippa lifted the mask and he was beginning to move his arms and legs. As the paediatric team rushed into the room, he began a wobbly cry that gained strength with his next breath. Pippa stepped back to let the paediatric consultant take over but she was smiling as she turned back to Ashley.

'Can you hear that?' she asked. 'That's your baby boy. He's doing well...'

She caught Lachlan's gaze again as she was turning.

His look was telling her that *they* had done well, too.

There was nobody else in the staffroom this soon after the shift change that day.

Just Pippa, who needed a moment to wind down before she got on with the rest of her day. She was sitting at the table, half a mug of coffee in front of her, just staring into space.

No wonder Lachlan looked surprised when he walked in and saw her.

'You still here? I would have thought you'd be hanging out to get home after a day like today.'

'I went to NICU to check on Ashley's baby.'

'Ah...how is he? I got caught up in Theatre after that excitement.'

'He's good. They're going to monitor him overnight, just to be on the safe side, but there's no indication of any neurological damage. Ashley would love a chance to thank you if you're going past the unit.'

'I'll make a point of doing that.' But Lachlan pulled out a chair and sat down opposite Pippa. 'As soon as I've sat down for two minutes. It's been quite a day.'

'It has.'

'I'm glad I've got the chance to tell you what a great job you did. I was...impressed.'

She ducked her head a little shyly at the praise. But then she risked an upward glance.

'So was I,' she said softly.

'It's not the first time I've thought that we make a

good team,' Lachlan said. 'Maybe we should celebrate that with another prosecco at the pub one of these days.'

Pippa gave him another one of those stern looks—like she had when they'd been having that first prosecco.

Lachlan looked over his shoulder as if he wanted to make sure they were still alone. They were, but he lowered his voice anyway.

'You did get a chance to check that rule book of yours, I presume?'

'Um…yes.' Pippa bit her lip. This wasn't the first time she'd regretted making that throwaway comment.

'And was it in the section for professional relationships or the one that deals with dating? No…let me guess. It was in both, right?'

Pippa nodded.

'I like dating rules.' Lachlan's tone was approving. 'I have a few of my own.'

'Like what?'

'Like keeping things *strictl*y casual. That's non-negotiable.'

'A "friends with benefits" kind of rule?'

'Exactly. But there's a time limit as well. And that removes any possibility that someone will expect commitment.'

'Sounds like a version of the "three date" rule.'

Lachlan made a sound that suggested he was intrigued. 'I think I've heard about that one somewhere.' He grinned. 'Probably in a dentist's waiting room magazine, but I didn't get time to read it properly. Do you use it? Is it as useful as the prosecco rule? What was the verdict on that one, anyway?'

Oh, help...

Pippa had dug herself a rather deep hole here, hadn't she?

Why on earth had she thrown in that stupid line about a 'three date' rule?

She knew why. It was automatic to pull any available cloak of protection around herself. Lachlan only had to talk to someone like Rita and he could find out she was single. Maybe she wanted to let him think that was by choice and not simply because she didn't have the courage to go anywhere near a relationship of any significance. How embarrassing would it be to admit she hadn't been in any kind of relationship, in fact, since her marriage had ended several years ago?

At least the question she needed to answer was on a different, imaginary, rule about going to a pub with your boss.

She caught his gaze again, fully intending to tell him that going out with the boss was definitely not permissible but…dammit…that eye contact unleashed one of those explosions of sparks. The man's attractiveness made him a kind of walking, talking firework, didn't it?

Pippa found herself shrugging. And saying something completely different.

'It could be up for negotiation.' She tried to sound as if success was unlikely. 'If the proper application forms are filled in.'

Lachlan nodded approvingly. 'Forms are good,' he said. 'Now…tell me how the "three date" rule works.'

She'd read about it herself. Quite possibly in a magazine.

'It does what it says on the tin,' she said. 'You get three dates and that's it. Both parties know the rules in advance, so it keeps things casual and makes it easy to back off but stay friends, if that's what either party wants.'

'Sounds perfect,' Lachan said thoughtfully. 'So…what about the subclauses?'

'Like what?'

'What constitutes a date? And…is sex on the agenda? On the first date even, given that the time limit's going to be rather restricted. I mean, this is kind of like a "friends with benefits" but with a use-by date, yes?'

Oh-h… Pippa couldn't respond to the query. He'd said the 's' word and her brain had turned to absolute mush. She was staring at Lachlan's hands, for heaven's sake. Imagining what it would be like to have his fingers trailing over her skin. It felt as if it could be dangerous. They might leave a flicker of tiny flames in their wake…

She cleared her throat. 'A date is any private meeting or shared activity that's agreed on in advance and… um…yes, it goes further than the boundaries of friendship, so it probably includes some form of…um…physical interaction.'

'Ah…so…if you happen to meet at a supermarket and end up in the pub drinking prosecco, it doesn't count?'

'No…' Pippa's tone was very firm. 'That was definitely not a *date*, Mr Smythe. If it's something that any friends can do, it doesn't count.'

He was smiling again. 'Clearly, I have a lot to learn,' he said. 'And from past experience I've found that the best way to learn something new is to give it a go. To get hands on.' His smile widened. 'So to speak…'

Pippa shook her head. 'Go for it,' she said. 'Did you have someone in mind to try it out on?'

Lachlan was looking up at the ceiling now, as if deep in thought. 'Absolutely,' he said a moment later. 'There is a contender.'

Pippa was, she had to admit, decidedly envious. She

was also dead curious, but she managed to keep her tone casual.

'Who would that be?'

Lachlan's gaze flicked back to capture hers.

'*You*, of course. Who else?'

CHAPTER FIVE

Lachlan had been correct.

This could well be *perfect*.

A time limit. Three opportunities to have time together that could be romantic. Physical. Pleasurable and unforgettable.

It was not only permission to indulge in the satisfaction of an unusually intense attraction, it also had the potential to end as amicably as it had begun.

He did need to confirm that it was a good idea, mind you. Or rather, to make sure that Pippa was genuinely on board for what could only ever be a friendship with temporary benefits. Just a bit of a fling to defuse an attraction that could otherwise become something of a distraction.

A workplace liaison wasn't ideal, of course, especially when he'd only just started in a new position, and particularly one in the department he was now the head of, but perhaps that was even more of a reason to get it out of the way. It was quite obvious that the physical pull was mutual. Lachlan had actually seen her pupils dilate when he'd asked whether a first date could include sex and the way she'd been so flustered and determined not to let the word cross her own lips had been…

…adorable.

But it was equally clear that she had her doubts, and

that was understandable. It *was* a bit of a minefield. If it went wrong it could damage not only his reputation at Queen Mary's but the excellent working relationship he was building with one of his most senior midwives.

Which turned out to be exactly what was making Pippa hesitant when Lachlan finally got an unexpected chance to speak to her in a place that couldn't have been more private. And secure.

The drug storage room—with a door that locked itself automatically when it closed behind the person authorised to enter. Pippa came in as Lachlan was about to leave. He didn't even need to raise the topic as he took a step towards the door. His raised eyebrows and a smile were enough to reveal that she'd been thinking about it. As much as he had?

'No,' she said. 'We work together. We'll still have to work together after the three dates. And you're my *boss*.'

'We're part of the same team,' he corrected her. 'I'm quite confident we're both professional enough not to let something personal interfere with our ability to do our jobs. Who knows?' He tried to amp up the charm in his smile. 'Getting to know each other better might *improve* our working relationship.'

'Can you countersign a drug for me, please? That way I won't have to wait for Sally.'

'Sure.'

Pippa used a code to unlock the cabinet where the controlled drugs like narcotics were kept. She took an ampoule of morphine from a box, recorded her action in the logbook and signed her name.

Lachlan scribbled his initials in the final column as witness to the drug and quantity that had been removed.

Pippa locked the cabinet again, put the ampoule into a kidney dish and then glanced up, her eyes narrowing.

'How do I know you're going to stick to the rules?'

'I'm good at rules.' Lachlan let himself sound slightly offended. 'I have my own rules about things. Like marriage.' He held his hands up. 'Not that I've had the same degree of trauma that you've had, but I'm on board with your aversion to it—and, presumably, to any long-term relationship that resembles marriage. I think we're on exactly the same page. I need to learn about this "three date" rule. I think it might serve me very well for the rest of my life. I can travel whenever I like, not collect any unwelcome baggage and… I might make some very good friends along the way—including you. Is that enough to convince you?'

'Hmm…' Pippa was adding an alcohol wipe, syringe and a needle to the kidney dish. The way she had her lips pressed together was giving away the fact that she was trying not to smile. Or appear too eager to give in?

Oh, man... Lachlan was seriously tempted to kiss Pippa right now. They were quite safe in here because there was no window on the solid door to get into this secure space and anyone coming in, like Sally was about to, would have to pause to use their swipe card. But that would hardly be the way to confirm that he was capable of behaving in a completely professional manner, was it? It was bad enough that he'd followed her into a locked room.

Not that she was making his restraint any easier. There was a glint in her eyes that told him she knew exactly what he was thinking and that she was not averse to the idea of being kissed. Something had to be done before this got out of hand, Lachlan decided. He was going to invite her to a first date. If her response made him feel like he was pushing her into something she was dubious about, he would back off and dismiss the prospect of even a single date with Pippa, let alone three of them.

'Let's do dinner,' he suggested. 'At the White Swan. I don't know if you noticed their blackboard menu, but they do steak and chips.'

Pippa lost the battle not to smile. 'I think you'll find that all pubs do steak and chips.'

'With an *egg*?'

She laughed. 'Maybe not always with an egg. Sometimes it can be with mushrooms.' She picked up the kidney dish. 'Excuse me, I've got someone who's pretty keen to get some more effective pain relief on board now that it's been charted.'

Lachlan stood between Pippa and the door for just a heartbeat longer. 'Is that a yes?'

'Will you stop waiting for me in locked rooms if I say yes?'

'Absolutely. Consider it a new rule.' He held the door open for Pippa.

She avoided making eye contact as she went past, and if anyone had been in the corridor outside they wouldn't have had any idea that her comment was about anything personal.

'Wednesday's probably good for me. Or Thursday. Let me know when you've checked your roster.'

Thursday.

Seven forty-five p.m.

Pippa was waiting, as arranged, by the bus stop near the staff parking area of the hospital—maybe a ten-minute walk away from the White Swan. Where she was about to go.

On a date.

With Lachlan Smythe.

Was it a date? She'd already been there with him, and that had definitely *not* been a date. But since then, that sizzling attraction had gone up by several noticeable notches. And he'd told her that he wanted to experience that imaginary 'three date' rule she had pretended to live by. It seemed that he was going to play by her rules and she had said that it was only a 'date' if there was some kind of physical interaction that wouldn't be appropriate if they were only friends.

A kiss.

More than a kiss.

A lot more than a kiss?

Good grief. Pippa was suddenly starting to feel all hot and bothered. Maybe this wasn't such a good idea, after all. But it was too late to back out now. She could see Lachlan striding towards her.

His smile was enough to make any doubts about what she was doing evaporate.

Dear Lord…the man was irresistible. Pippa decided she wasn't going to even think about any potentially negative consequences to this…date. Yep. She couldn't deny that she was hoping for an evening that would include some very inappropriate physical interaction.

'Hungry?' Lachlan asked.

'Starving.' Pippa nodded.

'Me, too.'

The words were a low, sexy growl. Pippa considered but then rejected making the suggestion that they skipped the pub and went straight to her place. She actually was very hungry. And this…anticipation was as delicious as any meal was going to be. Why not let it last a little longer?

The route to the White Swan meant they needed to cross one of the busy main roads that went through Richmond and had some residential houses with parking bays in front of them on one side and business premises on the other. Traffic was heading towards them from a distance as they crossed two lanes of the road to the central raised traffic island in front of an enormous supermarket delivery lorry and then waited for the bus that was coming in the opposite direction.

The blaring of an airhorn from the lorry was too close for comfort and they turned to see a car that was backing swiftly out from a parking space in front of a row of terraced houses, straight into the path of the truck. The driver swerved to miss the collision but was struggling for control as the huge vehicle rocked and it was already on the wrong side of the road. They could actually see the horror on the face of the bus driver as he realised what was happening. He was wrenching his steering wheel and the bus began heading straight for a big tree on the side of the road. The lorry hit the back of the bus with a sickening crunch at the same time the driver's end scraped past the tree with a screech of ripping metal and came to a shuddering halt. The impact was hard enough to shake the concrete island that Pippa and Lachlan were standing on.

There was noise everywhere now. Squealing from brakes being slammed on and crunching sounds from nose to tail collisions. There were horns blaring and people shouting. A faint scream was coming from inside the bus. A siren started as a police car in the distance raced to get to the scene. The thing that Pippa was most aware of in those first seconds, however, was that Lachlan's immediate reaction had been to grab hold of her.

To *protect* her.

And his first words, as he shielded her with his body, were to ask if she was okay.

'I'm fine,' she assured him. 'Oh, my God, Lachlan. We need to *do* something. Where do we start?'

'Triage,' he said. 'There'll be paramedics here in a matter of minutes but we can do a first sweep and at least make sure an airway is open if they're unconscious and get pressure on any uncontrolled bleeding.'

The lorry driver was climbing down from his cab that had jack-knifed after clipping the bus. He had blood streaming from a wound on his forehead. People were coming out of nearby shops, gathering to watch in horror. An elderly man on the other side of the road was standing beside the car that had caused the accident and drivers and passengers were getting out of their cars as they found themselves in a traffic snarl. A police officer was shouting at them to get back into their vehicles and move on so that the emergency services could get through.

'Come with me,' Lachlan directed.

The bus driver had managed to open the doors and he was leaning out.

'Help…we need *help*…'

Lachlan walked swiftly past the gathering crowd. 'There could be uninjured people coming out of the bus soon,' he told them. 'Keep them here and look after them until an ambulance arrives and they can be cleared.'

Pippa followed Lachlan into the bus through the back door. Shocked-looking people were sitting, immobile, still clinging onto the bars of the seats as if the bus was still moving. One man was standing in the aisle towards the back of the bus, bent over with his arms around his chest, and he was groaning loudly.

'If you can move, please make your way to the front of the bus,' Lachlan called loudly. 'There are people outside who will help you.'

The worst of the damage was at the back of the bus, where the side had been caved in and the windows shattered. A crumpled figure was lying across the back seat. A window on the other side had also been broken by a branch of the tree that was now inside the bus and someone was hunched inside the greenery, their hands covering their head.

People further up the bus were beginning to stand up and move cautiously towards the front door.

'Can you check the guy in the tree?' Lachlan asked. 'And have a look for anyone that might have slipped down between the seats as well. I need to get to that person on the back seat.'

But he paused as he went past the man holding his chest. 'Are you having trouble breathing?'

'It hurts…' The man groaned again. 'I was waiting to get off at the next stop and… I hit my ribs on the pole.'

Pippa could see Lachlan helping the man to sit down carefully on the nearest seat before he moved swiftly past. She had reached the man half-hidden amongst the foliage of the tree. She could see blood trickling through his fingers.

'Can you hear me?' she asked.

'Y-yes…'

'Did the branch hit you? Were you knocked out?'

'I…don't think so. But… I'm bleeding.'

'I can see that.' Pippa was breaking off the leafy twigs to clear a space. It looked as though this man had been incredibly lucky and the larger branches had only skimmed his head enough to give him the kind of scalp laceration that was notorious for bleeding heavily. 'Is it hard to breathe at all?'

'No...'

'Anything else hurting?'

'No...'

'Okay... Don't move. I'll be back soon, but there will be more help arriving any second.'

A lot of the passengers had managed to get off the bus now, with the help of the driver and people outside. By the time Pippa had checked the floor between the seats and turned back, she could see the flashing lights of both fire service and ambulance vehicles arriving. She could also see Lachlan perched on the back seat, his hands positioned to keep the airway of an unconscious person open. As she tried to get back to check on the man with the scalp wound, paramedics were coming in through both doors of the bus. One team went straight to Lachlan. Another to the man who was holding his ribs.

'Are you hurt?'

Pippa turned to the paramedic who'd come in through the front door.

'You're covered in blood,' they added.

'Am I?' Pippa glanced down and found that her pale green shirt was, indeed, streaked with blood. She shook her head. 'I'm fine... I'm a nurse. First on the scene with a doctor.' This blood must have come from the leafy twigs she'd been breaking and moving. 'There's someone with a scalp laceration beside that tree branch.'

'Right.' They were already moving. 'Thanks for your help. We've got this now.'

Pippa climbed off the bus. Someone jumped out of the

back of an ambulance and, having heard her story, gave her a pump bottle of hand sanitiser and a towel to clean any blood off her hands.

'Are you vaccinated for hepatitis?'

'Yes.'

The paramedic was peering at her face. 'You should be okay. Can't see any splashes around your eyes or mouth. I'm guessing you're well aware of protocols for contact with blood or body fluids.'

'I'll be fine.' But Pippa had a moment of concern for Lachlan. What was he still doing in the bus? Was he putting himself at more risk than she had? She stood to one side of the scene, waiting for him to appear, watching firemen and more ambulance officers entering the bus with equipment, including a rescue basket. A short time later, the most seriously injured passenger was brought out, strapped into the basket stretcher. He was in a cervical collar and had an oxygen mask covering his face. Lachlan was walking behind the stretcher and followed it to the ambulance, where it was loaded, the vehicle moving off seconds later with its lights flashing.

Pippa watched Lachlan turn to scan the scene as the ambulance left. That he was looking for her was obvious by the way his face relaxed when he spotted her. As he walked towards her, Pippa was aware of a curious melting sensation deep inside her body. She was remembering the way he hadn't hesitated to shield her as soon as he'd realised something dangerous was happening around them. How long had it been since anyone had cared for her like that?

Too long…

Lachlan noticed the blood smears on her shirt as quickly as the paramedic had.

'Not mine,' she assured him.

'I'm probably a mess myself,' he said. 'I certainly feel like I could use a hot shower and a change of clothes.' He took another glance around them. 'We're don't need to be here any longer but... I don't think we're going to get anywhere near the White Swan tonight.'

'No...we might need a rain check on that.' Pippa checked her watch. 'Good grief...it's after nine p.m. I had no idea we'd been here this long.'

'That guy in the back seat needed a bit of work. He regained consciousness but had enough of a head injury to be combative and need sedation.' He blew out a breath. 'Let me walk you home, at least.'

She shook her head. 'You'd be even further away from that shower and the clean clothes. I'll be home in a few minutes. It's all good.'

'If you're sure.' But Lachlan was hesitating. He made a rueful face. 'Not much of a first date, was it?'

'It doesn't count,' Pippa said. 'And, even it if did, it certainly wasn't boring.'

Lachlan was smiling again. 'It wasn't, was it? So I get another shot at a first date?'

Pippa could still feel the warmth of that being cared for feeling. She smiled back at him.

'It would be a bit rude to say no, wouldn't it?'

'Absolutely. 'Night, Pippa.' Lachlan dipped his head and brushed her cheek with his lips. 'We'll have better luck next time.'

Again, she was watching him. His back, this time, as he headed in the direction they'd come from. He lifted his hand in another gesture of farewell and Pippa lifted her own, even though she knew he couldn't see it. Then she found herself touching her cheek.

It hadn't been a real kiss but she could still feel its imprint.
She wished it *had* been real.
Both the date and the kiss.

CHAPTER SIX

THE FRUSTRATION WAS REAL.

The closest Lachlan got to seeing Pippa in the next couple of days was a photograph that appeared in the local newspaper, of the accident scene on the night of what was supposed to have been their first date, taken when she was getting out of the bus with all those blood stains on her shirt.

He hadn't forgotten the feeling of wondering whether she'd been injured herself, clambering around inside that bus. Or that overwhelming urge to keep her safe when he'd seen the dreadful accident unfolding in front of their eyes—so close it felt as if they'd escaped death themselves.

Was fate trying to warn him to stay away from her?

Was that why it was proving so difficult to catch even a moment with her during work hours, so they could at least find a time to try again?

It wasn't going to happen today, that was certain. Lachlan had checked the roster this morning—something that was perfectly legitimate for him to do, given that he was the HoD—and found that Pippa was on the first of two days off.

He'd worked late, being on call and having had an emergency Caesarean that he'd only just finished. He wasn't covering the night shift but the surgery had started just before the changeover and it had been a complicated and time-consuming case because the mother had dense adhesions from previous C-sections. She had lost a lot of blood and was being kept overnight in the ICU for monitoring due to a dip in the level of her kidney function. Lachlan wanted to check on her again before he went home for the night. By the time he was satisfied that she was doing well, it was nearly midnight and he was more than ready to go home.

Until he was on the way to the car park, when he spotted Pippa outside the hospital, sitting on a bench beside an archway that invited people to enter the garden area that was a feature of The Queen Mary Hospital's grounds. She was wearing scrubs and had a packet of sandwiches on her lap that looked as if they'd been spat out of a hospital vending machine.

'Pippa! What on earth are you doing here at this time of night? It's your day off, isn't it?'

'How did you know that?'

'Ah...' Should he look embarrassed that he'd been stalking her? The way she'd been when she'd paid attention to what was being said on the hospital grapevine. No... He sat down beside her instead. 'It doesn't matter,' he said. 'It's good to see you.'

'I'm not supposed to be here,' Pippa admitted. 'I came in last minute because they were so short-staffed, and I've got tomorrow off so I can catch up on sleep. They're being kind to me. They said to take as long as I like for a dinner break and they'll only page me if I'm really needed.'

'Excellent. That'll give us time to arrange another date. Oh, wait...it wasn't a date last time, was it?'

'No...' Pippa looked down at the sandwiches she was

holding. Lachlan could see that their corners were curled up and there was a tired-looking lettuce leaf poking out. 'Steak and chips sound pretty good right now.'

'I think I can do better than that,' Lachlan said. 'I think we deserve more than a pub dinner after the disaster the other night. What's the best restaurant in Richmond?'

'What's your favourite food?'

'Italian.'

'There are some amazing Italian restaurants in Richmond.'

'But what's *your* favourite food?' Lachlan hadn't forgotten the meal ingredients he'd seen in her supermarket trolley. 'When you go out, that is?'

'Probably French.'

'Is there an amazing French restaurant in Richmond?'

'There is.' Pippa was smiling, as if she was pleased with the direction this conversation was going in. '*Chez Anton*. It's right by the river and I've never been.' She hesitated, as if she was wondering whether to explain why that might be. 'It's a bit posh,' she added.

'Then that's where we'll go,' Lachlan said. 'Tomorrow night, seven p.m.'

'Okay… I can meet you there. It's an easy walk for me.' Pippa's eyes were shining and her lips were parted and…

…and she looked totally irresistible.

Lachlan couldn't look away from her eyes and it seemed as if Pippa wasn't about to break that eye contact, even when he leaned close enough to make it more than apparent that he was thinking of kissing her.

If anything, it felt as if she was leaning towards *him*.

It didn't matter. The important thing was that their lips were touching and…oh, man…it was just as delicious as he'd known it would be. He moved his lips over hers and could feel her response as a tiny gasp as he touched her bottom lip with his tongue. The pressure of the kiss changed and there was an urgent note to it now. They both wanted more...

Perhaps it was just as well that Pippa's pager sounded at the precise moment things were tipping into something far too intense, given that they were sitting where anybody coming out of Queen Mary's might see them. Lachlan might not know all the rules in Pippa's book but he could be fairly sure there could very well be something about keeping it private and protecting reputations.

That didn't magically erase the frustration, but it helped considerably that Pippa was feeling it, too. Lachlan felt her sigh against his lips as she broke the contact.

'I have to go,' she whispered.

'I know.' Lachlan found a smile as he remembered something that really did help deal with that unresolved tension. 'See you tomorrow night, Pippa.'

She couldn't stop thinking about it.

That *kiss*...

Every time she thought about it, her entire body felt as if it was melting. Especially when she finally climbed into her bed the next morning to get a few hours' sleep. Even more so in the evening as she got ready to go out.

On a date that was very likely to include another kiss.

Pippa had never felt quite this nervous about a date. Or taken quite so much care to look her absolute best. When her freshly washed hair was dry, she used her straighteners to turn it into a shiny fall that felt like silk rippling on her bare shoulders, because it was still warm enough on this summer's evening to wear a sundress that had spaghetti straps that were tied in bows, a shirred bodice and a long skirt that was full enough to swirl around her legs. It was her favourite colour, a soft olive green, with a print of tiny white daisies, and she kept her accessories simple, with leather sandals on her feet and thin silver bangles on her wrist. The walk along the towpath beside the river was one she loved but she barely noticed the boats or dog walkers or the band setting up to play live music in one of the restaurant gardens this evening.

All she could think about was Lachlan Smythe.

And that *kiss*.

He was waiting for her outside *Chez Anton* and he was looking as summery as Pippa, in a cream open-necked, short-sleeved shirt and sand-coloured chinos. They were shown to a table in the garden, shaded by a lush grapevine, that overlooked a grassy bank, the towpath and a wide stretch of the river and the waiter handed them menus.

'Can I get you something to drink?'

Pippa caught Lachlan's gaze. She wanted to ask for a glass of prosecco, but she had to make it seem as if she was following known rules for a casual relationship and having a drink that linked them as a couple had to be a no-no.

'I can recommend the house champagne,' the waiter said.

'Sounds perfect,' Lachlan said.

'Yes, please,' Pippa said.

Lachlan waited until the waiter walked away to wink at Pippa. 'Champagne is just the French version of prosecco,' he murmured. He opened his menu. 'And look... they do steak and chips.'

'It'll be *steak frites* here. No eggs.'

'Doesn't béarnaise sauce have egg in it?'

Pippa had to laugh. 'I do believe it does. Egg yolks, anyway.'

But there it was. Another connection. Was that why it felt as if there was a genuine friendship between them already? And was *that* what was making this attraction something unlike anything Pippa had ever felt, even with the man she had fallen in love with enough and ended up marrying?

They drank the champagne and ate the crispiest twice-cooked French fries with slivers of steak that were tender enough to melt in their mouths and deliciously coated with the tarragon and chervil flecked sauce. They had crème brûlée for dessert, along with another glass of champagne, and they still hadn't run out of things to talk about. The conversation had, in fact, naturally become more personal.

'I couldn't stay in Birmingham after my marriage ended,' Pippa told him. 'And it was the best thing I ever did to move here. I absolutely love being so close to the river. I walk along here on the towpath every chance I get.'

'Do you cycle?'

'I used to, when I was a kid.'

'I passed a place where you can hire bicycles. Think how far you could go on the Thames Path on a bike.'

'How far would you want to go?'

'Pangbourne Meadows.'

'What? Why?'

'It's supposed to be one of the best places for wild swimming near London.'

'Oh?' Pippa focused on scraping up the last morsel of her dessert. She wasn't going to let herself think about that snippet of gossip where the suggestion had been made that the new HoD might go swimming naked.

'Petersham Meadows is also good, apparently,' Lachlan continued. 'And that's probably walking distance from here.'

'Mmm...' Pippa was thinking of somewhere that was even more within walking distance.

Her cottage.

Her bedroom.

Suddenly aware of an unusual silence, she looked up to find Lachlan's gaze resting on her.

'Shall we head off?' he asked softly.

There was a new tension between them as they walked away from the restaurant.

Who was going to say something first? Or would nothing be said and they would get back to wherever Lachlan had parked his car and then they'd say goodnight and that would be the end of the date?

Pippa didn't want it to be the end.

The band that had been setting up as Pippa had been walking in the other direction was still playing as they went past. The lead singer was a woman with an amazing voice and they stopped to listen to her rendition of Prince's 'Nothing Compares 2 U'.

They were standing so close together that their arms were touching and it felt as natural as breathing to link their hands. And then Lachlan slipped his hand around her waist and...they were dancing. Just swaying together to start with, but then Lachlan lifted his arm and Pippa turned beneath it, stepping further away to let Lachlan pull her back, even more closely, into his arms. And then she rested her head in the hollow beneath his shoulder and he rested his cheek on her hair. When the song ended, they looked at each other and it turned out that there was very little that needed to be said.

Only four words, in fact, and it was Lachlan who whispered them.

'Your place or mine?'

Pippa's place.

The tiniest, cutest cottage Lachlan had ever seen, with its pink door between two square windows and a wisteria vine that had tendrils long enough to catch in his hair as he followed Pippa inside.

It could have been a garden shed for all he cared, mind you. He just wanted to be behind a closed door, in a space where he could be completely alone with Pippa. It felt as if he'd been waiting for this moment for…for ever?

He was holding her hand as they went inside. By tacit consent, they both stood there in silence, very still, as their eyes got accustomed to the reduced level of light. Until they could see each other just as well as they needed to.

Lachlan could see the shine of Pippa's hair and he wove his fingers into the thickness of it behind her head and let it ripple through them like silky ribbons. She closed her eyes as if she could feel it as well. Her lips parted and…

…and Lachlan was lost.

He touched his lips to hers. So softly it was no more than a breath. And then again, catching her lower lip between his and touching it with his tongue. A tiny sound came from Pippa—just a catch of her breath, but it was enough for him to cover her mouth again, and this time it was a real kiss. A conversation of pressure and response, lips and tongues, hands that were moving on bare skin and desire that was spiralling into a level that Lachlan had never known existed. Even if he had, he might well have avoided going anywhere near it, because it was redolent of a lack of control that was both unacceptable and intoxicatingly compelling.

Those stringy straps of Pippa's dress had bows and all it needed was a tug to undo them. He lifted his head enough to catch her gaze as he untied them because he needed to be sure that she wanted this as much as he did, but she was looking down, her fingers starting to unbutton his shirt. Maybe she felt the urgency in his gaze because her fingers stilled and, a beat later, she lifted her chin and met his gaze.

He could see the heat of desire in her eyes and there was no doubt that she wanted this to continue. There was a kind of wonder there as well, as though she didn't quite believe the power of what was happening between them and...oh, Lord...was that a hint of fear in there, too?

He hadn't expected that from someone who made her own rules and then followed them to the letter. He hadn't expected the...vulnerability he could see and that touched something that was deeper than purely physical.

He held her gaze and what he said came straight from his heart.

'You're safe,' he said softly. 'You can trust me.'

'I know...' She was the one holding *his* gaze now and the edges of any fear had softened. 'You can trust me, too.'

Her bedroom was on the other side of the narrow hallway down the centre of the cottage and there wasn't much space to walk around her bed, which was fine as far as Lachlan was concerned. The bed was the only space they needed. The rest of the world was about to become completely irrelevant.

They stood at the end of the bed to undress each other. He heard Pippa's gasp when his hands brushed her breasts as he pulled down the stretchy top of her dress. It was his turn to make a sound like a groan when she was undoing the leather belt of his chinos.

'Wait...' He reached into his pocket to find the foil packet that was inside his wallet.

'You don't have to,' Pippa whispered. 'I'm on the Pill.'

Lachlan leaned in to kiss her. 'Consider it an insurance policy,' he murmured. 'You can never be too careful.'

He never had—and never *would*—let anyone else take the responsibility for something this important.

Once he knew he was safe, that they were both safe, then he could let himself sink into what was promising to be the best sex he'd ever experienced. Ever...

Oh, *my*...

That was about as coherent as Pippa's thoughts were for quite some time.

It wasn't just the way Lachlan was touching her, with his hands and his tongue, his soft words and the sounds of pleasure—ecstasy, even—that he made. It was the feel of *his* skin beneath her hands and the taste of him and... the way they could move together that made it feel impossible that this was the first time.

It wasn't until she was lying there, waiting for her pulse and breathing to get a lot closer to normal, that reality began to take shape again.

Maybe it was the sound of Lachlan's breath that was halfway to being a sigh.

'Strike one,' he said.

Pippa blinked. 'What?'

'I'm guessing this counts as a date.' There was an amused note in his voice now.

'Oh...' Pippa turned her head. Her nose was almost touching Lachlan's. 'Yes,' she added. 'Definitely a date.'

'So that's number one.'

'It is.' Pippa tried to sound solemn but it was difficult when she was feeling this *good*. And happy. Lachlan wanting to experiment with the 'three date' rule meant that it could happen again.

Twice, in fact.

Lachlan was clearly following the same thought process. He kissed Pippa softly.

'Only two left,' he said.

Pippa nodded. But she caught her bottom lip between her teeth to stop herself smiling. Thank goodness she hadn't come up with the notion of a 'one date' rule.

'Okay if I have a shower before I head home?'

'Of course.'

Lachlan swung his legs over the side of the bed, but then he seemed to freeze. For long enough for Pippa to feel herself frowning.

'You okay?'

'I'm...not sure...'

Pippa propped herself up on her elbow. 'Why?'

'Ah...the condom broke.' His words were a monotone. 'That's never happened to me before.'

'It's okay,' Pippa said. 'Like I said, I'm on the Pill. And I haven't missed any doses recently. I've had years of practice.'

The glance over his shoulder was surprised enough to make Pippa blush.

'Not because I have an overactive sex life. And I've

never had an STI so you're also safe on that count. You're actually the first in quite a while.' Pippa pulled the duvet up to cover herself. 'I used to get irregular cycles, that's all. And menorrhagia. Enough to get anaemic.'

Lachlan was nodding. 'You're safe, too,' he said. 'So…' He got to his feet. 'All good, then.'

Pippa watched him walk to her tiny bathroom. Tall, lean and totally naked.

Yeah…it was definitely all good.

About as good as anything could ever get.

CHAPTER SEVEN

It was all very well having another two dates to look forward to, but it would be way too easy to use them up in as many days, wouldn't it?

Lachlan saw Pippa at the central desk as he walked past, the morning after date number one, and he could feel the burning embers from the night before as clearly as if he were walking over hot coals. It was extremely tempting to get to his office as quickly as possible and fire off a text message to find out if she might be free this evening for dinner or a show or something.

Especially the something.

Even the most fleeting flashback to the finale of last night's date was enough to cause flames to reignite from those embers and ramp up the heat. The kind of heat that should trigger a smoke alarm in the ward, let alone any internal warning system, but Lachlan was comfortable that this was safe.

For whatever reason—and he suspected it had a lot to do with the failure of her marriage—Pippa had strict rules about dating that she was currently following in her personal life.

Lachlan's were even stricter. He didn't know if he carried the Huntington gene himself. He'd never been tested and he didn't want to be. Having had years to think about it before he'd turned eighteen and could choose for himself, he'd decided it was preferable to live his life without knowing that the Sword of Damocles was hanging over his head. If he started to show symptoms, he'd deal with it then. What he would never do, however, was to let someone else get close enough for them to be affected as well because that would be as bad as passing the gene onto an innocent child. Almost...

He wasn't about to break the rules and try and extend the number of dates, no matter how much he might be tempted to, but even if he found the temptation irresistible he had the insurance policy that Pippa wouldn't be having a bar of it. This was a private and temporary arrangement and she was being very careful that their colleagues weren't going to suspect there was anything more than a professional relationship between them.

'Good morning, Mr Smythe.'

She wasn't giving the slightest hint of just how well they knew each other now. No wonder he was feeling so safe.

'Morning, Pippa.' Lachlan nodded at the staff members gathering for the handover. 'Rita... Sally—how are you?'

'I'm very good.' Sally grinned. 'Or so I've been led to believe.'

Lachlan gave a huff of laughter and kept moving, without looking back at Pippa.

Playing the game of keeping the 'three date' thing a secret might be as enjoyable as fighting the flames of desire every time they were close enough to be breathing the same air. It could add considerably to the anticipation of date two, in fact. How much hotter could things get, he wondered, if they kept each other waiting a bit?

A lot hotter, he decided when he managed to get to the cafeteria for a lunch break. Pippa was going in the other direction. He glanced at the plastic triangle sandwich pack in her hands and then lifted his gaze. It only took a heartbeat of eye contact to know they were both remembering the other night, when the first real date had been agreed on and Pippa had been holding exactly the same food. The subtle quirk of her eyebrow told him that, yeah…steak and chips might still be a preferable meal choice.

It felt like a private invitation to arrange another date.

The way her lips were curving into the merest suggestion of a smile as they carried on in opposite directions without even speaking to each other told him that his own expression had conveyed his intended message.

Soon. But not yet…

Who was going to broach the subject of a second date?

When several days had gone by without Lachlan saying anything, Pippa might have started wondering if he had decided that he didn't *want* a second date.

But she knew that wasn't true.

She could feel the hum in the air between them and she knew perfectly well that he could feel it as well. Fortunately, it was a hum that was quite controllable. It was automatically there as soon as they were anywhere near each other, but it came with a mental switch. It could be dimmed enough to be kept private, like when they were attending a staff meeting or they happened to be collecting sets of notes from the reception desk in Outpatients at the same time. It could be switched off completely when any personal interaction was totally inappropriate, which was any instance of them both being involved in a birth that required some medical intervention.

Or was it more that the personal hum was overridden by a professional one when that happened?

Because it did feel different to be working with Lachlan than with other consultants. Just having him in the room for the end of the second stage of a breech delivery, a week after their date, was enough to keep the atmosphere calm, even when it became apparent that a serious complication could be developing.

'You're doing really well, Amber. Baby's legs and bottom are born now. Take a few deep breaths and then have a wiggle and start pushing again.'

But Pippa was watching the baby's body carefully and there was no sign of the expected rotation that would put the back uppermost. She glanced up at the clock. The minutes were ticking past and it was a short window. There should be a steady descent of the baby's head and it should appear within three minutes of the umbilicus being born. Amber was pushing again but there was still no progress.

Pippa knew the three-minute mark had passed as Lachlan stepped closer.

'I'm just going to check on what's happening,' he warned Amber. 'Don't push. Take a few more breaths.'

The episiotomy Pippa had performed made it easier for Lachlan to slip his hand in as gently as possible. She saw his expression change moments later.

'Bilateral extended arms,' he said quietly.

The baby's head was stuck because of the extra room needed with the arms on either side. Pippa knew Lachlan would be trying to flex the baby's elbow and sweep an arm out. She also knew you only made one attempt.

And it hadn't been successful.

'What's happening?' Amber's husband was helping her to breathe in the Entonox. He was looking very pale. 'Why isn't the baby moving?'

'He's got his arms up,' Pippa said. 'Which is making things a bit tight. He needs some help to get going again.'

Lachlan was holding the baby's pelvis now, with his forefingers on the back and his thumbs around the legs. Pippa watched him perform a procedure he was clearly very familiar with, lifting the baby's body and rotating it in one direction and then back again. The manoeuvre was designed to unlock the impaction and bring the arms in front of the body.

Pippa held her breath. She could see in Lachlan's face the moment he felt the movement of the baby and then she could see the arms and shoulders being born. He adjusted his hold, cradling the tiny body on one hand and putting his fingers on the back of the baby's head.

He glanced up.

'Suprapubic pressure?' Pippa was already getting her hand in position on Amber's belly.

'Thanks.'

Pippa pressed down firmly as Lachlan corrected the flexion that was making the head difficult to deliver and, finally, the baby was born. She felt as if she was taking a first breath along with the infant and she could hear—and feel—the relieved breath that Lachlan expelled. In the blink of time before the baby's breath became a cry, she shared a glance with Lachlan and it felt like a smile. An emergency had been averted. Her trust in his skills had continued its climb and the feeling that they were, indeed, a good team became even stronger—a professional hum that was just as significant as a personal one, especially a personal one that had a distinct time limit of its own.

Okay...

Enough was enough.

It was well over a week since their night together and Lachlan wanted to lock in a second date. It didn't have to be in the next day or two but he wanted confirmation that it *was* going to happen.

He texted Pippa.

Do you like West End musicals? Fancy dinner and a show?

The response came back fast enough to suggest that Pippa had also had enough of waiting.

Sounds great. But not tonight—I've got an antenatal class to run. And I'm back on night shifts again next week.

No problem. I'll get tickets and let you know.

Lachlan checked Pippa's roster to see what date she was starting her week of night shifts and booked tickets for an evening where neither of them had work the next day.

Just in case they didn't get much sleep that night...

His registrar rang to let him know they were ready to start a ward round in the post-surgical ward but Lachlan took a brief detour on the way, to stop at the reception desk in the labour ward.

'I don't know anything about the antenatal classes we're running,' he said to Rita. 'Where are they? And who's in charge?'

'There's a training room attached to the physiotherapy gymnasium,' Rita said. 'It's all set up with lots of birthing balls and plastic pelvises and slightly weird-looking fake babies.' She smiled at him. 'You know…the usual stuff. It's a four-week course, on Tuesdays from seven to nine p.m., and it's for women from about thirty weeks pregnant. The midwives do the majority of the teaching and they have a roster for it.' She looked over her shoulder. 'It's Pippa tonight and it's a Session Three. From memory, that's about active birthing positions and breathing techniques. I've heard it can get quite physical. Maybe you should pop in and see it for yourself.'

It wasn't a bad idea. Lachlan had another viewing of the house near Marble Hill Park because he hadn't been able to forget those gorgeous views across Richmond Park from the upstairs bedrooms. The idea of a legitimate reason to spend time with Pippa at work when he wasn't in a professional role himself was quite intriguing.

Lachlan smiled at Rita. 'I might just do that.'

Lachlan had no trouble finding the training room in the physiotherapy department later that evening because he could hear the voices and laughter from some distance away. He let himself quietly into the room, where half a dozen pregnant women and their birthing partners were in various positions around the room.

Pippa was rubbing the back of a woman who was on all fours on a padded mat.

'Don't let your lower back sag,' he heard her saying. 'Curl it up and then straighten it. Pelvic tilts are great just for relaxation at the end of a long day, but they're also going to be great during labour.'

A father-to-be who looked young enough to still be a teenager was bouncing across the other side of the room on a large birthing ball. Pippa looked up and then started moving. Her eyes widened in surprise when she noticed Lachlan at the door, but she was on a mission.

'I hope you're not going to let Scarlett do that when she's in labour, Kyle. What did I say about bouncing?'

Kyle looked sheepish. 'That it can jam the baby in a bad position.'

'Close enough.'

'He's an idiot.' The pregnant young woman walking towards them was glaring at Kyle. 'Honestly, I can't take him anywhere. I have no idea why I let him get me pregnant.'

'You love me, babe.' Kyle was grinning. 'You couldn't resist my charms. Look… I know what to do. Rotate your hips, go from side to side. Do figure eights. I'm onto it.'

'Fabulous.' Pippa smiled at him. She raised her voice to get the attention of the rest of the class. 'Let's use the last bit of tonight's class to practise some of the breathing techniques we talked about earlier. Try the deep, slow, calming breaths. Inhale quietly. You can be as vocal as you want on the exhalation.'

She threw a grin in Lachlan's direction as loud groaning broke out, the birthing partners apparently keen to participate, and held up her hand, fingers splayed, to signal that she should be finishing up in five minutes or so.

Lachlan was more than happy to wait. He watched Pippa going from couple to couple, encouraging them, praising them and answering any questions they had. She was confident, friendly and warm and the class attendees clearly loved her, judging by their comments as they left.

'You're the best, Pippa,' one of them said. 'I'm keeping my fingers crossed that you're on duty when I come in to do this for real.'

'I didn't want to come,' Kyle confessed on his way out. 'But it was kinda cool.'

'I'll make sure he behaves himself better next time,' Scarlett said.

Pippa was smiling as she watched the young couple walking out of the room holding hands.

And Lachlan was smiling as he watched Pippa.

She was still in her working uniform of scrubs, with ugly but comfortable plastic clogs on her feet. Her hair was tamed into the familiar long braid and she was wearing no jewellery and minimal, if any, make-up and…

…and she was still one of the most beautiful women Lachlan had ever met.

But the sensation squeezing his chest right now was very different to the physical attraction that he'd been aware of from the moment he'd first laid eyes on Pippa Gordon. Attraction like that was something chemical. Something that would, inevitably, fade.

He respected how good Pippa was at her job and he really *liked* her as a person and they were both things that were very likely to get stronger rather than fading. Could they end up being real friends once the physical attraction wore off?

Close enough to at least partly fill that empty space in his life where special people should be?

That space that could feel so damn lonely sometimes?

His smile widened as the last couple left and Pippa walked towards him.

'What on earth are you doing *here*?'

'I heard about the classes. I thought a good head of department should be up to speed with everything going on. Plus… I was in the area. I went back to see that house off Richmond Road again.'

'Did you decide to buy it?'

'I did.'

Because it had happened again when he'd looked at the view over Richmond Park. The memories of times with his brother and his family had been even more vivid this time and it felt as if they had the power to shine a different kind of light into that empty space in his life. To be able to feel that those memories of the happiest time of his life were worth hanging on to—celebrating, even—instead of avoiding them because of the sadness attached to them was…well…it was breaking new ground for Lachlan. He could see clearly that, despite the pain that came later, he would never have chosen for that part of his life not to exist. He was, in fact, very grateful for it. He was going to welcome other memories. He might even go looking for old photographs that he could frame or hang on a wall. Because he was going to *have* walls of his own in the very near future.

'I put an offer in on it,' he told Pippa. 'And it was accepted.'

'Wow… Congratulations. That's exciting.'

Pippa started rolling a birthing ball to one side of the room. Lachlan went to pick up another one.

'It's certainly something to celebrate,' he agreed. 'And the White Swan will be my local in a matter of weeks.'

'Might need more than a cheeky prosecco at the local to celebrate something that big.'

'Perhaps we can find some champagne when we go to that show next Wednesday. I've got the tickets.'

'Oh, lovely… What are we going to see?'

'Let me surprise you. I'm sure you'll love it.'

'I'm sure I will.'

The look in Pippa's eyes made Lachlan think she wasn't referring to the latest musical extravaganza being put on in the West End and the flush of pink in her cheeks as she turned away to fetch another ball was all the confirmation he needed.

Perhaps she was going to be counting off the days to their second date with just as much anticipation as he would be. Not that he was about to admit that. Keeping things casual was obviously a foundation rule for the 'three date' game.

How good was it that they were both playing a game that had such well-structured rules? Neither of them was going to let things get out of control and when it ended—as it was destined to do—there would be no hard feelings and they would be able to remain friends.

Pippa could very well become the best friend Lachlan had ever had. Close enough for him to, one day, be able to tell her why anything more than friendship was impossible?

In the meantime, he could look forward to their next date and, inevitably, how their evening was going to end.

Lachlan had no reason to think that sex with Pippa wouldn't be as good the second time as it had been on their first date.

What was totally unexpected was that it turned out to be so much *better*.

Different.

Slower.

So much more intense.

He lay awake for a long time after he'd put Pippa safely into a taxi to get home from his apartment after an amazingly enjoyable night with a show they'd both loved, a riverside dinner—with champagne, of course—ending up in *his* bed, possibly because neither of them wanted to take the time to get back to Pippa's cottage in a different suburb.

It had felt like more than just sex.

In hindsight, it felt as if it had been dangerously close to being more than a purely physical connection.

It felt like they had been making love.

And that was breaking the rules that Pippa didn't know about. He was letting himself get too close to someone. If Pippa felt like this as well, she was going to end up being hurt.

Not nearly as hurt as she would be, however, if they went any further down the track of falling in love with each other. Or, heaven forbid, if she had to go through what he'd had to when he'd watched the struggle both his brother and his father had had to endure. To end up totally broken, like his mother, and simply give up on life.

Lachlan might not be able to protect himself if the worst was going to happen but he could protect someone he cared about. Tonight, he'd realised just how much he was starting to care about Pippa and it was enough for him to know he had to let her escape before any real harm was done.

He had to find a way to stop playing this game, preferably in a way that wouldn't have any negative impact on the friendship they were building and the professional relationship they already had.

He didn't quite know how he was going to do that.

He just knew that it was game over for him.

There simply couldn't be a third date and that was that.

The dream was so real, it was like making love to Lachlan Smythe all over again.

Pippa could feel the stroke of his hands on her skin and the slide of his tongue. She could hear the murmur of his voice and the groan of his pleasure. She could even feel the building of that exquisite pleasure that was almost pain, knowing that it was about to morph into a kaleidoscope of sensation that was simply pure bliss.

But then, in that odd way dreams could edit out chunks of time, she was watching Lachlan walk towards a door.

Naked—like he had been when she'd watched him walking to the bathroom in her cottage that first night. Except that she knew he wasn't going to a bathroom. He was about to walk out of her house.

Out of her life.

And it felt as if he was taking her whole world with him.

She tried to call out.

Don't go... Please don't go... Don't leave me...

The effort she put into trying to make a sound was so great that Pippa woke herself up.

She lay there in her bed, her breath coming in gasps, her body shaking, still caught by fragments of the dream, that fear of losing Lachlan so strong she knew exactly what it was.

She was falling in love with him.

This wasn't supposed to happen. This was supposed to have been safe. She knew that Lachlan wasn't remotely interested in anything more than a casual relationship.

He'd been even more interested in one that had a use-by date.

There was no denying that it *was* happening, however. To *her*.

In the space of two dates? How much worse could it get with a third date?

Good grief. Pippa deliberately pulled in a deeper breath to try and persuade her body—and mind—to shake off the fear.

It couldn't happen. Pippa couldn't go back into that space where you gave someone your heart and they stomped on it until it was completely broken.

The dream was a warning she couldn't ignore.

Damage control was required. Somehow, she had to find a way to make sure that third date didn't happen.

CHAPTER EIGHT

THANK GOODNESS IT was getting easier.

For the first week or so after that second date, Pippa could feel wisps of that dream messing with her head every time she saw Lachlan at work. The pull towards him was a kind of force field she was having to fight not to get sucked into. For a few days she even wondered whether it was too late.

Had she already fallen in love with him?

No, of course she hadn't. Even if it was possible to fall in love that fast, she had an insurance policy of the agreement that they were both on the same page as far as relationships that could be considered in any way serious. And falling in love was about as serious as they got, wasn't it?

The professional distance they had always kept during working hours helped a lot. Lachlan was friendly but appropriately distant with her, just the way he was with other colleagues like Rita and Sally and Peter and it was just the reminder Pippa needed that falling for a man like Lachlan was guaranteed to break your heart. Had dating him at all been a mistake? Why was it that men seemed to be generally better than women at being able to have a completely casual relationship that included sex or a bit of fun like a 'three date' game without emotions getting in the way?

No. Pippa couldn't convince herself it had been a mistake. Eventually, the memory of just that blink of time when she had enjoyed something so special might be enough to persuade her that she was brave enough to try again. With someone who might want something more than a casual fling.

Maybe Pippa just needed to channel some of that masculine skill to separate sex and emotion.

Or she could follow the example of Sally, who'd gone through a string of brief relationships since she'd started working at Queen Mary's and they'd become good friends. Sally had even fallen head over heels in love a couple of times and had been devastated when the men had walked away, but she had the ability to bounce back. She wasn't even afraid of trying again.

Plenty more fish in the sea, she'd say. *One day I'll find a frog to kiss who actually does turn out to be a prince.*

She even had the ability to make a joke out of having a broken heart.

Time for another pity party with Pippa, she'd said last time. *And try saying that fast when you've had a wine or two.*

She might need a pity party herself, Pippa thought—complete with chocolate and wine and a weepy romantic movie—if she couldn't get how she was feeling about Lachlan under better control. She was dreading a case where she had to work closely with him again and her heart sank like a stone when Dawn Grimshaw arrived in the birthing suite. Pippa was the senior midwife on duty and Lachlan was the obstetrician on call and Dawn was going to need the most experienced staff members available. She was thirty-four weeks and three days pregnant—with triplets—and declared herself to be in established labour as she met Pippa by the reception desk.

Pippa was already very familiar with Dawn's history. She'd met this couple right at the start of the pregnancy, when Dawn had come in at eight weeks gestation, feeling ill, bleeding and convinced she was miscarrying her third child. She had been there when the stunned couple were given the news that three heartbeats had been found on the ultrasound examination.

Lachlan had already met Dawn as well. He'd been on call when she had been admitted with a premature labour at almost thirty weeks. She had been given steroids to aid the babies' lung development but the other drugs administered had successfully stopped the labour so she'd been sent home again. It meant that Lachlan was familiar with Dawn's medical history and her determination to have a vaginal birth rather than a Caesarean and he would want to be involved with this delivery even if he wasn't on call.

'I'm sure it's the real thing this time,' Dawn said. 'The contractions are much stronger and longer and they're starting to hurt like hell.'

'The last ones have only been about three and a half minutes apart.' Dawn's husband, Graham, looked pale. 'I might have picked up a speeding ticket on the way here.'

'I kept my legs crossed,' Dawn said with a grimace. 'I also kept all my fingers crossed that Mr Smythe is in the building.'

'You're in luck,' Pippa said. 'He's not only in the building, he's on call. Rita? Could you bleep him, please? You'll find a plan in Dawn's notes for everyone else that needs to be called, too, like NICU and Paeds.'

Within a very short period of time, controlled chaos unfolded in the ward as a delivery suite was prepped, extra equipment was relocated, the neonatal intensive care unit was put on standby and additional paediatricians and midwives found to provide a team to care for each baby as it was born. Multiple births always created a buzz, especially when the mother wanted to avoid a surgical birth.

Lachlan appeared before anyone else, just as Pippa had got Dawn into the delivery suite and given her an initial assessment. It was Pippa's glance he caught first—just a graze of eye contact before greeting Dawn, but it was long enough for any misgivings she had about working with him to evaporate just as swiftly.

Personal feelings were totally irrelevant here. This was the man she wanted to work with. She might not trust him with her heart but she'd trust him with her life in an emergency and she had no qualms whatsoever trusting him to make sure these three identical boys arrived in the world safely.

'Dawn's five centimetres dilated,' she told Lachlan. 'Baby A cephalic. I'm about to set up the CTG and we've got a portable ultrasound on the way. Peter should be here any minute, and we've got Sally on standby for Baby B.'

Extra resuscitation units were being lined up to one side of the room to provide a space with oxygen, heating and light to assess a fragile newborn. They also had drawers full of the equipment, supplies and drugs that might be needed to fight for a tiny life.

'Who's Peter?' Dawn asked.

'He's one of our anaesthetists. I know how keen you are on having a completely natural birth, but remember how we talked about you having an epidural, just in case?

It would be too late by the time you're fully dilated and there's a risk that, after the first baby is born, the others can turn into a more difficult presentation.'

Dawn's face was scrunching into lines of pain as another contraction began. 'I think I do want one. It's all very well when it's only one baby but this could go on for hours, couldn't it?' She groaned. 'Where's the consent form? I'll have to sign it, won't I?'

'Peter will have the forms with him,' Pippa said. 'But we've got the gas and air here if you want to use it now.' She turned on the Entonox cylinder valve, watched the needle of the pressure gauge rise to indicate that the tank was full and then got a clean mouthpiece from its packaging and clipped it onto the tubing before handing it to Dawn. The information she needed to pass on was automatic as she set the equipment up. 'This is for self-medication,' she said, 'so you need to hold the mouthpiece by yourself. Put it between your teeth and close your lips around it. When you feel the need for pain relief, breathe in deeply and only through your mouth. Pain relief should be rapid and any side-effects, like feeling dizzy or having tingling fingers, will wear off quickly as soon as you stop breathing it.'

Dawn sucked a deep breath in. And then another. She groaned again as she lay back on the pillows, this time in relief as the pain of the contraction faded. 'How long will an epidural take to start working?'

'It'll take about ten minutes to insert and another ten to fifteen minutes for the medication to take effect,' Lachlan responded. 'Peter will put a cannula in your hand as well and Pippa will put a bladder catheter in. We'll need to monitor the babies and your contractions, so we'll put two bands around your tummy for heartbeats and one for contractions and we'll use a scalp monitor for the baby that's arriving first. Are you okay with all this? I know you want things as natural as possible but it's my job to make sure it's as safe as possible.'

Dawn reached for her husband's hand and was holding it tightly as she nodded. 'We trust you,' she said.

Pippa looked up from where she was now unwinding the bands for the CTG monitor to see Peter coming into the room.

'Good timing,' she said. 'We were just talking about you.'

An hour later, the first triplet was delivered. A small but healthy baby boy who was pinking up and crying as his cord was clamped and cut. Dawn got to touch her baby for a moment before he was whisked into the care of the paediatric team and then taken to the neonatal intensive care unit.

'He weighs just under two kilograms,' Pippa relayed. 'That's four pounds two ounces in the old money. He's doing well.'

'Adam…' Graham's smile was proud but wobbly. 'That's what we're calling him.'

'Because he's Baby A,' Dawn added. 'It's Ben's turn next. Then Callum's.'

But Baby Ben wasn't in any hurry to appear. When Lachlan checked with both a physical examination and then the Doppler ultrasound, Pippa saw his expression change as he watched the images appear on screen.

'Ben seems to have taken advantage of the extra space Adam left in there.' His voice sounded as though this was no big deal but Pippa knew it could be. 'He's managed to turn into what's called a transverse position, which means he's lying sideways inside the uterus and, in his case, he's got his back to the door.'

'Oh, no… Does this mean I have to have a Caesarean now?' Dawn burst into tears.

'Not necessarily. I can try and turn him. If it doesn't work from the outside, I can do an internal procedure. That means I put one hand inside the uterus and one hand on your tummy so I can shift baby enough to take hold of his legs and deliver him that way. If that's not successful, we have a theatre on standby and it will mean a Caesarean.'

'Please try,' Dawn sobbed. 'I don't want to go to Theatre.'

Pippa found she was holding her breath when the attempt to turn Baby B from the outside failed. An internal podalic version was a rare obstetric procedure and, while she knew what it entailed, she'd never seen one performed.

'You'll feel my hand inside,' Lachlan warned Dawn. 'But, with your epidural, it shouldn't be painful.'

His expression was one of intense concentration. He found the baby's head by palpating the outside of the belly and held it as he slipped his other hand into place to find the baby's feet and grasp them. Then both his hands were moving, gently but purposefully, shifting the baby so that he could be extracted. Pippa saw two tiny feet between Lachlan's fingers emerge and, only seconds later, baby Ben was taking his first breath. Again, his cord was clamped and cut, Dawn and Graham got a peek and the paediatric team took over.

He was bigger than Adam by a few ounces and, happily, his unusual entrance into the world didn't seem to have bothered him. They could all hear his loud protest as he was taken up to NICU to be with his brother.

Even more happily, the final triplet was in a perfect

position and was delivered only fifteen minutes later. This time, with the neonatal consultant's approval, Pippa was able to hold the tiny baby for a little longer, letting his parents touch and kiss him before carrying him to the warmth of the resuscitation unit. And this time she wasn't focused on the babies still to be born and her role as Dawn's primary midwife. She could look down at this baby boy in her arms, wrapped in soft sterile towels.

She guessed he was pretty much the same weight as his brothers and he was breathing well but not crying. His eyes were open and it felt as if he was looking right back at Pippa. And he was so little…

And so perfect…

None of the babies that Pippa had miscarried had got anywhere near looking like this, but for some reason this felt exactly like how she'd imagined it would feel to finally hold a live baby of her own and her eyes suddenly filled with tears. Perhaps it was because there had been so many babies in her hands in such a short space of time. Or that things had been tense when Lachlan had dealt with what could have become a serious situation.

Or maybe it was because she'd been feeling oddly emotional ever since…

…ever since that night with Lachlan that was only a couple of weeks ago.

Since that dream when she'd realised how dangerously close she'd come to falling in love with him.

Oh, dear Lord…

Had he *felt* that thought?

Could he see tears that were on the point of escaping when he glanced in her direction at exactly the same moment she glanced in his?

Somehow, she found a smile. A kind of embarrassed

one, as if she knew she was being less than professional by overreacting to the joy of a successful triplet delivery. It was good that she needed to turn away and hand the baby to the consultant. She stayed to watch as he assessed the third baby boy for his five-minute Apgar score because that gave her a moment or two to take a few deep breaths and centre herself.

By the time Dawn was through the last stage of her labour and could be taken to the NICU to finally meet her babies properly, Pippa found she was in a whole new headspace. She'd been through far worse things than a mild dose of heartbreak. Yes, there was a connection between herself and Lachlan but it probably wouldn't take any time at all for it to feel more like the bond of friendship she had with Sally.

As the days ticked past and it became apparent that Lachlan wasn't about to put any pressure on to make plans for another date, it felt as if the prospect had been put on a shelf—like a treat being kept for a special occasion?

If it was left there long enough to gather a bit of dust, Pippa thought, maybe it would be a mutual choice to simply forget about the still available third date and they could seamlessly pivot into being not only colleagues but real friends? That was, after all, the perfect ending when the mythical 'three date' rule was done and dusted, wasn't it? Lachlan would have no trouble at all finding someone who would be more than happy to have a friendship where those benefits weren't quite so limited.

Someone like Sally, perhaps, who came into the staffroom at the same time as Lachlan when Pippa was making herself a toastie for lunch.

'Have you heard?' she asked. 'That Lachlan's bought a house? In Richmond?'

'I had heard a rumour,' Pippa said cautiously. She kept her eye on the toasting machine to make sure Sally wouldn't see anything untoward in her face.

Pippa had been the first to know, hadn't she? Thank goodness nobody else knew that. Or that it was a house that had played its own part in what had happened between herself and Lachlan. She'd only bumped into him at the supermarket that day because he'd been to a viewing, and the day he'd put an offer in and it was accepted was the evening he'd come to that antenatal class she was running, with the tickets to the show that had been their second legitimate date. The one that couldn't be repeated because she'd discovered how close she'd come to falling in love with Lachlan.

She risked a quick glance at him. 'That's fantastic news. When do you move in?'

'It's a nice, quick settlement. I'll be in six weeks after the signing, so that's not far away now. Luckily, I've bought most of the furniture as well so I don't have to go on a mad shopping spree.'

'You are going to have a housewarming party, I hope.' Sally appeared from behind the fridge door, with her lunch container in her hands. 'And invite us all.' She grinned at Lachlan. 'Otherwise, our friendship might be over already.'

They all laughed, but Pippa still kept her gaze on what she was doing as she extracted her sandwich from the machine.

A cheese sandwich.

Like the one she'd made for Lachlan on the night they'd first met.

The night when the air had been so full of those sparks of attraction. Pippa didn't feel very hungry any longer. Why hadn't she recognised the danger of those sparks? The fire they could ignite and how difficult it might be to hose down any hot spots?

'Oh...*wow*...' Sally's eyes widened dramatically. 'How lucky are you, Lachlan? To be waking up every morning to that *view*...'

Everybody was staring through the windows of the master bedroom, as Lachlan gave his guests a quick tour of his house.

Everybody except Pippa. From the corner of his eye, he'd caught the way she'd turned her head to flick a gaze in his direction—as if she couldn't help herself.

As if she was thinking the same thing he was. That they still had a date available and it could end up right here. In this room.

In this bed...

Lachlan broke the eye contact instantly. Before Pippa could see how much he wanted that date.

'That's exactly why I decided to buy this place,' he told Sally. 'I've got a lot of happy childhood memories of Richmond Park.'

'It's a million-pound view, that's for sure.' But Peter was moving towards the walk-in wardrobe. 'No...you've got a dressing room *and* a full en-suite?'

'And four bedrooms?' Rita gave an audible sigh. 'I'm moving in, Lachlan.'

Pippa joined in the laughter, but she didn't catch his gaze again. Not that it stopped every cell in his body letting him know just how strong the longing was to make all these guests disappear and leave only himself and

Pippa in this bedroom. Was it possible she might be the last to leave tonight?

'Come downstairs again,' he said. 'Let me get you all a drink and get this party really started.'

He led the way downstairs, hoping that getting well away from his bedroom would dampen the physical as well as the emotional reaction to seeing Pippa so close to his bed. Things had been going so well, too. Pippa hadn't put any pressure on to arrange that last permissible date in the game they'd been playing and she'd kept any hint of anticipation well-hidden at work, but surely she had to want it as much as he did? Who *wouldn't* want another night of the most sizzling but, at the same time, so exquisitely tender lovemaking that he was still feeling echoes from that night that were powerful enough to be disturbing, weeks after the experience.

Someone who was just as averse to hurting someone who might start wanting more than they were able to give?

It could also be someone who was afraid they might be hurt themselves because they were beginning to want more?

Either way, it seemed as if neither of them was willing to take the risk of cashing in that third date voucher. Lachlan would have to ignore the voice that had just begun whispering in the back of his head.

One more time couldn't hurt... The novelty might have worn off and it'll just be like sex with any other gorgeous woman...

Lachlan didn't think so.

'Help yourselves to anything you like.' He waved at the array of ice buckets and bottles on a sideboard in the drawing room. 'There's red and white wine and...prosecco of course. And champagne...' He was careful not to look in Pippa's direction as he popped the cork on a bottle. 'This is a celebration, after all. And it's my very first house-warming party.'

'Really?' Rita held a flute out to be filled. 'And you look like such a party animal, Mr Smythe.'

'It's the first house I've ever bought,' he told her.

'And you've chosen Richmond.' Sally also held out a glass. 'That's great. It must mean you're planning to stick around.'

'I guess so.' Lachlan raised an eyebrow in Pippa's direction, ready to fill a glass for her, but she gave her head a tiny shake and reached for a bottle of sparkling mineral water. Was this a signal that she didn't want to play? That she wouldn't still be here when all the other guests had departed later this evening?

Don't give up, that traitorous little voice suggested. *Try again later...with that special bottle of the vintage French champagne you've got in the fridge...*

Lachlan managed to find a smile for Sally. 'Maybe it was turning forty that made me decide it was time to settle down,' he said.

'Or it might be those childhood memories you can see out of your window,' Rita said. 'After all those years of globe-trotting, maybe you realised it was time to come home.' Her smile was warm as she raised her glass. 'Here's to coming home,' she toasted.

It seemed like everyone could think of something good to toast. Richmond. The park. The Queen Mary Hospital in general and the obstetric department in particular. Even wild swimming got thrown into the mix, along with laughter and a cheeky enquiry about whether bathing costumes were mandatory. Lachlan relaxed into being the host as it became clear that everyone was clearly enjoying the party.

He had plenty of snacks available but he'd arranged for hot pizzas to be delivered later in the evening that received an enthusiastic reception.

'This is perfect,' Peter said. 'I'm starving. Ooh…that one with anchovies has my name written all over it.' He picked up a large wedge with one hand and took a bite. He picked up the box with his other hand and held it out. 'Pippa?' His words were muffled by a full mouth. 'You've got to try this…'

Lachlan saw the moment that Pippa actually turned pale after she'd shaken her head and Peter had turned to offer the pizza to someone else. He watched her press her hand to her mouth seconds later, and then turn to run out of the room.

He felt his stomach dropping.

Something was wrong with Pippa.

The thought made him feel ill himself. He put down the piece of pizza he was holding and turned to follow Pippa out of the room, but Rita touched his arm.

'I'll go,' she said.

Lachlan had to nod. And smile. It was far more appropriate for motherly Rita to follow Pippa to the bathroom she had presumably headed for. The last thing Pippa would want would be for him to be showing a level of concern for her wellbeing that might be a giveaway for how well they knew each other.

It was several minutes before Rita came back.

'She's okay,' she told Lachlan. 'She just feels a bit off.'

'I hope it's not something she's eaten. Like those salmon canapés. What if I've given you all food poisoning?'

Rita patted his arm. 'Nobody else is feeling sick. Pippa

said it was probably the smell of anchovies because she hates them with a passion, but I reckon she might have picked up that gastro bug that's going around. We had a toddler in Outpatients the other day who was throwing up all over the place.'

'Oh, no...'

'I'm going to take her home,' Rita told him. 'It's time I went and left you youngsters to enjoy yourselves anyway. Pippa said she doesn't want to make a fuss, so she asked me to pass on her thanks and that it's been a lovely party.'

The urge to stride out of the room and find Pippa so that he could see for himself that she really was okay was disturbingly powerful. Lachlan took a deep breath.

'Thanks for looking after her,' he said. 'Tell her I hope she feels better very soon.'

It had definitely been the anchovies.

Pippa felt quite well enough to go to work the day after Lachlan's housewarming party. She found some of her colleagues in the department's staffroom before handover was due to start. They were drinking what smelled like very strong coffee.

She grinned at Sally. 'So it was a good night, then?'

Sally nodded. 'You left early.'

'I wasn't feeling great. Me and anchovies don't get along.' She poured herself a mug of coffee and added milk.

'Ugh...' She glared at the mug after her first sip. 'Have we changed the brand of coffee or something? This tastes horrible.'

Sally laughed, reaching past her to rinse her mug and put it in the dishwasher. 'Tasted the same as always to me. Maybe you're pregnant.'

Pippa echoed her laughter. 'Yeah…right… Chance would be a fine thing.'

Sally's words came back to haunt her as she caught the first baby she delivered on that shift, however, lifting the baby girl to put her straight onto her mother's chest.

She'd never had any cravings in any of her pregnancies.

But she'd always gone off coffee. Big time.

It was impossible, of course. She was on the Pill and the chances of that form of contraception failing were only one percent.

Okay…the percentage went up if compliance wasn't perfect and Pippa did miss the occasional dose.

There'd been the issue of the broken condom too, but that was how many weeks ago? Seven? Eight? She would have had signs by now, even if the Pill had made her periods light enough to be barely noticeable sometimes.

Signs like going off coffee?

Throwing up at the smell of anchovies?

There were pregnancy tests freely available in the ward and, just to reassure herself, Pippa took one with her when she went for a bathroom break late that afternoon when her shift was over. She stayed in the cubicle, sitting on the toilet and staring at the little window on the stick for the three minutes it took to develop.

It didn't take three minutes, though. Clearly, she was excreting enough HCG hormone for the test line to develop almost as quickly and strongly as the control line. There was no doubt about it.

Pippa was pregnant.

CHAPTER NINE

'Are you okay, Pippa? You look a bit pale.'

'Yeah…all good, thanks, Rita. Just a bit tired.' Pippa kept walking. Out of the ward and out of Queen Mary's.

She'd been lying, of course. She wasn't okay. The last thing she'd expected—or wanted—was to find herself pregnant.

Again.

To be facing the pain, both physical and emotional, of losing yet another baby. Which would happen within the next few weeks, given how far along she was already. She'd never got past the first trimester. Sometimes it had been only days after a positive test that the bottom fell out of her world yet again.

Thanks to assuming her ultra-light periods were due to the contraceptive pill, she had to be only a couple of weeks away from the end point of her first trimester so she had every reason to suspect that the cramps and bleeding would start any day now.

Which meant that there was really no point in telling Lachlan that she was pregnant, was there?

Especially when it would ruin the friendship that seemed to be growing between them—the perfect common ground that would never derail her life in the way that falling in love with someone who was unavailable could have done.

She could hear his voice so clearly as she walked home that evening, telling her that he liked rules about dating. That he had a few of his own.

Like keeping things strictly casual. That's non-negotiable...

Casual. It would be unacceptable for someone to fall in love with him. Or to dream of a committed relationship or, heaven forbid, marriage or children.

Non-negotiable.

Nobody was ever going to persuade him to change his mind.

She'd been lucky to get as close to Lachlan as she had. Pippa had the feeling that it would be a rare privilege to be considered a good friend.

Falling pregnant had broken every rule Lachlan Smythe had about dating.

If she told him, he would never trust her again and they could never be friends.

She'd been through this herself often enough to know that she would survive. Doing it alone, in fact, would be preferable to the support of her ex-husband and the obstetrician who'd actually been sleeping with him at the time of her last miscarriage.

Pippa couldn't even tell Sally because if any hint got out, it could get back to Lachlan and he knew she hadn't been seeing anyone else. He would be able to add lying by omission to any other aspects of what would seem like a betrayal. He might even think that she'd been lying about being on the Pill.

By the time Pippa had arrived home at her little cottage, she was exhausted by overthinking everything. It was really quite simple. All she needed to do was to stay calm and carry on. This problem would be history within a matter of only a few days. Weeks, at the very most.

Whatever bug had targeted Pippa on the night of his housewarming party seemed to be having long-lasting effects. She certainly wasn't looking a hundred percent. She was still a little pale a week later and she seemed… subdued?

Not her usual self, that was for sure.

She was, however, still smiling and still caring for her mothers with the same focus and skill Lachlan had come to expect from her.

She'd called for obstetric assistance this morning and her summary was succinct.

'I have a thirty-six-year-old primigravida who's been in second stage labour for nearly three hours and getting very tired. We now have a non-reassuring CTG with a baseline heart rate between one hundred and one-oh-five and variable decelerations over the last twenty minutes or so that are lasting more than sixty seconds and are biphasic.'

'I'm on my way,' Lachlan said.

The CTG recordings were even more concerning by the time Lachlan arrived in the birthing suite and suggested that the level of oxygen the baby was receiving was not ideal.

'On the plus side,' Lachlan said, after explaining why Pippa had called for assistance, 'I know you feel too tired to carry on pushing but your contractions still have a good duration and intensity, which means you'll be able to help us if we try some assistance with either a vacuum cup or forceps.'

After a physical examination he told her that it might

be as simple as correcting the position of the baby's head. 'Your baby could be born within a few minutes,' he said. 'If we go for a Caesarean, even though you've got an epidural in place, it'll take quite a lot more time to get you up to Theatre and prepped for surgery. And the less time it takes, the better that is for baby, when oxygen levels might be dropping.'

The frightened first-time parents listened to the risk factors for both the procedure and the back-up plan for a C-section if it failed. He saw them both look to Pippa for reassurance.

'Mr Smythe is the best possible obstetrician you could have,' she told them, the sincerity in her tone completely genuine. 'If this was my baby, I'd absolutely trust him to choose the safest option for his birth.'

Within minutes, the consent form was signed. Peter arrived to top up the epidural anaesthetic and Sally arrived to assist Pippa.

'Paediatrics are caught up in Theatre and ED,' Peter reported. 'Someone will be here asap.'

Lachlan scrubbed in and got gowned and gloved. He could see that Pippa and Sally were both busy, getting the mother into position with her legs in stirrups, draping her legs and belly and inserting a catheter to make sure her bladder was empty. A trolley appeared beside him with all the equipment he needed.

He checked the gear, putting the cup of the vacuum device against his palm and pumping it to make sure it was functioning correctly and the vacuum pressure would hold. He carefully palpated the baby's skull, finding the triangular shape of the posterior fontanelle and the diamond shape of the anterior fontanelle near the forehead. He positioned the cup over the midline between the fontanelles. Looking up, he found Pippa's steady gaze on his and he gave her a single nod.

She was keeping a close eye on the CTG screen.

'Here it comes, Anika... Are you ready? Deep breath in and push. Push...push...push— You're doing *great*.'

Lachlan was applying gentle traction on the baby's head.

'Take another deep breath.' Pippa was taking one herself as if she was sharing this part of the labour with the mother. 'And...push...push...*push*...'

The top of the baby's head was visible as the contraction faded. They waited for the next one to start and Pippa was even more encouraging.

'Push as hard as you can. This one will do it. Push hard. *Harder*... You're almost there...'

Lachlan changed the direction of his traction to pull the head up. With his other hand he felt under the baby's face and as soon as he could feel the jaw he released the suction cap.

'Your baby's head is born, Anika,' he said. 'You can push his body out now.'

'One more,' Pippa said. 'Just one more push...'

And there he was. He heard Pippa's intake of breath as she noticed how limp and blue the baby was. Lachlan immediately clamped and cut the cord and Pippa scooped the infant into a sterile towel and took him straight to the resuscitation unit. The paediatric team still hadn't arrived. Sally took over monitoring Anika for the third stage of her labour.

'What's happening?' Anika cried. 'What's wrong?'

'Baby just needs a little bit of help,' Lachlan told her. He stripped off his gloves and was pulling on a fresh pair as he joined Pippa. The baby boy was dry and in the warmth of the unit. Oxygen was flowing and Pippa had a tiny mask over his face and was helping him with his first breaths. Lachlan could already see that the blue tinge to his skin was fading and he was moving—tiny arms and legs beginning to wake up. The disc of Lachlan's stethoscope covered half the little chest but what he could hear made him smile.

'Heart rate's over a hundred,' he told Pippa.

She lifted the mask and the baby took his first breath on his own. And then another that came with a warbling cry as it was released.

'Apgar of two at one minute,' Pippa said quietly. 'Up to seven at five minutes.'

'Can we see him?' Anika called. *'Please…?'*

Lachlan caught Pippa's gaze and gave her another single nod. She wrapped the baby in a fresh warm towel and gathered him into her arms to take to his parents. Lachlan found he was watching her rather than the baby so he saw the moment she had to blink back tears as she picked up the baby. It was then he remembered her reaction at the birth of the triplets last week, but this time he could sense an intensity that was…

…different, that was what it was.

But both those births had come with the kind of tension where a tiny life was potentially hanging in the balance. It was normal to feel the kind of relief that could bring a lump to your throat or a tear to your eye.

What was making him think that there was something more going on with Pippa? Making him feel as if he wanted to find out what it was. To ask for that third date so they could have a really private conversation? Pillow talk, even, where secrets could be shared?

No. That would be a bad idea. A really, really bad idea.

What he could do, though, was keep a careful eye on her and make sure she was okay. Because what if it had been something he'd done, or hadn't done, that had changed things? That it was his fault she was more emotional about her job and that she looked…almost haunted?

The twelve-week mark for the pregnancy finally arrived.

Then a few more days went past—so slowly that Pippa felt as if she was counting every single minute.

She'd never got this far in a pregnancy.

She'd never felt this…*good*…

That nausea was gone. She had more energy. And, from somewhere she couldn't control, Pippa began to feel flickers of…not hope exactly, but the first acknowledgement that maybe this time might be different.

That this, in fact, could turn out to be what she'd always dreamed of—the journey to becoming a mother. It kind of made sense. The father was different this time. Perhaps there had been some kind of chemical incompatibility in every one of those earlier pregnancies that wasn't there this time.

It was still far too early to be confident, of course. It was hard enough to believe she'd got this far. Maybe that was why, when the department was so quiet, late in her shift that day, Pippa decided to drink a large glass of water to fill her bladder, wait half an hour and then sneak into an unoccupied room and use the ultrasound machine—just to prove to herself that she really was still pregnant.

She angled the screen of the machine so that she could see it from the bed, propped herself up on pillows, pulled the elastic waistband of her scrub pants down and squirted gel onto her belly. Then she slid the transducer as low as she could and pressed it into the midline, angling it down to locate her bladder right behind her pubic bone. She held her breath as she changed the angle to find the uterus that was right beside the bladder and…

…and there it was. The dark fluid in her uterus and the unmistakable shape of a baby. She could see the head that looked too big and even identify tiny limbs. Legs that were actually *kicking*…

And the soft swish of a foetal heartbeat was filling the air.

'Oh, my God…' she whispered.

Pippa was overwhelmed. So focused on the screen and the rhythmic swishing she was oblivious to anything else, including the sound of the door being quietly opened and then clicked shut again.

She jumped, gripping the transducer more tightly at the sound of a voice in the darkened room.

'What the hell is going on in here?'

Pippa gasped. Of all the people who could have discovered what she was doing, this was the worst possible contender.

'*Lachlan…?*'

She couldn't move. The transducer was still on her belly. The image was still filling the screen. Lachlan walked towards the machine, sat down in front of it and reached for the transducer. Pippa's fingers went limp enough to let him take hold of the handle.

'I saw you coming in here,' he said, his tone expressionless. 'When you didn't come out, I started to wonder whether you were okay.'

Pippa could feel the pressure of the transducer on her belly deepen. She could see that Lachlan knew exactly what he was doing. He used the callipers to click on the frozen image of the baby, putting a marker on the tip of the head and another one on the rump. With the second click, a dotted line appeared and she knew that the machine was calculating the crown to rump length to provide a gestational age.

Lachlan was completely silent as he looked at the information. He changed the angle of the transducer and did a sideways sweep.

'Singleton pregnancy,' he said finally. 'Gestational age of twelve weeks, five days—give or take four days for accuracy.' His voice was just a monotone. It was icy. 'Is it mine?'

'Yes…' The word was a whisper. 'I'm sorry.'

Except she wasn't. Not now. Not when she could see this new life that had been created. When she could still hear that heartbeat.

But Lachlan lifted the transducer and the sound stopped. He sat there, the light of the screen making his face look ghostly. Frozen. He was sitting very still and the silence was deadly. Unbearable.

Pippa picked up a paper towel to scrub the gel off her belly. She needed to get out of here.

Lachlan turned the machine off and the screen went dark. He said only five words.

'You can't have this baby.'

The shock was electric. Pippa could feel it all over her skin—a horrible, prickling sensation. Sinking in to make her feel sick and create a weird buzzing in her head.

She was moving without giving her body any conscious instructions. Screwing up the paper towel. Pulling her scrub pants back up and swinging her legs off the bed.

She threw six words over her shoulder as her feet touched the floor.

'That's not your choice to make.'

And then she walked out of the room.

CHAPTER TEN

IT WASN'T A conscious choice to stay there staring at that black screen after Pippa had stormed out of the room.

It was simply that Lachlan couldn't move.

This was a body blow he hadn't seen coming. Even when he was going through the motions of clicking the cursor and taking the measurements that would reveal the gestational age of this unborn baby and it was sinking in that it could be *his* baby, he still hadn't seen this coming.

Something that was so huge, his world could never be the same.

It only lasted a heartbeat, but that was enough.

Enough for Lachlan to come face to face with something he'd managed to bury so deeply he hadn't even known it existed.

The strength of that longing to have a family of his own.

To be a husband. To be a father. To live, like most people could, without the fear of an unimaginably horrible disease becoming a reality—for a parent, for yourself or, even worse, for your child.

The fear was always going to win over any longing, of course, but that glimpse of what it could have been like had been the most painful blow Lachlan had experienced in too many years to count.

He'd seen the baby. Not just a shapeless blob with only the astonishing evidence of life that a tiny beating heart represented. Pippa's pregnancy was so far along that the outline of limbs was now clear, right down to minuscule fingers and toes. The button of a nose, the curl of developing ears. That was what had made the longing so fierce. And the fear so very real.

He'd had to hit back. It was self-defence. A shield that he pulled in front of himself. He hadn't intended that his words would come out as starkly as they had. Or as such a blunt commandment.

You can't have this baby...

Pippa had been perfectly correct in stating that it wasn't his choice to make. What she didn't know was that she wasn't making an informed choice herself. She had no idea of how much pain and suffering could be in her future. Or the child's. Or *his*, for that matter, which felt unfair when he'd been so determined—and careful—to make sure that this would never happen. That he would never have to go back into the space where he knew exactly what it would be like to live with the threat of Huntington's in the background of every minute of every day. A space he'd managed to lock the door on years ago. A space that he'd never the slightest inclination to re-enter.

Pippa had unlocked that door.

She hadn't given him any choice about going back in there either, because she'd *pushed* him in.

The longing was forgotten. Even the fear was fading. It was kind of like a game of emotional rock-paper-scissors.

Fear squashed hope. But anger could beat fear.

Lachlan could finally move again.

Okay, his words had been too harsh, given that Pippa did not know what had prompted them.

He owed her an explanation.

But he couldn't do that while he was feeling like this. The anger was another type of shield, and somehow he needed to find the courage to put it down before he would be able to speak to her.

It was the fastest U-turn Pippa Gordon had ever made.

Hopefully fast enough that the man at the other end of the corridor—Lachlan Smythe—hadn't seen her change direction in a very blatant attempt to avoid crossing his path.

She turned the corner at the end of the corridor and went into the first room she had access to, which was an unoccupied delivery suite. This was supposed to be her lunch break but Pippa had just completely lost her appetite. She needed to find a distraction and she could see one right in front of her. A neonatal resuscitation unit. It wouldn't hurt to double-check this vital piece of equipment and make sure nothing was missing from any of the external or internal components.

She flicked the switch to turn it on and check that the heater and lights were functioning. Then she checked that the oxygen and air cylinders were full and there were no signs of wear and tear on the hoses.

Her concentration slipped as she counted the towels and linen, however.

If she had to work with Lachlan, fine. She could deal with that, but Pippa had no intention of talking to him if she could avoid it and it wasn't anything other than a strictly professional conversation. She didn't even want to say hello to him.

She opened the first drawer under the bassinet mattress within its clear plastic walls. This was where the infant laryngoscopes were slotted, along with blades and introducers. There were the smallest sized plastic airways, too. And nasogastric tubes. They were all so miniature. The fight for newborn babies' lives was not just incredibly tense, it was so much more delicate because their airways and veins and arteries were so tiny and fragile.

How *dared* Lachlan tell her she couldn't have this baby?

Nobody was going to tell her what she could or couldn't do when it came to her body.

She was still furious, three days after he'd busted her giving herself an ultrasound examination.

Pippa took a deep breath as she opened another drawer and used her expert gaze to scan for any gaps in a wide range of supplies. Cannulas and bandages and splints. Syringes and needles and clamps and dressings. Every compartment of the drawer seemed to be well stocked and she finally let her breath out in a sigh.

Oh, she'd known Lachlan wouldn't react well to the news. He'd told her straight up that he was 'on board' with her assumed aversion to any long-term relationship that even resembled a marriage, and being linked to someone through parenthood was about as long-term as it got.

He had been amused enough to suggest that he was totally on board with her opinion that the old woman who lived in a shoe was 'stupid' because she had so many children. He'd laughed aloud. And making him laugh had added fuel to the fire of that instant attraction, hadn't it?

It didn't seem very funny now, though.

Okay...so he was the father of this baby. That gave him the right to know of its existence. To be part of its life if he chose to be, but it didn't give him the right to choose whether this baby was born or not. If he didn't want any part of being a father, well, that was fine, too. Pippa could cope perfectly well as a single mother, just like millions of other women managed to do.

Had she really thought he wouldn't have noticed her?

Lachlan had been aware that Pippa was doing her best to avoid him. He'd been doing the same thing himself in order to try and clear his own head, but seeing her practically running away so that she didn't have to walk past him was unacceptable. It was so blatant, people were going to notice. And start asking questions.

They hadn't had to work together closely in the last three days, largely thanks to him having a day off and some back-to-back meetings, but what was going to happen when they did? Was she going to turn around and walk away from a mother who needed assistance with a forceps delivery? Or stand at one side of the theatre, her body posture radiating hostility, while he performed an emergency Caesarean?

Lachlan had lengthened his stride, but by the time he reached the end of the corridor Pippa was nowhere to be seen in either direction and he didn't have time to stand there wondering how he was going to deal with this situation. He was due to start an outpatient clinic for high-risk pregnancies due to medical conditions.

There were women waiting for him who were desperate to have a child, despite the extra risk of congenital heart malformations, high blood pressure, renal failure or brittle diabetes. Brave women who deserved his complete concentration and best efforts to keep the pregnancy safe for as long as possible and ensure that both mother and baby stayed healthy.

His first patient was already waiting in the consulting

room and Lachlan picked up her notes as he went past the reception desk, pushing Pippa Gordon and *her* pregnancy completely out of his mind until the rest of his working day was finished.

Anna was a Type One diabetic and while she'd been managing her blood sugar levels well during her pregnancy, the complication of excess amniotic fluid had been noted at her last visit so she was being monitored more closely now.

'How are you feeling, Anna?'

'Not too bad. I'm getting a bit short of breath if I walk too far. Or do the vacuuming or something.'

Anna's husband, Clint, was smiling as they exchanged a fond glance. 'That's her excuse, anyway. I'm getting very good at vacuuming.'

'Have you noticed any swelling in your legs or feet?'

'No.'

'Indigestion? Heartburn?'

'Yes—but that's par for the course at this stage of pregnancy now, isn't it? I'm thirty-six weeks.'

Lachlan was scanning the report from the ultrasound examination Anna had just had. 'There's quite an increase in the amount of fluid from your last visit. Come and get up on the couch so I can have a feel of your tummy.'

Anna used the step to get onto the examination couch. Clint helped her get comfortable by rearranging the pillows and she glanced over to where Lachlan was washing his hands as she settled back.

'Is it dangerous?' she asked. 'It feels like we should be really worried with all these extra appointments.'

'We just want to keep a close eye on you, which is why we're getting you to come in so often. There is an increased risk of a premature birth or the baby being able to turn and become a breech presentation and we have to be aware of other potential complications like a cord prolapse or part of the placenta becoming detached.'

Clint nodded. 'Our midwife gave us a list of everything to watch out for and she told us not to hesitate to come in and get checked if we're worried about anything. She's really lovely. Pippa Gordon, her name is. Do you know her?'

'I do indeed.' Lachlan nodded as he reached for some paper towels. 'She's a wonderful midwife.'

For a split second, as Lachlan dried his hands thoroughly, his focus slipped. He could so easily imagine Pippa making sure someone like Anna was fully informed and she would know what she was talking about as far as risk factors to either baby or mother. If she didn't know enough about something like polyhydramnios, she would do whatever research was needed to get up to speed.

Was that the problem with this stand-off they were in?

Just giving her the bare facts, as he'd intended to do, and explaining that going ahead with a pregnancy was unacceptable if a test confirmed the risk of Huntington's Disease might well not be enough for Pippa.

She deserved to hear the whole story.

Even if that didn't change how she felt about the situation she had the right to know the risks she would be facing in the future. It was a moral duty on his part to make sure that she *was* fully informed, however hard that was going to be.

He'd finally reached a stage in his life where he'd found a very welcome peace. Where he could experience a memory, like bike riding with Liam, that could bring joy rather than push him back into the space where the worst of the other memories had been filed and locked away.

Telling Pippa everything could risk undermining this new peace so much that he might never find it again. But he had no choice, did he?

Pippa deserved an explanation.

She also deserved an apology for what he'd said to her.

Not that she was going to let him get close enough to have any kind of conversation at work, and that would be entirely inappropriate for the extremely personal discussion he intended having with her. She was just as unlikely to accept an invitation from him to meet somewhere else, so there was really only one solution. He would simply have to turn up on her doorstep and force her to listen to him.

And there was something else he would have to do first.

Something that would have to wait until this clinic was completed and he was satisfied that there was nothing he needed to do urgently to keep all these high-risk mothers and babies safe.

'Let's get started,' he said aloud, screwing up the paper towels and dropping them into the wastepaper basket. 'Did you have a BGL finger prick when you went for your blood tests earlier?'

'No. They mentioned things like renal and liver function. I do have an appointment at the diabetes clinic in a couple of days. I am noticing that my insulin levels need adjusting more often at the moment, which is a bit of a pain.'

'I'll test it now, if you're okay with that. I'd just like to double-check it against your continuous monitor for accuracy.'

'No problem.'

Anna held her finger out to get a drop of blood collected. Then Lachlan wrapped a blood pressure cuff around her upper arm. He was going to do a thorough obstetric check-up and had set aside plenty of time to explain the possibility of inducing labour earlier—possibly as early as next week if the baby kept growing this fast. The need for a C-section was another possibility that they needed to be aware of.

His patient after Anna was Caitlin, who'd had a congenital heart defect corrected as a child and was now also well into her third trimester. The final couple he saw needed extra time simply to reassure them, not only because they were expecting twins, and multiple pregnancies were automatically higher risk and therefore received more frequent monitoring. This couple had been trying to get pregnant for more than ten years and had finally achieved success thanks to IVF treatment in another city. They were understandably highly anxious so it was much later than normal business hours by the time they left, but Lachlan had a phone number that he knew he could use to make this particular call.

The person he spoke to was a very senior doctor at London's Regional Genetics Centre—one of the specialist services for the diagnosis and management of genetic conditions.

'Of course I remember you, Lachlan. And your family.' His tone was gentle. 'What can I do for you today?'

'I'm ready,' was all Lachlan had to say. 'Could I possibly make an appointment to come and see you tomorrow?'

CHAPTER ELEVEN

IT HAD BEEN a long day.

Eighteen-year-old Kayley, who'd become pregnant accidentally and had no intention of keeping her baby and no desire to go through the process of giving birth, had come in with regular contractions that had continued for several hours with little progress. The atmosphere in the room was tense and miserable, which wasn't helping anyone.

'The gas isn't working. I want an epidural.'

'You're not quite dilated enough to have an epidural yet.' Pippa had estimated it to be barely two centimetres on last examination. 'We need to be sure you're in established labour. If things don't get going again, we might need to send you home for a while and we can't do that if you've had an epidural.'

'I don't want to go home. I want a Caesarean.'

'You really don't, Kayley. Not unless it's really necessary. It's major surgery that can be very painful afterwards and it takes a long time to recover. Let's get you up and walking around. That might help.'

'You'll be lucky.' Kayley's mother was flicking through a magazine as she sat beside the bed. 'It's hard enough getting this one out of bed on a good day.'

'Would you like me to get one of the doctors to come

and see you, Kayley?' Pippa sent a silent wish into the ether that it wasn't Lachlan on call today. His days off had overlapped hers and she wasn't sure if he was even back in the hospital yet. She wasn't feeling nearly as angry as she had been, but she was still hoping to avoid working with him for as long as possible.

'What for?' Kayley muttered.

'To talk about options for pain relief. Or helping to get your labour established.' Beneath the surliness and lack of cooperation, Pippa could see the teenager's fear. 'I know this isn't easy for you, sweetheart,' she said gently. 'We all want to help.'

'Do what the nurse says, Kay.' Her mother dropped the magazine. 'I'm going home for a bit to see what chaos your brothers are creating but I'll be back later, okay?'

'Whatever...' Kayley picked up the Entonox mouthpiece and dragged in a deep breath. Then she dropped it over the side of the bed. 'It's *still* not working. It's useless...'

It turned out to be Sandy on call and she was brilliant with Kayley. She made the teenager feel as if she was taking some control of the situation as they made a plan to break her waters, start an oxytocin drip and get an epidural in place sooner rather than later.

Six long, hard hours later, an exhausted Kayley was holding her baby in her arms, and Pippa's heart was squeezed hard at the pride in this young mother's face.

'Look at him, Mum...'

'Yeah...he's pretty cute. You don't want to keep him now, do you?'

'I dunno... This doesn't feel like I thought it was going to.'

'You don't have to make any big decisions yet,' Pippa

said. 'The whole team will be in tomorrow with all the people you need to talk to, like your counsellors and psychologist and social worker. It's time to rest now. You've done a brilliant job, Kayley. You should be very proud of yourself.'

Kayley smiled at her for the first time since she'd arrived this morning. 'I guess I am. Well tired, though.'

Pippa was well tired herself. She got home, kicked her shoes off, opened the door of the fridge to see what she had available to cook for dinner and then pushed it shut again. Cooking was a step too far. Her phone was in the pocket of her coat hanging by the front door. After a day like today, she deserved to order something hot that would be delivered, hopefully before she fell asleep on the couch.

The knock on her door as she reached into the coat pocket made her jump. Opening the door to find someone standing there with paper bags that were clearly full of takeout food was nothing short of a miracle.

The only problem was that the person holding the bags was Lachlan.

'We need to talk,' he said quietly. 'Can I come in, please?' He lifted the bags. 'I come with food. Did you know *Chez Anton* caters for takeout? I thought you might let me in if I brought posh steak and chips.'

Oh-h...

He was smiling at her and for a moment Pippa was pulled back to that dream she'd had. The one when she'd been so devastated when he walked away from her and it felt as if her world had shattered.

She'd had her suspicions then that she might have already fallen in love with him and, while she'd dismissed it, it was more than a suspicion at the moment. But she was overtired. Pregnant and hormonal. He had arrived with hot, delicious-smelling food and he was smiling at her.

Caring for her...

What woman wouldn't fall in love with a man like this?

She was too tired to even try and summon the shock and anger she'd had at his reaction to finding out that she was pregnant with his baby.

She tried. She tried to remind herself that she preferred the idea of being a single mother to having anything to do with Lachlan Smythe ever again. She opened her mouth to tell him to go away and leave her alone. But she found herself saying something rather different.

'You'd better come in then,' she said.

He'd even brought sparkling mineral water for her to replace the champagne they'd had to accompany exactly this meal they'd had on their first date. Oddly, it felt even more delicious to be curled up on the couch, still in her scrubs, with bare feet, eating the crispy twice-cooked fries and slivers of steak with her fingers. She knew Lachlan wanted to talk but they ate in a companionable silence with nothing more important being said than how perfectly cooked the food was and how good was tarragon and chervil together in a sauce?

But then the meal was over, the containers piled back into the paper bags and their fingers wiped on the serviettes that had come with the meals. Pippa found herself curling further back into the corner of her sofa. Lachlan leaned forward, his hands on his knees and his head bent. He let his breath out slowly.

'I need to tell you a story,' he said.

'Okay...' There was something in Lachlan's tone that

tugged at her heartstrings enough to make her want to reach out and touch him. To reassure him?

To let him know that she could care for him the way he'd just shown he could care for her?

Whatever it was, Pippa resisted it. She hugged her arms around herself instead. Around her belly and the baby she needed to protect.

'I had a younger brother,' Lachlan said quietly. 'His name was Liam and he was three years younger than me. By the time I was five, he was old enough to be fun to play with and I was his favourite person in the world. He'd be waiting for me at the gate when I got home from school with some awful present like a soggy, half-eaten biscuit he'd saved for me and...' he cleared his throat '...and I loved him so much that I'd eat it and pretend it was the best present ever.'

Lachlan didn't lift his head so he didn't see that Pippa was smiling. She knew that kind of love that could exist between siblings.

'He was so excited when he started school, but that was when people noticed that something wasn't right. He was a bit clumsier than the other kids and sometimes he walked oddly. One of his teachers said he looked like a little old man. She thought it was cute, but what did worry her was his learning problems. They did all sorts of educational tests and thought he might have ADHD. He got sessions with a psychologist and a speech therapist.'

Pippa was listening quietly. Watching Lachlan. She could feel his pain even though his voice sounded perfectly normal. Calm. In control. The way he was with patients when he was taking charge of a potential emergency. Exactly the skilled professional you wanted to be in charge, and that meant keeping an emotional distance so that his focus couldn't be derailed.

'He had a seizure one day at school and that took things to another level. He was given an MRI and they suspected Huntington's Disease.'

Pippa's inward breath was a gasp. 'In a *child*?'

Lachlan turned his head just enough to give her a graze of eye contact. 'It's rare but it happens. They call it "The Devil's Disease"—the cruellest disease known to man.'

Pippa swallowed the huge lump in her throat. She didn't want to hear any more of this story.

But she couldn't *not* hear the rest of it.

'My parents got tested and my father had a positive result for the disease. He was already well into his forties so he knew he was likely to start getting symptoms by the time he was fifty, but he refused to talk about it. It was Liam that mattered. His son. The child he was supposed to protect, and it was his fault that he now had this terrible disease. I remember seeing him cry for the first time. And seeing him look at me as if he was wondering whether he was going to lose both his sons before he died himself.'

Pippa could actually feel the blood draining from her face. Had Lachlan been tested? Was he working up to tell her that he also had Huntington's and therefore the baby she was carrying had a fifty percent chance of having inherited the genetic disorder? It had to be. She could still hear the hollow tone of his voice, as if she was doing something completely unthinkable.

You can't have this baby...

Lachlan threw another glance at Pippa, as if he'd guessed what she might be thinking but he wasn't ready to answer that unspoken question yet.

'Liam's seizures became more and more frequent,' he continued quietly. 'In general, the younger the child is when the symptoms appear, the shorter time they survive, and the progression was rapid for Liam—only ten years from diagnosis. I was eighteen. Liam was fifteen.'

Pippa closed her eyes. 'I'm so sorry, Lachlan,' she whispered.

'It was my mother I was most sorry for in the end,' he said. 'She had devoted her life to caring for Liam. Both she and Dad were devastated when he died and...and we thought that Dad's depression was part of his grief. Until the other symptoms began to appear. I was lucky. They wouldn't hear of me not going away to university and then medical school. The progression of the disease could take decades. It didn't, but it still took too long before my mother finally admitted she couldn't cope with caring for him at home. He spent his last year in a home, unable to talk or move or even swallow. He was still the centre of Mum's life. She visited him every single day and...when he died, she just seemed to fade away. Her official cause of death was a heart attack. It's not very scientific, but I believe it was more like a broken heart.'

Pippa had tears rolling down her cheeks.

She had to touch Lachlan, and when she reached towards him he took hold of her hand, gave it a squeeze, but then let it go. He wasn't finished. Pippa took a deep breath. He was going to tell her what she desperately needed to know. She couldn't let the breath out until he did.

'They didn't test me as a child,' Lachlan said. 'Unless you're symptomatic they won't do it until you're eighteen and can choose for yourself. I'd seen what Liam went through and I didn't want to know if it was going to happen to me, so I chose not to get tested. I watched what happened to my father and my mother, who didn't even have the disease, and that only confirmed that I'd made the right decision for myself.'

Pippa had to let her breath out, but it wasn't a sigh of relief. She still didn't know. Fear was digging its claws in.

'It's the toss of a coin.' Lachlan shrugged. 'Heads, you're fine. You can live a normal life. Tails, you're facing a degenerative, life-threatening brain disease and life will never be normal again. I preferred to live with the hope I might be free of it.' He let his breath out in a sigh. 'I knew if I got symptomatic I'd have no choice but to face it and I was okay with that. Because I would be doing it by myself. I wouldn't have a partner that would have to live through it and have their own life ruined like my mother's was. Above all, I was going to make damned sure I never risked passing it on to a child because I felt that was a social responsibility as well as a personal one. The only way, so far, to eradicate the disease is to stop passing it on. And yes, I could have found a partner and tested embryos and terminated pregnancies that were affected, but how could I willingly give my partner and healthy kids the prospect of having to live with me when it was my turn and I knew how horrendous it would be?'

Lachlan got to his feet. He turned and, for the first time, he made direct eye contact with Pippa. And held it.

'I've had the test now. It could take weeks to get the results, but if I'm negative there won't be any repercussions for the baby.'

Pippa was holding her breath as well as Lachlan's gaze.

If he was negative, wouldn't that mean that there was no longer a reason for Lachlan to fear letting anyone close enough to him to be swept up into the horror of watching him slowly die? No reason for him not to have his own family and be a father?

But the grim tone of Lachlan's voice was more than enough to warn her that it was far too soon to go anywhere near that kind of hope.

'If I'm not negative,' he continued, 'prenatal testing is available through amniocentesis from fourteen to eighteen weeks, but that's an ethical minefield we can discuss if it turns out to be necessary.'

Oh... *God*...

Pippa had done this.

She'd pushed Lachlan into a space where he had to face his worst nightmare. When any hope of living a normal life without the fear of this dreadful disease could be taken away from him. They might both have to live with the fear that their child could be affected. She cared deeply about this man and *she* had done this to him.

Pippa's overwhelming emotions must have been written all over her tear-streaked face because she saw the tight lines of Lachlan's face soften a little.

'I'm sorry I told you that you couldn't have this baby,' he said. 'I had no right to say that. But now you know why I said it.'

She could see the muscles of his throat moving as he swallowed. Hard. Was *he* trying not to cry? Did he need to escape? Was that why he was already heading towards the door?

The urge to follow and put her arms around him was so strong, Pippa could feel herself starting to move and it was in that moment that she realised how much she loved Lachlan.

How much she wanted to be with him—for better *or* worse.

But she also understood how impossible that was.

Lachlan was never going to let anyone that close.

Ironically, the more he cared about someone the less likely he would be to want to spend time with them, let alone make a lifetime commitment. The more he cared, the more effort he would put in to sparing them having to potentially watch someone *they* loved suffer so much.

She'd gone an even bigger step further into the forbidden territory of relationships. She was the person who'd forced him to break a vow and risk the worst thing he could imagine doing in his life—passing on an unthinkable future to an innocent child.

Even if going through this testing ended up releasing him from the fear of letting someone get close enough to create a family with, maybe it wouldn't be with *her*, because she'd done something so cruel to him.

'I'm sorry, too,' she whispered.

But Lachlan didn't hear her. The door was already closing behind him.

CHAPTER TWELVE

'How are you feeling, Anna?'

'I'm okay... I think...'

Anna was lying on the operating table as her surgeon came in, gowned, gloved and masked, his hands held carefully in front of him so as not to come into contact with anything that wasn't sterile. She couldn't see that Lachlan was smiling at her as he spoke but he hoped she might be able to hear it in his voice.

Anna's husband Clint was holding her hand. The anaesthetist was at her head, monitoring her spinal anaesthetic and the two IV lines that had been placed, one for fluids and the other for administering insulin and glucose to keep Anna's blood sugar stable. A scrub nurse was arranging instruments on the sterile surface of a trolley and others were pinning up the drapes to screen off the surgical field from the parents. Anna's midwife was also close.

'All set, Pippa?'

'Yes.'

Pippa met his gaze steadily. He couldn't tell if she was smiling because of her mask, but he *could* tell that she wasn't angry with him any longer. She was over trying to avoid him. There was something else in that split second of eye contact, but this was no time to wonder what effect sharing his story with her last night might have had.

Oddly, it hadn't thrown him into as dark a place as he'd expected. He could almost feel confident that he wasn't going to lose any newfound peace with his past—or his future? He might keep it very well hidden, but a part of him had always been prepared for the worst. If his test results were positive, he could still hope for the best for his baby and support Pippa in raising the child for as long as he possibly could. If his results were negative…

No. He wasn't going to let his mind go there, even for a nanosecond. Not just because he was about to focus completely on the surgery ahead of him but because he knew the fishhook that could be hidden in hope. Buried so deeply in your heart that when that hope was ripped away, it took far too much of your heart with it.

Pippa was all set. She had finished her preparations for this emergency C-section. All she needed to do now was to pick up the sterile towel and be ready to take the baby as soon as it was born. She was pleased to have her presence acknowledged and more than relieved to meet Lachlan's gaze. She hadn't seen him since he'd brought dinner to her cottage last night to share his harrowing story, and she'd had an almost sleepless night, not just feeling broken-hearted for him but worrying that he had far more reason than she'd ever had to prefer that they didn't work together.

There was no sign of him resenting her presence in Theatre, however. If anything, the way he had just acknowledged her felt as if there was a new connection between them. That anything private they knew about each other was exactly that. Private. It didn't have any bearing on them working together but it had inevitably deepened the level of trust between them.

Lachlan nodded at his team. 'Anna came in with the first signs of going into labour this afternoon and an ultrasound has revealed that, due to her high level of amniotic fluid, her baby has managed to get into a transverse lie, which is why it turns out today is going to be his birthday.' He held out his hand. 'Scalpel, please, Suzie.'

Pippa was aware of the concern regarding the effect of stress and the emergency surgery on Anna's blood sugar levels as well. Both she and the baby would be monitored very closely in the next twenty-four hours, and the sooner this surgery was safely over the better.

The first incision had been made through the skin and Lachlan was moving swiftly but surely as he navigated through muscle, fascia and the peritoneum to open the uterus. Pippa saw his hand going in and expected to see the baby emerging seconds later. Instead, she saw a small arm appear and then the frown lines on Lachlan's forehead deepened. He pushed the arm back inside and his whole hand disappeared into the incision. It seemed that the baby had managed to wedge itself into a difficult position.

'You're doing very well, Anna.' Lachlan's voice gave no hint of the effort he was putting into trying to extract this baby against a ticking clock. 'You're going to feel me doing a bit of pushing and pulling but it shouldn't be hurting.'

Pippa wasn't the only person to be glancing up at the clock. The length of time and how difficult it was to extract a baby could be a significant factor in a birth injury or worse, a fatality.

Lachlan was twisting his own body as he reached even further inside the abdomen.

'I'm just trying to find a foot,' he said. 'That's the only way to be sure I've followed the leg and not an arm. Ah…there it is.'

His hand appeared, two tiny ankles locked between his gloved fingers. He was applying gentle traction and rotating the baby at the same time as he brought the legs out first and then the body of the baby boy. He lifted it up as the cord was clamped and cut and Pippa almost gasped.

The baby hung in his hands like a ragdoll, the head and limbs dangling, completely limp. Pippa took the infant into the towel she was holding and took it straight to the resuscitation unit.

'Page the Paeds team,' she heard Lachlan say behind her. 'They're on standby.'

The specialist neonatal team was in the theatre within what felt like only seconds. Pippa was still drying and trying to stimulate the baby. Someone ripped open a mask and another doctor had a stethoscope disc in place on the chest.

'Heart rate's just on a hundred,' they said.

The neonatal consultant was positioning the baby's head and clearing the airway with suction from a bulb syringe.

'Still not breathing,' she said.

The mask fitted over the nose and mouth completely. The ribs on the small chest were visible as it rose and fell with each rapid puff that was delivered.

The stethoscope was back in place as the seconds ticked past into a minute. Pippa was aware of more frequent glances coming in their direction from where the surgeon and his team were working to deliver the placenta and then close Anna's abdomen.

The first sound the baby made was like a bird chirping. And then it was a gargle. Finally, they could all hear the unmistakable sound of a newborn announcing his presence in the world and Pippa had never felt quite this relieved. She wrapped the baby up when the paediatric team were satisfied he was stable and she put a little woollen hat on his head to help keep him warm. Finally, she could take this precious bundle back to the operating table and show him to his parents. She held the baby close to Anna's face.

'He's gorgeous,' she told them. 'And he's absolutely fine. He was just a bit shocked at the way he had to come out.'

Pippa had been shocked, too.

And it hadn't been simply on a professional level. She had felt a connection to the baby in her own womb in that moment she'd seen the frightening limpness of the baby in Lachlan's hands.

She'd known, without giving it any conscious thought, in the split second before she took Anna's baby into her hands that she was going to fight for her own baby, no matter what battles might lie ahead. She was going to love it with all her heart and be the best mother she could be. For ever, hopefully. But certainly for as long as she possibly could, if fate had other plans in store for her or her child.

She was going to take a leaf out of Lachlan's book and live as if their baby was free of the disease. She would deal with whatever happened, if it happened, but until then she didn't want to know.

She did, however—at some point—need to let Lachlan know.

* * *

When Pippa told Lachlan a few days later that she needed to talk to him, he suggested a walk. Tomorrow, when they both had a day off. Well away from the hospital.

He drove them to Richmond Park and took a path that was still familiar, even after so many years.

'I learned to ride a bike here,' he told her. 'And I helped Liam learn to ride his. And that little forest of oak trees over there? That was our favourite spot for family picnics.'

It was where they stopped, grateful for a shady break from a surprisingly warm autumn afternoon.

'It looks like someone mowed the grass for us,' Pippa said as she sat down.

'More likely, it's been eaten down by the deer. We'll need to keep an eye out for them at this time of year. It's rutting season and the bucks can be more aggressive.'

'Is it safe to be here?'

'We'll hear them. Or see them. We can move away and keep our distance.' Lachlan smiled at her. 'I'll keep you safe, I promise. Although I'm not so sure about the weather. There are some rather black looking clouds not that far away.'

Pippa shrugged. 'What's the worst that could happen? We're not going to melt if we get a bit wet.'

'True.' Lachlan sat down beside her and tipped his head back to enjoy what was left of the sunshine streaming through leaves that were beginning to take on their autumn colours. 'What was it you wanted to talk to me about?'

'Um…the test.'

'I don't have the result yet. The DNA that gets extracted from the blood samples has to be sent to a specialised laboratory for analysis. It can take four to six weeks.'

Pippa nodded. 'Yes, you told me. But it's not your test I wanted to talk to you about. It's the baby's.'

'That will only need to be done if my result is positive.'

But Pippa shook her head. 'I don't want to have it done,' she said quietly. 'Even if your result *is* positive.'

Lachlan felt a chill run down his spine. He could feel his muscles tightening. Was it anger? That, again, she wasn't giving him a choice? Or was it fear—for his own diagnosis and then for that of his child?

His words were even quieter than Pippa's had been. 'Why not?'

'Because I don't want to know. I want to live in hope. Like you've been able to do…' Pippa was biting her bottom lip. 'Until I came along and made that impossible for you.'

Lachlan was still grappling with his emotional reaction to what she'd said.

'And there's another reason.'

'Which is?'

'There's a risk with having amniocentesis done. For miscarriage.'

'A very small risk. Less than one percent.'

'It's not a small risk for me.' Pippa wasn't looking at Lachlan now. She was letting her fingers drift through the blades of grass beside her. 'I've had miscarriages before,' she told him. 'Too many.'

Lachlan blinked. '*How* many?'

'Five…'

He swallowed. Hard. How could he have not had any idea of the kind of challenges Pippa had faced in her life?

How did she manage to find so much joy in delivering and being with other people's babies?

Why had he made a stupid joke about her husband leaving her for her obstetrician when the guy had just been rubbing salt in what had to be a gaping wound? Had the end of the marriage coincided with yet another unhappy end to a pregnancy?

It broke his heart to think that Pippa might have had to cope with that on her own.

'I had *no* idea,' he said slowly. 'I'm so sorry… I can't begin to imagine how hard that's been for you.'

Pippa's nod only acknowledged his sympathy. Her face was showing no expression. 'I never got past eleven weeks,' she said. 'And they never found a reason for it. I didn't have any abnormalities with my uterus. I didn't have any hormonal issues and there weren't any genetic problems. I'd never smoked and I gave up alcohol and coffee. I'm just one of the fifty percent or so of women who have recurrent miscarriages and never get to find out why.'

Lachlan let his breath out in a long, slow sigh. 'So that's why you waited so long to tell me that you were pregnant? Because you thought you wouldn't actually need to?'

Another nod.

'And then I got to twelve weeks, but I couldn't believe that it was real. That was why I was doing that ultrasound on myself—the one you walked in on.' Pippa finally looked up. 'This is kind of a miracle to me,' she said. 'I tried for so long, again and again, despite the heartbreak, because it meant everything to me to have a baby. This wasn't supposed to happen. What are the odds of two forms of contraception failing at the same time? But it did happen and…it feels like it was meant to be.'

The odds were almost zero, Lachlan had to admit.

'I know I might have a terrible price to pay for being able to have this baby and love it with every bit of my heart.' Pippa had to pause and clear her throat. 'But I'm prepared to pay that price because…' He could hear a hitch in her voice now that suggested tears were even closer. 'Because that's what life is really all about, isn't it? Loving people? Taking that risk?'

A sudden gust of wind was a warning that the temperature was dropping fast as the sun went behind clouds. But was that the only reason why Lachlan felt a chill?

Hadn't he thought something along the same lines not that long ago? When he'd come to the point where he could embrace memories of his brother instead of avoiding them? When he'd realised that he wouldn't want to have missed that part of his life? Given the choice in hindsight, he had decided that the price was worth paying, so how could he blame Pippa for making that choice in advance?

But had he really missed what was *most* important about life? What about being the best person you could be? Or being the best doctor you could be and helping as many people as you could?

Pippa filled the silence. 'I know you don't feel like that and I understand why and…and I'm sad for you, but if I can keep this miracle going and carry this baby long enough, I'm going to love him or her enough for both of us.'

Lachlan still couldn't find any words. He was caught on the fact that she was feeling sorry for him. For what he was missing out on.

'I don't know what's going to happen,' Pippa said, her tone suggesting that she had said almost everything she wanted to. 'But... I can't throw hope away. For this pregnancy or for the future of my baby. I don't want the joy to be stolen from everything that happens in the next who knows how many years and... I know you can understand that because it's what you've chosen for yourself. And you can still do that. You don't have to tell me the results. You don't even have to find out yourself, if you can still be okay with that?'

Could he?

'I don't know,' he admitted. 'I'll have to think about that. It's different now.'

'Because of the baby?'

He nodded. 'It was absolutely better not to know for myself. But for a baby? Watching them grow up? Waiting for every milestone like that first smile and starting to walk and going to school or learning to ride a bike? Maybe I need to know, because otherwise the black cloud on the horizon that's always been there for myself will be so much bigger. And blacker. Close enough to block the sun, maybe—like those real clouds are doing at the moment.'

As if to join the conversation, those real clouds chose that moment to part and unleash more than a mere shower. Huge, fat raindrops began to fall, heavy enough for the leaves of the oak tree to offer little protection.

'Shall we wait it out or make a run for it?'

Pippa was already scrambling to her feet. 'We'll get far too cold if we try and wait it out.'

They got far too cold, anyway. And far too wet. Lachlan cranked the heater up when they got back to his car and headed straight for Pippa's cottage so that she could get dry and warm. She was shivering uncontrollably now despite the efficient heating of the car and the last thing he wanted was for her to end up getting sick. She had more than enough to deal with right now.

He got out of his car to make sure she got inside fast as well, because her hands were cold enough to be fumbling with her keys.

'Are you going to be okay?'

'I'm fine.'

But she didn't look fine. If she couldn't manage her key, how was she going to get her sodden clothes off and into a hot shower fast enough?

'I'm not convinced,' he said. 'And it was my idea to go on that walk. I'm coming in to make sure you *are* okay.'

He knew where the bathroom was. He knew how to turn on this shower because he'd done it before. On their first date.

On the night that Pippa had become pregnant.

Oh, God…she was fumbling with the metal fastener on her jeans now, her fingers shaking.

Lachlan could feel how slippery the slope he was stepping onto was, but he couldn't stop himself. He covered Pippa's hands with his own.

'Here…' The word came out as a kind of growl. 'Let me…'

He peeled the wet denim off her legs. And then she held her arms up like a child so he could lift the wet shirt over her head. The small bathroom was filling with steam as she stood there in her bra and knickers and Lachlan knew this was when he should step out, but he couldn't move. His gaze ran down Pippa's body. There was no hint of a pregnancy bump yet but she looked different, somehow.

Even more gorgeous than she had on that first date. Or the second…

She was looking up at him, water dripping from her hair to trickle down her face. Her lips were parted and her eyes were so dark—her pupils dilated with…desire, that was what he could see.

What he could feel in every cell in his own body.

An intense desire that felt like flames licking his skin and made him shiver.

'You're cold, too,' Pippa whispered. 'You can share my shower.'

Pippa had never had sex in a shower before.

She'd never had sex knowing that she was pregnant, either.

Or when she was cold enough for the hot water to feel as if it was burning her skin, and Lachlan's hands were cold enough to be creating an oddly similar kind of burn. Together, the sensations were unbelievable. Like the rain of hot water on her face as it was tilted up to meet Lachlan's lips and what felt like a ripple effect when the heat of his tongue met hers. How wet their bodies were and the slide of hands that were slippery with shower gel was another dimension that was off any charts that might record physical arousal, or satisfaction.

It was, without doubt, *the* most astonishing sex she'd ever had.

Scorchingly hot. Astonishingly intense. And over far too soon.

It seemed like Lachlan was thinking the same thing because when they'd almost exhausted her supply of hot water, he wrapped them both in towels and then carried her to her bed to do it all over again.

This was where it had all started.

And this had to be where it all ended, didn't it?

There was something very poignant about the smile that Lachlan gave her after a slow, exquisitely tender kiss a long time later.

'I guess this counts as date number three,' he murmured.

Pippa's huff of laughter could almost have been a tiny sob.

'I guess it does.'

CHAPTER THIRTEEN

The later it got, the more tempting it became to let his mind wander.

Lachlan Smythe was in his office, trying to get a presentation on high-risk pregnancies ready as a guest speaker for an upcoming midwifery conference.

He had a well-drawn, colourful illustration of the anatomy of the uterus on his computer screen and he was adding arrows and text that would appear with a click of a mouse, to make it a slide for the presentation. He was recording prompts on another document to make sure he didn't leave out any of the key information he wanted to impart.

'Here we have the three layers of the uterus,' he said aloud, as he typed into the second document. 'The endometrium on the inside, the myometrium in the middle and the perimetrium on the outside. The endometrium is where the placenta is implanted, and what I'm going to talk about today is where this implantation can go wrong and result in placenta accreta, increta and percreta.'

He needed to start a new slide to describe the different degrees that a placenta could grow past a normal implantation, but it was a word he'd just said that continued to hang in the air, like the aftermath of a bell tolling.

Okay...his focus was gone but the word was still there.

…wrong…

Wrong, wrong, wrong.

Had he been following an ill-advised track in his personal life, for the whole of his adult life? Pippa seemed to think so and it had prompted him, over the last couple of days, to think more about his philosophy on living than he had since he'd been an angsty teenager, grappling with the meaning of life as he'd navigated the grief of losing his brother and then having to watch his father pulled slowly away by the appalling grip of Huntington's Disease.

Pippa hadn't experienced that, so it was all very well for her to tell him that the most important thing in life was having people to love and that it was sad that he felt he had to keep others at a safe emotional distance, but she had no idea what she could actually be facing in the future, did she? No idea at all.

Lachlan rubbed at his forehead with his fingers.

'The recognised risk factors for developing accreta lie with scarring of the endometrium from previous Caesarean sections or surgery for fibroids,' he said, redirecting his focus yet again. 'Or due to a placenta praevia, where the placenta has attached itself to the lower segment of the uterus where the walls are thinner.'

He was typing bullet points onto the slide as he spoke, trying to ignore an insistent unrelated thought that was doing its best to disrupt the flow.

A voice that was asking him how on earth he had come to the conclusion that Pippa had no idea at all about grief?

She'd lost five babies.

Five.

He knew better than to dismiss the degree of emotional fallout because she'd never got past her first trimester.

She'd been dreaming of having a baby and she'd had to grieve the loss of both the baby and the future as a mother that she wanted so desperately every time every one of those pregnancies had failed.

She'd been brave enough to try again, though, hadn't she?

Again and again.

Until, to add insult to injury, she'd found her husband was cheating on her—with, presumably, the person who was treating her recurrent miscarriages—and she'd lost her marriage as well.

Which was why she'd subscribed to that 'three date' rule, of course. And why he'd felt so safe to play the game with her. She had been just as reluctant as he was to engage with someone on an intimate level.

But she was prepared to risk far more than the fallout of a relationship that hadn't worked. The future she was actually hoping she could face was a much bigger deal.

There was a baby involved.

A baby that might—or might not—one day have to face the decisions that were playing havoc with Lachlan's concentration right now. Because thinking about Pippa raised an even bigger temptation.

That he could take up her suggestion to cancel the testing process and keep living the way he always had.

With hope…

It would be a perfectly acceptable thing to do as far as the genetic clinic staff were concerned. You were allowed to pull out of the process at any point.

But if Lachlan did that he would be stealing the potential joy that would be there for Pippa if the result showed that he didn't have Huntington's himself and couldn't have passed it on to a baby. Pippa would never have to live with the cloud he'd been under for as long as he could remember and his own cloud would evaporate. Just like that. Poof!

A whole new world could open up for him.

One where he could allow himself to fall in love. To *be* loved. To have a whole family of his own, which was something he'd never allowed himself to dream of.

And, if that was the case, it would be Pippa that he would choose to share his life with. That was a given.

But it was a flip of a coin. And the other side from that joy was the grim confirmation of a slow death sentence that would also open up a whole new world he would have to step into.

The circle of his thoughts always came back to the same question. Was it really better to live with hope for as long as possible? Or, as Pippa had suggested, was he only living half a life and missing the most important part?

With a sigh, Lachlan hit save on the work he'd started and then shut down his laptop. He'd go into the diagnosis and management of placental tissue that could grow far enough to escape the uterus and invade the bladder later—maybe when he got home. Part of this presentation would be covering the massive blood loss that could happen with attempting the removal of a placenta accreta and it was even more likely to make him think about Pippa and that dramatic night they'd first met if he was still here in his office.

And thinking about Pippa would only lead his tired brain back onto the same path that just kept going round in the same loop. It wasn't as if he actually had a choice. Because this wasn't just about him any longer. Pippa might not want to know what the future held but, to Lachlan, it felt like part of his responsibility as a father. How could you protect someone to the best of your ability if you didn't know what you might be up against?

Lachlan could hear the raised voices as soon as he left his office and he felt the hairs on the back of his neck rise. Violence against hospital staff was increasing everywhere and the labour ward had its fair share of abusive and uncooperative patients and relatives. He'd been told they had a great security team at Queen Mary's, but nobody could be everywhere at once and trouble in the emergency department could mean that these well-trained guards were unavailable in other areas of the hospital.

He lengthened his stride as he heard the aggressive note in a male voice. It sounded as if it was coming from the reception desk that was just inside the entrance to the ward. Rita would be at that desk and the thought of their motherly and warm-hearted receptionist being subjected to abuse like this was totally unacceptable.

'Don't tell me you don't have the keys. I *know* you've got them—you're just being a bitch...'

A crashing sound came just as Lachlan turned into the reception area. Rita was looking terrified. The computer screen that was normally in front of her had been pulled across the desk, ripped free of its cables and was lying on the floor.

'My girlfriend *needs* drugs.' A tall, very skinny man in ripped jeans and a hoodie started swearing at Rita. 'She's having a *baby*. Everybody gets drugs when they're having babies. The stupid nurse isn't getting them fast enough so, guess what? Turns out it's your job...'

Rita jumped back from the desk as he reached across the desk to grab her. She saw Lachlan coming and cried out.

The man's head swung around and Lachlan saw the

spiderweb tattoos across his face and the piercings in his eyebrows and nose. There were two large spikes on either side of his mouth, below his bottom lip.

'Who the hell are *you*?'

Lachlan saw Rita picking up a phone. He knew she would be calling for help. He just needed to buy some time.

'I'm a doctor. What's the problem here?'

'A *doctor*, huh…?'

The man was suddenly very still, his eyes narrowed. It felt as if a bomb was about to be detonated. Without moving his own head, Lachlan scanned the area around them. There was no sign of any of the night shift staff. No sign of anyone else. What he could see, against the wall beside him, was an abandoned wheelchair.

The trigger came when shouting could be heard coming from Room Three. As the man launched himself in Lachlan's direction, he grabbed the handles of the chair to put in front of him as a barrier. When he saw the man pulling out a knife, he shoved the wheelchair forward and the metal footplates smacked into his legs. The man shrieked in pain but stepped back, looking over his shoulder as if he expected an attack from behind as well. He had to be able to hear Rita shouting into the phone as clearly as Lachlan could. He would be able to see the face on the other side of the doors that needed swipe cards or for Rita to deactivate the lock from the desk. Sally must have been coming back from a break and she was staring through the glass panels of the doors, horrified.

The man with the knife in his hand could see that there were people on three sides of him. With another stream of profanity, he took off in the only direction that was clear. He wrenched the first door he came to so hard

Lachlan could hear wood splintering as he slammed it shut behind him.

Lachlan ran towards Rita. 'Are you okay?'

Her nod was jerky.

'Have you called Security?'

She nodded again. 'They're on their way.'

Another glance at the door showed that Sally had turned her head. Was she watching the arrival of the security guards?

'Is his girlfriend in Room Three?' That was the best place for them both to be.

'Yes...' But Rita's voice was a frightened whisper. 'So's Pippa...'

The knot that suddenly formed in Lachlan's gut was tight enough to cause pain. Big enough to stop him being able to take a proper breath. He wasn't going to wait for anyone else to arrive.

He couldn't.

Pippa was in trouble and protecting her had just become the thing that mattered most in his life.

The only thing that mattered...?

They were drug seekers.

The woman, Kardi, *was* probably six months pregnant but she wasn't in labour, despite her dramatic entrance to the labour ward a short time ago, clutching her belly and screaming in pain, with a man helping her to stay upright. Pippa was walking through the reception area, on her way back from the staff toilet, when Rita had opened the door to the panicked request of the new arrivals and she'd had no choice but to take them straight into a room to assess the situation. The screaming had to be upsetting everybody, including the woman Pippa was caring for in Room Two that she'd only intended to be away from for a minute or two.

'Can you get Sally or anyone else that's free to come and help, please, Rita?'

'Sally's on her break but I'll find someone.'

But nobody had arrived and Pippa knew she might be in trouble as soon as she was alone in Room Three with the couple.

'I'm Pippa, one of the midwives here. What's your name?'

'Kardi. With a K.'

She'd stopped screaming. The man with her was standing with his back to the door of the room.

'Let's get you into a gown and up on the bed so I can see what's happening. How far along in your pregnancy are you?'

'Dunno. 'Bout seven months.' She moved towards the bed but stopped to bend forward and groan loudly. 'It *really* hurts. Where's the gas?'

'You need more than gas, sweetheart,' her companion said. 'Morphine. That's what you need.'

'Yeah…that's what I need. Or methadone'll do. Haven't had enough today, you know?'

Pippa managed to sound much calmer than she was feeling. She opened a cupboard to find a gown. 'Put this on, Kardi. I'll get you comfortable and then I'll go and find a doctor. I can sign off on any drugs like that.' She put the gown down on the end of the bed. 'I can see you're in real pain,' she said. 'Let me go and call a doctor now.'

She turned towards the door, only to find that Kardi's partner was standing right in her way.

'You're not going anywhere,' the man said. 'Kardi, you come and watch the door. I'll go and get what we're here for. Give this nurse a kicking if she tries to go anywhere, right?'

'Yeah…go on. Hurry up.' Kardi turned back to Pippa. 'So…where's the gas, then?'

'Right here.' Pippa pointed to the other side of the bed. 'I'll set it up for you, shall I?'

She edged carefully around the end of the bed, knowing she could be attacked at any time. She didn't have to look over her shoulder to know that the door of the ensuite bathroom was open. Pippa knew there was a lock on the door. Not that it was ever used, but it seemed that bathroom doors automatically came with a locking system. Kardi's attention was on the mouthpiece she was taking from its sterile packaging. Holding her breath, Pippa turned as if she was about to find the tubing to attach the mouthpiece to, but she dropped it on the bed instead, ran into the bathroom and shut the door behind her. She twisted the lock just as Kardi started banging on the door.

She heard another door banging only seconds later. And shouting, from the two people in the room—at each other, as they realised their plan was going wrong—and from outside the room. Male voices. Pippa could only hope they were from Security, but she was so terrified her mind was playing tricks on her and she could almost imagine that one of those voices was Lachlan's. Then it was drowned by the thumping of someone's body slamming the bathroom door.

'Open it!' The command was a scream.

Pippa had been leaning against the door from the inside, but feeling it move made her retreat until she had a solid wall behind her back. She slid down to sit in the small space between the toilet and the shower and squeezed her eyes shut.

She might die, she thought. If these violent drug seekers got to her first. She could hear Lachlan's voice again then. From just the other day, when they were in the park and she'd been a bit nervous about the possibility of being amongst male deer in the rutting season.

I'll keep you safe, I promise...

If only...

But thinking about it was enough to comfort her. And thank goodness he wouldn't be here at this time of night.

Except he did stay late sometimes, didn't he? Pippa's mind was racing now, back in time. It had been in this room that he'd arrived like a knight in shining armour to rescue her from a situation that had been so scary.

Not as scary as this one, though...

Pippa put her hands over her ears. She couldn't bear the crashing sounds and shouting that was going on out there. She could still hear it, though it was getting steadily quieter, fading into the distance.

Until there was silence.

Pippa's heart skipped a beat as someone tried the door handle.

'Pippa?'

It was Lachlan. And she could hear the fear in his voice.

'Are you okay? Can you open the door? You're safe... I promise...'

CHAPTER FOURTEEN

THIS...

The moment he could take Pippa into his arms and hold her so tightly he couldn't tell where his body ended and hers started.

This *feeling*...

It was bigger than anything. Bigger than *everything*.

'Oh, my God, Pippa... I thought... I thought I might have lost you.'

He could feel her trembling in his arms. When Sally, with a security officer right behind her, came to the door of the bathroom, Lachlan gave his head a tiny shake and mouthed that it was okay.

He had this.

Sally looked from Lachlan to Pippa and back again. She turned and walked away, forcing the security officer behind her to move far enough away so that she could shut the door quietly. She had a rather misty smile on her face, as if she knew exactly how big this moment was for Lachlan.

And for Pippa?

Lachlan's lips were against Pippa's hair. 'I can't lose you,' he whispered. He pressed his lips to her hair. 'I love you.'

Pippa's words were muffled because she was still

pressed so hard against his chest. 'I love you, too,' she said. 'I thought I was going to die and all I wanted was… *you*. And I could remember you telling me that you were going to keep me safe and… I just played that over and over in my mind and…' Her voice was choked with tears. 'I *did* feel safe…'

Lachlan knew his own voice was thick with the overwhelming emotion that had pushed its way through what now seemed like flimsy barriers protecting his heart.

'But I can't…' He hauled in a breath before saying the words he least wanted to say. 'I might *not* be able to keep you safe. Or give you a future.'

Pippa lifted her head. Her eyes looked huge in her pale, tear-streaked face but the look in them was melting something inside Lachlan.

His fear?

'You're giving me *this*,' she told him softly. 'This moment. And it's the biggest and best moment of my entire life. And even if I never had another moment like this, it would be worth it because I can remember it for ever and—' She pulled in a distinctly shaky sounding breath. 'If I ever have another moment where I think I'm not going to be alive much longer, *this* is what I'm going to remember. You telling me that you loved me and me saying it back and that—in that moment—life couldn't have been any more perfect.'

She was right, Lachlan realised with absolute certainty. Life *was* made up of moments and the best ones were… priceless. They became memories that could be treasured for as long as you lived. But the others…?

'Could you take that risk?' he asked quietly. 'That there might be a limit to moments like this?'

'I thought I was never going to have *this* one.' Pippa

was smiling through her tears now. 'And I'm going to kiss you now and that's going to be another one.'

Lachlan started to dip his head. He wanted that kiss too. *So* much...

But Pippa pulled back in his arms, just enough to keep their eye contact.

'We'll make the most of every moment,' she said. 'For as long as we can. It's all anyone can do, isn't it? It's just that some people have more idea of what could be around the corner and...and maybe that's not such a bad thing, because every moment like this will make us realise how lucky we are. And...' Her eyes widened, as though she'd just had an even better idea. 'If you really love someone, doesn't that mean that you don't leave them to face bad stuff alone?'

She loved him *that* much? That she wouldn't want him to be facing the bad stuff by himself?

He could see the answer to that in her eyes. He could feel it in his heart at the same time because...because he loved *her* that much. And she was right. He would never want her to face anything that could be distressing without him being close enough to comfort her.

Lachlan could taste the salt of tears on Pippa's lips but he didn't know if they were his tears or hers.

Not that it mattered. They had this moment and he could only hope that this kiss was making Pippa feel as cherished and...hopeful...as he was feeling.

When a polite knock on the door reminded him that there was rather a lot of witness statements and paperwork and finding replacement staff to cover the rest of this night shift that needed to be done in the wake of a major incident in the department he was the head of, he ignored it.

Just long enough to make this moment last for another heartbeat.

The next knock was louder.

'Are you guys okay in there?'

'We're good,' Lachlan called. 'We'll be out in just a second.'

He needed that second.

He smiled at Pippa. 'I think I need a date.'

'A *fourth* date?' Her eyebrows rose. 'You do know that's breaking the rules, don't you?'

His smile widened. 'Not a fourth date. I mean an actual date. On a calendar. The kind you can draw a circle around.'

'But is it a date for a date?'

'No...' Lachlan's smile wobbled, just a little. 'A date for our wedding. If you'll marry me, that is?'

Pippa caught her bottom lip between her teeth, but her arms tightened around Lachlan's neck and she was coming up on her tiptoes, clearly intent on kissing him again.

'I think that's actually in the rule book,' she murmured. 'The fourth date is for the proposal and the answer is always yes.'

That worked for Lachlan.

He was more than happy to ask the big question again. He'd have a perfect ring ready because Pippa could help him choose it. He'd go down on one knee and he'd know the things he really wanted to say so that he could tell Pippa the whole long list of every reason he loved her this much.

And how she had changed his life, because he was going to make the most of every special moment. He could look back and find comfort in moments from the past and he wouldn't look too far ahead because they weren't there yet and why would you spoil something as perfect as what was happening right now?

Another blink of time stolen from the world outside.

Another kiss.

The envelope had been there for weeks now.

On the desk at home, hidden under a pile of medical journals that were still waiting to be read because life had been so very busy.

Pippa had moved into Lachlan's new house and they'd had a wedding to prepare for that had turned out to be the best day ever. Even the weather had cooperated enough to allow them to go and have their wedding photographs taken in Richmond Park, and the one he would treasure for ever was under the now bare branches of that huge oak tree, with Pippa in her gorgeous white dress on a carpet of autumn leaves, some of them red enough to be an echo of her hair that was hanging in ringlets as Lachlan was tipping her back to kiss his bride yet again.

He'd forgotten completely about the envelope that day. He hadn't thought about it during the week they'd been on honeymoon on a gorgeous Greek island, either.

But they were home again and settling into their new life together and…he was almost ready. He hadn't been ready when the results of his test had become available. He'd been offered another counselling session at the Genetics Centre to discuss the results but he'd declined. What he did request was to have the results sent to him so that he could open the envelope in his own time.

On his own.

Because when he'd had the phone call to say that they had arrived, he'd come to what felt like a compromise he could live with in an ethical dilemma that was so difficult to resolve.

At some point soon, Lachlan needed to know so that he could prepare for the future in a way that meant he could protect the people he loved the most.

Pippa.

And their daughter. He'd felt the baby move last night for the first time, his hand resting gently on Pippa's now noticeably rounded belly.

They'd agreed to avoid even the slight risk to the pregnancy that the amniocentesis represented. They would live in hope for this baby. Even if Lachlan was carrying the gene, there was still a fifty percent chance that their baby would not be. The odds of a paediatric form of the disease were low enough to be acceptable and who knew what advances in medicine could happen in the decades to come? Lachlan couldn't steal the hope that was shining in Pippa's face as she put her hand over his to feel the kick of tiny feet, or maybe it was the prod of an elbow. A nudge to remind them to make the most of another one of those moments.

No. He wasn't going to steal that hope.

But he was going to find out the result. Because he needed to know. And if he was clear, he could offer Pippa more than simply hope.

He could give her the gift of making the sun shine brightly enough to blitz those black clouds and give them both the clear skies that most other people got to live with.

If he wasn't clear, he wasn't going to tell Pippa.

That would make the hope she was living with his gift instead. He could keep the result hidden for as long as possible because he loved her that much.

When he was sure Pippa was asleep, Lachlan slipped

quietly out of bed and put his bathrobe on. He went to his study and turned on the desk lamp. He pulled the envelope out from under the journals and held it in his hands.

For a long, long moment, he stared at it. Taking in a very deep breath.

Steadying himself.

The soft voice at the door made the breath leave his lungs in a rush.

'Is that what I think it is?' Pippa asked.

'Yes.'

'You were going to open it without me?'

Lachlan's heart broke at what he could see in her eyes.

'I didn't want you to know,' he said quietly. 'If it was bad news.'

'That's not fair...' Pippa came closer. 'If you get to protect me and I can't do the same for you.' She held out her hand. 'I love you, Lachlan,' she said steadily. 'And my life is in that envelope as much as yours is.' Her voice dropped to a whisper. 'Let me open it?'

Lachlan couldn't say anything past the lump in his throat. Silently, he handed the envelope to Pippa.

She opened it and withdrew a single sheet of paper.

And then she stared at it.

Frowning.

Lachlan felt the world stop turning. 'It's bad news, isn't it?'

'I don't know,' Pippa said. 'I don't understand. What are CAG repeats?'

'It's a DNA code for the chemicals that the Huntington's gene contains. Most people have a level that's low enough that they're not at risk for the disease. Some are a bit higher, which means they're not likely to get the disease themselves but they could still pass it on to their children. If they're really high they already have it and, the higher the level, the younger it can start.'

'Okay. So that range is the twenty-seven to thirty-six repeats in the brackets here.'

'Yes.'

'So...' Pippa looked up, her eyes filling with tears as she held the piece of paper out to Lachlan. 'Twelve is good, yes...?'

Dazed, Lachlan looked at the result.

There it was, in black and white.

He was clear. He was not going to get the disease and there was no way their baby could be affected.

The clouds were breaking apart and vanishing but they were leaving a few drops of rain behind.

Or were they tears?

Of joy?

That was certainly what it felt like as Lachlan wrapped Pippa in his arms, the paper slipping through his fingers to drift to the floor.

This was another one of those moments.

And it felt like the biggest one yet.

EPILOGUE

Four months later...

'LACHLAN? ARE YOU AWAKE?'

'I am now, darling.' Lachlan snapped on a bedside light and propped himself up on one elbow. 'Are you okay?'

'Um… I got up to go to the loo but then this happened…'

Pippa was standing in the door of the master bedroom's en-suite bathroom. She was wearing a soft tee shirt that was pushed up so far by her belly that the elastic waistband of the silky boxer shorts she was wearing as well was visible. Pale pink shorts that Lachlan could see had a dark stain on them that was growing rapidly bigger. He dropped his gaze and…yes…there was a puddle on the floor where Pippa was standing.

'Your waters have broken.'

'You think?' Pippa grinned. 'Thank goodness I married an obstetrician.'

Lachlan was out of bed. He pulled a jumper on and then reached for his jeans. 'We'd better get going. Where's your bag? How far apart are your contractions?'

'Haven't had one yet. Oh…wait.' Pippa was biting her lip as Lachlan pulled up his jeans. She let out a groan as she released her breath. 'Yep…that's a contraction, all right.'

'Thank goodness I married a midwife.' But Lachlan wasn't smiling. He looked, Pippa decided, rather adorably scared stiff.

She had to cling onto the door frame then, to ride out the rest of an unexpectedly strong contraction. Had she somehow slept through hours of the early stages of her labour?

'What do you want to wear?' Lachlan asked. 'To go to the hospital?' He turned back to pick up his phone. 'I'd better let them know we're on our way.'

'Not yet.' Pippa blew out a breath as the pain finally began to subside. 'The first thing Rita's going to ask is how far apart my contractions are. *Oh…*'

'What? What is it? What's wrong?' Lachlan was right beside her and Pippa grabbed hold of his arm instead of the door frame.

'Another…contraction…' she gasped. '*Oh-h…*'

The pain was fierce. Back-to-back with the last contraction. It was then that Pippa realised they weren't going to make it to the birthing suite at Queen Mary's. Despite being a partnership of an obstetrician and a midwife, they'd never even considered a home birth. Possibly because they both wanted to be in the safest possible place for the arrival of what felt like the most precious baby in the world.

Pippa felt her knees giving way beneath her. Lachlan took her weight until she was safely on the floor, on her hands and knees.

'I need to check your dilation,' he said. 'Don't push, okay…?'

'I don't think I need to,' Pippa groaned. 'Get my shorts off. I can feel the baby's head… I *need* to push…'

'No...wait.' Lachlan's voice was a command. Authoritative. Calm.

Pippa could feel her clothing being removed. She could feel his hands on her body. She could feel pressure. Lachlan was pushing back on the baby's head. Trying to slow the delivery. She could feel another contraction beginning to build and she put all her focus into not giving in to the urge to push, opening her mouth and taking short, rapid breaths. How many times had she coached women to pant like this to try and slow labour down to prevent tearing or provide the chance to check that an umbilical cord wasn't wrapped around a baby's neck?

'You're doing great, hon,' Lachlan said. 'Oh, man... she's not to going wait, is she? Here we go...'

Pippa gave in to the push, knowing that the safest pair of hands imaginable were waiting to catch her baby. When had Lachlan had time to grab one of the towels from the bathroom? And how did he manage to turn her so that she was now sitting on the floor, ready to take her baby into her arms and hold her against her breasts? It was all a bit of a blur for a while then. She was shivering almost as much as she had been the day that they'd got caught in the rain.

No hot shower for her this time. Lachlan ripped the duvet off the bed and wrapped that around her. He'd called an ambulance.

'They've got an ETA of about five minutes,' he told Pippa.

'That's okay... We're fine...'

Their daughter wasn't crying, but she was breathing well and moving her arms and legs. She lay in her mother's arms and her eyes were wide open. She was simply lying on Pippa's skin and looking up at both her parents.

'Aren't you gorgeous?' Lachlan whispered. 'As gorgeous as your mum.'

Pippa looked up for the first time since she'd been given her baby to hold. She looked straight into the eyes of her baby's father as she leaned back into the circle of his arms.

'I love you,' she said softly.

'I love *you*.' Lachlan pressed a soft kiss onto Pippa's head. 'I can hear the ambulance arriving. I'll have to run downstairs and let them in.'

But he didn't move for a moment. And Pippa didn't want him to.

The realisation that they had just become a family was sinking in. They both looked down at their daughter. They had chosen her name long ago.

'Welcome to the world, Hope,' Pippa whispered. 'We love you, too.'

*****

*If you enjoyed this story,
check out these other great reads
from Alison Roberts*

Paramedic's Reunion in Paradise
City Vet, Country Temptation
Falling for Her Forbidden Flatmate
Miracle Twins to Heal Them

All available now!

MILLS & BOON®

Coming next month

A DADDY FOR HER BABIES
Becky Wicks

'Twins,' Theo announces, before Dr Priya can.

She nods and lets him wheel the monitor closer so I can see better.

Twins.

The word echoes through the room, doubling itself in my mind. Twins? I turn to Theo, who's still grinning in a way that makes him look ten years younger and twenty times more handsome. Here they are, right here. Two little beings, my babies, dancing in their own private universe.

'Twins are a huge part of my family. They have been for generations, but somehow I never really thought...' My voice trails off. I'm lost in a swell of emotions now, just looking at the screen. I am completely mesmerized by what I'm seeing and soon I'm hearing it, too—two tiny hearts beating in sync.

'They're cooking along nicely, Carter,' Theo says proudly.

'Would you like to know the genders?' Dr Sharma asks. My palm is warm and clammy now from my nerves, glued to Theo's. He's still mouthing the word *twins* to himself, and there's a look of disbelief and wonderment on his face that I've never actually seen before. Am I ready? I think I am. I tell her yes. I think I'm feeding off Theo's excitement.

Dr Sharma begins with another swirl of the cool wand over my abdomen. 'You're having a boy and a girl.'

'One of each, no…' Theo lets out a laugh, just as I do.

A boy and a girl. This is crazy. More tears gather in the corners of my eyes. 'Just like Rose dreamed,' I remember suddenly. Weirdly, Rose said she had a dream the other night, in which I announced this exact thing. I wish she were here now. She'd be wrapped around their little fingers already, too.

'Congratulations, Carter,' Theo whispers. I know I'm emotional, but his words tingle my ear and send a flush of adrenaline to my nerves. I can't help missing my sister, but I'm so relieved that someone's here to witness this. That *Theo* is here to witness this.

'Congratulations, *both* of you,' Dr Priya says, making me a printout so I can show Rose. She's going to be so thrilled. Just wait till she… Wait… *What did she say?*

'Oh, no,' I insert as it hits me what this lady just alluded to. 'Theo's not… I mean, we're not…'

'They're going to be so loved, right, wifey?' Theo finishes for me. He's still marveling at the screen. He really does look fiercely determined now and I let the comment go.

They will definitely be loved. But my friend and colleague has just been mistaken for the father of these babies, and more concerning, for a hot fleeting second there I caught myself wishing he really *were*.

Continue reading

A DADDY FOR HER BABIES
Becky Wicks

Available next month
millsandboon.co.uk

Copyright © 2025 Becky Wicks

COMING SOON!

We really hope you enjoyed reading this book. If you're looking for more romance be sure to head to the shops when new books are available on

Thursday 22nd May

To see which titles are coming soon, please visit
millsandboon.co.uk/nextmonth

MILLS & BOON

FOUR BRAND NEW BOOKS FROM
MILLS & BOON MODERN

The same great stories you love, a stylish new look!

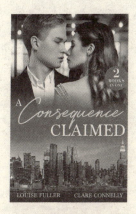
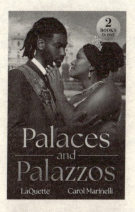
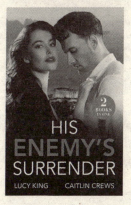
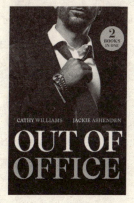

OUT NOW

Eight Modern stories published every month, find them all at:
millsandboon.co.uk

Afterglow Books is a trend-led, trope-filled list of books with diverse, authentic and relatable characters, a wide array of voices and representations, plus real world trials and tribulations. Featuring all the tropes you could possibly want (think small-town settings, fake relationships, grumpy vs sunshine, enemies to lovers) and all with a generous dose of spice in every story.

♪ @millsandboonuk
◉ @millsandboonuk
afterglowbooks.co.uk

#AfterglowBooks

For all the latest book news, exclusive content and giveaways scan the QR code below to sign up to the Afterglow newsletter:

afterglow BOOKS

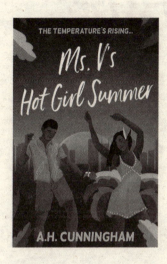

✈ International 💻 Workplace romance

☯ Opposites attract 🚫 Forbidden love

🌶 Spicy 🌶 Spicy

OUT NOW

Two stories published every month. Discover more at:
Afterglowbooks.co.uk

LET'S TALK
Romance

For exclusive extracts, competitions and special offers, find us online:

- **f** MillsandBoon
- **X** @MillsandBoon
- **◉** @MillsandBoonUK
- **♪** @MillsandBoonUK

Get in touch on 01413 063 232

For all the latest titles coming soon, visit
millsandboon.co.uk/nextmonth